A SCANDALOUS DILEMMA

"I must confess that I do not understand you entirely, Charity, but I mean to." And as William arrived beside her, he slipped a hand about her arm, and stood very close to her. His touch almost burned and she drew in her breath sharply. Suddenly she felt very frightened and vulnerable. She was not in the least experienced but she knew enough to understand that to be so very close to a man could be very dangerous to one's heart!

She tried to move away, but he held her arm fast, slipping his other hand about her waist. She felt her throat constrict with emotions she did not understand, for she felt like crying and laughing at the same time, and all of her schemes fell swiftly away at his mere touch. How was it possible that he could command her so completely?

"Charity," he whispered, "will you not love me but a little?"

THE BEST OF REGENCY ROMANCES

AN IMPROPER COMPANION   (2691, $3.95)
by Karla Hocker
At the closing of Miss Venable's Seminary for Young
Ladies school, mistress Kate Elliott welcomed the invitation to be Liza Ashcroft's chaperone for the Season at
Bath. Little did she know that Miss Ashcroft's father, the
handsome widower Damien Ashcroft would also enter her
life. And not as a passive bystander or dutiful dad.

WAGER ON LOVE   (2693, $2.95)
by Prudence Martin
Only a rogue like Nicholas Ruxart would choose a bride on
the basis of a careless wager. And only a rakehell like Nicholas would then fall in love with his betrothed's grey-eyed
sister! The cynical viscount had always thought one blushing miss would suit as well as another, but the unattainable
Jane Sommers soon proved him wrong.

LOVE AND FOLLY   (2715, $3.95)
by Sheila Simonson
To the dismay of her more sensible twin Margaret, Lady
Jean proceeded to fall hopelessly in love with the silver-
tongued, seditious poet, Owen Davies—and catapult her
entire family into social ruin : . . Margaret was used to
gentlemen falling in love with vivacious Jean rather than
with her—even the handsome Johnny Dyott whom she se-
cretly adored. And when Jean's foolishness led her into the
arms of the notorious Owen Davies, Margaret knew she
could count on Dyott to avert scandal. What she didn't
know, however was that her sweet sensibility was exerting a
charm all its own.

Available wherever paperbacks are sold, or order direct from the
Publisher. Send cover price plus 50¢ per copy for mailing and
handling to Zebra Books, Dept. 2824, 475 Park Avenue South,
New York, N.Y. 10016. Residents of New York, New Jersey and
Pennsylvania must include sales tax. DO NOT SEND CASH.

Reluctant Bride

VALERIE KING

ZEBRA BOOKS
KENSINGTON PUBLISHING CORP.

ZEBRA BOOKS

are published by

Kensington Publishing Corp.
475 Park Avenue South
New York, NY 10016

First printing: November, 1989

Printed in the United States of America

Dedication

*To Marlena de Bouville
and to my kindred spirit,
Marlene King.*

"A little rebellion now and then is a good thing."
—*Thomas Jefferson*

Chapter One

"Miss Charity, it is The Gentleman! *Mon Dieu*, what will you do?" The petite woman, her English speech laced with an elegant French accent, leaned forward slightly to peer through the front window of the post chaise. Her eyes were very dark and of the moment round with horror as the carriage slowly drew to a stop before a mysterious and quite strangely costumed highwayman.

Charity Holwell stared in disbelief at the tall figure standing in the road, the setting sun at his back obscuring his face with shadow. He wore a long, curling black wig, which gentlemen of an earlier century were known to wear, but even in the failing light of the early April evening, she could tell that he wore a half-mask to disguise his face. He stood firmly before the carriage, his stance wide, his arms folded across his chest, a pistol held casually in one hand. Charity's cousin, Penelope, had warned her that such a man frequently accosted ladies of gentle birth, but it was still so shocking to see the specter for herself that she could not resist the impulse to take hold of her maid's small gloved hand and hold it fiercely.

"Oh, Marie!" she cried, her own speech also touched lightly with the shadings of an accent. "It is the notorious Gentleman! And Penelope warned me that I ran the very

7

great risk of happening upon him were I to travel in the late afternoon. I should have attended to her!"

On either side of the road, the wooded hills about the Hertfordshire countryside were bathed in a red, dusky glow, the sun just preparing to descend over the horizon. Beside Charity upon the seat of the post chaise, lay a small box, and as the carriage drew closer still, she took in a sharp breath and with fingers that trembled, opened the box in a hurried manner. Wrapped in silver paper lay a beautiful half-mask of white silk, embroidered with gold thread and seed pearls. Trailing from a cluster of lilies of the valley at the top right corner of the mask were several narrow white ribbons, knotted at each end. This was the mask she wore when she performed the ballet but never in her wildest fancies did she imagine that it would also be used to disguise herself from an infamous highwayman who was believed to be a gentleman of the *beau monde*.

Pressing a hand against her bosom in a futile attempt to still the wild beatings of her heart, she lifted the mask from the box, and instructed her maid to tie it quickly about her black curls. Marie most willingly obliged her for as much as it appealed to her romantic nature to have this daring man accost her mistress in this completely scandalous fashion, she still knew quite well that the English were not so forgiving of even an innocent kiss, and certainly not one received from a highwayman! And that he always kissed his victims was the very cause for so many excited protestations, palpitations, and swoonings amongst the gently nurtured females of Mayfair. No, far better that Miss Charity remain unknown to the bewigged devil who, merciful heavens, possessed such very broad shoulders!

When the post chaise came to a complete stop, Charity sat very still beside her maid, her gaze fixed upon the form of the tall gentleman. The highwayman, now satisfied that the carriage was fully stopped, handed his pistol to his servant who was waiting by the side of the road astride a fine bay horse. And as the bandit approached the post chaise, Charity noted with a growing sense of hostility that his gait was at once firm yet arrogant. She disliked him excessively for the various reports she had heard of him convinced her that he was without the least sensibility with regard to his victims, kissing them violently and then demanding as much as fifty pounds from them for his services, which he bade assure them went to an orphanage in London. He was a philanthropist, or so he professed! But Charity hadn't the least reason to believe him to be anything but a conceited rogue, who had fallen into debt and was using this scheme to settle his affairs.

And she didn't think it at all fair, or gentlemanly, that he knew full well who his victims were, calling them by name, but keeping his own identity a secret by sporting a mask of his own, as well as a costume more befitting a masquerade than a robbery. He was dressed in a full-skirted burgundy velvet coat, with lace in a froth about his neck and wrists. And covering muscular thighs were tight riding breeches and ancient top boots that were pulled up over his knees and seemed to accentuate the very obvious fact that he was a man of sport, his legs shapely and lean.

But why, Charity wondered, had he accosted her? Penelope had said that he seemed to know when and where his victims were traveling which was why he was reputed to be a member of the *ton*. And yet, he could not have known who she was for she had not been to London in years. Behind him, his companion in arms, also masked, though wearing the garb of a country farmhand, remained astride his horse, holding the reins of the highwayman's fiery black steed, and leveling a pistol at the postillion's sweatstained head.

The postboy, sporting a shock of yellow hair, did not seem to be the least concerned that his life was in danger. He stood beside his lead horse and kept the team of four in check, rubbing a sleeve over his brow and rolling his eyes. If the truth were known, he was bored by the proceedings as well as irritated by the thought that his supper would no doubt be cold by the time these coves had done with the ladies. Not but what the black-haired wench was a beauty of no mean order, but he'd rather have his stomach full and a tankard of ale slipping down his throat than have to wait for these highwaymen to play at being bandits.

Charity waited, her hand pressed to her bosom again, her heart sounding furiously in her ears. The Gentleman's hand was upon the door, and as he peered in at her, he stopped in his movements, drawing back slightly, apparently surprised by what he saw. Charity thought perhaps her own mask had shocked him a little and for that she was grateful as she returned his stare with a lift of her chin.

But a slow smile, even faintly familiar to her, overtook his features and he wasted no time in jerking the door open. And with a lowborn voice, quite at odds with his elegant bearing, the highwayman cried, "Well, well! A raven-haired treasure and hidden so mysterious-like behind a mask! And I can tell, even in these shadows that you ain't the female I wuz expectin'! But you'll do. Indeed, you will! Come!" And glancing at Marie, he inclined his head to her and added, "I'll return yer mistress to ye in nought but a shake of yer fist."

And with that he took Charity's arm firmly and with a steady pressure began drawing her quite easily from the coach. Having accosted a number of ladies before, he had become skilled at the matter and the moment she gained the doorway of the post chaise, he possessed himself of her hand and with a sharp little jerk caused her to lose her balance so that she fairly tumbled into his arms, the rascal! But how neatly he caught her, smiling broadly upon her, holding her fast in an embrace that brought a blush to Charity's cheeks, the full length of his person pressed most despicably against her own body.

"Such a light, delicate flower as I've found!" he exclaimed, apparently delighted with her. "And a beauty, I might guess, by your raven locks! And those eyes! Faith, even in this light—as clear as spring water."

Charity decided in that moment, that she would not submit tamely to this monster's devilish sport, but would do everything she could to rid herself of his verminous presence. And she would start, she decided, by speaking with an intriguing French accent, at which she was most proficient because she had spent the past four years living in Paris and studying the ballet with her dancing master, Monsieur Bovin. He had taught her, in addition to excellent technique, the necessity for emotion and expression in communicating the essence of her dance. It was with little difficulty then, that she brought tears swimming to her eyes and in a light whisper she cried, "Monsieur, I beg you will let me go. You have said yourself that you were waiting for another woman. Pray, allow me to continue on my way!"

"I'd be nought but a bacon-brained gudgeon to do so, what with you speaking like a Frenchy an' promising pure enchantment from these rosy lips!"

Charity tried to keep from becoming tense within the very distracting circle of his arms at this most pointed reference to his intentions—that he meant to take a kiss from her—but she was not as successful as she hoped for he said, with a low chuckle, "Nay, don't go pokering up, Missy. It don't become you. And I'll not hurt a hair on your head, if that's what's troubling you. And most females enjoy me ways."

Charity, using every instinct that Monsieur Bovin had taught her, let a tear trickle from the corner of her eye, down her cheek and when it had passed beyond the edge of her white mask, she continued, "Monsieur, I am no woman of experience as you seem to think. I am innocent!

11

Pray do not do this wretched thing." If she could only catch him unawares she might kick him harshly upon his shin and escape. Although what she thought she would do with his servant who was still brandishing the highwayman's pistol, she did not have the faintest notion. But she was strongly of the opinion that one ought to cross but one bridge at a time, and she continued, "I have suffered greatly these many years in my country, my family, all gone—" She let the words hang, hoping that he might believe they had been destroyed during the course of the revolution.

Her voice, and the tear that he wiped away from her cheek with a soft, gloved hand, seemed to give him pause and he relaxed his hold on her slightly. Charity seized the moment and let go with a hard kick of her half-boot against his own booted leg. He cried out, though she could not determine whether it was in surprise or in pain.

The results, however, were quite inadequate, for his top boots, of the finest leather, protected him sufficiently and he merely cried, "Whoa!" as though he were addressing a spirited horse. "How's this! Tryin' to escape The Gentleman, eh? I like a female with spirit! Like a fine, mettlesome mare what only needs a bit of tamin' to bring her about!"

Charity did not appreciate being likened to a horse and responded hotly, "If Monsieur thinks for one moment that he can put the bridle on me, he is much mistaken!"

The sounds of an approaching mail coach caused the highwayman to again hold her roughly as he said in a whisper, "That I only had a stretch of time to prove different, but I've not more than a few seconds." And he placed his surprisingly gentle lips on her own.

Charity tried to endure the reprehensible feel of the highwayman's kiss by concentrating in an objective fashion on the cold, damp air promising rain in an hour or so, upon the sounds of the postboy squawking about missing his supper if the *gent don't get on wi' it,* about the sounds of a yard of tin blasting out a loud greeting not a quarter of a mile behind them.

But something strange seemed to overtake her senses, and her ability to concentrate faltered dramatically as she found the gentle, sweet search of his lips reaching into her heart, fastening its tender claws about memories she had forgotten completely, and pulling at feelings she had believed long since buried. Her mind filled suddenly with visions of William riding alongside her through the long gully near her village, of William at Christmas and his present of the most fragrant scented gloves perfumed with ambergris, of his warm smile that had caused her to love him from the time she was but a girl of eleven. William. And she threw an arm about the man's neck, the feel of his wig through the wool of her royal blue pelisse quite an odd sensation as he held her even more tightly still. William.

A sudden blast of the horn, sounding shrilly next to the post chaise, tore them apart as they both cast startled eyes upon first one another and then the mail coach that burst by in a maroon blur of tremendous speed. Two or three frisky gentlemen atop the coach, cheered and waved, applauding the performance of the masked lovers, one of them crying out that he, too, enjoyed a truly excellent masquerade.

The highwayman bowed low to the coach as it moved swiftly away and, turning back to Charity, frowned at her, giving his head a shake as though he was trying to solve a puzzle. His expression grew quite thoughtful, even kind, but as he made a motion to step near her, a hand extended toward her, Charity leaped backward and cried, "Monsieur. I forbid you to touch me again. You have taken your stupid kiss and now pray permit me and my maid to continue on our journey."

At these words, the highwayman smiled in an irritating

fashion, as though he found all women to be grossly hypocritical, and effecting a very grand bow, gestured her toward the door of the coach. As she began mounting the steps, he said, "And now, my pretty Mamzelle, the needs of me poor orphans are small—fifty quid would nick the nick!"

Charity answered with a lift of her brow, "Monsieur, I am terribly afraid that you shall be gravely disappointed for I carry nothing on my person. My cousin warned me most strongly about a ridiculous highwayman who accosted females of gentle birth, kissed them, and then demanded payment for his services. And as for the orphans . . . Bah! I spit on you for using innocent babes to disguise the true nature of your crimes! You are an evil, Monsieur! A great evil." She then lifted her chin and directed her gaze toward the front window-glass.

Before the bandit closed the door upon them, he leaned toward Charity and took one of her hands. Holding it gently within his own, he forced her to look at him and in a low voice said, "I'll not quarrel with ye, Miss, though I do enjoy seeing yer eyes spark fire, but as fer me orphans," and at this his voice dropped to a whisper, some of the coarseness to his speech disappearing, and he continued, "I assure you, Mademoiselle, they do indeed exist, painfully so. I only wish that you might see them for yourself to comprehend my mission." And with that, he placed a kiss upon her fingers and before Charity had so much as a chance to realize what he had said to her, he took his leave at a run, mounting his horse with all the spirit of an adventurer, both servant and master disappearing into the beechwoods beside the road.

Charity sat forward upon her seat, her heart feeling strangely desolate as her gaze searched the woods for The Gentleman, but to no avail. A grayness had fallen over the countryside, for the sun had set, and the woods were black with shadows. And what silence seemed to surround her when but moments before, the very air crackled with the highwayman's presence. One of the horses snorted as the postboy mounted the lead horse and Charity sank back into her seat. For one brief moment, when he had spoken in a whisper, Charity not only believed him to be sincere, but wished for him to stay, to remain with her, if but for a little while.

As the post chaise lurched forward, then began moving steadily upon the graveled road, Charity dismissed her thoughts as absurd. He was an unprincipled, ungovernable, arrogant creature who robbed young maidens. That they were always young ladies of wealth had been one aspect of the business which had always intrigued Charity. Of course, a *gentleman* would not rob impoverished maidens, but on the other hand, a man of chivalry would rob no one! She shook her head; there was simply no comprehending the man! But why had he taken to kissing wealthy young ladies in the first place?

And worse, for how was it that such a man, or perhaps such a kiss, should have brought so many feelings coursing through her heart? About William and her childhood days and his sweetness toward her when she was but a little girl. She touched her lips with gloved fingers and felt a sadness rage through her, for William had changed so very much in the past ten years, that she no longer knew the man who treated her own dear cousins, Penelope and Anne, with such overt contempt. And however dear were the memories that now haunted her, she knew that the affection which had once existed between herself and William could never be again.

As the post chaise gained speed over the firm bed of rock on the well-maintained highway, Charity untied the strings of her mask. After she had replaced the mask carefully within the silver paper, she could not resist turning around to gaze at the woods, the silliest hope burning in her heart that just perhaps the highwayman would follow her post chaise. But the shadows were still, the woods quiet, and the bandit gone.

Marie turned to her and begged to know if she was feeling quite well after so brutish an embrace. Charity regarded her maid and seeing the twinkle in her Gallic brown eyes, tweaked Marie's arm and said, "And it is just like you to find the mauling I just endured quite romantic."

"And you did not?" Marie asked, regarding her with a doubting expression on her face.

Charity felt a flush creep up her cheeks, as she stumbled slightly over her words. "I—that is, I take it very unkind in you to mention the matter at all." And as she cleared her throat and straightened her cuffs, she continued, "I won't pretend that I did not find the experience somewhat . . . that is—oh, do stop laughing at me. But what I wish most particularly to know is how could a gentleman actually take to kissing maidenly females when the discovery of his activities most certainly will mean his ostracization from society forever?"

"Mais, cherie, do but think. If you dance the ballet upon the stage at Drury Lane, as you intend to, will you not suffer the same fate as this highwayman were you to be discovered? Will not society be as unforgiving to you as it will one day to this man? And why, I ask you, do you wish to risk your future among polite society? And do you really think that this mask," and she tapped the lid of the box resting between them upon the seat, "will protect you from discovery? No, *cherie,* I hasten to assure you that the gentlemen who see you upon the stage, particularly with your pretty legs exposed so completely, will be wild to know who the ravishing ballerina is."

Charity swallowed hard for her maid had spoken the truth and though her intention to dance the ballet was not considered a crime under the King's Law, such as the theft of fifty pounds was, the *haut ton* would never forgive her

16

performing at Drury Lane. It was strictly forbidden that any young lady of quality appear upon the stage. And her heart turned over completely, as it had a hundred times since her arrival in England but a fortnight earlier, because her ambition was now nearly within reach. For if Monsieur Bovin was to be believed, she had but to audition before the directors of the Drury Lane Theatre and her success was assured. Had she made the right decision to pursue a life upon the stage? Or was she casting away a life that was more important to her than she truly understood, for Marie was right in this one thing: Charity's mask, which she intended to wear during each performance, could not, by the very nature of public curiosity, sustain her anonymity for any considerable length of time.

Chapter Two

William Sandridge, fifth Earl of Redbourne, tore the black curled wig from his head as his horse galloped toward the familiar White Swan Inn. Letting the cool night air dry the sweat on his brow, the wig having been unbearably warm, he let out a cry of both satisfaction and pure pleasure. As the lights from the village sprang into view, he stuffed the wig into a leather satchel attached to his saddle and untied his mask. Bringing his horse to a stop some two hundred yards or more from the village, which was obscured from view by a dense shrubbery, he dismounted his horse, removed the velvet coat as though it were infested with bugs and began stripping off his boots. His servant, having already dismounted, tethered the horses lightly to the shrubs and handed the earl a pair of modern top boots and a coat of blue superfine.

William could not contain the excitement he felt as he hopped about on one leg, trying to get a boot on from a standing position and having the devil of a time accomplishing the task. But he laughed, not caring in the least that he appeared as mad as Bedlam, for his spirits soared with the pleasure of the French girl's kiss. Faith, if he didn't know better, he would swear he had fallen in love with her the very instant his lips touched hers. And the fragrance of her skin reminded him of the scent of ripe peaches, a delicate perfume that he thought he would remember forever.

The servant, a young man nearly as high-spirited as William, merely shook his head at his master's antics, a broad smile on his lips. He had attended the earl on all of his adventures, and set about folding the burgundy coat into a tight bundle and stowing it within a valise slung over the pommel of his saddle. The boots followed shortly thereafter and within minutes, William was astride his horse, both of them trotting the remainder of the distance to the White Swan.

A few moments more and William dismissed his servant to see that both horses were properly bedded down for the night, and on a firm, brisk step, entered the ancient timber-framed inn.

As the innkeeper came bowing up to him, Lord Redbourne cried, "A bottle of your very best brandy, my good man. I've cause for celebration."

"Yes, m'lord. Indeed, m'lord. Right away, m'lord," and the barrel-bellied, gray-whiskered man snapped his fingers to a nearby lackey. Straightening the linen towel he carried over his arm whenever Lord Redbourne graced his humble inn—which had certainly been often enough during the past year—the innkeeper asked, "And may I be so bold as to inquire of yer lordship precisely what good fortune ye might be celebrating?"

Standing before a small gilt mirror in the short hallway before the parlor he had hired for the night, William tidied his hair in a few, deft motions as he responded, "You may, indeed! For I have just kissed the most unearthly French creature. And though I have as yet seen only the sparkle of her blue eyes and the sweet cherry color of her lips, I know that she is far lovelier than Venus. She wore a mask, you see, sporting pearls and a little dangle of ribbons off to the side. And what spirit!—a quality I admire enormously. I

20

only wish that I knew who she was."

"Ah," the innkeeper nodded wisely. "A Frenchwoman. Wearing a mask. Enchanting, indeed yes." And he received the bottle of brandy from the stableboy who always served in the taproom whenever the earl stayed at the inn.

As William turned toward the door to the parlor, he inclined his head to the innkeeper and said, "Mr. Boles, I perceive you are a man of excellent taste."

The innkeeper beamed upon these words and stuttered happily over at least a half-dozen different expressions of gratitude as he followed Lord Redbourne into the parlor. But before he had quite finished his speeches, the earl gave a loud whoop and cried, "Hugh, by God, you came! I'm devilishly glad to see you. How do you go on?" And the innkeeper moved to a sideboard near the door and began preparing two snifters of brandy.

Hugh Bramfield rose from a settle by the fire, where he was lounging quite at his leisure and awaiting the arrival of his friend. He was clearly one of the tallest men of Lord Redbourne's vast acquaintanceship and had served in his majesty's army for a number of years, distinguishing himself in several battles, including Waterloo. But after this decisive victory against Bonaparte, he sold out and settled down, as many a spirited army officer did, to the rackety pleasures of a tame London existence. He was quite handsome, with curling brown hair and deeply set blue eyes which had more than once twisted the tender heart of a pretty English maid. His voice was richly timbered, as he advanced toward William, a hand outstretched to the earl, "And you! I suppose you've been up to your usual masked adventures."

William cast a sidelong glance at the innkeeper who was bustling about the sideboard and straightening the towel over his arm, then reverted his gaze to his friend. "Well, I've not been to a masquerade in ages as it happens, but tell

21

me about yourself. I haven't seen you in weeks." Only then, as the earl took Hugh's elbow and guided him back to the fire where they both reposed themselves, did William notice the rather pinched appearance to the lines about his friend's eyes.

Hugh stretched out his long booted legs before the fire, and, running a hand through his thick locks, took the bowl-shaped glass of brandy from the innkeeper and said, "I must confess that I've been spending half my hours at Drury Lane, for nothing is quite so charming as the ballet." And a mischievous smile lightened the somewhat somber air that seemed to weigh upon him.

Lord Redbourne sat in a comfortable chair, upholstered in what was no doubt once a beautiful red velvet, but now, especially in the candlelight of the small, oak-panelled room, appeared almost brown. He, too, stretched his legs out before a crackling fire made up of hornbeam logs and taking a brandy from the innkeeper, dismissed the landlord of the White Swan, answering his companion, "And is it possible that the *lure* of the ballet in this case might happen to be a certain lively female with bright coppery hair?"

"What?" Hugh cried, astonished. "Oh her? I apprehend you refer to Daisy." And he tossed his hand in the air in a dismissing gesture. "She was far too demanding for my pocketbook and I had had quite enough of her sullens to last me a lifetime. No, Daisy is now dipping quite happily into Somers' purse."

"Impossible!" the earl cried. "How could she, after gracing your bed, entertain a man who wears creaking Cumberland corsets and possesses the longest nose hairs I have ever seen?"

"My dear fellow, though I do appreciate the obvious loyalty of such a remark, I hasten to remind you that Somers is both titled, which lends mightily to an opera-dancer's prestige, and as wealthy as Croesus, which will improve the temper of even the worst termagent. I only wonder that she did not jilt me sooner."

Hugh settled further into his seat, the glass of brandy resting upon his chest and balanced just above a brass button on his bottle green coat. "You are the perfect friend, are you not? Well, as it happens the dibs haven't been in tune for quite sometime and little Daisy, of the sweetest smiles ever, had the worst shrewish temper I have encountered yet. She grew impatient with my lovemaking when I could no longer keep her blue silk-lined phaeton and white horses."

William nodded wisely and Hugh cried, "But enough of her! For as I mentioned, I am still charmed by the ballet."

"Ah. And what is her name?"

"Francoise. Francoise Minon." And his gaze took upon a rather mooncalf expression, his smile soft and warm.

William frowned. "She is French?"

"Every delectable inch of her."

For some unaccountable reason, Will felt a sharp twisting of his heart as he sat up quite straight in his velvet chair and frowned upon his friend. But a few moments ago, he had kissed a Frenchwoman and an odd fear gripped him that he had just been saluting his dearest friend's mistress. Still frowning, he asked, "She would not possess a crown of black ringlets, would she?"

"Francoise? No, no. A very pretty light brown hair, wispy and angelic, eyes of a startling green and her voice— that breathy quality that only the French language can supply and which drives me utterly mad!"

William sighed with profound relief as he remembered his own encounter earlier and nodded his head. There was something exciting about the way the drift of the language played upon one's ears, he thought. And the young lady's lips, so provocative and insistent. Lifting his glass, he proposed a toast, "To our Gallic neighbors who have given us so many fine things and from whom in the future,

23

we dearly hope to receive many more."

Hugh smiled broadly at this as he lifted his glass to William and afterward emptied its contents. But he soon seemed to fall into a brown study, his deeply set blue eyes again appearing quite pinched as he gazed at the fireplace. Every now and again, the logs would crackle and hiss and shoot up a burst of sparks, the smell of the burning wood filling the small square chamber. Above the fireplace was an old painting of a hunter marching through the beechwoods and carrying a brace of pheasant slung over his shoulder. Several fat candles sputtered on the mantel. Hugh's gaze drifted to one of the candles, where a runnel of wax had formed into a lake at the base of the candlestick. In the quiet of the room, he said, "There's only one bit of mischief, though. Damme if I'm not in love with the wench and all I can think about is carting her off to Gretna Green."

William, who had been sipping his brandy, choked upon the fiery liquid and when he spoke, his voice sounded hoarse, "Good God, man, what are you saying?"

"And why shouldn't I wed her!" he cried, though William could see that he was not so much addressing him, but rather trying to convince himself of such a course. "I'm in love with her, I tell you, and she makes me laugh, and she is so very sweet besides not caring for baubles in the least. And more than once when I've been too long at hazard or faro, I make my way to her rooms— God knows how, for I'm always in my cups—and I sleep in her chambers which are scarcely fit to house a family of rats, the poor thing. You don't know what she's like, Will. She's kind and gentle and I don't feel so damned careworn when I'm with her—and, damme, she was maidenly when I—I seduced her." He rose hastily to his feet and setting the snifter upon the mantel, took a turn about the room his hands shoved deeply into his pockets. "I love her I tell you! Is that so very bad?!"

24

William was so taken aback by his friend's distress, that he sat staring at him with his mouth slightly agape. Was this Hugh? Sensible, controlled Hugh, who continued his military regimens of exercise even after selling out, rising early to swim every morning, taking his horses out daily, supper at White's precisely at eight o'clock every evening? Was this him, marching about the parlor of an inn, an anxious expression digging deeply into the lines of his face? Taking a sip of his brandy, the earl said, "If you don't have a care, my dear friend, you shall surely punch holes in the pockets of your coat. I can see through the fabric that your hands are clenched into very tight fists!"

Hugh paused in his steps, and glancing down at his pockets saw that Will was right and he removed his hands with a laugh. Grimacing at his friend, he said, "Have you ever known me to make such a cake of myself?"

William answered with a smile, "Only once, when you were fully in your cups at Almack's and tried to kiss Lady Jersey."

"The devil take you, Will. Why must you put me in mind of that truly wretched incident? I lost my vouchers for the remainder of the season." And he returned to the settle where he again stretched out his feet toward the fire.

The men laughed together and though Will wished to be of some assistance to his friend, he knew by the manner in which Hugh changed the subject entirely, that he did not wish for further discussion regarding the pretty Francoise. Instead, he regaled William with an account of one of the riders during a race at Newmarket he had recently attended, who had been thrown from his horse and carried off the course upon a hurdle, both legs broken. Will made no demur but instead entered into a lively discussion of the various dangers of riding in general, and racing in particular.

After a moment, when the gentlemen were fully satisfied that they agreed completely upon every aspect of horse racing, Hugh asked, "And now tell me, Will, for you are powerfully silent upon the subject, have you spoken yet with Lord Datchworth?"

Will was startled by the question, not so much because it was unexpected, but because his own adventure of the afternoon had completely superseded the astonishing news that very soon he would most likely be engaged. "Yes," he responded with a bewildered shake of his head. "But you will not credit it when I tell you that for the past several hours thoughts of Charity Holwell or her uncle have not so much as entered my brain." He then related how he had somehow managed to stop the wrong post chaise and instead of finding the young woman he meant to harass, had found instead a most intriguing young Frenchwoman. Hugh listened with delight and when William had finished the short history, he said, "Then you can comprehend a little of my feelings for Francoise."

Will responded with a smile. "My good man, if the kiss I shared with Francoise's compatriot were any indication, I no longer wonder that you wish to rush your opera-dancer to the altar. What bliss such a marriage would entail!"

"Then you do understand the nature of the dilemma I face, but tell me why you have then offered for a female you have not seen in years? You cannot possibly be in love with her."

"Oh, no . . . at least, I don't know what my feelings for her may yet become. I only remember her as a little girl. But I am no longer sanguine in my hopes that I will one day fall magically in love for Cupid seems unable to pierce my hide with any of his arrows! I'm certain it is my fault entirely that no female has yet won my heart—"

"No, no. The truth is that you have been too much pursued for your rank. It is a common enough failing amongst the matchmaking Mamas of our society. But are you certain you are being wise?"

"What? To have chosen a marriage of convenience, one

that, I will point out, pleases my dear mother immensely. It was she who, this Christmas past, pointed me in Miss Holwell's direction for she mentioned quite by chance that she rather thought Charity would be returning to London this season. I had always known that she and Charity's mother had wished for a match, but it is greatly to Mama's credit that she has not once in recent years said as much."

Barely disguising a yawn, Hugh rolled his eyes and said, "As much as I respect your mother, I cannot but feel the very worst reason to marry is to please one's parent."

"I consider this aspect of the business not a reason, but a happy benefit. If it has not escaped your notice, I am three and thirty and now wish simply to set up my nursery. The Sandridge estates fell to me by default, not by birthright, as you well know—"

"A younger son always has a birthright. I don't know what you mean," Hugh said, as he snuggled more deeply still into the cushions of the settle, the snifter still upon his chest.

How could William explain to anyone his feelings regarding the earldom which he never truly believed belonged to him. His brother John had inherited the title, and perished not six months later from a virulent bout of the influenza. And that was some ten years ago, just as William was preparing to enter the army with his good friend, Hugh Bramfield. He had never wanted anything else than a career alongside Hugh and it hadn't occurred to him once in his comings and goings that his father or John would die. But they had, and that within a year of one another.

And John had been on the brink of matrimony, as well. So, as the only remaining son, William had been thrust into a role he neither wanted nor was in the least prepared for. But undoubtedly the worst aspect of the matter had been how thoroughly the attitude of the females of his acquaintance shifted dramatically. He had felt from the first that no longer was he William Sandridge, but a bit of golden merchandise displayed at Almack's, the Royal Italian Opera House, and every fashionable drawing room in Mayfair. And how much he missed the earlier days with Hugh, of high spirits and reprehensible pranks, like the time they stole a bear from a gypsy camp and frightened all the villagers at a Maying near his country seat. He tossed off his brandy and as the image of John's betrothed took possession of his brain, he felt such a loathing within his heart, that he nearly crushed the glass in his hand. Penelope Ware. How could John have loved her for her heart was carved out of ambition—not once in the past several years had she relented in her pursuit of him.

Penelope had been his first victim as The Gentleman, and how much he had enjoyed inflicting his kisses upon the coldest fish that ever existed and with such relish did he watch her part with fifty pounds as though he had just chopped off her leg. And her words, spoken to what she believed to be a lowborn thief, confirmed his every opinion of her, *I don't give a fig for your orphans or anyone else's. Why should I? They ought not to have been born in the first place and merely reflect the gross immorality of their parents.* He had been dumbstruck, though not entirely surprised by her opinions, and he would have demanded another fifty pounds in penance for the coldness of her heart, but a black curricle appeared in the distance, traveling down the road at a spanking pace. Flourishing a bow he hoped appeared full of mockery, he could not resist calling her a fish and disappeared into the woods. He looked back only once and found her standing beside the post chaise a model of outraged maidenhood as she watched him depart, stamping her feet in a childlike frustration. And Penelope was Charity's cousin! Well, perhaps a small part of him, too, wished to see Penelope writhe under his choice of a bride, for though Charity

28

certainly by dint of her connections, was worthy of his rank, Penelope's station in society, as the daughter of a viscount, as well as her former engagement to his brother, had a far greater claim to such worldly rewards as a title and all the privileges which would attend a peeress of the realm. And had only she been less obvious in her desire to secure just such a position, Will rather thought he would have given her serious consideration for she was an elegant creature in every respect, save the heart.

Rubbing his forehead with the tips of his fingers, William considered Hugh's question again—why had he decided to marry? He said, "Though I have never been completely at ease with my circumstances, the irony is that I wish for a son of mine to inherit the earldom. I may not have wished for it myself, and a dozen times I may have cursed the title for its limitations and strictures, but damme, I want my flesh and blood to possess it." He shook his head with a laugh. "Perhaps I feel more deeply about my inheritance than I realized. How odd that I should, only now—" What a very odd noise that was, he thought, and as he looked over at his dearest friend, he saw that Hugh's eyes were closed, the brandy snifter was still sitting upon his chest, and his lips were popping open in the most amusing manner, followed by rumbling snores.

Will rose from his chair and in a quiet voice said, "I take it most unkindly in you that you must fall asleep when I am speaking with such eloquence about my own dear self." And taking the snifter from its precarious station, he decided to let his good friend remain gently within his sleep. As he regarded the creased brow and the deep lines etched beside Hugh's mouth, William frowned. Only that morning had he learned that this distinguished officer was on the brink of financial ruin.

Chapter Three

Charity paused in the doorway and stayed the butler from speaking for the barest moment. She wanted to take it all in at once, to observe her cousins and aunt grouped about a very fine inlaid table of burr walnut, before her presence was made known to them. They were involved in a homey task, arranging flowers in an elegant blue and white vase, and Penelope was speaking in a low tone to her mama. And though Lady Datchworth wore an expression of grave concern upon her face as she listened intently to her eldest daughter, the picture still held all the warmth and tenderness of a family party which Charity had missed sorely over the past four years.

Anne and Penelope stood over a vase, which was thick with an abundance of spring flowers, and were struggling with the placement of a final pink rose. Anne cried out that she had just pricked her finger and Penelope begged her not to stain the embroidery beneath the vase with droplets of blood which Anne would surely do if she did not take great care! Anne responded to her sister's sharp tone by pouting at Penelope and sucking upon her finger, while Lady Datchworth, who was seated beside the table, placed a hand upon Penelope's arm, and said, "But never mind that! Are you certain she will not wish to marry him?

Oh, dear. And after your father promised! What shall we do?''

"I don't know," Penelope said, shaking her head, so that her delicate brown ringlets, drawn up into a knot atop her head, seemed to dance about her pretty face. "But you had best permit me to speak with her first. You see I know her sentiments quite well because of all my correspondence with her." Lady Datchworth nodded and the ladies then fell silent and still Charity refused to give Hinx permission to announce her. She hadn't the least notion to whom Penelope was referring, but all she wanted of the moment was to enjoy this pleasing sensation of coming home after so long a time.

The drawing room was alive with furniture and flowers all jumbled together in a haphazard fashion, at least a dozen small bowls of violets scattered amongst several large bouquets of ferns, yellow daffodils, pink and red roses, and peonies. The scent of the roses assailed Charity with a warm remembrance of saying good-bye to her beloved relatives in this same chamber when she had left upon her adventure to France. Charity found tears smarting her eyes as she glanced from one beloved face to the next—to Anne who had grown quite stout, though her warm smile and sweet expression were as welcoming as ever, to her somewhat vain and flighty aunt, who wore an exquisite turban of orange silk draped with several strands of small matched pearls, to Penelope who was at that moment sliding the recalcitrant rose, whose thorns kept clinging to the other flowers, into the crowded vase. How elegant Penelope was, presenting a truly Grecian aspect in her white empire gown embroidered in gold floss about the hem in the classical Greek key pattern.

Only when Lady Datchworth, as though sensing Charity's presence, turned her head toward the doorway, did Charity signal the butler to announce her.

A delighted smile suffused her aunt's features as she rose

from a blue and white striped chair, to greet her niece. "My dearest child!" Lady Datchworth cried as she rushed toward Charity and began chattering as though a matter of days instead of years had separated them. "I forgot how pretty you are and how black your hair is! And that bonnet, very *a la mode* and are they wearing so much of just this shade of blue in Paris? It is quite becoming for it matches your eyes. Well, you shall certainly set the *ton* by the ears and tomorrow we must all do a little shopping for we have so many treats in store for you this season that you will not credit how gay we all shall be! And I have in mind for you this lovely cashmere shawl, of the palest peach color, which most certainly would enhance any of your Parisian gowns!" And after kissing Charity's cheek, though having to bend at an awkward angle to keep the turban from becoming entangled in Charity's poke bonnet, she cried, "Come!" And she took Charity's hand, pulling her forward into the room to greet her cousins.

Beyond the flowers, the drawing room was a fine example of Lady Datchworth's impeccable taste, for the long chamber was decorated in white scrollwork and molding, papered in a delicate print of light blue and gold stripes, while the drapes were entirely in gold and hung with large tassels. The furniture, which was a scattering of settees and chairs arranged for the entertainment of a veritable crush of guests, was in a variety of patterns of blue and gold with an occasional burgundy spray of flowers that complimented the various occasional tables of cherrywood.

Anne did not hesitate to enfold Charity within the circle of her plump arms. "Dearest cousin, you have been gone far too long. Oh, do but let me have a look at you." She pulled back slightly, still holding each of Charity's hands and squeezing them as she said, "You are by far more beautiful than ever I remembered, is she not Pen?"

Penelope's well-modulated voice drifted across the table

which separated them. "Indeed, yes. But I have always known that our Charity would grow into an enviable example of womanhood."

Charity looked from Anne to Penelope and felt her throat constrict painfully as she said, "I have had so many wonderful experiences in Paris and I was surrounded by many of Furney's cousins and I was so busy that I scarcely kept track of the days even when we were buried up to our ears in snow. You cannot imagine! But until this very moment, I did not realize how much I have missed you both, and you dear Aunt!" And with that, tears spilled from her brimming eyes and all the ladies found it necessary to scatter about the chamber in search of kerchiefs.

Once they had all sniffled into their lace handkerchiefs and laughed at one another, Anne cried, "Oh, pooh! And we had promised one another not to become watering pots and here you are making it quite impossible to be anything but!" She then slipped her arm through Charity's and walking beside her led her to a cosy group of chairs and a settee by the fire where Charity soon found herself relating as many scandalous *on dits* of Parisian society as she could possibly remember. But as she asked about each of the three women and about whether Almack's had continued to be as exclusive as ever, Charity was again struck with how precious these friends from childhood were. She wanted never to be separated from them again, and with that the thought of her own intentions to audition at Drury Lane in two days time brought her up so short that she felt the blood drain from her cheeks, her head growing quite dizzy.

"My dear, you look very ill of a sudden. What is the matter?" And though she heard her aunt speak these words, Charity thought that Lady Datchworth's voice sounded strangely muffled as though she had addressed her from a great distance. Nodding in an attempt to reassure her aunt that there was nothing wrong with her, Charity soon found Anne's vinaigrette beneath her nose and Penelope patting her hand.

Pushing the gold vinaigrette away from her, Charity cried, "No, no, please! I am perfectly well, thank you. It is only that—" And she broke off, aware that she could not possibly tell either her cousins or her aunt that she had been studying the ballet in Paris for the past several years and that now she meant to perform upon the stage at the Theatre Royal in Drury Lane! Taking a deep breath, and attempting to smile, she said, "It is just that I am so very excited to be here."

Penelope narrowed her eyes at Charity and appeared as though she meant to ask her if anything else was amiss but at that moment, Lord Datchworth burst into the room and in his jovial fashion, as he rubbed his hands together with delight, cried, "So, Abigail, where have you hidden her? Ah, there she is! Couldn't see her for all these curst flowers! Don't know why my home must smell like a succession house!"

"Because of Charity's party, of course," Lady Datchworth answered in a rather cold manner.

Charity was a little surprised by the reserved inflection in her aunt's voice, but she had always held Lord Datchworth in much affection and smiled happily upon him as she watched him approach.

Lord Datchworth was a tall gentleman, and quite handsome for his five and fifty years, with dark, playful brown eyes and a fine crop of light, silvery hair. "Uncle Stephen!" Charity cried. "How dashing you appear in your black pantaloons and coat and is that the style of neckcloth known as *trone d'amour*? Oh, but you must still be a considerable favorite with the ladies." And for the barest moment, Charity felt the form of her aunt, who remained seated beside her, stiffen alarmingly, as though Charity had touched a delicate nerve between her aunt and uncle.

Lord Datchworth, who by now had reached the perimeter of their small coterie, responded with a smile hidden behind his brown eyes. "Why, of course I am! Could you ever doubt it?" And with that, he cast his wife a triumphant, challenging look which effectively brought a rather stoney appearance to her aunt's expression as Lady Datchworth again pinched her lips together and cast her pale blue eyes toward the carpet.

The tensions which now crackled in the air were impossible to ignore, but Lord Datchworth, though resting a concerned gaze upon his wife's bowed head for a moment, chose to direct his attention fully to Charity as he took one of her hands and pulled her to her feet. "Now, let me have a look at you!" And holding her hand outstretched much as Anne had done earlier, he cried, "Now how is it that my wife and daughters have kept you sitting here in your pelisse and, good God, what an enormous poke bonnet. All the crack in Paris no doubt! Pretty pink ribbons though!" And he flicked one of the ribbons with his finger still smiling upon her. "And you've grown into a beauty, damme if you haven't! Though you're nearly as thin as Penelope! What is it with young ladies today? Hardly enough flesh upon you to squeeze!"

"You are very naughty, you know!" Charity responded and pulling free of his hand, gave her uncle a quick hug. "Wicked, wicked man!"

"That's a good girl," he said, returning her hug in his brisk fashion. But when he tried to kiss her forehead the top of his head collided with her bonnet. "Confounded hat of yours nearly knocked me over." And without a moment's hesitation, he tugged gently upon the bow, until the pink satin ribbons hung in two streamers, and in a deft manner, lifted the bonnet from her head. "But this I will say, I've not the smallest doubt but what William will be immensely pleased with you!"

At these words, Anne and Penelope both gasped while Lady Datchworth cleared her throat and in a quiet manner, began, "Stephen—"

But Lord Datchworth had a mission to accomplish and merely lifted a hand, saying, "In a moment, in a moment!" And to Charity he said, "Now off with your pelisse and let's see if Furney has you turned out in style. I was always quite a judge of the ladies' fashions, you know."

Charity was glad to be relieved of her pelisse, for the drawing room had grown quite warm of a sudden and what could her uncle have meant by his reference to William? And even as she busied herself in removing her pelisse, her thoughts turned to the earl and much to her chagrin she felt a blush suffuse her cheeks. If only her uncle would not notice, for he was exceedingly playful and would be quite content to twit her about any blush that might play havoc upon her fair skin, the rascal!

But her uncle was quite a perceptive man, as he took her chin in hand and gazed at her cheeks. "I see that they've told you! And what do you think about heaven's fortune smiling upon you in this manner?"

Charity cocked her head slightly as she cried, "But I don't understand? We've not exchanged a word about— about William!"

"Stephen, for heaven's sake! The child has just arrived!"

Lord Datchworth regarded his wife with a startled expression. "Do you mean you have said nothing to her? Not even in your correspondence?" And taking the pelisse from off his niece's shoulders as Charity turned slightly away from him, he regarded her with a rather joyous expression as he said, "By Jove, then, you've the sweetest surprise awaiting you, my lovely Charity! For if you've a mind to, and I've little doubt but what your answer will be—for you were always chasing after William with your petticoats muddied and your knees scratched and dirty—"

37

"Stephen!" his wife called to him sharply.

Lord Datchworth frowned as he turned to his wife, but seeing her expression of grave reproach, he coughed twice and after saddling her with Charity's pelisse and bonnet, he said, "That is, I'm certain your aunt will be happy to tell you everything!"

"But Uncle!—"

He patted her shoulder. "There, there! I won't say another word for my wife is like to scratch my eyes out if I don't let her deliver the good news herself!" And after eyeing his wife warily, he coughed again and sputtered, "Well, well. We are certainly glad to have you amongst us and I don't mean to be uncivil."

He pulled a silver watch from his waistcoat pocket and popping the lid open, exclaimed, "Is that the time! Zeus, but I promised old Langley I'd meet him at White's half an hour past!" Replacing his watch in his pocket, he again kissed Charity upon the cheek and turning to his wife, placed a rather tiny peck upon her cheek as well and after telling the ladies not to gabble themselves hoarse, he was gone.

Lady Datchworth rose to her feet and walked slowly to the door where she set the blue pelisse and poke bonnet upon a long table of cherrywood. Charity watched her, at the hint of a stoop to her aunt's shoulders, and she felt as though her warm welcome to London had dimmed quite suddenly. Her aunt was clearly distressed by some difficulty with her husband. Anne and Penelope were watching their mother as well, only Anne wore the worst, most conspiratorial expression upon her face as she turned toward Charity and whispered, "I shall come to your bedchamber as soon as my maid has tied my mobcap about my curls, and tell you everything!"

And with that Charity had to be content. But as for the hints her uncle had dropped, she could not imagine why William should have any interest in her after so long a time. Why it almost sounded as though he had offered for her but that was quite impossible. They took part in a few scrapes when she was a child and he was but in his salad days, scooping her up to ride before him upon his horse, climbing walnut trees and gathering the nuts for Cook— and how shocked Mama had been at her unmaidenly conduct and yet somehow pleased for she couldn't abide the wan complexions of young ladies who never enjoyed the least exercise. And how very many times had Charity and William gotten caught in the rain when he was teaching her to ride as a girl of twelve. At least a dozen! But he was going into the army soon, and wanted to see her properly instructed so that when he returned they might ride out together. And how was it they had become such fast friends, for she was but a child in comparison to his two and twenty years—he was a man, in fact.

But they had shared adventures—perhaps that was both the rhyme and the reason—and perhaps he had recognized in her a similar spirit, a longing for life to hold an excitement that seemed to be lacking in the decorous lives of those around them. But he would have his adventures, for he would very soon become a cavalry officer!

And then all had changed quite suddenly, her mother had perished of the consumption within six months of learning of her illness and John, William's brother, had died when a virulent influenza ravaged the countryside. And with this thought she glanced at Penelope who she believed had never stopped grieving for her betrothed, for Penelope's future had been brightest of all, for had John lived she would now be the Countess of Redbourne.

None of their lives had gone unaffected by these two deaths, and what disparate paths they had each taken, so at odds with the initial dreams of youth: William had become an earl, his longed for career in the army cut off; Penelope had grown in to a spinster, though she had received at least six offers of marriage since John's death;

39

and Charity, well, she had lived in Paris for four years, her intent to master the ballet so that she might pursue a career upon the stage!

Lady Datchworth remained in her contemplative stance for only a few seconds and then, catching sight of herself in the mirror above the table, smiled suddenly, pinched her cheeks several times and when she turned around to face her niece and her daughters, her spirits seemed completely restored. "I don't know how it is that your uncle, my dear Charity, can always succeed to throw me into a fit of the megrims, but alas, he knows me far too well and has merely to say a well-chosen word or two and I am mad as fire! But enough of that!"

Lady Datchworth returned to the group by the fire where she stood near the mantel and regarded Charity as though she were deeply perplexed. When all three young ladies were staring at her, she finally said, "I only learned from Penelope but a few moments earlier that your sentiments with regard to William are not what either myself nor your uncle supposed them to be. Indeed, when we remember that you were a particular favorite of his from the time you were a child, well, you may imagine our surprise. You do know that he inherited the earldom some time ago when his brother, John, died of the influenza?"

Charity glanced at Penelope who sat in a winged chair of yellow silk, her body unearthly still as though held suspended by some inward thought, her long white fingers rippling faintly over the spokes of a painted wheel fan. Charity was saddened by the distant expression on her cousin's face and felt that her suspicions were confirmed yet again that Penelope still loved John.

Answering her aunt's question, Charity shifted her gaze back to Lady Datchworth and said, "I daresay everyone knew that William had come into the title."

Lady Datchworth regarded Charity in a searching manner, her own brow knit in concern as she said, "It is very important to me that I know precisely what your sentiments regarding William are. You were fond of him at one time, were you not? And is Penelope correct in her belief that you could not love him?''

Charity tried to keep her fingers from trembling and hoped that her face was as expressionless as she wished it to be. Clasping her hands together tightly and grateful that her soft kid gloves covered knuckles which she was certain had turned white with her distress, she took a deep breath and said, ''I have had so many mixed reports of William over the years that now I scarcely know what to think of him. Until John's death, I must confess that I loved Will very much, like a brother, and after my own mother died and I removed to Kent to reside with my cousin, Furney, I had very little contact with him, save for the appearance of little presents he would send to me now and again, and about once a year for three or four years, a hastily drawn letter. I had no reason to feel anything but kindness toward him until I removed to Paris. Since that time, however, I have heard such dreadful news of him that I cannot but say that my affection for him has been considerably tempered.'' She lowered her gaze to regard the delicate folds of her white muslin walking dress. She was begowned in the latest mode of fashion for the year 1819, with several rows of ruffles gracing the hem of her gown.

Penelope began fanning herself with the wheel fan, and in a quiet voice said, ''I am to blame, then. I have been too open, too opinionated. You have been overly persuaded by my misfortunes and would still hold him in affection had not I written to you about his treatment of me.'' And turning to her mother, she said, ''I have said too much to her. It is my fault if she refuses him!''

Charity frowned at her cousin and turning to her aunt, said, ''But what does this mean? Of what are you speaking? Almost I begin to think that William has made a formal offer for my hand in marriage, but that is quite impossible!"

"There you are out!" Lady Datchworth cried. "For he was closeted with your uncle in his office on Thursday last for over an hour, and made precisely that—a formal, quite generous offer for your hand in marriage! It was the most fantastic thing and quite set your uncle into a spin! I don't think he is yet fully recovered. First he blessed himself and then you since he is your legal guardian! And though I can comprehend how my daughter's experiences at his hands might have persuaded you that he is not a man you can love, I feel it my duty, as your aunt, besides believing that I stand in your mother's stead at this moment, to recommend to you that you think his proposals through most carefully before you give him an answer. And though I believe it a wonderful thing to marry for love, having done so myself and only occasionally regretting it, the very real benefits of becoming the next Countess of Redbourne are a prospect not to be discarded without due consideration."

Upon these words, Charity could not restrain the sudden anger that overtook her as she rose to her feet, and moved to stand beside Penelope's chair. "I can scarcely credit that this has happened at all! And though I believe you are quite sincere in what you say, for I do realize that a sense of duty would oblige you to advise me to consider Lord Redbourne's proposals, I simply cannot comprehend why William would offer for me at all! The man who has publicly humiliated both my cousins, and that upon more than one occasion, has actually had the audacity to ask for my hand in marriage? It is unthinkable! Has he grown conceited as well as cruel and inconsiderate of the sensibilities of others? I begin to think him quite insufferable or perhaps merely stupid! Does he think that I am not without loyalties, that I do not know where my duties and obligations lie—?"

Lady Datchworth cried, "Pray calm yourself! I can see

by your heightened color that you are quite angry, and perhaps understandably so, only do not make your decision hastily. After all, you do not need to accept his proposals or reject them for some time. I am certain that he will want you to reacquaint yourself with his mother who is in town for the season."

"Lady Redbourne is here? For the season? But I thought she was an invalid."

Lady Datchworth nodded. "I understand she has come up to London upon his request—to see you."

"Oh, no! And all for nought! Poor woman! Well, this is just another example of his extreme selfishness."

Lady Datchworth wanted to say more, but her niece's ideas seemed so fixed that she thought it better to wait, and merely responded, "Perhaps you can meet him at the soiree we are holding in your honor on Thursday evening. Then you may judge for yourself if he is beyond redemption in your eyes."

And though Charity inclined her head to her aunt and told her that in this situation she would certainly abide by Lady Datchworth's decision, she had, in her heart, already judged for herself. William Sandridge, Earl of Redbourne, was not the sort of man who could possibly make her happy. And though she had any number of truly fond memories of him from childhood, nothing could prevail upon her to accept his proposals. Nothing!

Later that evening, the young ladies linked arms and mounted the stairs together, Anne laughing the entire while for she had partaken of more wine at dinner than she ought to have and somehow found amusement in everything. Charity and Penelope exchanged several glances whenever Anne would fall into a fit of giggles and when they had arrived at the landing, Penelope whispered, "Charity, come with me to my bedchamber for I have something I must ask you."

She then tried to encourage Anne to go to her bedchamber directly, but Anne was sufficiently in command of herself to know that she was being got rid of and insisted upon joining them in Penelope's room. "After all," she cried, "I promised Charity that I would tell her about Mama and Papa!"

Once inside Penelope's chamber, Charity stopped upon the threshold and exclaimed, "How very elegant!" For the room was decorated entirely in gilt, white, and burgundy. Scrollwork of Grecian urns and acanthus leaves adorned the furniture, mirrors, and picture frames, as well as the molding about the ceiling. Even the counterpane was embroidered with gold floss. Everything sat tidily in place, no dust marred a single surface. As Charity glanced about the room, she was struck in a rather odd manner that though the bedchamber was perfection in the Classical mode, it seemed to be lacking an essential warmth or vibrancy. Seating herself upon a chaise longue of white silk, she regarded Penelope and thought that the bedchamber was very much like her cousin, though Pen of course had a warm heart. Charity had always held her cousin in the highest esteem for Pen was a model of refinement in which every sensibility was kept carefully in check so that always she presented herself to the *beau monde* as the epitome of elegant womanhood. She was a tall creature, taller than Charity by a full two inches, and very thin so that the gauzy muslins and draped silks which were the current mode lent her the appearance of a goddess. She had light brown hair which she wore in precisely the same manner every day, with a fringe of wispy curls upon her forehead, and the remainder of her curled locks drawn up into a knot at the top of her head, and pinned in a Grecian drape of curls almost to her shoulders. No romping here, Charity thought.

Penelope drew forward a small, Empire-style chair, and

seating herself near Charity, regarded her with an amused expression and asked, "And what, my dear, dear Charity were your secret thoughts this evening, which you hoped to keep hidden from my mother! And don't pretend you do not comprehend of what I am speaking for there was nothing in my description of the Almack's Assembly Rooms which could possibly have caused you to pale so dreadfully as you did! And don't try to tell a whisker for I am not easily gammoned!"

Anne wrinkled her brow at Penelope and said, "Oh, Pen! What are you talking about? Charity told us she was merely excited to be here, to be home with us! Is that so very hard to comprehend?"

Charity looked from one cousin to the other, her thoughts tumbling quickly through her mind. She could not tell either of them about her schemes to dance at Drury Lane—at least not yet. She knew she had to devise some sort of story to satisfy Penelope, but what? And suddenly she realized that she had the perfect solution and as Anne sat down beside Charity upon the chaise longue, she swallowed hard—for she was not at all used to pre-varicating, and addressing Anne, said, "Your sister is quite right! I was hoping to conceal a matter which caused me a great deal of distress this very afternoon!"

Opening her eyes wide, Anne cried, "Oh, but how absolutely delicious! Pray tell us at once!"

Charity said, "As it happens, I chanced upon The Gentleman this afternoon! Yes, you may stare! And given the truly reprehensible manner in which he accosted me, I am certain you cannot wonder that when I recalled his attack my heart nearly failed me!"

Both ladies immediately exclaimed their horror at the incident and Anne, her blue eyes wide with excitement, cried, "Good gracious! You do not mean our notorious highwayman! He stopped your post chaise, and—and ravished you?"

Charity was so taken aback by her cousin's choice of expression that she gasped, "Anne Ware! No, of course he did not. A kiss, merely, I assure you!"

Anne's shoulders seemed to slump. "How very unromantic!"

Charity and Penelope joined in a remonstrative chorus as they cried together, "Anne!"

Penelope added, "You cannot possibly know what you are saying! Ravished, indeed!"

But Anne ignored this rebuke and with her eyes sparkling as she pressed a hand to her bosom, she said, "Oh, do but think how exciting it would be were such a man to abduct you to a sailing ship and whisk you across the seas!"

Charity knew at once that her cousin truly did not comprehend the full import of such an abduction and she responded with a twinkle in her eye, "Well! I am very grateful he did not for I am always violently ill upon crossing even a very short channel—and that in the calmest of waters!"

Penelope, her own complexion whiter than usual, said, "I can see that you mean to joke us about so distressing an attack, but I am seriously disturbed to know that The Gentleman still means to continue his onerous activities!" Charity saw that her cousin was very much upset by the incident and was not surprised that Pen rose to her feet and began pacing the room. "For some time now Mama and I have been considering contacting Bow Street to see if something might not be done about this horrid bandit! You may be assured that when Mama learns of this, she will not hesitate to send one of our servants round to the runners! I shall see to that myself!"

Anne, whose plump face and blue eyes had taken on the dreamiest of aspects, now pressed both hands to her large bosom, and closing her eyes, said, "Well, I can only hope that the runners are not too successful, at least not right

46

away, for I wish that I might be The Gentleman's next victim. Oh, were I to be kissed just once by so wicked a creature! Charity, did you know that I was with Penelope when our highwayman first accosted her? And he was about to kiss me, too, when that stupid old man in the tilbury stopped and cried out, *Ho there, are you in need of some assistance?* Now why is it, I ask you, that when you *do* require the aid of a perfect stranger, one is never to be found, but at the very moment that a little civil disinterest would win the day, the entire world must cry out, *Ho there!* Well, I need not tell you that such a kindness soon put The Gentleman to flight and I was left to dream about the very thing you and Penelope have had the great good fortune to experience. I was never so disappointed in my entire life as when the bandit eased his horse through a break in the hedge of buckthorn and then disappeared into the wooded hills." She sighed gustily, her eyes wearing a mooncalf expression.

Penelope clicked her tongue at her sister but merely commented that she wished for the sake of those ladies who might possibly be less romantic than Anne, that the highwayman's activities be brought to a halt.

Charity said, "I am very sure you are right and I would be happy to speak with one of the runners myself if you think it might help. But now, I simply must know what has gone amiss between my aunt and my uncle and why did my aunt seem so distressed this evening?"

Anne went off into a peal of laughter and cried, "Because my Papa is pretending again to have a mistress!" She laughed again, this time at Charity's expression of horror and cried, "Oh do but look, Pen, how very shocked Charity is!"

"Do hush, Anne. You speak far too frivolously about a serious matter!" Penelope reseated herself upon the small chair covered in a burgundy damask and spoke somewhat impatiently, "For years now, my parents have been

47

playing at this truly wretched game—Papa feigns possessing a mistress, when all he does is go to White's and lose at faro until one or two o'clock in the morning, splash perfume upon his person, and return home with an air of worldliness!"

"Whatever for?" Charity cried.

Anne giggled as she continued the explanation. "Mama, you see, tends to ignore him during the course of the season, for she becomes quite caught up in cardplay herself. Why, last year she lost over a thousand pounds! And Papa does not wish her to gamble as she does, for indeed she seems to possess a true gamester's spirit. For several seasons he badgered her, trying to force her to stop, but his efforts only seemed to make the situation worse. And one day, he threatened to take a mistress, for he could see that she loved her cards more than she did him, and instantly she settled down, the fever disappearing almost entirely. Ever since then, we have enjoyed watching this charade immensely, have we not, Penelope?"

"I cannot profess to have taken any enjoyment in it whatsoever. But now we have another matter to contend with, do we not? Charity, I wished somehow that I had been able to prepare you for William's proposals. Whatever will you tell him?"

Anne puckered her brow and pursed her lips. "Yes, cousin, what do you mean to do?" She shook her blond curls and said, "I was so certain you loved him! You were always hanging upon his coattails when you were young!"

"I was used to be very fond of him when I was a child, I would never deny that," Charity said, a very odd lump forming in her throat as she thought of William. "For he was exceedingly kind to me after Papa died." Her father, who had been quite dear to her, had perished some twelve years earlier on a walking expedition about the Cumberland fells. He had been too hasty when confronted by a deceptive climb amongst boulders near a waterfall, and had fallen, breaking his neck and dying instantly. He had been a gentleman of great spirit, full of adventure and daring, and his many friends had mourned his passing with heartfelt grief.

Anne regarded Charity with a sympathetic smile as she said, "And do you know, I think your Papa would have approved of William! Do you remember the time when we were all at Chisley Hall, and the pair of you came in dripping wet from having taken a toss in the duck pond! And did John give William a dressing down for having nearly drowned you! Though how you could possibly have perished in but two feet of water, was never quite clear to me! Still, John was ready to draw Will's cork!"

Charity had forgotten that escapade of theirs. And how angry her dancing master had been when she had come down with a dreadful cold two days later. She was about to remark upon it when Penelope cried, "Anne! Such a vulgar expression. Wherever do you learn such wretched things? *Draw his cork*, indeed! I daresay, however, that George Meesden uses such cant phrases all the time!"

Charity was surprised, as she regarded her cousin, that Penelope's tone of voice could harbor such a measure of bitterness. Next to her, Anne's entire form had grown stiff with anger, her hands clenched into fists, as she cried, "How dare you say such a thing! And you know very well that Mr. Meesden would never speak to me in such a manner!" Her tone grew almost insolent as she responded, "He may only be the third son of a baron, but I had far rather he courted me than your moldy old viscount Meares!"

Penelope could not let this pass. "But at least my beaux are mature, grown-up men, instead of boys scarcely out of university!"

Charity regarded the sisters with no small degree of astonishment. How very much the congenial family atmosphere had altered since her departure for Paris so long ago. She knew that both her cousins were quite willing to continue quarreling, so she lifted a hand and said, "I hope you don't mean to pull one another's hair out on my first night here. Could you possibly wait until tomorrow?"

The ladies turned to regard Charity as though they had forgotten she existed, and both of them had enough grace to blush slightly as well as to beg Charity's forgiveness for their unseemly conduct. But it was quite clear to Charity that this battle had been raging for some time and would no doubt resurface as soon as the occasion presented itself. Biting her lip, she looked from one face to the other. She had scarcely been in London for three hours and already the Datchworth household seemed fraught with difficulties. And worse! For she was herself about to add to the abundant tensions already present. And she wondered just how long she would be able to keep her own identity as a ballerina secret?

Chapter Four

Charity had never seen so ugly a man in her life as the Bow Street runner who stood with his shoulders squared before Lord Datchworth. The runner identified himself as a former barrister who had developed a considerable liking for the profession of thief taker because he found he enjoyed doing battle with the underworld. He was of medium height, and had a short, though quite pronounced scar upon his left cheek that was reddish in hue and in stark contrast to his pale skin. Curly black hair, which was unkempt, hung about an unruly face composed of a wide flat nose, bushy black brows, and the odd angles of a jutting chin, a square forehead, and uneven cheekbones. He was missing a tooth and as he enumerated his excellent qualifications to Lord Datchworth, Charity could not help but notice that several of the rest of his teeth had not seen quite enough tooth powder in the man's forty years. In every respect, but most especially because he was well-muscled from his thick neck to his heavy thighs, he presented an appearance of menace.

Charity, Penelope, and Lady Datchworth stood, almost knit together, near the window that fronted Grosvenor Square, the morning light behind them flooding the small chamber. And as they gazed upon the runner, even Lady

Datchworth whispered that she wished Bow Street had sent over a more appealing man than the cretin which kept scanning nearly every object in her husband's office.

The viscount's office was a particular refuge of his and was paneled in a beautiful mahogany wood. In the center of the room, Lord Datchworth sat behind a large curved desk of golden walnut. He seemed out of patience with the runner, as he listened to the man's recital, leaning forward in his chair, his hands folded as he tapped his thumbs together. In a tidy row at the edge of his desk sat a silver inkwell, a tray of pens, and an ancient blotter with a bold *D* engraved upon the handle.

The runner was in the process of listing what strides thus far had been made toward the apprehension of The Gentleman, making it quite clear that the greatest inhibitor to Bow Street's progress had been the inaccurate information the ladies were wont to give, saying that the description of the bandit ranged from medium height, dark, and swarthy to an almost Norse appearance of fairness with the highwayman's stature at such a magnitude that only an Olympian god could have fit such a description. His eyes had been described as brown, blue, and hazel and one particularly volatile young miss had seen quite clearly that the highwayman's eyes were a fiery red and smoke poured from his nostrils!

Upon these last words, Charity placed a hand over her mouth and took a deep breath to keep the laughter that threatened her countenance from overtaking her. Good gracious! Smoke from his nostrils!

The runner's gaze then shifted to the pens on Lord Datchworth's desk and afterward, each in turn, the blotter and the inkwell.

Lord Datchworth, his hands still folded and sitting atop a desk pad of maroon leather, flicked his thumbnails one against the other, and cried, "My good man! Will you not regard me directly for you have the worst habit of shifting your gaze everywhere but upon my face! Damme, if I don't think you're calculating the value of every article in my possession!"

The runner was not the least daunted by these harsh words and even smiled with a certain degree of pride as he straightened his shoulders slightly and said, "I am sorry, indeed, if my mode of conducting this matter offends you, but I have been trained in methods of observation and I apply them whenever I have the smallest opportunity." He tapped his head with his forefinger and added, "It keeps my cannister sharp and rapier-like!"

Lord Datchworth rolled his eyes slightly and gestured to Charity to come forward, instructing her to answer any questions which the runner might deem fit to ask her.

Charity stepped away from the window, regarding the unattractive man directly for she refused to be intimidated by his piercing stare and dark teeth, and immediately said, "I hope that I can be of some assistance to you, but I am afraid that his eyes were not in the least a fiery red, nor did his nostrils smoke—at least not to any noticeable degree."

The runner smiled in a friendly manner and as he regarded her carefully, taking in her glossy black curls, the pretty light blue gown made high to her throat and edged with lace, the clarity of her exquisite eyes, he cleared his throat and said, "And meaning no disrespect to you, Miss Holwell, but if I was a notorious highwayman who had taken to kissing young ladies, your post chaise would have been one of the first ones I'd have looked for!"

Both Lord and Lady Datchworth each made a noise as if to protest the complete audacity of the man's remarks, but Charity understood their harmless nature and merely answered politely, "Why, how very kind of you to say so!"

Mr. Stokes, however, colored at his words for he seemed to realize that he had not said the proper thing to the young lady, given her gently nurtured upbringing, and glancing sideways at Lady Datchworth, bowed to her and said, "Meaning no offense, ma'am. Truly!"

He then gestured for Charity to be seated upon a wing chair of a rust and black tapestried fabric, and asked her if she would acquaint him with all the particulars of the dreadful attack.

Charity's recital of the highwayman's attempt to rob her was very brief, but the runner's true expertise was soon evident as he began asking any number of questions upon the relative size of the bandit and his servant, the horses involved, the precise location of the attack. His questions were concise and penetrating and after some thirty minutes had passed, he had filled at least a dozen pages of a small red notebook with his scribblings and appeared satisfied with the interview. Rubbing the side of his nose, he was about to speak when a rapping upon the door stopped him.

Lord Datchworth, emitting an impatient sigh, called out, "Yes, what is it?" Only to have Hinx open the door and inform the viscount in his quiet, stately voice that Lord Redbourne had arrived and was wishful of speaking with Lord Datchworth.

"Redbourne?" Lord Datchworth called to him, casting an annoyed glance at Charity. "One moment." He sat drumming his fingertips upon the desktop, regarding Charity from narrowed brown eyes.

For her part, Charity barely prevented herself from crying out in surprise at the mere mention of William's name. It was one thing to correspond with Penelope about his doings, or to argue with her uncle over his proposals, but to have him so near, and that without any notice at all, was unsettling in the extreme. She was in no way prepared to speak with him for the news of his proposals was still little more than a shock to her.

And as for her uncle! Good gracious, breakfast had been a nightmare what with Lord Datchworth, a piece of toast in hand, storming the length of the morning room after he learned the nature of Charity's sentiments. He could not credit his ears that she was actually desirous of refusing William's proposals.

Her uncle had been mad as fire, as he flung the toast back on his plate, leaned his hands on the table and glared at his niece. "Not accept Redbourne's addresses when you've loved him since you were a child? Don't gammon me, Charity! I've watched you with him dozens of times over the years and I don't give a fig that you were so young! And don't you remember that occasion when you were nearly out, at my wife's niece's wedding? You were a very grown-up seventeen at the time! There, I can see by the blush on your cheeks you know damn well what I am referring to—that you sat in our pew scarcely able to take your eyes from William's tall figure. And he didn't precisely ignore you himself, for after the nuptials, he spent half an hour chatting with you and pushing you on the swing behind the rectory! I sent Pen out to get you lest you create a scandal of your own, with half the ladies in the drawing room tittering over the pair of you smelling of April and May for you were in clear view of all of them from the windows!"

"Oh, Uncle!" Charity cried, pressing her hands to her cheeks. "Not only had I nearly forgotten about that episode but I had no idea that we could be seen by anyone! Oh dear!" And she turned to Penelope and said, "You were very kind to have rescued me!"

Penelope sipped her tea slowly, in a gracious manner that many a matron had held up as an example for their awkward daughters to follow. And when she had dabbed at the corner of her mouth with a linen table napkin, she said, "William knew quite well that at least a dozen Tabbies could see the pair of you. He was merely hoping to stir up some mischief."

"And speaking of mischief!" Lord Datchworth cried as he shook a finger at Penelope, "I'll thank you kindly to hold your viper's tongue. Mischief, indeed! Well, I don't care what the reason," he continued as he turned to regard Charity, "I saw enough that day to convince me even now that you're a match if ever heaven made one."

Charity lifted her chin slightly as she said, "I will always count Lord Redbourne as a friend. I am grateful for his kindnesses to me when I was young, but I am not persuaded we should suit."

"Not persuaded you should suit!" Lord Datchworth cried, as he ran a hand through his hair in a fit of extreme exasperation. "I don't know! I don't understand! What is it with young ladies these days? Why, between you and Penelope, who has turned away more suitors than I could shake a stick at—and tempting Fate in the most reprehensible manner possible—I begin to think the world has gone mad. And if you don't have a care, you'll both become ape-leaders of no mean order. Meares won't wait forever, Penelope! He's a line of succession to think of and he's nigh on forty if he's a day! And as for you, Charity! I should never have let you run off to Paris like that for look what has come of it! Refusing Redbourne more because he never did take to Penelope than because you don't love him! Tell me you don't love him, Charity! Bah! Well, I wash my hands of you, though I demand that you don't refuse him right away. Give the man at least a few days to speak for himself, and if you still can't abide the thought of being leg-shackled to him, then I won't say another word on the subject! Bah!" And he quit the chamber on his hasty stride, his voice booming down the hallways as he called for his horse. "And be quick about it!" ·

Charity shuddered at the memory of the morning and then regarded her scowling uncle whose gaze now was directed toward his hands as though he were trying to solve a difficult riddle. Leaning back in his chair suddenly and pushed himself away from his desk, he cried, "Hinx! Show Redbourne in here at once!"

56

Mr. Stokes regarded the viscount with considerable surprise and said, "Do you wish me to leave, my lord. I'm certain I've enough information for the present."

"No! I want Redbourne to hear what has happened. He was used to be an excellent friend of Miss Holwell's and he may wish to direct several questions to you as well."

"Very good, my lord."

Charity sat opposite the door and thought that never had her heart pounded so fiercely as it did as in that moment. Footsteps echoed upon the black and white tile in the entryway and she knew it was but a matter of seconds before the door would open and she would see him. The light from the window dimmed as clouds drifted in the path of the sun, and the footsteps ceased. The heavy carved door opened slowly. Hinx announced the Earl of Redbourne and suddenly he was there, standing in the room and regarding her with a look of surprise.

She had forgotten he was so tall and that his hair was just that shade of blond that it looked sailor-streaked, and had he actually grown more handsome than she remembered? His eyes were hazel and flecked with gold, his nose aquiline, his cheekbones high and pronounced, and his smile of the moment as warm as ever she remembered.

"Charity?" he asked, as though disbelieving that she was sitting in front of him, and that she was now three and twenty instead of a chit of eleven.

Every memory seemed to rip through her in that moment, but only as though she was observing them, for she could see herself in her mind's eye, astride his horse and could hear herself giggling as he galloped them both through the woods and into the valley below. And later, at Chisley Hall, toppling into the duckpond, water flying up her nose. And how easily William lifted her to her feet and afterward gave her his kerchief when she began sneezing.

Without thinking she rose to her feet and said, "It has been a very long time, Will. How do you go on?" Her heart felt full of summer as she regarded him, the affections from childhood flooding her. But as though drawn by a force she didn't understand, she turned to regard her cousin Penelope and at least a dozen dissimilar memories, of letter upon letter, surfaced in her mind—tearstained missives of the hurt that her cousin had endured at the earl's hands—and she cast her gaze quickly to the floor, a dark blush covering her cheeks, so many emotions overwhelming her at once.

Her uncle intervened immediately as he rose to his feet and spoke in his somewhat booming voice, "Redbourne, I brought you in here because I thought you should know, given the nature of your interest in my niece, precisely what happened to her yesterday!"

Lady Datchworth crossed the room and, greeting William in a quiet voice, slipped an arm about Charity's waist as Lord Datchworth began informing William of The Gentleman's attack upon her.

Though she made every effort to concentrate solely upon her uncle, Charity found it impossible to do little more than watch William's face as he listened in shocked silence to the short history. His complexion seemed to pale, his cheeks appearing quite drawn of the moment as he shook his head any number of times, his expression one of incredulity. He seemed incapable of believing what he was hearing, but at least twice, when he regarded her directly, Charity could have sworn that a quirky smile played at his lips. Did he not take the attack quite as seriously as her aunt and uncle did? And she bit her lip in an effort to stay a smile that would be most inappropriate given the presence of the Bow Street runner.

Rounding the corner of his desk, Lord Datchworth addressed the earl, "I can see by your expression that you are quite as dumbfounded as I was. And how could it have been possible that the highwayman would have known that Charity was traveling upon that road? No one knew, for she is just now come to London."

Lord Redbourne could not resist giving way to at least part of a smile, as he regarded Charity with a soft expression in his eyes and said, "A happy accident, perhaps. Perhaps The Gentleman was waiting for another female entirely, and merely mistook Miss Holwell for his intended victim." Charity shook her head at him for speaking with such frivolity, but to little avail for he smiled more broadly still until she answered with a smile of her own and then quickly averted her head to regard the scrollwork upon a mahogany secretaire near the fireplace. She felt as though they were sharing secrets together, though what secrets she was not certain in the least.

William again addressed the viscount, "I trust Bow Street is doing all that it can to apprehend this monstrous criminal, this *great evil* that has been afflicting the delicately nurtured young ladies of our society!"

Charity's gaze flew back to the earl upon these words, for they were the very ones she had used in addressing the highwayman on the evening before. Was this, too, a happy accident, and the silliest suspicion crossed her mind, but she dismissed it immediately. The William she knew from Penelope's letters, a man who tolerated little nonsense from the females of his acquaintance, would no more have posed as a highwayman than Penelope would have danced the ballet upon the stage.

Mr. Stokes throughout Lord Datchworth's recital had remained silent, but spent those few minutes in regarding each detail of Lord Redbourne's person with great care— his intricately tied neckcloth, the elegant cut of his coat of blue superfine, the buff breeches, and gleaming Hessians. And when Lord Datchworth introduced him to the earl, he said, "I wish to assure you that I am taking it upon myself to see that everything will be done about this dastardly bandit and I am fully confident that within a fortnight I shall have your man. I'm new on this particular case, you see, and having read all the various reports, I think I've discovered some common threads that, with a little judicious review, will bring a satisfactory conclusion in no time at all. I mean to begin with a search of the area Miss Holwell described to us. As it happens, I am myself familiar with Hertfordshire, having grown up in Stevenage. And from the description," he referred back to his notes, frowning at them in a contemplative manner, "I would put the actual attack near a small village just north of Welwyn. Now, I don't know the name of that village but there's an inn there I'm familiar with called The White Swan. I intend to begin my investigation there."

William cried, "The White Swan? Are you certain? I was there only last evening with a friend of mine. It's in the village of Little Digswell."

Mr. Stokes again rubbed the side of his nose as he frowned in a thoughtful manner upon the earl. "Aye, that's it. And though it would be highly improbable that you would have actually seen a masked highwayman, did anything of an unusual nature occur that night?"

Lord Redbourne merely shook his head and he remarked on the fine quality of the brandy to be found at the inn, as well as the fact that his friend, Hugh Bramfield, had fallen asleep in the midst of a fascinating anecdote he had been recounting to him. "But other than that, the inn was very quiet and after permitting Mr. Bramfield to sleep for an hour or so, we completed our journey to London."

Mr. Stokes nodded twice, making several more notes, and then excused himself saying that he would be in contact with Lord Datchworth over the next few days to let him know precisely how his investigation was progressing.

When the door closed behind him, Lord Datchworth said, "A dreadful business, this! And I'm sorry if I shocked you, William, but I knew you would want to know."

The earl was at that moment regarding Charity with an

odd expression on his face and realizing that the viscount had addressed him, he said, "What? Oh yes, I am very grateful that you informed me of this truly wretched event, but I was wondering if you might permit me to have a few words alone with your niece." He turned to regard Lady Datchworth and smiling upon her, asked, "That is, unless you object to it since the lady has not yet accepted me?"

Lady Datchworth, still holding Charity's waist, turned toward her slightly, and said, "I think my niece should decide for herself if this is an appropriate time or not, for she has just arrived you know, and we are hardly settled in our routines yet."

Charity regarded her aunt and then Penelope who was watching her with a horror-stricken expression, and she did not know precisely what to say, but she thought that it would be the grossest incivility on her part to refuse so polite a request from someone who had so recently offered for her. Finally, she said, "If you wish for a few words, of course, William, for we are friends."

He frowned slightly at her words, but bowed to her then moved to open the door for Penelope, Lady Datchworth, and Lord Datchworth, the latter of whom, as he passed through the doorway, turned back and with a scowl upon his face, shook his head at Charity in a fierce manner.

As they filed from the room, Charity moved away from the door and walked to the window where she lifted the gold silk drapes back slightly and stared up into the gray clouds. She had been so surprised at seeing William, that her emotions had become quite numb with the shock of it all. And that he no doubt wished to make her a formal offer for her hand in marriage, only increased the bemused sensation that had wrapped itself about her heart.

William closed the door with a quiet snap and turned to regard Charity. The past few minutes had held so many surprises for him that he wasn't certain how to assimilate it all. And as for Bow Street's intention to capture The Gentleman, well, that was something he would have to consider quite carefully, but not at this time, not with the woman he hoped to make his wife standing before him. She was wearing a light blue muslin morning gown, with a pretty demi-train edged in lace trailing slightly behind her. The back of the gown was gathered in a great many tiny pleats, and flowed in a ripple, from the very high waist of the gown to the Aubusson carpet. The long sleeves were also edged with lace and gathered in several tiers from puffed shoulders and though the gown was made high at the neck, a delicate border of lace clung to her throat while a cascade of delightful black curls rose from the crown of her head to fall in a trail down the middle of her back. The portrait was as pleasing as it was soft and desirable to William who still could not credit that this was the little girl he had taught to ride and the nearly grown schoolroom miss who had chatted so artlessly with him in the rectory garden following the wedding of one of his cousins.

But above everything was the knowledge that this was the very same Frenchwoman he had kissed but a day earlier. And why had Charity felt it so necessary to hide herself behind a mask, unless of course she simply wished her identity left unknown to The Gentleman. Such a desire he could comprehend quite easily for she had certainly made it clear to him that she did not approve of his activities. He shook his head slightly, was this truly his Charity?

She was an exquisite creature, almost wraithlike for she was very thin, the light pouring over her black curls as she looked out the window. And the kiss they had shared had been equally unreal, dreamlike. He wanted to tell her instantly who he was, but as this thought entered his mind, so did a sudden awareness that he could not tell her the truth just yet—if ever! Good God! His adventures, which until this moment, had been necessary to his soul, now seemed sullied in the presence of Charity and the goodness she represented, the sweetness and purity. Would she ever understand why he had taken to accosting some of the females of his acquaintance? Would she ever love him?

Of course she would. He had seen the affection on her face the moment he entered the room and spoke to her. She loved him. But how, precisely, was he to explain himself to her? He did not know. But as she glanced over her shoulder toward him, a questioning expression upon her face, he knew one thing more certain than any other, that he desired nothing more in his life than to hold her again in his arms, and on a firm tread he made his way toward her.

Charity watched his approach and could not deny that in his hazel eyes, was a fire that threatened to consume her. And that he had clearly but one purpose in mind was not a matter for dispute at all as she turned fully to meet him. Taking a small step backward, the short, ruffled demi-train of her gown wrapped slightly about her feet, she lifted a hand at his approach as though she might ward him off. But he came at her, with the force of a strong gale as he gathered her up in his arms and without so much as a by-your-leave, pressed his lips upon hers in a rough, demanding kiss. Heaven help her, what was she to do, for there resided in her heart, this traitorous being who wanted nothing more than to feel his lips roving so harshly over her own as he crushed her within the circle of his arms. And how sweet his breath was as he pulled back slightly and began just barely touching her lips with his. Tears smarted her eyes as he whispered, "I know now why no other woman seemed to please me. Charity, you've come home!" And his mouth was upon hers again in so burning a kiss that she was not at all certain that her feet were still anchored to the floor.

She felt her body betray her as she returned the pressure of his lips. She wanted his kisses more than she wanted life in that moment and she struggled mightily to keep from throwing her arms about his neck as he held her in a fierce embrace, his lips releasing her, but only for a few seconds, as he cried, "You will marry me. You must. All those years lost while you were in Paris. I should have eloped with you at that wedding when you were seventeen. Do you remember how I teased you about it until Penelope came upon us and whisked you back to the parlor? Marry me, Charity." And he kissed her again.

Tears burned her eyes as thoughts of poor Penelope began tearing at her mind and with a faint sob, she pushed him away, her eyes cast down, as she said, "Pray leave me alone, Will. I don't know my heart in this situation. I don't know how to answer you."

She felt his body hovering about her, his arms reaching out to her and then falling back as he said, "What is it? Why are you sorely distressed? Surely you will marry me?"

Charity, her eyes swimming with tears, looked up at him sharply at these words and said, "Were you so very certain of success when we have scarcely exchanged a half-dozen letters in these five years and more?"

His face was contorted with bewilderment as he ran a hand through his hair and said, "Should I have written more? But you see, I had no notion, no intention of offering for you until but recently. You were only a shadow in my life, residing in Paris as you did, a friend, a childhood acquaintance— Oh, the devil take it, I am making a great mull of this."

"Do you love me?"

His mouth fell slightly agape at this question, for though he might have said as much to several of his past mistresses, he could not speak these words so readily now. "To say, *I don't know,* will no doubt do more harm than good, but you must believe me when I say that I had meant originally for this to be a marriage of convenience of sorts, because I did hold you in such affection when you were much younger. I never thought to have feeling as I have now, but to call it love—Charity, you must realize that whatever is said between us now, I want to be true and not a heedless remark to win the day. I don't know what it is I feel, but that I want you to be my wife—and yes, if that is love, then I do love you—is the only thought I have in this moment."

Charity fingered the smooth silk drapes between her fingers. "Then you will understand when I say yet again that I do not know how I feel and I cannot give you an answer at this time. But I promise you that you shall have an answer before Lady Datchworth's soiree on Thursday evening."

He touched her gently upon the arm, but she pulled away and said, "Pray, William, for my sake, will you not leave me alone now?"

"Of course," he said, his voice sounding hurt, though he did not move away from her. "There is but one thing I must know before I leave, do you hesitate because of Penelope?"

Charity pressed a hand to her cheek and answered him, "I hesitate, William, because I do not know who you are. But I will not deny that the pain my cousin has suffered at your hands cannot but have an effect upon my decision."

William's voice seemed very distant and cold to Charity as he answered, "I see." She expected him to say more, to perhaps try to persuade her that she had not mistaken his character. Instead, he turned on his heel and was gone.

Chapter Five

Penelope stood at the front window of the drawing room, which was situated on the first floor of the townhouse, and gazed down into the square. She was waiting for William to emerge from the house, her heart cold and angry at the man who had robbed her of so precious a title and position in society. She was dressed in a pale pink morning gown of a soft muslin, ruffles encircling the neck of the gown and crossing over the bodice to travel in a gentle flow about the high waist. William had not even looked at her when he entered her Papa's office. His eyes had been only for Charity, and she felt her chest tighten to an alarming degree. She still could not believe that after all her efforts in attempting to win William, not only had he spurned her at every turn, humiliating her in public on several occasions, but he had chosen as the future Countess of Redbourne, her own cousin! Not that she wished to deny Charity every happiness in life, but this was beyond bearing!

And why had John died, cheating her so completely of the place amongst the *ton* that had come to mean everything to her. She had never been able to let her dreams go. They were as much a part of her existence as breathing and sleeping and though she could not even remember what John looked like, the life that was to have been hers was burnt into her mind and would never be forgotten. She was, in her heart, the Countess of Redbourne and she had walked through the halls of the Sandridge houses over and over in her imagination, worshipping an ancestry that went clear back to the Conquest.

She still could not credit that Fate had tricked her so ruthlessly in giving her John's love and the hope of so noble a future for herself, only to wrench both from her in a stupid epidemic of influenza.

In her hand she held a delicate lace kerchief. She always had such an article close to her, for this was one of several mannerisms that she had adopted in order to present a gracious, elegant portrait of herself to the *beau monde*. John had taken great pride in her, in all her efforts to achieve a feminine ideal. But William had laughed at her, at what he called her simpering affectations! William was cruel and heartless and she had never understood him, nor why she had failed so completely to please him. And what was he anyway in comparison to John? He was wild and ungovernable and at first she truly believed that she could control him and that he would soon grow to love her as John had loved her, once he had an opportunity to be with her more.

But almost from the first, he seemed to despise her, though she had done nothing whatsoever to earn his contempt. And her attempts over the years, to intrigue him, to enchant him, to show him her worthy qualities, had only served to push him further away. And now he had actually offered for Charity! She felt sick inside, almost queasy at the thought. She could not permit matters to end thus, to have her cousin, dressed in white satin, lace, and orange blossoms, step lightly down the aisle to become the next Countess of Redbourne! She could not permit that to happen!

On the street below, one of Lord Datchworth's footmen

was walking William's fine black horse to and fro and occasionally the rather small young man would turn back to the spirited horse and speak to it. He would gesture in what to Penelope seemed a placating manner, in hopes of keeping the gelding from bolting. William was very much like that horse, she thought, as the gelding reared back and danced in a reprehensible manner upon the flagway. She could hear the footman shouting several interesting epithets at the horse as he struggled to bring the beast under control. But it was clearly evident, even to Penelope, that the footman was losing his battle as the horse whinnied and snorted and tossed his head.

And just as the reins slipped from the servant's hands, William walked from the house, planted his feet firmly upon the stone flags as he drew on his gloves and in a single command brought the horse, its long neck bowed in submission, mincing toward him.

Penelope despised William no doubt as much as he despised her. And she would prevent this marriage by means of the same sort of intensity she had used in pursuing William over the past ten years, only now she would cast a rub in William's way at every turn. Straightening her shoulders slightly, Penelope schooled her features to her habitual expression of complete composure. No one knew the depths of her feelings and she hadn't the least intention at this late hour of letting such sentiments be known even to her mother who was of the moment the only other occupant of the drawing room.

Turning around, she realized with a laugh that even had her features been contorted with pain, her mama would not have noticed, for Lady Datchworth was absorbed deeply with her own concerns as she stared into the gilt-edged mirror by the door, smoothing out the skin about her eyes in a gentle circular motion with her fingers.

"Oh, dear," the viscountess moaned. "And there is yet another wrinkle. I have just now decided that I shall never smile again, for everytime I do the wrinkles grow deeper and more pronounced." And she alternately smiled then frowned in rapid succession in order to watch her wrinkles appear and disappear. "And very soon your father will proclaim me old and bracket-faced and will give the widow Baldock a *carte blanche!*"

Penelope, who was nine and twenty, and quite beyond an age when such notions would have caused her to blush, merely responded quietly, "And you know very well that Papa loves you very much and that he does not pay the least heed to something so inconsequential as either a wrinkle or that unmentionable female!"

Lady Datchworth turned to regard her daughter with a delighted smile. "And what a generous thought, my dear! I only wish you were right. But your papa is forever scrutinizing every female who should happen to cross his path, ogling them with his quizzing glass and making his pronouncements upon their relative youth, clear complexions, or smooth skin! And then he will turn to me in that odious manner of his and ask in an innocent voice whether or not I think crushed strawberries applied to my face liberally every night would not be of some assistance to me? The wretch! I am all out of patience with him!" She was begowned in an amber silk morning dress, bordered about the bodice with a delicate Brussels lace and upon her head she wore a matching turban dressed with three long white feathers.

"And you know very well that he says these things only to twit you, particularly after you have been playing at whist all night with Lady Eversley."

Lady Datchworth crossed the room to stand before the fireplace where a small pile of coals had turned to white ashes. Removing a brass-handled poker from a stand upon the hearth, she began pushing the coals about and after a moment, said, "Sally Jersey saw him speaking with Harriette Wilson not two days ago, and I'm certain that

70

that Cyprian has quite turned his head. He means to have her, I know it. I can *feel* it!"

"But do think, Mama," Penelope said, as she moved to a settee near the fire where an upright tambour frame was stationed, "That a woman known as *Silence* will no doubt have made a great deal more of Papa's encounter with a Fashionable Impure than probably occurred." And sitting down, she drew the tambour frame forward and regarded an elegant peacock, sporting one very bold, golden eye which stared back at her. The drawing room was still rich with the scent of the flowers, the roses vying for supremacy with the recent addition of lavender, and the violets continuing to bloom with large healthy blossoms.

Penelope continued, "And speaking of Lady Jersey, did she perchance give you Charity's vouchers to Almack's for I had the most delightful notion that it would be very charming, even before her soiree tomorrow evening, to introduce Charity at the assembly rooms. How surprised everyone would be, and her party tomorrow would be an absolute crush because of it."

It was these very last words which seemed to have a strong effect upon the viscountess, for she immediately ceased her task, replacing the poker to its stand, and turned around to regard her daughter with a speculative gleam in her light blue eyes. "What an excellent thought and, as it happens, I have only this morning received the vouchers from Emily Cowper." She crossed the room quickly to a cherrywood table near the door and retrieving the vouchers along with a second letter, added, "And here is a missive from Charity's cousin, Miss Pelham-Furneux."

The door opened quietly and Charity entered the room, a somewhat thin smile upon her lips. "From Furney?" she asked. And though she affected a happy countenance, Penelope could see from the slight puffiness of her eyes, that all had not gone well with William. Had he kissed her, she wondered? But of course he had, for he was wild to a fault and would not hesitate to take such advantage of her cousin. Poor Charity, she thought, having to endure a mauling at the hands of such a beast.

Charity, for her part, however, had quite a different reason for wishing that William had not kissed her for the truth was that the moment she felt his arms about her, all rational thought fled her mind. She was incapable, with his lips upon hers, of choosing a sensible path for her feet. But in the end, when they had exchanged at least a few words, some of her sense had returned to her.

Lady Datchworth handed the letter to Charity, and also the vouchers as she said, "Penelope has had a delightful notion that we ought to attend Almack's this evening, and I concur. But what I wish to know is whether or not it would please you?"

"Almack's?" Charity cried. She had for so many years heard about this exceedingly fashionable weekly subscription ball, where the ladies all dressed in their finest silks and jewels and the gentlemen were required to wear satin knee breeches, that with alacrity she responded, "Yes, oh, indeed yes. You cannot imagine how much I have wished for it, particularly after all of Penelope's letters of the past several years." But even with these words, Charity was reminded yet again of other letters that hurt even with this brief remembrance of them, correspondence full of William's misdeeds.

Penelope, who was gently guiding a needle into the wing of the peacock, said, "And though I have not said anything to Mama, I don't think she will mind in the least if I tell you that I was also thinking that were you to ask William to attend you there, you might better be able to judge for yourself the sort of man he is. I know that his past treatment of me must be weighing heavily upon your mind and I still blame myself for revealing so much to you. I should have been more circumspect in my letters." And pressing her kerchief to her forehead, she bowed her head, apparently overcome with emotion.

Charity saw the expression of anguish upon Penelope's face and her heart went out to her. Poor Pen, she thought. "You mustn't blame yourself, Penelope!" Charity cried as she went to sit beside her cousin and slipped an arm about her waist. Penelope sniffed into her kerchief and dabbed at her eyes as she said, "But I feel as though I have ruined your affections for Lord Redbourne and had I not, you would even now be engaged to him."

Lady Datchworth returned to sit across from her daughter and said, "You are being too harsh with yourself, Penelope my dear. Indeed, Charity ought to know everything and I agree with you that your idea has merit. Charity ought to have every opportunity of seeing William and how he conducts himself in public before she accepts him or not."

Lord Datchworth's voice intruded upon them all in this moment as he boomed, "What's this? What scheme are you now hatching?"

Lady Datchworth, who had cried out at his sudden appearance, let out a sigh of exasperation and responded, "We are merely discussing the possibility of attending the assemblies at Almack's this evening."

"And will Redbourne be there?"

Lady Datchworth said, "I shall send a note 'round to his house, of course, for he will want to see Charity I am sure."

Lord Datchworth stood several feet away from them, his hands clasped behind his back, as he rocked upon the heels of his black top boots and scowled at them. "I can see by the expression on your faces, that all three of you have some little plot brewing and I don't like it! And you!" he cried, shaking a finger at Penelope. "If I find that you've taken it upon yourself to create more mischief than usual I shall take my riding crop to you! You let things be! Attend to Meares, for if you don't bring him up to scratch this season, you may consider yourself past your prayers forever!" And as he nodded his head to his daughter, he then turned to his wife saying that he would be grateful if she did attend Almack's for she could hardly lose a thousand pounds while waltzing, but when his gaze came to rest upon Charity, he pursed his lips together so tightly that his face began turning quite red. And after sputtering something about the incongruities of the female mind, he marched from the room with all the ladies smiling at his retreating form.

When Charity returned to her bedchamber later that morning and closed the door behind the various concerns of the house, she quickly broke the blue wax seal of Furney's missive and read the contents with her heart in her throat. She stood in the middle of the comfortable chamber which was decorated in gold and burgundy. A tall, scrolled, canopied bed, draped with a warm burgundy velvet against the chill spring nights commanded notice with carved acanthas leaves upon each bedpost. Beside the window, a tall secretaire housed two dozen volumes of books including the works of Jane Austen and Sir Walter Scott, though tucked in the corner of the bottom shelf was a forbidden volume of Lord Byron's poetry, several pages of which Anne had marked especially for Charity to read.

As the details of Furney's letter became clear to Charity, for her cousin was a poor correspondent and very unfortunately in charge of arranging the practical aspects of her audition at Drury Lane, the young woman seated herself at the secretaire. Taking a pen, she dipped it in the inkwell and began copying certain portions of the letter— the address of the small house which her ballet master, Monsieur Bovin, had hired for use during rehearsals, the address of rooms Furney had hired near Drury Lane to which Charity would retire before and after her audition, and finally a small note reminding herself to inform her aunt that her dearest cousin and companion, Miss Pelham-Furneux, would not be attending them this season because her mother was quite ill, besides possessing a weakened hip, and needed her in attendance for an unspecified length of time.

The letter on this point read, *I know it goes sorely against the grain with you to have to tell a whisker, but until you decide with great finality that you will give up forever your place in society for a career upon the stage, both M. Bovin and myself feel that as long as it is possible, you must live out this dual existence. And I wish to impress upon you again that this is no decision to be made without enormous consideration of all the consequences.*

Charity set down her pen in the tray in front of her, and placed her head in her hands. The difficulties which had seemed to pour over her from the moment she arrived in London now drifted away as thoughts of her Parisian life assailed her. A dual existence, for she rehearsed incessantly it seemed every morning quite early and only without detection because of Furney, but in the afternoon and into the long evenings she enjoyed French society in the same manner as did so many other well-bred young ladies of her acquaintance. Her dear cousin, Agnes Pelham-Furneux, had been a strong support from the first and Monsieur Bovin had been with her since she was a child. Her dancing had been as inevitable as a summer shower during an al fresco nuncheon, for she had acquired her mama's love of dance, who herself had been quite addicted to the ballet from the time she was a young girl as well.

But it was Furney who had made the impossible possible—to study the ballet in Paris, hiring a house, serving as companion, and keeping the talemongers from ever guessing the truth that Charity had aspirations upon the stage. And as for Monsieur Bovin, he had originally been a refugee of the French revolution, for even though he was but remotely related to the Compte de Rameau, and had served as ballet master to the Royal Paris Opera House for several years, his life had been imperiled and he came to reside with Charity's mother's family, who were distant relatives of his, some thirty years earlier. And years later, as Charity grew up before his eyes, he recognized very early that she possessed a considerable gift for dance and though he taught all of the young ladies about Hertfordshire the intricacies of the quadrille, the simple movements of the country dance, and eventually the scandalous embrace of the waltz, he could not resist persuading his cousin, Marie Holwell, to permit him to instruct Charity in the ballet.

Charity took at once to the discipline of the daily work, to the grace and fluidity of movement that was always a part of the master's teaching, to the extraordinary innovation of stiffening the toes of the ballet slippers so that she soon mastered the new art of dancing *sur les pointes*.

But everyone felt a measure of guilt and excitement over the secretive aspect of Charity's study of the ballet for it was forbidden for any gently nurtured female to even contemplate such an activity because the opera-dancers in London were notorious. Still, they all continued for there was a magic in Charity's abilities that entranced them; what emerged from her dance was not heavy acrobatics but a clean light drift of movement that resembled the similar movements of a rising young ballerina upon the Paris stage by the name of Maria Taglioni. Both ladies shared an ethereal quality, a romantic expression and line of physique that Monsieur Bovin was certain would change the course of the ballet forever. He referred to it as the Romantic Ballet but all Charity knew was that when she became absorbed in one of her ballet master's creations, life was infinitely sweet and she could not imagine living without her dance. But where in polite society could her passion for the ballet and her love of all her friends and relatives possibly meet? It was one or the other, certainly not both, but as was her habit in the past, she quickly set aside the impossibility of the choice before her and instead turned her attention back to Furney's letter.

Rising from her chair, she slipped the addresses into her green beaded reticule, and taking Furney's letter, did not hesitate to walk to the fireplace and toss the missive upon a heap of red and white coals. How quickly the letter, containing so much information which could destroy her place amongst society in the barest blink of an eye, crumpled into a burst of flames and disintegrated into a blanket of ashes upon the coals. Tomorrow her life would change forever, if she wished for it. But the truth was, having once again taken up her place within the affectionate bonds of her aunt and uncle's family, she was no longer as certain as she had been in Paris that she could give up so very much for a few years upon the stage.

As the ashes became absorbed into the heat of the coals, Charity turned away from the fireplace and rang for her maid. She had another pressing matter to attend to, though of a much lighter nature than whether or not she should become a famous ballerina like the amazing Taglioni, for now she must choose which balldress to wear to Almack's.

That evening Charity found herself caught in the midst of a swirl of delight, for she had forgotten that by now so many of her friends from schoolroom days in Hertford-shire, as well as Anne and Penelope's friends, composed a large portion of fashionable London society. And before ten minutes had passed, when the Datchworth coterie was gathered at the entrance to the ballroom, a veritable swarm of acquaintance rushed at her, welcoming her home from Paris, and exclaiming over her fashionable gown of a lavender satin that had seven rows of pleated ruffles encircling the hem. So many voices begged all at once to know why she had absented herself from England for such a dreadfully long time, and so many demands were made for her dances, that Charity found herself quite overwhelmed with so much interest and affection.

Only then, in the midst of all the confusion and loud clattering of friendly voices, did Charity become aware of William. He was standing off to one side, his streaked blond hair gleaming in the candlelight, his white neckcloth arranged in perfect folds, his black coat and satin knee breeches seemingly molded to his athletic form. It was no wonder that several of the ladies clustered about her also turned in his direction, and regarded his tall form carefully, several fans fluttering over suddenly flushed cheeks.

Charity felt her heart go to him, and she did not feel it unreasonable at all that so many of her friends would find it nearly impossible not to stare at him. He was very handsome as was the tall gentleman next to him, who sported a healthy head of curly brown hair, and smiled in a rather dazzling manner at each of the ladies near Charity.

William, for his part, regarded her with a warm smile and when he knew that he had caught her eye, he bowed slightly to her, an elegant movement that, in the funniest way, brought forcibly to mind the highwayman who had accosted her post chaise—was it only but two days ago? But whether it was remembering the bandit so suddenly or merely the kind expression on the earl's face, Charity could not resist returning his smile and inclined her head in a gracious manner to him. Surely in all her correspondence with Penelope some error in understanding had occurred. Surely this man who smiled so sweetly upon her was not so bad as she believed, that Penelope had merely misunderstood a number of their encounters.

There was a sudden pressure on her arm, and turning in the direction of the perpetrator, Charity realized Penelope was trying to gain her attention in order to whisper something to her.

Leaning very close to her, Penelope said, "I shall bring William to you. But wait here."

Charity thought this was rather odd, for she had little doubt that William would approach her soon enough. But as she watched Penelope circle about the fringe of the crowd of well-wishers, an anxious feeling entered her heart. It was obvious from Penelope's letters that William could scarcely tolerate Penelope and she could not imagine anything good coming out of this action on her cousin's part. In fact, based upon everything Penelope had related to her over the years, this sort of boldness on Pen's part would no doubt anger William.

And the moment Penelope curtsied before the earl, Charity knew that in this she had been right. With a growing sense of uneasiness, she watched as a cold, indifferent expression overtook William's countenance, so much so, that for a moment she did not even recognize him.

Charity's heart felt as though someone had just weighed it down with a heavy stone. For in that moment, she saw the man Penelope had written to her about—arrogant, disdainful—his expression incredibly heartless as he addressed a few words to Penelope, bowed curtly and moved away from her with the tall gentleman in tow. But much to the other man's credit, he turned back to Penelope and with a hopeless gesture seemed to extend to her his silent apologies. And between the two men, Charity knew instantly which was a gentleman and which had so completely confirmed again that he had the manners and heart of a wild boar!

For a moment Penelope remained where she was as though she had been struck physically, the blow rendering her completely paralyzed. And when finally she was able to move, she returned to Charity's side, her eyes cast down, her cheeks suffused with a dull blush.

The clamor about Charity was still as noisy as ever and she was unable to offer her dearest cousin the commiseration she needed, but she was able to at least take her arm and press it in an encouraging manner before they were both whisked off to enjoy a country dance.

Hugh caught his friend's elbow as they both bowed to the Princess Esterhazy, and the moment they were beyond the ears of this formidable patroness of the assembly rooms, he spoke in a low tone, "Isn't Miss Ware, the young lady to whom you just delivered a remarkably biting set down, a relative of Miss Holwell's?"

"Of course, she is Charity's cousin! Why do you ask?"

Hugh appeared quite astonished as he released William's elbow and said, "I am only a little surprised that you go about charming your prospective bride in such a manner. I should hardly call giving Miss Holwell's cousin a set down an act designed to win her heart!"

The earl turned slightly to regard Hugh and in a half-laughing manner exclaimed, "But why do you appear so disapproving? Don't tell me you think I was actually unkind to Penelope Ware? For one cannot be unkind to such a female, in the same way one cannot be unkind to a tree by offering it the cut direct—save of course unless you are using an axe, and then the cut direct would be deadly indeed!" He laughed at this witticism and begged his friend not to be so serious.

But Hugh was not quite so amused as he responded wryly, "But to a female who is quite on the shelf, to offer her such a set down, would it not be equal to taking your axe to this symbolic tree and chopping it down?"

"Oh, you refer to her position in society. I was referring to her heart. Solid hornbeam, if you ask me, and all deadwood!"

"Lord Meares does not apparently think so. The *on dits*

have it that he intends to wed her if he can."

"And he is welcome to her, I'm sure! But then he has hardly known her for as many years as I. Perhaps I ought to drop a word in his ear!"

"How very obliging of you, I'm sure!" Hugh regarded William with a frown as they progressed about the rim of the ballroom floor. The candlelight shimmered upon the satins and jewels of the dancers as the pair continued a slow progress, and the orchestra measured out the beats of the easy country dance. The gentlemen attracted a great deal of notice for they were both very tall, though Hugh was taller still, and there was scarcely a young lady in the room who did not wish in the secret place of her heart that one or the other would ask her to dance for then her place in society for that season would be positively made.

Three such hopeful young ladies rose from their chairs not ten feet in front of the gentlemen and were trying to hide their giggles, for they were all just emerged from the schoolroom and suffering from terribly high spirits. It came to William as something of a shock when the ladies formed a line in front of their path, and upon a whispered cue of *now* from the middle young lady, all three, dressed in soft white jaconet muslin, flipped their fans open at the same moment in a flurry of pretty, brightly painted butterflies. Each fan had been decorated with red, yellow, and blue butterflies, laced in the background with dark green ivy leaves, and the result was charming, at least to one of the gentlemen anyway. The ladies then could not contain their giggles and hid their faces behind their butterflies, moving beyond the earl and his friend.

William was startled, but responded as he always did, with a very depressing lift of his brow, his nostrils flaring slightly as he watched the ladies pass by.

Hugh, on the other hand, had laughed outright when they whisked open their fans, and could not resist lifting his quizzing glass, which hung about his neck on a white silk riband, and ogled each of them in turn as they walked past him. The ladies were delighted as they returned Hugh's broad smile, but all of them were soon covered in confusion as they directed their glances back to the Earl of Redbourne, and their laughter slowly died away as they hurried toward the exit of the ballroom under William's austere gaze.

"How's this! What the devil has gone amiss?" Hugh cried. "Why did they run away? I meant to ask the middle one to dance, for she had such lively green eyes!" But glancing back at William's stony expression he did not hesitate to say, "Good God! I'm only surprised now that they each did not drop at my feet in a dead faint. You look positively saturnine my dear friend! And these poor girls were devilish pretty and out for a lark. How could you stare at them in that boorish manner? Why, they're just schoolroom chits."

"Then I think they ought to learn a little conduct!"

"My, what a fusty old woman you've become! How is it I've not noticed this before! What's become of you, Will! You, of all people, what with your masked adventures and the like, distressing young ladies in so wretched a fashion. It's not like you!"

"And what do you know of the matter!" William cried. "I suppose on the surface it would seem that I am being cruel. But you can't imagine what it is really like for me. One smile, and all her friends would have it that I had fallen violently in love with the chit. All I am doing is merely saving myself and the ladies a great deal of trouble!"

Hugh returned with a light tone, "And at my expense, I might add. But I promise you I won't utter a word about how completely ridiculous you are behaving, nor will I point out that if Miss Holwell has seen any of this, she'll surely not have you now."

At this William turned to regard his friend with a smile.

"Oh, she'll have me all right, even if she did utter some nonsense this morning about not knowing me."

"Eh, what's this? Do you mean she didn't accept you immediately?"

"Well, no. But I'm certain it was merely a show of modesty or the like!"

"But this is promising!" Hugh cried. "And I for one dearly hope that she will refuse you. I'm afraid you need taking down a peg or two, m'boy! You've grown a little high in the instep."

William knew his friend was joking and in a like manner responded, "And I suppose next you will tell me that if Charity does not lower my sense of self-consequence that you will be happy to do so! But name your seconds and I'll gladly meet you—swords, pistols, or fisticuffs. You have but to say the word!"

Hugh clapped him on the shoulder and with a teasing huff of his voice, said, "Nay, lad. I wouldn't want anyone to be on the brunt end of the thrashing I'd deliver!" And the men laughed together. But as Hugh searched the ballroom floor, his eyes found the very pretty face of Charity Holwell, and he frowned slightly. She was very graceful, as she went through the movements of the dance in much the same manner as Francoise; she held her head very high, her carriage quite the most elegant of all the ladies present, and in every respect she seemed confident and poised. But was she a match for Will? He had absolutely no way of knowing. However, he hoped sincerely for her sake that she was spirited and forceful, else he feared his dear friend would crush her within a sennight of the nuptials. For though he loved William, his friend was quite one of the most stubborn, obstinate, and properly named creatures of his acquaintance, for Will was willful indeed!

* * *

83

The simple movements of a country dance lent themselves to idle ballroom chatter and gossip and also to observation. The latter was now causing Charity no small degree of distress. And though she continued to listen attentively to, and smile at, her freckled partner, her thoughts continued to drift to the young ladies and their butterflies, to Hugh and his playfulness, and, as she ground her teeth, to William and his disdain. This was clearly not the young man who had fallen laughing into a duck pond with her. This was someone else who had robbed her childhood friend of his easy temper and loving kindness. And she did not like this man in the least and meant at the first opportunity to tell him so.

It was therefore with a measure of relief, once the dance had ended, that she saw William making his way toward her. And as she again saw him lift a brow to another innocent female who deigned to smile at him, her first thought was to deliver a brilliant set down, something like, *Oh, there you are My Lord Arrogance. And do you intend also to humiliate me? And don't you think it would be a great deal more sensible to perhaps deliver a general set down to the entire assembly for that would certainly make your task a great deal easier, would it not?* The truth was she was furious with his complete disregard for the feelings of other people, her own anger evident as she fanned herself very briskly, the white feathers of her fan just touching her chin.

He was smiling as he made his approach and she smiled in return, very sweetly she hoped, and she wondered if any of her anger showed in her eyes. Had Furney been present, she could have warned William that Charity's sword was sharpest when it was sweetened with a smile.

She extended her hand to him, feigned a look of great adoration as she batted her eyes, and sank into a deep curtsy. Ah, what pleasure to see the slight frown enter his eyes as he lifted her to her feet and whispered, "Was that necessary?" and glanced about him to see if anyone was watching.

Everyone was intrigued and Charity was enjoying herself immensely. "Do parade me about the ballroom floor, Will. For I wish everyone to see me upon your arm. Your consequence," and here she turned to again regard him adoringly as she continued, "will add so much to my otherwise impoverished place in society."

"What nonsense is this?" he asked, taking her arm and directing them upon a similar route as he and Hugh had just navigated.

"Nonsense?" she queried in an innocent voice. "I should never refer to your consequence as nonsense. Now it is you who are speaking nonsensically." And as they made their way about the ballroom, she bowed with great mockery to many of their mutual acquaintance, waving her fan in a grand gesture of acknowledgement that soon grew to irritate the earl.

"What are you doing with that curst thing!" he whispered. "What are you about? Stop this at once!" And he laughed, but his laughter was strained as though he was on unfamiliar ground.

Charity stopped in mid-step and whirled toward him, her expression aghast. "Oh, good, my lord! Have I displeased you? Oh, dear, and I thought you would be so happy that I have made the most of your consequence. But if you do not like my fan, I throw it away at once." And with that she tossed it on the floor and it landed at the feet of Princess Esterhazy.

Charity heard the gasps and was pleased, but she regarded no one but William. He, for his part, was utterly bemused, as he stared back at her and she could see that anger was vying for supremacy over stupefaction but was not winnning the day as he remained mute before her. It was the Princess who spoke next, "Redbourne, the lady has dropped her fan. What will you do about it?"

The question seemed directed toward the very essence of his being and William turned to stare at the white feathers lying beside the Princess's emerald-studded shoes. He regarded them for some time, and Charity remained with her attention fixed solely upon him. He seemed uncertain what to do, and a crowd began growing about them.

Finally, he asked Charity, "Madame, do you wish for your fan?"

She responded, "No, I do not!" Another gasp arose from the crowd and many began whispering, shocked at Miss Holwell's tone of voice as she answered the *Earl of Redbourne*.

He said, "Then, if you have no objection, may I keep it as token of this moment, for I have a fondness for duels?"

Charity again curtsied deeply. "I beg of you to please yourself, m'lord, though I daresay you always do." And as she rose to her feet, she again smiled ever so sweetly as she said, "And I wish to inform you that I hereby accept your gracious hand in marriage!"

Chapter Six

By this time, William had regained his composure and regarded Charity quite steadily as the growing crowd about them became a hubbub of whisperings, exclamations and cries of, *I didn't hear what she said! What did she say? What? She's to marry Redbourne? Never heard a thing about it. Pitching it a bit rum, don't you think?*

Princess Esterhazy exclaimed, "This is quite beyond bearing, Miss Holwell. What do you mean that you stand there, staring up at Lord Redbourne with that ridiculously simpering expression and then tell him you'll marry him! What nonsense is this! It isn't done! One does not accept a proposal of marriage while one is tossing one's fan about as though it were a cricket ball. I've never heard of such a thing!"

Lord Redbourne turned to the Princess and bowing in his elegant manner, said, "You must forgive my betrothed. You see she has but recently returned from Paris and does not yet know how to go on in society. I intend to instruct her myself."

"See that you do!" the Princess answered with considerable asperity. "We cannot tolerate such hoydenish behavior as this."

After bowing slightly to her, the earl bent down to

retrieve the fan. And as he did so, Charity assumed the air of a complete innocent as she addressed the Princess, saying, "And I am certain that so worthy a gentleman as my Lord Redbourne will be able to instruct me in many things. For instance, in how to retrieve objects from a ballroom floor. Look how he does it with such grace, such elegance of demeanor, such efficiency. I am quite overwhelmed by his excellent example. I shall learn so very much, I am sure, under his tutelage. I tremble at the very thought of so much knowledge waiting to be imparted to me."

And turning away she espied her cousin and cried, "Did you hear that, Penelope. William and I are to be married, and he intends to instruct me. But you must help me fashion my bridesclothes." And she turned back to William, who was regarding her with a measuring eye, and said, "Dearest William, you really must excuse me now, but Penelope and I have so very much to discuss."

He bowed to her, very slightly, and said, "You are too good to me, Madame. I don't deserve so much kindness."

If he hoped to discompose Charity by these words, he was greatly mistaken. For she merely regarded him with a honeyed expression which completely mystified most of the people present as she said, "Yes, you are so very right." And she turned on her heel and walked away from him.

William watched her link arms with Penelope and rapped the fan against the palm of his hand. He was very deep in thought and did not realize that the Princess was speaking to him at first until she caught hold of Charity's fan, forcing him to look at her as she repeated her question, "I ask you again. Are you indeed engaged to this young lady?"

"So it would seem."

"This is all very odd and quite unlike you, Redbourne. I was used to think you one of our more proper young men and now I am not so certain. And all of this nonsense about picking up fans, and how elegantly you accomplished the task. It made no sense at all to me. None whatsoever!"

William glanced at several of the people still gathered about him, and with a gentle withering expression, soon had scattered the onlookers to various corners of the ballroom. To the Princess he said, "Perhaps if you regarded this fan, not as an innocent tool with which to cool your brow, but as a gauntlet, albeit a feathered one, Miss Holwell's speeches might be better comprehended."

"A gauntlet you say? But why? Why does she accept your hand in marriage, and then throw a gauntlet down before you!"

"That, Madame, is a question I wish answered even more than yourself."

The response to Charity's announcement that she had decided to marry William was indeed mixed. And though any number of her acquaintance at Almack's congratulated her with great enthusiasm, the reponse amongst her nearest relatives was not entirely sanguine. Having returned to the safety of the townhouse, the family retired to the drawing room where Lord Datchworth, his brow furrowed, tossed off at least two glasses of brandy and began pacing the length of the long chamber. Once he nearly overset a bowl of violets sitting alone upon a tripod table near one end of the room and cursed the flowers soundly. He was clearly upset but as yet had not made known his sentiments to his family.

Lady Datchworth, Anne, and Penelope sat grouped together upon a blue striped settee near the fireplace, exchanging looks of trepidation, whilst Charity stood by the fireplace, her heart beating rapidly and her mouth quite dry.

"Am I given to understand, then," Lord Datchworth

cried as he paused momentarily in his marches, "that you threw your fan at Princess Esterhazy and then announced that you would marry Redbourne?"

Charity swallowed very hard, for she could see that her uncle was quite angry, and clasping her hands before her, the lavender silk feeling rather cool to her skin, she replied, "I suppose anyone near the incident could possibly have described it thusly. As it happens, I had not meant to throw my fan at the Princess, only to toss it away from William. He expressed a certain repugnance toward my feathered fan, or rather, I suppose, my manner of waving it about!"

Lord Datchworth scowled at her as he placed his hands on his hips, trying to make her out. "And since when, even in Paris, has throwing one's fan in a ballroom become the accepted mode of conduct?"

"I should not have done so, and I do indeed apologize to you and to my aunt."

He seemed slightly mollified by Charity's admission of guilt and her subsequent apology, but he was not satisfied and resumed his pacing, shoving his hands deeply into his pockets.

"I don't like this," he muttered. "I don't like it at all!" And walking straight up to Charity, he held her gaze quite fiercely, and said, "Did Penelope suggest this to you? Has she some scheme in mind that I don't know about?"

"Papa!" Penelope cried. But she got no further, for her father hushed her with a backward wave of his hand all the while still regarding Charity with his brown eyes flashing his irritation.

Charity laughed lightly, though she did not at all care for being scrutinized so closely by her uncle, and said, "No, of course not. What could Penelope have suggested to me anyway?"

"Then why did you accept him so suddenly when you were, only this morning, intent upon refusing him?"

Lord Datchworth was by far too needlewitted to let much escape him, and though Charity thought that she could fool her aunt and most of her friends, she knew that her uncle and Penelope would be the most difficult, if not impossible, to persuade that her motives were innocent. Giving her uncle stare for stare, she decided the best course was to answer him with as much honesty as she could and she responded simply, "Because when I watched him saunter about the ballroom, I made up my mind that I wished for it. Truly, it was nothing more than that. I may at some point perhaps regret so hasty a decision, but it is done."

Lady Datchworth intruded, "Stephen, why do you badger the child! Isn't it enough that she has done as you wished?"

He huffed at his wife, and harrumphed several times, as he turned away from Charity and resumed pacing the drawing room, his hands again shoved into his pockets. "I know I should be content with that, but somehow I am not! Charity has a shrewd cast to her blue eyes tonight and were it Penelope, I wouldn't have the least doubt that some truly wretched scheme was afoot and I would lock her in her bedchamber for a fortnight. And it didn't escape my notice that William was in rare form this evening, first giving Pen a set down and then casting his cold eye upon three innocent chits. . . ." He seemed to be speaking to himself upon these points as he walked briskly to and fro, every now and again removing a hand from his pocket to stroke his chin, and then shoving it back into the unfortunate pocket. Charity thought that in the morning her uncle's valet would find the seams ripped through, and she found herself smiling.

This was not quite pleasing to her uncle, whose scowl deepened as he cried, "And why do you seem so happy of the moment! I forbid you to smile for I am enormously upset by the manner in which this business was conducted. And pray tell me, if you would, why it is being bandied about that your fan was some sort of gauntlet—that Redbourne referred to it as such? Am I now to expect more of this sort of hoydenish behavior from you? Why, I heard such tittle-tattle flying from mouth to ear all evening that I was sick to death of it. I suppose this means that the rest of the season will be hell to pay! And you listen to me, Missy! I don't know why you've decided to lock horns with Redbourne—nay, don't go protesting that you've suddenly tumbled in love with him—but I do ask you to please consider your aunt and cousins and, if you can manage it, try not to make too great a fool of yourself! Well, that is all I have to say upon the matter, and now I mean to retire to my bed—though I daresay I shall be besieged with nightmares about feathery fans and butterflies and gauntlets. Good God!"

And upon these words, as he regarded the ladies of his house, he threw up his arms in a hopeless gesture, begging to know why he had not been blessed with sons and nephews instead of cursed with females, and stalked from the room.

Lady Datchworth rose upon his exit and shook her head in bewilderment. "That man is as mad as Bedlam! Whatever was he speaking of? First Charity and then three young ladies whom I don't think I am acquainted with and then fans and gauntlets. Really, I begin to think I should send for the doctor to physic him." But turning to Charity, Lady Datchworth soon forgot about her husband and moving toward her, possessed herself of her niece's hands and said, "You will be very happy, I am certain of it. I know that William has a tiny little fault, that he perhaps is a trifle boorish at times, but I know that you will be able to correct this lack in his manners in a trice! I am certain of that, I can *feel* it!" After that, she expressed her raptures for several more minutes and promised Charity that as soon as possible, perhaps on Friday after the soiree on Thursday, they might call upon the dowager Lady Redbourne. And after feigning a yawn, she bade the young ladies goodnight, adjuring them not to sit up too long, though she herself understood quite well the need they might have for a lengthy chat. She then crossed the room on a light, happy step, sighing with much satisfaction as she repeatedly said, *my niece a countess*, checked her image in the gilt mirror by the door and finally was gone.

Anne sat with an embroidered pillow clutched to her stomach, regarding Charity with her blue eyes so wide that they appeared nearly ready to pop. Penelope also stared at Charity in wonderment, and in a quiet voice finally said, "I could not credit my ears when I heard you actually accept William. And though you may tell Papa whatever you like, I know that you have a great deal more to impart on the subject than this. So, I shall ask you, why did you do it?"

Charity regarded her cousin, the drawn appearance to her features, the almost blank expression to her brown eyes, the pale cast to her complexion, and she said, "And I thought you at least would understand."

Anne cried, "Well, I know I don't understand at all."

Charity continued to regard Penelope and said, "When first he treated you so unkindly at the very beginning of the ball, I must confess that I was truly shocked, for until that moment, I had had only your letters to reveal his nature to me. But to see his arrogance and cruelty with my own eyes, well, I can't explain how deeply it affected me for I would never have suspected that the William I grew up with could have grown so utterly hard-hearted! And that is not all, for later, those poor young ladies, who meant only to tease the gentlemen but a little, to receive such a cutting *look* from William was more than I could bear!"

Anne cried, "But what did they do? Oh, why did I have to be eating one of those dry little cakes at such a moment, when so much excitement was going on in the ballroom!

But pray tell me what they did! I am all agog to know!"

Charity shook her head. "It was utterly charming. They were barely out of the schoolroom and had painted their fans in brilliantly colored butterflies, and stepping in front of William and his friend—who I later learned was a gentleman by the name of Hugh Bramfield—the ladies unfurled their fans all at once and began giggling." Here Charity stopped, for she was still so horrified by what followed, by the image of her beloved William treating them in so biting a manner, that for a moment she could not continue. Burnt in her mind forever was the look of humiliation upon the girls' faces, and the arrogant, cold expression upon William's haughty features as he sent them about their business with a mere lifting of his brow. She continued, "I was never more shocked than to see William behave in so ungentlemanly a manner. What could possibly have happened to him in all these years that he must stoop to hurting innocent young girls?"

"Oh, dear," Anne said in a quiet voice. "That was not very well done of him, was it?"

Charity replied in an equally subdued manner, "Not at all."

"What do you mean to do then?" Penelope asked, a little of the color beginning to return to her cheeks. Her brown eyes even seemed to sparkle a little as she shifted her gaze away from Charity. She was sitting near a vase of flowers and ferns and reached out to an errant frond, gently pushing it deeper into the arrangement. She added, "For though I apprehend that you are exceedingly angry with William, I cannot imagine what you intend to do. After all, you have accepted his hand in marriage." She then returned her gaze to Charity, regarding her almost as intensely as Lord Datchworth had done earlier.

Charity, with great relish, held back her answer until both ladies leaned forward slightly in their seats. "Why, I mean to lead him a merry dance for the next few weeks and at an appropriate time, I think I shall simply decide that we should not suit!"

Both Anne and Penelope gasped in horror. Anne cried, "But you cannot! Oh, Charity why you would be ruined forever in doing so. To play the jilt!"

At these words, Charity turned around to face the fireplace, for she did not wish her thoughts detected in the least. How could she explain to her cousins that when she saw William's cavalier treatment of the ladies, a daring scheme involving her decision to dance upon the stage had taken shape in her mind. There was no doubt that William's manners needed improving, that somewhere he had lost an essentially kind part of his being, and that her own intention to dance at Drury Lane might just be the mending of his ways.

After a moment, she turned back to them and said, "I know that I have not discussed this with you before, and perhaps you won't quite understand when I say that I don't think I shall ever marry. I don't desire to wed or to take a husband."

Anne cried, "Not wish to marry! But that's impossible! Every young lady wishes to marry, why, it is all we think about from the time we are children."

"Yes, I know, and I can't explain all my feelings to you, at least not yet, but I'm certain in the course of the season, I will be able to. But for the moment, I intend that my dear betrothed will have the great pleasure of receiving as many set downs, cold expressions, arrogant bows, and curt remarks as I can possibly deliver in the next few weeks."

Penelope said, "You are certainly speaking in riddles this evening. But whatever the cause, I am only grateful that you were not taken in by William for I know that at times he can be very persuasive! And as for your current scheme, I would only suggest that you do not let Papa see or hear you doing anything so wicked as what you have just described."

Charity said, "I make no promises whatsoever."

Penelope lifted her brow at this and said, "And I was afraid that our society would bowl you over. But here you are full of rebellion and spirit and prepared to do battle to the death. But what I wish to know is what you have *not* told us this evening. For you haven't satisfied my curiosity in the least, but rather you have piqued it enormously."

Charity then smiled at her cousin and said, "I only wish that I had more to tell you, but I am afraid you will have to wait until my future is more clearly settled within my own heart."

On the following morning, Charity escaped from the house with Marie in tow, with the explanation that she had a great deal of shopping to do before the soiree that evening. And begging her hackney driver to *spring 'em*, she was soon with Monsieur Bovin in Hans Town where she endured the rigors of a final rehearsal before her audition. Afterward, with her ballet master on one side of her and Marie on the other, the three of them traveled quickly to Furney's rooms in the City where Charity donned her complete costume of a long gauzy tutu, a powdering of her black tresses, and the final adornment of her pearl-embroidered mask. Over the costume Furney arranged a long, hooded black wool cape so that Charity was able to enter another hackney without creating a great deal of notice. Only then, as the coach rumbled toward the Drury Lane Theatre, did Charity find her nerves growing increasingly taut, the work of her lifetime coming to a very sharp conclusion. But was she prepared to take this step and so alienate herself forever from the people and the society she loved?

Charity had never known such misery as this, her

stomach in a knot of apprehension as she waited now in the wings of the Drury Lane Theatre for her audition to begin. How much deception had brought her to this point and how much her heart seemed to wreak havoc against her ribs. She was both hot and cold. The tips of her fingers felt as though she had placed them in freezing water, so nervous did she feel. She was certain she would forget the order of her steps. She would trip just walking to center stage. Oh, why had she wished to take part in so madcap and scatterbrained a scheme?

Glancing out into the darkened theatre, she could discern the slightly stooped shoulders of her aging ballet master. Rows of seats and richly dressed boxes formed shadows behind him as he spoke to several faceless gentlemen, governors of the theatre.

Would the audition never commence?

The stage manager stood behind her and in a superior manner, said, "I hope that yer performance is acrobatic. Them governors like it when a female can spin like a top!"

Charity feigned a French accent. "Then I greatly fear that they shall be disappointed! Monsieur Bovin has an entirely different concept of the ballet."

She gripped the sides of her ankle-length tutu and was well aware that a number of feminine faces on the opposite side of the stage were regarding her with great hostility. Her reception backstage had been very cold but her disguise at least helped to lessen the effect of so much antagonism. She was wearing her pearl-studded mask, the ribbons dangling to the side, and the first words she had heard from a member of the *corps de ballet* was, "La, but someone ought to tell her that she is in the wrong century! A mask, indeed! What airs!"

Monsieur Bovin turned away from the governors and nodded to the man seated before the pianoforte. Beside him stood a flutist and an elegant female running her fingers silently next to the long strings of her harp. The musicians seemed completely disinterested in the proceedings and waited patiently, with ill-disguised boredom, for the sounds of the pianoforte to prelude their own performances.

Charity wanted to cry, her nerves stretched to their thinnest as she watched the man at the pianoforte glance to see that the others were at least aware of what was going forward, if not attentive. Would that her dancing might evoke some emotion from their apparently sated sensibilities.

"Take your place, Mam'zelle Novarre," the stage manager whispered to her. In all of their discussion about her anonymity, it had finally been decided that she would, in addition to her mask and her powdered hair, use a false name as well. "Julian, what plays that overgrown harpsichord, just nodded his bushy gray head. 'Tis time to gladden a few hearts with a sight of them pretty ankles!"

Charity took a deep breath and had the greatest fear that her feet would refuse to move. But somehow, as she regarded the very spot, center stage, where she would begin her ballet, she found herself moving, arms outstretched in two delicate arcs, her feet silent, as she crossed the stage in very brisk, precise steps.

Curtsying quite low to the gentlemen seated several rows into the theatre, she slowly stood up, the line of her body perfect and graceful as she set her chin toward the upper balconies.

Mama, she thought. How odd that at this moment she would remember her mother. Suddenly she saw her, tripping through the meadows about her home in Hertfordshire, chip hat in hand, red silk ribbons trailing through the long grass, the summer sun glistening on her black hair. "Charity, my pet, you should dance. And I do not mean the assemblies but oh, if only you could dance the ballet. Did I ever tell you that I wished to be a ballerina?"

"Yes, Mama. A hundred times."

"What a foolish dream. And yet your papa never scolds me or thinks it foolish. He loves the delightful ballets that flit throughout the operas, almost as much as I do." She had sighed, her sweet smile bringing time back to Charity in a long, flowing ripple. "I suppose that is why we have brought Monsieur Bovin here when we knew he had been exiled. You should dance Charity."

Letting out a deep breath, Charity nodded to Julian and the music began. *Andantino*. She thought she heard the faintest snigger as the pianoforte took the place of the orchestra, and the harp and flute waited for their parts to begin. Mozart's *andantino*, from a concerto. An odd piece for a ballet, yet perfect, for it was easy, gentle, and very romantic. She could not hear it without feeling as though the music also took her back to that last summer with her mama.

Her heart suddenly full, her slippers now acted of their own accord and transported her to a field of bluebells, to her mother's laughter, her feet on half-points and then full-points, as she glided across the stage, in pursuit of butterfly, an elusive, scattering creature which she mimed again and again. And how much the delicate movement of the harp floated with her as she moved in undulating rhythms, on full-points again and again, her arms freely, yet precisely, extended and rippling.

And as the butterfly escaped her, she slowly gave up pursuit only to have the tiny creature land upon her shoulder and she whirled and danced and pirouetted across the stage, the butterfly now, in mime, dancing with her, pursuing, pursued, the entire dance coming at last to a gentle rest as she sank to the wooden floor, the butterfly now alight upon her raised hand, the pianoforte playing a final musical phrase.

Charity remained in that position, as though seeing the butterfly and then her mother's face. *Mama.*

At first she did not hear the applause until a distinct *bravo* sounded from behind the curtains and Charity slowly let her surroundings seep into her consciousness as she watched the butterfly leave her hand. And now she heard the three musicians honor her with quiet rappings upon their respective instruments. They no longer appeared in the least bored, but alive, their faces considerably animated.

Charity rose to her feet and sank into a deep curtsy as she faced the shadowed governors. And after regarding her ballet master, her eyes dimmed with tears. She fled the stage to the safety of the nether regions, and hid in the veriest hole of a dressing room.

She had been been alone for a few minutes, trying to still the pounding of her heart, when a gentle tapping on the door distracted her impatient fears.

"Entrez!" she called in French.

Another feminine voice, very shy and breathy, answered in the same tongue, *"Pardon,* Mademoiselle Novarre, but your dance, it was so *merveilleux!"*

Charity answered her in her native language, the extreme flutterings of her heart subsiding a little, a hint of perspiration collecting across the concealed bridge of her nose. "Oh, please do come in."

"I will only stay for a moment. But you are English?" The young opera-dancer stopped, a look of surprise suffusing her sharp, fine-boned features.

Charity stood up immediately and cried, "Is my accent so poor then? Pray, keep my secret if you will. I wish it known that I am French."

The young woman curtsied very slightly and promised to keep Charity's secret most faithfully and after introducing herself as one Francoise Minon, an orphan of the

French Revolution, she cried, "But I did not come to speak of myself but of your *petit* ballet. How beautiful it was, so very *romantique,* so very French!" She was a small young lady and Charity thought that she was at least five and twenty but no more. Her wispy, light brown hair was pulled into a knot at the top of her head and her pretty features, though thin and angular, were considerably augmented by a pair of brilliant green eyes, that glimmered with life even in the dull light of three candles that illuminated the dressing room.

And in the next moment, as the door burst open, it seemed that the small dressing chamber was filled with young women, all opera-dancers, congratulating Charity on her performance.

She could not credit that the same females who had been regarding her with undisguised dislike one moment could actually be complimenting her so sincerely the next. And then, as though each of them had the same thought, every pair of eyes fell to her stiffly embroidered ballet slippers and one girl cried out. "I counted them! You were *sur les pointes* for no less than twenty steps at a time! And that more than once! How did you do it?"

Charity immediately removed her slippers and let the young women handle them. She tried to sound very French. "It is done only occasionally at the Paris Opera but I believe that one day it will be performed always! And you can see how stiff my slippers are."

Another voice cut in, "But you also turned on your points!"

"Enough!" Monsieur Bovin's voice cut through the feminine chatter and in a few broad gestures accompanied by a string of French words, ushered everyone from the room, though quickly grasping Charity's slippers from one of the opera-dancers as she playfully tried to take them from the room, hidden behind her back.

Monsieur Bovin stood regarding Charity with an expression in his small brown eyes that nearly caused her to weep. She knew him so very well, and he was saying so much by the look of affection and pride with which he regarded her. He was bent slightly with his seventy years, but was thin and energetic. His shirtpoints were starched as though he were a young man of twenty, his neckcloth tied in an elegant, yet simple fashion, his carriage refined, his thinning gray hair cut short and swept toward his temples as was the fashion of the day. He approved of her this day, she could see that clearly in his face, and without so much as a thought for the propriety of her actions she went to him and embraced him, thanking him for this moment in her life.

"And I thank you, *cherie*. Such an audition. Exquisite. And what were you thinking of, I wonder? You did not hesitate once and you gave yourself fully to every movement." He held her very close and Charity had an odd sense that this was not a beginning for her, but an ending of sorts, even though his next words confirmed that the governors had been enchanted with her performance.

Releasing her, he said, "They wish you to dance the *divertissement*, this very dance that I choreographed for you."

Charity still clutched his arms, not wishing this moment, which they had all worked so very hard for, to end. "That is wonderful! That is more than I hoped for. I thought perhaps the *Corps de Ballet*, but this!"

Drawing away from her slightly, he tapped her slippers together and then handed them to her. He was frowning and Charity felt her heart jump within her breast. Something was wrong and she begged him not to spare her feelings.

He said, "It is about the mask and your hair." He waved

102

a hand over Charity's disguise. "The governors, while believing that they can make excellent use of your anonymity for a short period of time, will not hear of it continuing indefinitely. They will expect, as part of a grand scheme of promotion, for you, at their command, to unmask. They foresee a great furor of interest in the near future, as well as a dramatic rise in the theatre's popularity and therefore, its profits."

Charity sat down on a hard wooden chair, her back to a wide mirror, the room smelling of old stage makeup and cheap candles. She regarded the shredded wood of the floor and felt the exhilaration of the moment collapse upon her. But what else could she have expected?

Monsieur Bovin went to her, taking her hand and pressing it very hard. "You still have time, my child, to forget this scheme. No contracts have been signed. Marie told me that you accepted Lord Redbourne's hand in marriage. Is this true?"

Charity looked up at him sharply and responded, "Yes, but it is not quite what you think. I don't intend to marry him."

The ballet master narrowed his eyes at her and said, "I don't think I quite understand, but in any case, this step you take today, will alter your life forever. But I know you—you have considered the choices before you. Still, if you need more time—"

Charity fondled his hand, which was white and wrinkled and she pressed it to her cheek. "I was so certain when I was in Paris that this was what I wanted, but the moment I saw my cousins and my aunt and uncle, everything became confused until today when I stepped out on the stage and danced. I must do this, Monsieur, and I think you know that."

"Yes. I do know it. So be it, then. I will speak with the governors at once."

103

"That is what I wish, but as for the unmasking, beg a few weeks, and if at all possible, if I could but dance only one evening for the first few weeks—"

And for the first time, Monsieur Bovin smiled very broadly as he said, "They will do whatever I say, for they see the profits dangling before them. Your success is assured!"

Chapter Seven

The gauntlet. Charity sat very straight in her blue damask chair by the fireplace, smoothing out her gloves of lavender kid, the very thought of the battle to come stirring her heart up, much as the coals had been stirred just a few minutes earlier. She wished for this contest in a manner that would certainly have shocked her aunt. And even Penelope, whose own will was quite as sturdy as her own, would have been surprised at the heat of her thoughts as she reviewed in her mind yet again the scheme which would begin her own fierce campaign against the arrogant creature who had overtaken her beloved Will's heart.

The drawing room hummed with the chatter and nonsense of the ladies clustered about her. Of the moment, they were discussing in a lively manner the precise shade of The Gentleman's eyes. For herself, Charity was grateful that the general conversation had turned away from her own experiences in Paris and was now full of the highwayman, for the scrolled mahogany clock sitting upon the mantel and reflecting from its glass cover the brilliant candlelight of the drawing room, not one minute earlier had struck ten, the hour at which William was expected to arrive.

At the far end of the drawing room, two mock

Corinthian pillars flanked the opening of a cosy ante-chamber where Lady Datchworth was seated at a small table along with three other matrons. They were women of rank and wealth, wearing the finest lace and satins while diamonds and emeralds glistened upon their bosoms. Graceful ostrich feathers adorned at least two satin turbans and nearly met in the center of the table as the players bent over their cards. Charity again let her gaze drift to the small antechamber, for she was waiting for Marie to appear and signal Lord Redbourne's arrival.

The little room had an entrance into the hallway, and earlier that afternoon, Charity had walked the distance around the two rooms and the hall in order to feel perfectly comfortable with her current scheme. But as she watched her aunt give a little shout of triumph at some discard or other, Charity sighed yet again, for her maid was still not present. And why now must William be late?

Letting her gaze return to the drawing room, where a veritable swarm of guests moved amongst her aunt's daffodils and ferns and roses, Charity could not help but be pleased with the progress of the evening thus far, for the soiree was indeed *a crush*, and even Lady Datchworth had been so very happy with the number of guests in attendance, that she had slipped her arm about Charity's shoulder and given her a quick hug. "You are cutting quite a dash, my dear. And though I was a little afraid that Princess Esterhazy might have been excessively displeased with your conduct at Almack's, it would seem that very few persons have paid the least heed to her complaints. But what else could I have expected when it is already become known that you are engaged to William! You will discover, my dearest niece, that his mantle provides a great many advantages for his bride-to-be!"

But these words, far from causing Charity a thrill of pleasure as her aunt had no doubt expected them to, served instead to strengthen her resolve to act out this first of her several stratagems for bringing her beloved betrothed to task for his cruelty and indifference to the many females of her acquaintance.

From across the room, Charity watched her cousin Anne speaking in an animated fashion to a short young man with dark brown hair. Her plump arms danced about her as she related an anecdote to the somewhat portly young gentleman who laughed several times during the course of her recital. Wondering if this was the Mr. Meesden of whom Anne had spoken several times since Charity's arrival two days ago, she was about to ask Penelope, who sat to her right upon the light blue-striped sofa, when Anne, turning her direction caught Charity's eye, and soon afterward took the young man in hand and began pulling him toward their group by the fire.

But before they had progressed even halfway across the room a grave point of dispute arose amongst the ladies present. One of the young ladies, a fairy-like creature by the name of Merrie Thorley, insisted quite firmly that the highwayman had eyes of a startling blue, for when he had attacked her equipage but a few miles from London not six weeks ago, it was very early in the day and she saw his eyes most distinctly. "They were blue, I tell you, and quite piercing. Of course, I remember so little after—that is, after he accosted me so brutally, for he then threw me into my traveling chariot where my dear companion, who was used to be my governess and so knew the delicacy of my nerves, caught me and held her vinaigrette beneath my nose. And such palpitations as I endured for *days* afterward!"

Elinor Widford exclaimed, "And I tell you that his eyes were definitely green, just like mine!" And she turned about the group so that everyone gathered there might witness for themselves both how pretty her large green eyes were in the dazzling candlelight as well as to judge for themselves whether or not they thought The Gentleman ought to have entrancing green eyes or dullish blue ones.

But this only made Merrie quite angry and in response she said that it was impossible for the highwayman to possess such cattish eyes. Whereupon Elinor remarked on how very commonplace blue eyes had become and afterward both ladies leaned forward in their seats, preparing to scratch one another's eyes out which seemed the only poetic means possible for ending such a hopeless argument.

But Penelope lifted an elegant hand which had the astonishing effect of silencing both females, their mouths slightly agape, their words cut off completely. Charity regarded her cousin with no small degree of wonder, for the ladies most certainly were on the brink of war, and their deference toward Penelope spoke very highly of her esteem amongst her friends and acquaintance.

Penelope did not speak for a moment, as the ladies' attention gathered toward her. And when all eyes were turned her direction, she smiled sweetly and said, "But we have one amongst us who can settle this business quite easily, for she had the extreme displeasure of meeting our horrid bandit not two days ago on the Great North Road. I speak of my cousin, Charity."

Several gasps and exclamations followed this speech, and Charity soon found several pairs of astonished eyes directed toward her as the ladies demanded nearly in unison to be told the whole of her adventures and precisely why she had been so silent upon a subject that had for months now never been far from their hearts. Wasn't The Gentleman the most elegant yet miserable creature that ever existed? And hadn't dear Miss Holwell been frightened nearly out of her wits?

"No, I was not," Charity answered readily. "I was far too angry to be frightened. Such a man ought to be brought before the magistrate at Bow Street and suffer the consequences of the King's Law."

One young lady who sat at Penelope's right hand, and who had scarcely spoken a single word for she was clearly just out of the schoolroom, spoke in a shy yet rapturous voice, "But did he kiss you, Miss Holwell? And was it perfectly awful?"

Charity could not help but laugh, for the entire discussion was absurd in the extreme. For all the ladies, save Penelope, were expressing both their abhorrence of the highwayman all the while giving the very distinct impression that such were their nightly dreams as they tucked their hands beneath their cheeks, and snuggled their mob caps deeply into soft down pillows at night. Oh, to be kissed by The Gentleman!

Charity responded, "I kicked him very hard upon his shin, but to little avail. He kissed me, and though he did not precisely *throw* me into the post chaise, he left quite abruptly when a coach came into view."

"Why, how very brave of you," the young lady responded, clearly disappointed at this recital. The rest of the ladies merely responded with a very sad, "Oh."

Charity did not even try to conceal her smiles as she said, "But as to the color of his eyes, I think they might have been gray perhaps even hazel."

Both Merrie and Elinor took great exception to this callous judgment upon The Gentleman's eyes, for gray or, heaven forbid, hazel were colors of the most indifferent. But at least Charity's opinion had the happy effect of joining the combatants together in a loud protestation that it was Charity now who erred.

However at that moment Anne approached the group by the fire and cried, "Oh, no. You are all quite mistaken for I saw the color of his eyes clearly when he attacked our post chaise nearly a year ago, and his eyes were brown! A very deep, entrancing color." And upon these words, she turned back to the stodgy young man at her elbow and gave him a very sweet smile.

Only then did Charity notice that her beau had very dark brown eyes, and the compliment so charmingly given, was meant exclusively for him. He even blushed, which endeared him to Charity forever.

Anne then turned to her cousin and said, "And may I present Mr. Meesden to you, Charity? He is a—a very good friend of mine for several years now."

Charity greeted George Meesden, who was a young gentleman of but two and twenty—younger by three years than Anne!—and whose general demeanor was quite at odds with his youth for he gave the appearance of a portly man who had been on the town for years. He spoke in a measured voice very precisely, and the only sign of his youth was his tendency to color over just about anything. He did so now as he said, "And may I wish you every happiness, Miss Holwell, in your forthcoming nuptials? I understand that Lord Redbourne has had the very great honor of winning your hand in marriage."

Charity had nearly forgotten about William, and as the clock upon the mantel struck the quarter hour, she glanced toward the antechamber, only to find, much to her dismay, that Marie was there, waving to her in a frantic motion. And after catching Charity's eye, she disappeared immediately into the hallway.

Swallowing very hard, Charity rose to her feet, and after thanking Mr. Meesden, said, "But I do beg you will forgive me, but I believe my aunt wishes to speak with me." Mr. Meesden bowed slightly. Charity inclined her head to him, and with an apologetic smile, moved carefully out of the tight cluster of ladies by the fire.

Not daring to look toward the entrance to the drawing room, Charity wended her way as quickly as she could toward the antechamber and heard at least one person call out, "Oh, do but look! Redbourne has arrived with Mr. Bramfield!"

Charity did not even glance in her aunt's direction as

she passed by the card table, but instead walked quickly into the hallway. Marie then turned the corner to observe the traffic of the guests, and Charity watched the back of the maid's head, holding herself rigidly, as Marie gauged the precise moment when Charity should make her flight.

From the sounds emanating from the drawing room, Charity could hear the rumble of guests as several called out to the earl congratulating him upon his engagement, and even one slightly foxed masculine voice cried, "But where the devil is Miss Holwell! Saw her not a minute ago in the middle of a bevy of beautiful young chits, but now she's gone! Vanished!"

Charity leaned slightly against the wall, her heart beating loudly in her ears. What would William think when her absence became known? Would he suspect her treachery? Her gaze became fixed upon Marie's dark brown curls, her tense shoulders, and one hand held behind her back as she made ready to give Charity another signal.

Charity knew she ought not to be playing such a reprehensible trick upon William, however ignoble his behavior. It was very bad of her, and yet she wanted nothing more in this moment than to execute her schemes for somehow it put her in mind of summer days in Hertfordshire when she would tease the William she had once known, so many long years ago, by hiding in the beechwood until he was so angry that he would threaten to flail her alive. But he always forgave her. She had always, somehow, been able to make him laugh.

But that was so very long ago, and as the greetings continued to flow about William, though growing less distinct as he apparently made his way into the drawing room, Marie's hand twitched quite suddenly—the signal! —and Charity bolted around her, running to the top of the stairs, looking neither right nor left, lifting the skirts of her royal blue satin gown, and bouncing upon the very

111

tips of her slippers down the stairs to secrete herself, under the disapproving eye of Hinx, in Lord Datchworth's office. Closing the door behind her, she leaned against the door, her heart suddenly full of excitement and mischief and she actually found it necessary to cover her mouth, lest she burst out laughing and alert several new arrivals to her presence! If only she could trust Hinx not to betray her. But she was fairly confident that the butler would remain silent, for Marie had discovered him nipping at the cooking sherry only that morning. Ah, what thrills life could contain if one were but a little daring! And if somewhere in her mind a small voice called out to her that she was being unmaidenly and rebellious, she quickly stilled that voice, adjuring it to silence, as she let the excitement of her schemes flow through her. And a very odd thought occurred to her that this must be how The Gentleman felt when he accosted the young ladies in their post chaises. And what if it were true that he was a member of the *beau monde*? And suddenly she wished more than anything to know who he was for she felt quite certain that such a man would understand her own love of adventure, her own longings to dance upon the stage.

Hugh Bramfield watched Charity disappear through a doorway upon the lower floor of the townhouse, and felt mildly surprised. He had been in the process of searching for his quizzing glass which he discovered had slipped from its riband, when, coming out onto the landing, he noticed a dark-haired female, a servant, watching the stairs with a rather animated smile upon her lips until she discovered his presence. Then she turned toward him, her features drawn together in an anxious expression, curtsied, and afterward fled the landing to disappear into the hallway at the back of the townhouse. What was amiss, he wondered, and that was when he had turned to see Miss

Holwell disappear into a chamber located to the right of the front door. Now what scheme was afoot? And a broad smile suffused his face.

The truth was, from the little he had seen of Miss Holwell, besides the very obvious fact that she was clearly a diamond of the first stare, he liked her. And the manner in which she had accepted William's hand! Was nothing more poetic than that, for William had just made the worst cake of himself in cutting those three charming young ladies at Almack's. Faith, Charity seemed to have quite as much spirit as the earl and Hugh now had great hopes for an engagement, which by its very nature as having begun as a contract of convenience, now promised to afford the entire *haut ton* a great deal of amusement over the next few days and weeks.

Silently wishing Charity well, Hugh turned upon his heel, and headed back to the crowded rooms where just beside the door he saw his quizzing glass and stooped to pick it up. And as he bent over, he discovered a pair of shining black shoes standing very near his hand. *Damn*, he thought, a measure of anger coursing through him. He knew full well what face he would find connected to the shoes studded with several small diamonds.

Rising to his full height, he at least had the advantage of looking down upon the thin-nosed gentleman as he said simply, "Tewin." And that was the most greeting he intended to give the somewhat gaunt smiling gentleman who sported a head of thinning black hair brushed forward in the current Brutus fashion, his black eyes small and gleaming.

"Ah, my dear Bramfield. So it is you, though to be sure I wasn't able to recognize you fully until you stood up, still the parts seemed familiar enough."

Hugh despised the pale arrogant man who continued to smile at him in a maddening fashion. Nodding curtly to him, Hugh made a movement to step beyond Mr. Tewin, but he did not count upon finding Tewin's hand upon his arm, holding him back with a firm pressure. "One moment, if you please," he cried. "I wish to beg one or two words with you, surely you can spare me that consideration for it has been so long since I last saw you and we were used to be such great friends. And when was it that we last spoke—" he laughed slightly. "Or should I say, when was it that we last sat down to a game of faro. Of course, I remember now. Damme if it hasn't been a fortnight to the day! Can you imagine that so much *time* has actually passed between our meetings?"

Several newcomers were advancing at that moment up the stairs, and Hugh removed the hand upon his arm quite carefully, feeling as though he were handling a very slimy object as he cast the hand away from him. "Don't ever touch me again, Tewin, or you will answer for it!"

Hugh stepped aside to permit the latest guests to enter the drawing room and would have followed them into the chamber, but Mr. Tewin stopped him by saying, "I am growing short of patience, Bramfield. I want my money or you may book passage upon the next packet to Dover!"

Turning back to the thin, small-eyed creature who was known to cheat at cards, Hugh bore down upon him, backing him against the doorpost with his mere physical presence, and hissed at him in a low voice, "I have no proof of your methods, Tewin, but I know you marked your cards. And if you care to live one more day, I should think twice about ever again threatening me."

Tewin glared at him, his white complexion growing paler still, his features twisted in bitterness. "And you are like so many great officers that have come back from the wars, still doing battle and gaming away your properties. I will forgive your slur about marking my cards, but you can't gammon me that you've the ready to pay your debts or that I am the only one you owe money to. I just want to be the first when you do finally set about discharging your obligations." And with that he disappeared amongst the guests, his thin form gliding between clusters of gentlemen and ladies.

Hugh stood for a moment in the doorway, trying to collect his thoughts. He had never before been approached in so hostile a manner, but the fact was Tewin had the right of it. He may have been a weasel, but others to whom he owed gaming monies were not. He kept promising quarter day funds, for he had a small independence, but even now the property in the miserable fenlands was mortgaged to the hilt and he didn't know what he was going to do. And Tewin's suggestion that he book passage upon a packet was not so far-fetched an idea as he had once thought it was. Even Beau Brummell had succumbed to a gaming fever that had cost him his entire existence among the *haut ton* and the Beau now lived in Calais, elegant but impoverished, exiled from England forever.

Huffing out a deep breath, he set aside his fury with Mr. Tewin and went in search of William. He found the earl deep in conversation with George Meesden, and when he approached them discovered that they were involved in discussing the merits of Mr. Coke's modern methods of farming and Hugh sighed with impatience—a pair of dull dogs indeed. He wondered how William, with his exploits as a highwayman and his high-handed manner with the ladies, could possibly find anything like farming to hold the least fascination for him.

Glancing about the drawing room, Hugh searched for any sign of Charity, thinking perhaps she might have returned to her soiree, but he found no evidence of her. He could not then resist interrupting the gentlemen, who had begun arguing about the merits of pigeon dung, and asked, "And where, might I ask, is Miss Holwell? I should like to be formally presented to her for at Almack's, as you know, Will, she linked arms with Penelope and walked away before ever I could beg an introduction!"

He was smiling as he spoke and his taunting words resulted in a gratifying response as William cried, "Oh, the devil take you, Hugh! You're as bad as Tewin who was here not a minute before spouting some nonsense about hoping that Charity will make me a comfortable wife! But as for her whereabouts, I haven't yet found her. Perhaps she is in the library. Have you seen her yet this evening, George?"

Mr. Meesden said, "Yes, earlier, as it happens. But as to her whereabouts of the moment, I cannot say. Just before you arrived, however, she mentioned that her aunt seemed wishful of speaking with her. Lady Datchworth, I believe, is engaged in playing whist in the antechamber. She might know where Charity is." His cheeks grew flushed at this speech and Hugh raised a brow wondering how it was the boy, who never ceased to remind him of his own portly parent, blushed whenever he was spoken to.

Hugh addressed William, "Perhaps we should seek out Lady Datchworth then." Oh, but he was very wicked to be leading William on this chase, but then, his friend deserved such ill-treatment when he so effectively ruined his chances of getting up a flirtation with the butterfly chits of the evening before.

The progress from one end of the drawing room to the next took at least fifteen minutes, for everyone wished to congratulate William upon his engagement. But Hugh's smile, which had begun to grow each time they stopped, grew broader still when it became generally known that Miss Holwell was not present to greet her betrothed. Some titters were heard as well as teasing remarks that Miss Holwell was no doubt merely *bashful.* This ironic comment sent any number of ladies and gentlemen into peals of laughter. For it was by this time well known that Miss Holwell had accepted Lord Redbourne's hand in marriage in an excessively peculiar manner, and in front of any number of disinterested persons who had each repeated the occurrence until the story now popularly bandied about that Charity had taken to hitting everyone present with her fan, finally throwing it at the Princess Esterhazy, and lastly shouting at the Earl of Redbourne that she meant to accept his proposals.

Of course, little if any of it was true, but it was still quite amusing to have Charity's absence now contrasted with her theatrical manner of having accepted William's hand in marriage. Hugh could not help himself, as he followed behind Will, and he could even admit to himself that he was behaving very badly, but of the moment nothing afforded him more pleasure than watching his friend's expression as the earl grew increasingly angry over the various comments that were made to him regarding the *bashful* Miss Holwell.

And when they finally reached the whist table, William had to try several times to gain Lady Datchworth's attention, for she was engrossed deeply in her play, a decided frown between her pretty arched brows as she chewed upon her lower lip.

After the third attempt, Lady Datchworth finally looked up from her cards, her pale blue eyes blank and staring, her ostrich feather hanging limpy from her turban as she snapped, "Yes? What is it? Oh, it is you, Lord Redbourne. What do you want?"

If William was at all perturbed by this indifferent reception, he did not show it, but bowed politely to her and said, "I apologize for disturbing your play, Lady Datchworth, but I wish to know where Charity is. Have you seen her recently? Mr. Meesden seemed to think you had spoken with her at least once during the past half-hour."

Blinking twice, her eyes still quite blank, Lady Datchworth said, "I have just lost my high card. How could I have done so? Charity? No, no, you must be mistaken. She was here not five minutes ago. She ran out into the hall. I am certain of it. Now do go away. Shoo, shoo!" And with a sweeping motion of her hand she turned back to the enthralling game, the ostrich feather swinging in front of her nose and causing her to sneeze.

Hugh backed away from the table, swallowing very hard. He could feel his eyes bulging as he repressed the laughter which threatened to consume him and made haste to leave the chamber and pass into the hallway. And to think of the Earl of Redbourne being received by his betrothed's nearest relative as though he were a flea! It was a deal too much to bear and how very much Will's pride must be smarting. He nearly collided with a servant bearing a tray of iced cups of champagne and when he reached the hall he gave way to his mirth. It was too ironic! And what pit had William fallen into by becoming engaged to Charity? Perhaps Nemesis had come upon him, exacting vengeance for William's pride.

But William did not seem greatly overset by Lady Datchworth's lack of courtesy to him as he regarded Hugh with a questioning glance. "And what do you find so amusing?"

"I should not have teased you so, but it was quite worth the effort when Charity's aunt regarded you as though you were one of the servants. As it happens, and I should have told you sooner—"

Hugh got no further, for at that moment Lord Datchworth rushed from the antechamber and cried, "Redbourne!" Catching up with William he hooked his arm saying, "You must forgive my wife. She's been in this state for the past hour. A gaming fever! It happens every season." And he released the earl's arm, turning back to scowl at his wife and shake his head. "I must do something about this, but damme I hate to, for she gets this sad expression in her eye and then we start quarreling again. But what can I do? I love her, don't you see?"

As all three gentlemen gathered about Lord Datchworth, William said, "I have myself upon occasion become caught up in a spirited game of hazard or faro to know how very irritating any intrusion can be—"

"Eh, lad, that's very kind of you to say so," Lord Datchworth cried with a friendly smile as he clapped William on the arm. "Now, regarding this business with my niece. I can't help but feel it was done in a hurly-burly manner. I don't really know what got into the chit to accept you like that, at Almack's of all places! Why, one minute she was complaining that she didn't know her heart and the next—well, I just don't know what to tell you. You might want to give her her head a bit, though, and let her wear herself out with whatever machinations she's intent upon—taking a bit after Penelope if you ask me—but don't hesitate to pull in the reins hard and tight! Charity's a spirited filly, but I suppose you know that for you were used to romp with her a bit when she was a little girl and as full of mischief as any boy you'd ever see!" And puffing out his cheeks he ended his speech with, "Females, bah!"

The gentlemen all looked at one another in a mystified manner and Hugh wasn't at all certain what Lord Datchworth was trying to relate to his future nephew, but in the midst of this tangled discourse, Hugh heard a distinct warning.

William said, "I realize that your niece has had some reservations with regard to my proposals, but what is more to the point, where is she right now? I'm certain in time that I can relieve any concerns she might have about our forthcoming marriage, but first I must have an opportunity to speak with her. However, of the moment, no one seems to know where she is."

119

"Eh, what's this? What do you mean?"

Mr. Meesden said, "We cannot find her, though I think next we ought perhaps to try the library." And he gestured behind him for across from the drawing room was Lord Datchworth's well-appointed bookroom.

Hugh said flatly, "She's not in there."

Lord Datchworth said, "You've seen for yourself? You've been there already?"

"No. As it happens, I saw where she went just shortly after our arrival here."

"Why, whatever do you mean?" Lord Datchworth cried.

Hugh said, "There is a chamber to the right of the front door, is there not?"

"Yes, my office. William was there yesterday morning."

Hugh nodded, trying to restrain the peculiar enjoyment he felt at this moment. And though he had a slight prickle of his conscience which said he ought to remain silent for Charity's sake, he thought it would be vastly more amusing to discover just what either William or Charity's uncle might do upon finding her secreted in the viscount's office. Clearing his throat and schooling his features to what he hoped was an irritating expression of indifference, he said, "Charity is within that chamber, even as we speak. She entered it in a furtive manner, not one minute after Will and I crossed the threshold of your drawing room and I strongly suspect she means to remain there, but for what purpose," and here he regarded William, no longer able to restrain a smile, "I cannot imagine in the least."

William turned upon Hugh and narrowed his eyes at him. "You knew all along, didn't you. *Where's Charity, I wish to be presented to her!* What a rascal you are and I would immediately show you my displeasure in a punishing manner, if I did not feel it was more expedient to speak with her first! But after that, you'll answer for this piece of tomfoolery!"

And after William and Lord Datchworth decided to go to the office together and discover precisely what Charity meant by her very odd behavior, Hugh watched them descend the stairs with a very pleased sensation. Damme if he didn't think that his good friend had met his match and in a quiet voice he blessed Charity, hoping that she might be the means of bringing William about!

Chapter Eight

Charity's black curls still tickled her ear, for Marie had arranged her hair so that her long tresses, while pulled into a knot at the top of her head, cascaded not down the back but to one side, several wispy tendrils fluttering at her ear. More than once she had given her head a slight shake, hoping to dislodge a particularly tenacious curl, but to little avail and with the singular result that, earlier that evening, when they had been enjoying a family dinner before the soiree, Lady Datchworth had exclaimed that she was tossing her head like a spirited mare, "Though to be sure I have never seen so enchanting a coiffure and I am quite certain Lord Redbourne will be cast into raptures, only do try to have a little more conduct!"

And even Charity's royal blue satin gown had quite astonished them all for it was a very bold color for such a young lady, but even her aunt said that the very rich shade of blue enhanced Charity's eyes and contrasted charmingly with her black hair. "Only there you are again, tossing your head! Whatever is the matter?"

"The curls are tickling my ear!"

"Well, have your maid arrange them differently next time, but for this evening, I expect you to ignore this mild discomfort for you do not wish to give Redbourne a disgust of you! Not that he would cry off from the engagement because you are throwing your head about in this unseemly manner, but a lady ought always to be elegant and composed. You must follow Penelope's lead in this."

Charity bowed her head meekly and assured her aunt that she meant to behave very prettily this evening for she had but one hope, that she might please her beloved future husband in everything!

Lord Datchworth, who had been lifting a fork loaded with small green peas to his mouth, cleared his throat ominously, dumped the peas from his fork, and shook the implement at his niece in a menacing fashion. "Just see that you do, Missy! I'll have none of your nonsense this evening, nor Penelope's! No tossing of fans or the like!"

Charity could see that her uncle was upset and did not hesitate to assure him that she would take great care with her fan, even offering to leave it in her bedchamber if he so desired.

"What I desire is that you behave in a properly brought up fashion!" After this he began spearing the peas on his plate with his fork and muttered something yet again about feminine wiles and schemes.

Charity now stood before the fireplace in her uncle's office thinking about her wiles and machinations and the scheme which had brought her to hide within the darkened chamber. And, try as she might, she could not feel badly about what she had done. In fact, for the past twenty minutes, as the sounds of laughter and the ebb and flow of drawing room chatter hummed through the walls of the townhouse, Charity realized she was enjoying herself immensely. What was William thinking? she wondered, for by now he must be aware that she was missing. And she felt the sweetest sensation within her breast of revenge. And if her conscience burnt her a little, she had only to remember the butterfly chits at Almack's and how very much William's behavior had offended her own sense of what was right and good and yes, even proper.

A very faint glow of coals burned in the grate, and illuminated only the back of Lord Datchworth's chair as well as the planked floor immediately in front of the hearth. The rest of the chamber was quite dark save for a flickering of light at the window where the flambeaux which burned outside the house on either side of the front door shone through. But as her eyes had adjusted to the darkness, she could discern the faint outlines of the flowers upon the table by the window, the golden light from the flambeaux catching just the edges of the vase.

And then, much to her horror, the door opened and Charity saw the shapes of two men standing in the doorway, the light from the entrance hall glowing behind them and casting their faces in shadow. But even as dark as the shadows were, Charity knew at once that the first gentleman was William and that, oh, heaven help her, the second was her uncle and she gasped aloud, her fluency with the French tongue betraying her as she cried, "Oh, *mon Dieu!*"

Lord Datchworth nearly pushed William aside as the two gentlemen entered the room, and he exclaimed, "And what the devil do you think you are doing in here? Good God, it is as black as midnight! Redbourne, close the door immediately and when you've done that, you'll find the tinder box upon the mantel. Light one or two of the branches there, and any others that take your fancy whilst I have a word with my niece." He then held his hand out to Charity and commanded, "Come!"

Charity did not hesitate to move toward her uncle, regarding the viscount's severe expression with a measure of trepidation. The faint glow from the fireplace caught the contours of his face—his well-marked cheekbones and cleft chin and the several deep wrinkles that marked his years as well as his displeasure with her. He was dressed in a black coat from Weston's, well-shaped to his shoulders which, though a trifle padded at the chest still gave him an elegant appearance.

Drawing Charity to the window where the light from the flambeaux still flickered across the several glass panes, he frowned down upon her and in a whisper, cried, "What mischief are you brewing, my dear? Is this any manner to treat your betrothed? I am shocked and this very scheme resembles Penelope's mind so nearly that I cannot but wonder if it was she who told you to do this thing—and whatever did you hope to accomplish?"

Charity glanced toward William who was struggling with the tinder box, then reverted her gaze to the window as she answered in a low voice. "You must not blame Penelope, Uncle. This is my doing, no one else's. You must believe that."

He reached toward her and held her arm at the elbow as he whispered, "But why? I don't understand. If you did not wish to wed William, then you should have refused him, but these cat and mouse games—well, I cannot approve of them at all."

Charity was silent for a moment as she watched the amber light drift across the glass in waves as the breeze ruffled the flambeaux. Finally, she whispered, "Can you tell me why every season you pretend to take a mistress?"

"Oh, but that is quite different!" he protested immediately. "You see my wife—" he broke off, his brow puckering, his face coming more clearly into view as William lit the first branch of candles. "What is it you are trying to say, Charity?"

Regarding her uncle directly, she said, "I won't pretend that my actions are honorable, for that would be the worst sort of hypocrisy, but all I can answer you in this case is that I have a purpose in what I do."

Lord Datchworth puffed out his cheeks again as he

released a breath of air. "You were supposed to protest your innocence, not argue with me in this reasonable manner. However, I must express my grave concern to you, that you are a moth flying haphazardly near a candle that burns exceedingly hot. I don't wish to see your wings singed, for then you are bound to fall."

Charity smiled a little as she said, "But if I fall, at least I can admit to you now that I am fully aware that it will be of my own doing."

"Bah!" he answered, his habitual retreat into a pretended incomprehension of the feminine mind returning in full force. "Females! Well, I wash my hands of you." And turning toward William he said, "She is yours to do with as you please. I can't make the least sense of her and I leave you alone to battle this out."

And upon these words he harrumphed once at his niece, turned on his heel, and quit the room.

By now, the chamber glowed with a warm candlelight that spilled over the paneled walls, the floor, the table, and the vase of flowers that smelled of fragrant lavender and roses. Charity straightened her shoulders slightly as she let her fingers run over the soft petals of a red rose. Stealing a glance at William, regarding him beneath a fringe of black lashes, she found his expression somewhat inscrutable as he watched her intently. He was standing directly in front of the fire, a branch of candles upon the mantel, glowing just over his left shoulder. He clasped his hands behind his back, his feet planted firmly apart, as though he was preparing to dig his heels into the floor and resist whatever it was she meant to say to him.

He was dressed with his usual grace in a well-fitted coat of black superfine, a white waistcoat, black pantaloons and black slippers. His neckcloth was intricately tied, the shirtpoints starched and his blond hair combed into a carefully brushed shape about his temples. He was clearly a man of consequence in appearance and bearing, though even as he stood regarding her from speculative hazel eyes, Charity knew that behind the man who smiled almost warmly upon her, resided an arrogant creature that could spring to life at any unbidden moment.

He did not speak at first and when he did his words overset Charity almost completely. "How beautiful you are in this chamber that glows with but a dozen candles. Your hair touching your shoulder in that manner, I find altogether pleasing." He moved from the hearth and began a direct saunter toward her, his pace slow, his hazel eyes almost glittering in the dim light, as he regarded her intently. "My dearest Charity, and bride-to-be, how very short our moment was at Almack's last night when you accepted my offer of marriage. I only wish that I had had more time to express my gratification at your sudden decision." His voice held just a hint of amusement, as though he were expressing a joke he knew she would appreciate, almost as though he understood the absurdity of the situation and Charity felt a small hope rise in her breast.

Feeling very confused, Charity turned toward the flowers, the fragrance of lavender assailing her further and seeming to add to the bemusement that overtook her. This was not how she wished for these next few minutes to progress with William.

When her uncle had made it clear that he meant to leave her alone with the earl, she had at once thought that she would make the very most of this time and confront William directly about his cruelty to Penelope as well as to the innocent young ladies at Almack's. Instead he told her she was beautiful and pleasing, and the truth was she couldn't bear the flashing of his eyes as he approached her on so purposeful a step.

He continued, "I must confess that I don't understand you entirely, Charity, but I mean to. I intend to discover the depths to your mind." And as he arrived beside her, he slipped a hand about her arm, and stood very close to her, touching her arm lightly with the tips of his fingers. His touch almost burned, and she drew in her breath sharply. No, she had certainly planned none of this. He said, "I could berate you for not greeting me above stairs, but to what purpose when the light from the window there is shining on your black hair and teasing me so. I know you must have had an excellent reason, as I have an excellent reason for wishing to set aside our differences during what will no doubt prove to be an all too short moment together. How much I value your uncle and his professed inability to comprehend you!" He stepped closer to her still, so that the length of his body touched hers, and she felt suddenly very frightened and vulnerable.

She was not in the least experienced, but she knew enough to understand that to be so very close to a man could be very dangerous to one's heart!

She tried to move away, but he held her arm fast, slipping his other hand about her waist and holding her close to him. She felt her throat constrict with emotions she did not understand, for she felt both like crying and laughing at the same time, and all of her schemes fell swiftly away at his mere touch. How was it possible he could command her so completely? And instead of trying to determine ways in which she could further her campaign against him, her thoughts became focused instead upon minute things like the gleam of light upon a single petal that was beaded with water, like the sensation of safety which his arm that was holding her engendered within her, like the smell of fine soap that emanated from William. How strangely close to tears she was.

"Charity," he whispered. "Will you not love me but a little? Am I so very bad that you must hide from me and taunt me at Almack's? What have I done to cause you to turn against me, but above all, what do you mean by accepting my hand in marriage and then treating me with such disdain?"

There was a lightness to the tone of his voice that told Charity a great deal. Mostly, that though he believed what he was saying, he did not credit that she might have reasons of merit, that it was not conceivable that she would have valid motives for her actions. His attitude was clearly quite frivolous. But the worst of it was for Charity, that the closer he drew to her, the less she cared. She had only one desire, as he began playing his own game—a sport of seduction—that he not leave her side for a very long time. And oh, how was it possible that she could one moment despise him for his scurrilous treatment of many of her acquaintance, and the next moment, wish that he would hold her in his arms that she might lose herself in his embrace forever?

She was hopeless, beyond remedy as he leaned his head close to hers and in the most delectable manner, began placing a trail of whisper kisses upon her ear, his breath very light, causing shivers to engulf her.

"No, William, pray do not!" she whispered.

But he laughed softly in her ear and clicking his tongue said, "But my dearest, if you are free to play at such a wicked game then I insist that I be permitted to engage in a certain favorite sport of my own. You see, I have kissed you before, if you remember! And that young lady was not so indifferent as your actions this evening would indicate! Besides, I claim my right as your future husband, to greet you in any manner I choose fit!" And he again kissed her ear as well as her cheek, and began a slow burning progress down her neck.

"William," Charity said, her voice sounding a trifle hoarse. "Will you please stop! This is most unseemly. What if someone were to walk in, my uncle, for instance!"

"Your uncle would know to leave as quickly as he had come!"

Charity drew in her breath, for he had just found an incredibly tender spot just beneath her ear and she sighed. Her protests grew weaker still as he continued this onslaught to her delicate skin. And even when she made a half-hearted effort to lean her head away from him, he followed her movements smoothly, his breath now warm against her throat.

He said, "I ought to warn you, Charity, that if you persist in your schemes, I will resort to even more drastic measures than this."

"Oh?" Charity inquired, though not truly understanding what he had just said for he had begun nibbling upon her ear. "I suppose you must do what you feel is best." How fuzzy her mind felt, her senses wrapped completely up in the touch of his lips.

Somewhere from a great distance, Charity heard more guests arrive and she tried to push William away as she said, "You ought not to be doing this. It is very wrong. I beg of you to stop. Oh, you are kissing my brow, how very sweet!"

Charity realized that these words, far from causing him to cease his lovemaking, were more of an invitation to continue as he laughed into her hair. And when Charity had the good grace to offer a giggle of her own, he did not hesitate to turn her around, pulling her into his arms and holding her fast. She thought he would kiss her immediately, indeed she wished for nothing more, instead he held her gaze for what seemed an eternity, and only when he appeared to have satisfied some inner desire, did he slowly lean forward and place a kiss upon her lips.

What heaven, Charity thought, his breath almost hot as he moved his lips over hers. And how gentle he was, his arms feeling safe and comfortable as he held her close to him. She could no longer resist the impulse to lean into him, nor to slip her arms about his neck, returning his kisses fully, her own traitorous desires completely

131

overwhelming her.

After a very long moment, he pulled away from her, his features heavy with desire as he said, "I think we ought to have a very short engagement."

But these words so effectively brought Charity's mind back to her present schemes, even forcing her to remember in that she would very soon dance upon the stage as a masked ballerina, that she gasped, took a hasty step backward only to collide with the table, nearly oversetting the vase of flowers. But she caught them in time and breathed deeply. Good heavens! So many thoughts poured in upon her at once that she could hardly think. Her feelings for William were so strong and yet she knew she could not deny that there existed between them a monumental difficulty, for she would never marry any man who could be as heartless as William had proved himself to be.

And when she looked up at him, toying with the notion of simply stating her grievances and asking him to please apologize for his hundreds of unkindnesses to Penelope and a dozen other females, a somewhat satisfied expression overtook his face as he said, "But I think there is something else we must concern ourselves with first, and that we should begin with an apology."

When he spoke these words, Charity's first thought was that he had come to his senses and seen the error of his ways. But his voice was laced with a measure of arrogance that made her pause to consider upon what she based this tremendous hope. Did she, for instance, really believe that he saw anything wrong with how he had behaved at Almack's? Good gracious, of course not, and her spirits fell correspondingly as she realized he was the one who was expecting to receive an apology.

Donning one of her sweetest expressions, her blue eyes wide with a false innocence, her words honeyed, she said, "I suppose when you refer to an apology that you mean that you wish me to apologize to you?"

"Of course," he said with a friendly smile, obviously well-pleased that she was going to be so very reasonable.

Charity touched the round table with the tip of a gloved finger and began tracing a pattern of inlaid scrollwork upon the wood. She was very wicked and she was growing every moment to realize just how wicked she was, for she was enjoying herself immensely and felt a decided surge of pleasure as she said, "But William, have you not considered that an apology would mean that I regret what I have done, and, forgive me, my lord and master, but I regret none of it!"

She felt, rather than saw him move away from her, since she kept her gaze fixed to the table. And the distance that he now put between them relieved a great tension which had built up within Charity and she sighed with relief. She was intent upon battle, particularly since he had dared to demand an apology from her.

He stood several feet away, near the tapestried chair where she had sat the morning before, a very faint frown appearing then disappearing upon his brow. After glancing about the chamber, his hazel eyes shifting quickly from one object to the next and finally landing upon a globe of the world near Lord Datchworth's desk, he said, "Am I to understand that you will not offer an apology for this evening's stratagems? But why ever not, when you were so clearly at fault? Even your uncle took great exception to your machinations! Nor do I at all comprehend this absurd manner in which you address me, for your tone of voice and that horridly simpering expression upon your face do not match the insult of your words. What do you mean by it?"

"I mean only to reflect your glory, my lord, as any true and good wife will. I only do as you yourself choose to do, though my performance happens to be directly solely toward you and not toward three young ladies just emerged from the schoolroom." She waited, her heart beating rather quickly in her breast, to see just how this speech might affect him.

He seemed quite astonished as he answered, "I begin to understand at long last—you were expecting an apology from me because of the butterfly chits. Well, if you think I regret having set the young ladies on a proper course, you are greatly mistaken! What I do I will not have subjected to your scrutiny or anyone else's. They were wrong to have accosted me."

Charity, in a highly theatrical manner, curtsied deeply to William, pressing one hand against her bosom as she said, "And I repeat, my lord, I am determined therefore only to reflect your image. And now, if you care to escort me to the drawing room, I shall be happy to play your contented bride-to-be."

"Madame," William said, his upper lip curling ominously, "I find of the moment that I am of a mind to leave and will do so very shortly once I have collected my good friend, Mr. Bramfield."

Charity rose to her feet, and made a slow elegant progress across the room as she answered him cheerfully, "Well, I am certain you must please yourself, for you always do, but if you should desire it, I will be happy to inform Mr. Bramfield that you await him on the flags." And when he inclined his head to her, his nostrils flaring, she opened the door and passed through with her head held very high.

Chapter Nine

William left Lady Datchworth's soiree in Grosvenor Square with the profound feeling that his world had suddenly taken an unexpected and considerably unpleasant turn. Never, in his entire existence had he believed that Charity, the sweet, vivacious young girl whom he had taught to ride, should become such an arrogant, high-handed, and damnably mulish young lady—and he was engaged to her!

Parting company with Hugh, who had an assignation at Drury Lane with Francoise, his green-eyed operadancer, the earl went first to a fete in Upper Brook Street where two or three smiling acquaintance asked if it were true that his fiancé was terribly *bashful*. This remark seemed rather cryptic, until, having left the fete, he walked out onto the flags and realized with a start that his friends must have been referring to Charity's disappearance at her own soiree and a fury took possession of him. How dare she humiliate him in this manner before the *ton*!

The evening was damp and a light mist swirled about the oil lamps that barely lit the street. It was past the midnight hour and the streets of Mayfair still clattered with the wheels of barouches, hackneys, and town chariots, for the members of the *beau monde* kept late hours indeed during the season. William, carrying a walking stick with the ivory handle carved into the shape of a dog's head, drove the cane sharply into the flags with each step he took. Besides his anger at being so ill-used by his betrothed, he felt something nagging at him, a ticklish thought that though a constant irritation, refused to take shape in his mind.

Damn and blast! What was Charity about? What could she possibly hope to accomplish? Did she intend to bring him to heel? Well, she certainly had a great shock coming if that were the case. But damme if he didn't think that the entire affair resembled Penelope's scheming mind more nearly than the sweet young girl he had decided to make his wife. But there it was again, that nagging thought which refused to surface. He shook his head. He had not considered Penelope Ware's influence before, and now his engagement and particularly the ramshackle manner in which it was conducted suddenly took on a shading that was not in the least desirable. Was Penelope to blame?

He let the cool evening mist flow over him, which seemed to have the happy effect of soothing his exacerbated sensibilities and, deciding to go to his club, he signaled a hackney across the street.

As he was climbing into the coach, the hay-strewn floor smelling damp and musty, a curricle rolled by him bearing two bucks, their collars pulled up about their necks to ward off the chill April air. One of them cried, "What ho, Redbourne? Has your bashful bride-to-be recovered from her shyness?"

Their laughter seemed to flow into the hackney and remain with him the entire distance from Upper Brook Street to St. James Street. How quickly one's affairs became known amongst the *beau monde*. And when he walked into his club, he could tell by the manner in which every head turned toward him that someone had been beforehand in relating the evening's events.

He paused upon the threshold and taking a deep breath entered the well-lit chambers. His friends smiled at him, lifted their glasses, toasted his future bride, and at least two gentlemen, known to dislike Redbourne, sniggered and laughed outright.

Mr. James Widley, a longstanding friend of William's, had set up a faro bank and was shuffling the cards with great vigor. He was a lean gentleman with bright curling red hair, light blue eyes, and a face full of freckles which lent him a boyish appearance even at the age of one and forty. Upon seeing the earl, he glanced up at him, and gave a half smile, while beckoning him to join the other players gathered about the table covered in green baize.

When the several gentlemen had placed their bets as to which order the cards would appear from the top of the deck, Widley regarded the earl with a wry twist to his mouth, his blue eyes warm with laughter as he said, "And did you find Lady Datchworth's townhouse quite *full* of guests?"

Nearly all of the gentlemen chuckled, their eyes half-glazed from having imbibed in copious amounts of claret. The muffled laughter which rose up about the room ended the earl's attempt to ignore all the efforts to get a rise out of him. Confronting the situation in a direct manner, he spoke in a purposefully carrying voice and said, "Miss Holwell did not greet me in the drawing room, if that is what you mean, James, though later I spoke with her in private."

Widley could not keep from saying, "So you were able to find her after all! The *on dits* have it that her uncle set you all on a search of the townhouse for her!"

William glanced about the room at any number of friendly faces who had paused in sipping their Madeira or halted a game of cards merely to watch his reactions, and a funny thought passed through his mind that each of these men, whether taunting or curious or even malicious, seemed to be initiating him into some sort of inner circle.

Lowering his voice to a normal level he let out an exasperated sigh and addressed James, "I hope you have not emptied the cellars for I am greatly in need of some of that very fine wine you are all drinking so greedily."

The general laughter and well-meaning back-slappings that accompanied these words somehow soothed the earl's quite lacerated feelings, while several sympathetic gentlemen said that it was high time he met with a female who intended to lead him a merry chase! They'd all known such females, and usually they were dashed pretty girls, too, just like Miss Holwell. However, it was recommended that if he did end up marrying the chit, he ought to prepare himself for a great deal of mischief in the future as well.

Lord Redbourne saw the laughing faces of his friends and acquaintance and stood up and bowed to them all. He was then applauded for his graciousness in enduring the brunt of their jestings, and afterward the cardplay was resumed, as well as a general clinking of glasses as various friends toasted one another. But William's mind was filled with thoughts of all that had happened, and the room grew hazy at the very edges of his vision. A servant set a glass upon the table before him and uncorking the wine, poured out a measure of the rich red claret. Redbourne took the glass and let the wine roll about his tongue and finally swallowed as he blocked out the sounds of the dying laughter. And as the flavorful liquid warmed his throat, he nodded to the servant who then filled his glass and left him to the enjoyment of the superior wine.

As Widley began drawing the cards from the top of the deck one after the other, a series of groans, whoops of triumph, and curses succeeded the appearance of each card. William was lost to the play as he stared into his glass. And that nagging thought finally made its appearance for though he could not imagine what mischief Charity was brewing, a powerful feeling entered his breast

138

that marriage to her would not be as orderly as he had planned and the sensation of this newly formed idea, much as his friends had just suggested to him, did not entirely displease him. In fact, he found his heart quicken to the idea, his blood rising as it did in the midst of an exciting hunt.

Sipping his claret, the earl suddenly smiled broadly and Mr. Widley, watching the expression on his face, cried, "Now what the devil are you thinking, Redbourne. I know that expression. I saw it once when you rousted Tewin in a match of rather fierce swordsplay, as I recall!"

William regarded his friend full in the face and said, "How odd that you mention it, James, for I was just thinking that I am in the most urgent need of improving my fencing technique. My skills seem quite shabby of the moment. A not uncommon occurrence when one has been bereft of a worthy opponent for so long a period of time."

Mr. Widley removed another card from the deck, the familiar responses again issuing from the half-foxed gentlemen, as he said, "I apprehend you refer to Miss Holwell."

Lord Redbourne, his smile playing about his lips in a most reprehensible fashion, answered him, "Indeed I do." And he lifted his glass in salute.

Mr. Widley raised his glass in response, as did the others about the table and one poor soul, quite in his cups, his voice considerably slurred, cried, "And may the best man win!"

The play continued for an hour or so, one of the gentlemen finally toppling over on the table in a drunken stupor. Two muscled servants came forward at once and removed him from the table, propping him up in a chair toward the back of the room until he should regain consciousness. Mr. Widley, pleased that the bank was winning, expressed his pleasure in this occurrence and then said, "I say, did any of you hear that Bow Street found an article believed to have been used by that rascally highwayman fellow in his most recent robbery?"

William, who had been draining his glass, choked upon these words, and was spared having to explain this odd occurrence for the entire table broke into a discussion of the vileness of this fellow who went about kissing innocent young maids.

Clearing his throat, William was finally able to say, "I cannot but think this thief is the worst scoundrel and rogue that ever existed, but did you happen to learn precisely what they found?"

Mr. Widley stroked his chin in a contemplative manner as he again gathered the cards together and began shuffling them. "A mask, I think. Found it in one of the hedgerows just outside of Little Digswell and it seems to have fit several of the descriptions."

William sat very still, and though he was regarding James, his thoughts flew back to Tuesday evening and how wild and free he had felt after kissing—faith, was it really Charity?—and afterward galloping into the wind. He remembered tossing his mask away, unthinking, uncaring. Bow Street had seemed so uninterested in solving the case before, but now! Could they possibly trace that mask back to him? He didn't think so, for it was commonly used at masquerades and had no distinguishing embroidery to set it apart from a hundred others just like it. Still, it was quite disturbing to think that the runner had been so very thorough.

Widley said, "I've heard that several of the parents of the offended ladies have joined together and promised Bow Street a large fee for discovering the identity of the thief. A thousand pounds, so I've heard!"

One of the gentlemen at the table, whistled softly at these words, then said, "Wish I had that much right now! Damme if I've not lost a thousand already!"

Widley ignored the man as he regarded William

directly, a frown between his light red brows as he said, "There's a rumor, too, that they have a suspect in mind. I believe he's a particular friend of yours, Redbourne—Hugh Bramfield. It seems he was at the White Swan Inn that very night following the robbery."

William knew that he had paled, for the skin on his face felt very taut. All the moisture seemed to immediately dissipate from his mouth, so shocked was he. Blinking several times, he found himself completely unable to think or to speak, and could only sip at his wine in hopes that the turmoil he felt would not be visible to everyone. Even his tongue was stuck to the roof of his mouth! So Hugh was suspect. He looked away from Widley at that moment, his eyes fixed on the deck of cards in front of James as he turned the top card over—a knave! How poetic, for he felt nothing less than that to have actually endangered Hugh in his own foolish schemes!

"But what proof could they possibly have," William said finally, though to a great degree he was speaking to himself trying to find a thread in the midst of his jumbled thoughts that he could hold to. "A mask in the shrubbery and my good friend just happening to be at an inn where the incident occurred—the merest speculation!" And he directed a piercing gaze at James.

"You needn't eat me!" Widley cried. "Merely telling you what Mr. Tewin was bandying about only this afternoon at Hyde. Can't say where he got his information, but you must admit that it's very suspicious, what with Bramfield being all to flinders."

William worked his jaw, trying to keep from letting his temper get the better of him, for of the moment he was furious. But not with Widley, in fact he was grateful that he had heard this news tonight, instead of later when it might be too late to do anything for Hugh. No, he was angry only with himself, for begging Hugh to meet him at the White Swan when Hugh knew damn well what he was doing. He drained his glass and, setting it on the green baize cloth in front of him, rose to his feet and begged to know what his losses were.

"A mere monkey, Redbourne. Send a check 'round if you like. It's of little consequence."

William inclined his head in an absent manner for he was still nearly beside himself with a frustrated sense of rage that he had provoked this stupid farce. "Widley, I . . . that is . . . thanks for saying something to me. Bramfield and I have been friends since Eton. You've done me a great favor."

Widley nodded his head several times, his light blue eyes narrowed slightly. In a quiet voice, he said, "Thought you should know, that's all."

"I am indebted to you."

Lady Redbourne felt a film of perspiration cover her brow as William lifted her from her bed. Today the pain in her joints had been quite steady, increasing as the afternoon wore on. Traveling even so short a distance from Hertfordshire had been of nightmarish proportions but she had been determined to partake of this one last season in London and to greet officially the young lady her son had chosen to make his bride.

"Am I hurting you, Mama?" William asked as he cradled her easily in his arms, for she was exceedingly thin believing that the disease she was forced to endure did not need the distress any additional flesh would undoubtedly cause.

Lady Redbourne spoke with a breathy quality to her voice, "Don't be absurd. Of course you are not hurting me!"

"Mama, such a whisker! For if you could see the expression on your face you would be the first to admit the truth!"

Ordinarily, she would have argued the point with great vigor, but of the moment the pain in her hips seemed to radiate in horrible pulses all the way to her feet and it was all she could do to say, "I don't know what you are talking about!"

Lady Redbourne closed her eyes as William walked very slowly toward the sitting room adjoining her bedchamber. Years ago the room next to hers had been occupied by her dearest Frederick, her husband of what now seemed a brief four and twenty years. But three years after his death William had so very sweetly refurbished the room into a sitting room. All about the walls of the square chamber trailed a paper of dark green ivy and lavender flowers— lilacs and purples being favorite colors of hers. The furniture was mostly gilt and covered in soft purple velvets while the windows were hung with white silk. The effect was cheerful and when William had first shown the room to her, his face appearing boyish and very proud, she remembered crying, initially in gratitude for his thought-fulness and later, when she had been left alone upon the chaise longue, the door shut firmly behind William and her maid, Miss Finch, her kerchief was wet with tears of heartsick bitterness at these wasted years of her life.

But that was a long time ago, and now the dowager faced her existence with a tolerable amount of peace, taking pleasure in each day she was given. It was unfortunate that the pain today was worse than usual, for however much she tried to keep it from William, he always seemed to know the degree of her suffering. And today, most particularly, she wished to have a comfortable cose with him, undisturbed by his concern for her well-being. He could, she realized with a sigh, be as old-maidish as Finch.

Lady Redbourne leaned her head against her son's shoulder. She may have accepted her lot in life, but she still despised the rheumatic complaint which had so twisted her body, leaving her daily in varying amounts of pain. But never would she admit to anyone the harshness of the disease and she added, "You make such a fuss, William, when you know very well that I am perfectly comfortable."

William answered in a soft teasing voice as they passed through the doorway, "Then perhaps I ought to set you on your feet and teach you to waltz! It is all the crack, you know, even at Almack's!"

"Wicked boy!" she cried. Touching the lapel of his blue riding coat with a swollen knuckle, she could even laugh at herself for she was no more able to dance than she was able to climb out of her bed by herself. She could not resist adding, "However, I wish very much that I could have learned the waltz. It is the prettiest dance that has come to England in ages! I had Bracken and Finch perform it for me!"

"You cannot be serious!" and he gave a shout of laughter that rippled through Lady Redbourne's entire frame. And lowering his voice, he added, "I should like to have seen them dancing together, in fact I shall ask them to perform the steps for me right now."

"You will do no such thing!" she cried in a whisper, for Lady Redbourne's personal servants were waiting for them in the sitting room. "I will not have you teasing them."

She patted William's chest again. For a long time now the gnarled fingers of her right hand had refused to function separately. The most she could do was rap at things, anything, including her son's coat, and the task of correspondence had become impossible save through the use of her companion, Miss Bracken, whom William had thrust upon her a year ago. Her son was very attentive, for which she was exceedingly grateful. But there were times when he was nothing short of a nuisance for his actions served quite frequently to remind her that she was indeed an invalid. And the moment he had become aware that not only were her letters short but that her previously constant flow of correspondence had dwindled to a frightening, illegible drip, did he immediately quit London, hurrying back to Hertfordshire where he determined for himself the true state of affairs—the disease had taken a turn for the worse—and the result was the addition to the dowager's staff of a tall raw-boned creature by the name of Miss Theodora Bracken.

Bracken and Finch, William would often call out merrily to the two efficient ladies who cared for his Mama, *And that has the sound of a fine shipping firm. Bracken and Finch. Have you considered setting up in business?* Of course William had charmed them both, a most unfortunate occurrence for the dowager knew quite well that in addition to her own correspondence, William received daily accounts of her welfare from Bracken.

William took her to the purple velvet chaise longue where he set her down very gently so that she leaned against a mound of lavender striped and flowered pillows. Both servants immediately swooped down upon the dowager, covering her legs with a peach cashmere shawl, and tucking pillows behind her knees until she nodded to them that she felt quite comfortable. And though she was dressed in a chemise robe of dark green wool with a white gown of ruffled cambric visible from below the three-quarter length of the robe, she still needed the extra warmth of the shawl. She never seemed to be quite warm enough.

Dismissing her maid and her companion with a nod, she thanked them for their attentions and turned to her son, saying with a smile, "And so Charity has accepted you." She held his gaze, wondering if everything she had heard of the young lady's manner of accepting her son's proposals were true. After a moment, she asked, "But have I heard it correctly, that upon agreeing to become your wife, Charity threw her fan, hitting the Princess Esterhazy upon the mouth?"

"No!" William exclaimed with a laugh. "And who told you that bit of tittle-tattle? It is all jumbled up!"

"Then you do not deny that she threw her fan?"

"No, of course I do not, but I do assure you that the *weapon* landed only at the Princess's feet. It certainly did not strike her."

Lady Redbourne lifted a hand in a gesture of exasperation. "I knew it was servants' gossip to a degree, but it is very odd just how many interesting facts they do discover in the space of only a day or two." She broke off for a moment and begged him to sit down beside her for she had something of a particular nature to say to him. William seemed a little surprised, but pulled a chair forward, sitting down and regarding her intently.

She continued, "Not that I begrudge the servants their tittle-tattle, especially since my own invalidish state makes it impossible for me to learn very much of anything without such gossip among the houses of Mayfair. I am, in effect, dependent upon Miss Finch and Miss Bracken for all my contact with the *beau monde*. But beyond your betrothed's ability to throw things, I heard a completely separate bit of news that concerned me deeply. Miss Bracken informed me of this matter first, and later, when Emily Cowper paid a very gracious visit upon me earlier this afternoon, I begged her to tell me what she knew of it. As it happened, a young friend of Emily's, a schoolroom chit I believe you would have called a young lady, was at Almack's on Wednesday night, at about the same time that you were there, so perhaps you may recall her, or more precisely, what happened to her. You see, this young lady and two of her friends had spent the entire week decorating their fans with some absurd little butterflies in very bright colors and had been practicing together some trivial movement which they meant to perform *ensemble*.

"Now Lady Cowper told me that had she known what

the young ladies were about she would have put an end to such silliness before ever they reached Almack's but as it was they were in high spirits and it seemed that in the process of displaying their fans *ensemble* they offended a certain peer which Lady Cowper said had most unfortunately grown quite high in the instep in recent years. The girls were mortified, one of them in tears as she sipped her lemonade. And the other two, finding themselves the objects of much tittering, could scarcely keep the color from their cheeks. Now, when I questioned Emily about this particular peer, she refused to tell me his name, though she did say that but a few minutes later, his bride-to-be threw a fan at the Princess Esterhazy." She paused for a moment as she regarded her son with narrowed eyes and said, "What an intriguing evening you had, William. Only, what does it all mean? I am completely mystified to make it out."

William rose from his chair and turned away from his mother, as he moved to stand by a mahogany table near the window. A brisk spring rain had begun pummeling the windowpanes and he held one of the white curtains aside slightly, looking down into the street in an unseeing manner, his jaw working strongly.

"I don't know how to answer you," he began finally. "And to a large degree, I feel almost too angry to speak at all, for what right had Lady Cowper to come here and disturb you—for I can see that you are overset by what you have heard—regaling you of the most trivial nonsense!"

Lady Redbourne watched her son. "You are right, of course. She had no business speaking to me of the matter at all, and probably would not have, but I asked her to. Perhaps then it was wrong of me to wish to know precisely what had happened. But I must confess, William, that I found it difficult to understand why you would have disapproved so strongly of the young ladies. Especially since you cannot be unaware of the tremendous power you wield in these young ladies' social careers. I cannot believe you meant to be so cruel."

"Cruel?" he responded with a laugh. "There you are very wrong, for I have done them a great kindness in not perpetuating certain false hopes of theirs that one or the other of them, merely by painting her fan a brilliant shade of blue or red, and behaving outrageously at a ball in order to attract my notice, will then very soon be able to march me to the altar—or any other peer. And you know it is all such utter nonsense anyway! This had nothing whatsoever to do with me, with who I am! It is all because of this stupid role I have assumed. Were I a mere Captain Sandridge, the ladies would not have bothered to cast a single eye my direction!"

"My dear William, I could chasten you for your incivilities, but I am more concerned with your heart. That you, who once stole a bear from a gypsy camp, should turn on a group of pretty young girls and give them what amounted to a cut direct, speaks to me of a heart that has grown quite ruthless and insensitive. And I don't fear for the young ladies, they will recover soon enough and have no doubt burnt their fans in effigy, but I think I would rather have heard that you tried to kiss one of them than that you actually gazed upon them, as was related in Miss Bracken's history, as though they were beneath contempt!"

William turned away from the window, the rain still hammering at the glass. His hands were clasped behind his back and his expression seemed considerably sobered as he said, "I can see that you don't approve of what I did, but I assure you that my motives were not malicious." He frowned at the floor, his brows knit in consternation. "And you are not the first person to take me to task over this matter. Why is it no one can see that I intended only to dampen such pretensions as can do none of these ladies the least bit of good?"

148

"William, do you think it possible that your most unfortunate experience with Penelope Ware has perhaps colored all your thinking with regard to us poor females? And was there a sadder case than Miss Ware? Not that she was indifferent to your brother, but I fear she loved the notion of becoming his wife more than she loved him. And she is such an organized female that it seemed the most natural thing for her to shift her affection from one brother to the next."

William regarded his parent thoughtfully, for she had struck a chord within his heart that seemed never to be still. "Mama, I hated her for that. John was hardly in his grave when she made it clear she had set her cap for me."

"If you remember, my dearest son, she was very young then. She was but nineteen. I don't mean to defend her, for what she did was very wrong, but in all of this you seem to have gained so little understanding of the frail human heart." At this point, as he came to sit beside her again, she said, "I only ask that you think on what I've said, that perhaps your actions are harsher than they need be. But enough of this! Tell me about your future bride. I understand she is *bashful!*"

William looked at his mother sharply and, seeing the glint of amusement in her eyes, he groaned aloud and said, "So you have heard of that as well. Why do I feel as though I live my life stark naked!"

"William! What a dreadful manner of expressing yourself, however apt! No, it was not fair that you had not been trained up for this peerage, as John was—and oh, how very much he was prepared to take your Papa's place! Too much, I often thought. He was an old man in his bearing and speech before ever he had attained his sixteenth year! So you see, I do understand, my dearest boy! But now I wish to hear everything about Charity. Is she quite as beautiful as I have heard?"

William turned his thoughts inward for a brief moment

149

as he remembered again just how Charity had looked when she stood by the flowers, her features glowing with the light from the candles, her black hair gleaming and trailing over one ear, her regal countenance as she waited for him to speak. She was so very graceful, in much the same manner as the elegant *prima ballerinas* who were beginning to perform regularly at The Royal Italian Opera House—exquisite creatures that were year after year growing more graceful and ethereal in their appearance and in their mode of dance. Charity had just such an appearance, carrying herself with a lightness of step and a straightness of posture that was so utterly pleasing.

Finally, after conjuring up so complete an image of his betrothed in his mind, he said, "She is quite beautiful and more elegant in her countenance than any other female of my acquaintance, even Penelope."

Chapter Ten

"It is very wicked of you, Mademoiselle! But so exciting!" Marie, her head bowed low over the skirt of Charity's pink balldress, was at that moment kneeling upon the carpet and pinning several green and brown plaid bows to the body of the dress. She was smiling and evidently enjoying her mistress's current scheme.

Charity tried to return her smile, but she could not. From the moment William had quit Lady Datchworth's soiree on the evening before she had felt very alone, as though a part of her wanted more than anything to go with the earl. And only after she had bade the last of her aunt's guests good-bye, laughing brightly as many of them teased her about being bashful, did she finally admit to herself that she missed the William of her childhood enormously. But that exuberant devil-may-care young man seemed to be gone forever. In his stead resided a stranger upon whom she intended to wreak as much havoc as she could, much in the same manner that he had bruised the hearts and tender sensibilities of so many of her dear friends, as well as her beloved Penelope.

She stood before a gilt-framed mirror in her bedchamber and regarded the reflection of Marie's industrious form as the abigail pinned another bow to her gown. Wearing a false expression of asperity, Charity spoke in a teasing voice, "You were at least supposed to pretend to be shocked at such a hoydenish stratagem as this, and certainly not to appear as though you wished you were committing this heinous crime yourself!"

Marie leaned back on her heels and looked up to regard Charity. With a clicking of her tongue she said, "You are being quite ridiculous as you very well know. Now turn, if you please. Ah, that is much better. These bows may be very ugly, but they should at least be placed upon the gown in a careful arrangement."

Charity was now facing her maid, and she glanced down at Marie's rich brown curls, waiting patiently for the next bow to be secured to the gown. It was now nearly eight o'clock, at which time William was due to arrive, for he had asked permission earlier that day to escort Charity and any of the ladies who wished for it to Lady Dunford's ball in Berekeley Square. Lady Datchworth had accepted graciously, for her husband, still quite angry with her for having become so miserably engulfed in her game of whist at Charity's soiree, had refused to escort his wife anywhere but meant instead to attend Drury Lane because he had a sudden desire to see the opera as well as the charming dances which were performed throughout the evening! *The very charming dances* which he had emphasized could only mean that he intended to scrutinize the notorious opera-dancers, many of whom frequently became the mistresses of the gentlemen of the *haut ton*.

Lady Datchworth had shed tears upon these words which were spoken quite angrily in front of all the ladies. But her husband remained unmoved by her display of guilt and remorse and completely ignored her pleas that he refrain from going. And by seven o'clock the entire household knew that Lord Datchworth had dressed in his best opera clothes and had left for a mysterious rendezvous at Drury Lane. Poor Lady Datchworth, regretting infinitely that she had so given in to her passion for cards—not to mention the fact that she had lost a full five hundred pounds!—cast herself upon her daybed in her bedchamber of rose silks and was only able to revive through Penelope's ministrations, as her daughter pressed cloths soaked in lavender water upon her brow.

As Charity watched Marie pin the very last bow upon her gown she felt a sudden twinge of conscience, for though this atrocity of a balldress was directed solely toward her errant husband-to-be, Charity knew that her poor aunt would be greatly shocked by the gown. And as Marie rose to her feet and untied a heart-shaped, pink velvet pincushion from about her wrist, Charity considered quite seriously that she ought perhaps to set aside her schemes for one night, merely for her aunt's sake.

Just as she was preparing to command Marie to remove the bows at once, though, a light tapping sounded upon her door. When she called out for the visitor to enter her bedchamber, she was soon met with Penelope's astonished gaze, her brown eyes wide with horror as she looked over Charity's gown several times. Finally, she placed a hand upon her cheek, a lace kerchief held lightly between her fingers, and spoke in her quiet controlled manner, "Good heavens, what an interesting creation. But do not try to tell me that this is the very latest fashion from Paris for I will not believe you!"

Charity smiled. "No, of course it is not!" Penelope, of all her relations, should be able to appreciate her purposes, and she twirled about, upon her toes—and her whirls almost became a traitorous pirouette—so that her cousin might better be able to see for herself the charming gown in its entirety.

"How very graceful you are, Charity!" Penelope cried after a moment. "For though this is quite the most miserable balldress I have ever encountered, still you move in it as though it were the most beautiful gown ever created. Why, I was remarking to Anne when we were sitting together and observing you dance the quadrille at Almack's with Lord Wadesmill, that you have a certain polish and elegance to your movements completely unequaled by anyone upon the dance floor. I suppose I must attribute this to your many years in France."

Charity knew that she was blushing for she felt her cheeks almost burn as she turned away from her cousin and sat down before her dressing table. Marie was immediately beside her recommending that she wear perhaps the rubies which would further reduce the acceptability of her costume and Charity agreed at once, hoping Penelope would ignore the heightened color of her cheeks.

But Penelope walked slowly up behind Charity, holding her gaze in the reflection of the mirror, her brown eyes slightly accusing as she said, "My dear cousin. You cannot fool me in the least. You have some scheme or other in progress and I do not refer to this gown nor to William. For several days now I have found you at times utterly distracted in your thoughts, and blushing when you should not blush, and nervous when you normally are perfectly at ease."

Feeling as though her heart was about to burst into a thousand little pieces, Charity said, "Why, I cannot imagine what you mean save that I am fully involved in composing all manner of devilment with which to taunt William. And this gown is but one of several schemes I have in mind." Hoping to divert Penelope's suspicions she asked, "Do you not think that William will be greatly shocked?"

Penelope stood very close to the dressing table that she might be able to look Charity in the face, rather than at her reflection, and peering down at her she said, "Undoubtedly. In fact, I daresay Lord Redbourne will fly into a fit of rage! His consequence could not possibly tolerate such a gown. But you are still concealing something, my dear." And she smiled faintly. She was dressed in an exquisite gown of burgundy silk, a necklace of diamonds resting gracefully upon her chest in several loops, her breasts high and well-formed, revealed modestly by the conservative décolleté of her gown. She was an example of feminine perfection, her hair gathered into its habitual knot of curls that were arranged in Grecian ringlets cascading from the crown of her head and enhanced with a wispy fringe of curls gracing her creamy brow.

Charity said, "I will not pretend to you, my dearest Pen. We have been friends as well as cousins for so long now that I daresay you know my thoughts even before I speak them. But I cannot tell you all the dreadful things that I do. I only promise that when it becomes expedient, I shall certainly reveal everything. Will you not trust me in this but a little?"

"Of course, my dear. I only ask that when you decide to unburden yourself that you will tell me first since you are my dearest friend. For by now you must know that I am positively burning with curiosity!"

Charity nodded her head and promised to do so. But remembering her concern for Lady Datchworth, she said, "I understand that my aunt is quite blue-deviled this evening and I was wondering if I ought not to subject her to this gown right at this moment. I needn't hurry my schemes with regard to William, and I don't wish to inflict more pain upon my aunt."

Charity watched her cousin's eyes closely, hoping to see her cousin's answer first within the expression of her eyes. But Penelope was, and perhaps always had been, somewhat inscrutable to her. The brown eyes merely scanned the various bows about the skirt of Charity's pink ballgown, and after a moment Penelope said, "I have been with Mama for the past half-hour and she is perfectly well, I assure you. She is even now dressed in her finest blue satin gown for she is determined not to permit Papa's own stratagems to overset her. She is quite determined to go to the ball and her spirits are considerably restored. Besides, she had already promised Lady Dunford that she would make up one of a game of whist. Mama did not feel she ought to cry off."

Charity was a little startled as she said, "But is this very wise of my aunt? Why I understand she lost five hundred pounds in her play of last night."

Penelope dismissed this with a wave of her kerchief, saying that her mother ought not to be denied her pleasures. She then said with a slightly mischievous smile that the real reason she had come to Charity's bedchamber was to inform her that William had arrived.

Charity rose to her feet abruptly at these words, nearly turning her chair over, so hasty were her movements. "William has arrived? Oh, why didn't you tell me at once?"

Penelope laughed at her as she gently touched the light brown fringe of delicate curls upon her forehead. "I felt it would be quite the thing, given your intentions toward him, to make him wait."

Charity returned her cousin's smile. "You are very wicked, you know, almost as bad as I am!" And the young ladies laughed together.

As they quit the room and began a slow saunter down the hall, Penelope said, "And I almost forgot, for I do have an amazing treat for you, cousin. One of my beaux, Lord Meares—you have heard me refer to him upon more than one occasion—has just returned from his property in Shropshire, and he wished to invite all of us to attend him at Drury Lane tomorrow evening. He said that he heard from one of the governors of that theatre that an intriguing ballerina by the name of Mademoiselle Novarre would be making her debut in the *divertissement*. And you will not credit this, Charity, but he also said that the *on dits* have it, that the ballerina in question is actually a member of the *beau monde!* Can you believe anything so absurd as that?"

Charity could not even feel her feet as she walked beside her cousin, for she was deeply shocked. Somehow, the fact that Penelope had been the first one to mention her own impending performance brought reality so suddenly and harshly upon her that she felt a tremendous dizziness assail her.

After a moment she was able to gather enough of her wits together in order to respond, "Quite absurd." But she wasn't certain if she had spoken loud enough for Penelope to hear her, for her cousin glanced at her with a decided frown between her brows. For a moment, Penelope appeared as though she would speak, but then she gave her light brown curls a toss of her head, as though the idea that had just entered her brain was ridiculous in the extreme.

Charity finally took a deep breath and said, "I have been meaning for some time to tell you and my aunt that I will not be here tomorrow nor Sunday. You see, I received a letter from my cousin Furney and her mother has grown worse. Poor Furney is quite beside herself and has begged for me to join her in Tunbridge Wells for a day or so— perhaps longer. And I really feel I ought to go, for my cousin has been so kind to me over the years that it seemed the very least I could do." How much these lies smote Charity's conscience. And was this what she had sunk to, telling whiskers to her cousin? Yet what choice did she have, for she could hardly blurt out that she was Mademoiselle Novarre. Swallowing very hard, she continued, "But please extend my apologies to Lord Meares for I had so looked forward to meeting him. Will he perchance be at Lady Dunford's ball this evening?"

"I am afraid not. But never mind. You will meet him soon enough, I daresay. I only hope that Mrs. Pelham-Furneux recovers quite soon."

"What? Oh, I hope so, too. At least—" Charity broke off realizing that she was about to expose herself completely, and finally she said, "Pen, I am so very nervous of a sudden. Are you certain your Mama will not be greatly distressed by this gown?"

They were by now at the hallway just before the landing and Penelope, her brown eyes almost elusive as she said, "Of course she will not! She will most likely believe it is merely a recent Paris creation!"

Lady Datchworth's drawing room seemed very quiet to William as he stood chatting with Anne Ware and George Meesden. The night before, at Charity's soirée, the room had hummed with a constant flow of chatter, and the crush of guests had been so thick, and the champagne had flowed so freely, that the hum had quickly grown to a loud constant clattering. But now the chambers were silent, Lady Datchworth sitting in a chair of blue damask by the fireplace and smiling, though the rather taut appearance of the lines about her eyes betrayed that some unhappy emotion was working strongly within her. William noticed that the viscount was absent which perhaps accounted for some of Lady Datchworth's ill-concealed misery.

The drawing room also was not nearly so full of flowers as it had been, and even those that remained seemed a little brown about the leaves, petals drooping and colors darkening slightly. But it was the quiet that bespoke that all was not well, and William wondered what was keeping Penelope and Charity.

Anne and George had bent their heads together slightly and were arguing with great good humor upon whether or not Charity would care to see the lions at the Tower of London. They had all the appearance of having fallen deeply in love and daily William was surprised that no announcement had been made regarding an engagement. He looked at George, who was a fine young man with a small independence, the third son of a baron of excellent lineage, and realized suddenly the nature of the delay for he would wager a thousand pounds that somehow Penelope had impeded Mr. Meesden's pursuit of Anne; the daughter of a viscount most certainly could not marry the third son of a baron. The first son, perhaps, but the third? Never!

Thoughts of Penelope brought back to mind his earlier conversation with his Mama, and forced him to reconsider the harshness of his attitude toward Penelope. But could anyone know what it was like to have Penelope always ready with a determined smile or word no matter how cross he might be with her? He was convinced that she had never given up her dogged pursuit of him and even now, when she could have Viscount Meares with a mere lifting of her finger—and for a lady of nine and twenty, she ought to bless herself for his interest in her—he would still find her staring at him, her brown eyes cloaked, her controlled smiles readied upon her perfect lips. Was it any wonder that he sneered at her?

But if he understood his Mama, she was not so much concerned with Penelope, but rather with his attitude in general, that he was attributing Penelope's motives to all females. And as he considered the young ladies at Almack's, he tried to imagine for a moment just what it would be like to have a peer lift a critical brow—particularly if you were a chit just out of the schoolroom—and for the first time he thought that perhaps he had been a trifle harsh with them. In fact, was there anything he despised more himself, than some person of rank coming the crab over him?

The door to the drawing room opened upon this thought and the first inkling William had that something had gone awry was the expression on Anne's face, since she faced the door and William's back was turned slightly away. The pretty color to her cheeks faded quite ominously, her blue eyes growing wide and staring as she gazed at some unknown object and finally gasped loudly, covering her mouth with one of her gloved hands as she cried, "Oh, dear God in heaven, what has Charity done?"

And just as William turned around to search for the reason for Anne's dismay, Lady Datchworth rose abruptly from her chair, an embroidered kerchief upon her lap sliding down the shimmering satin of her balldress to the carpet on the floor as she cried, "Take that off at once! Of all the absurd starts—! Charity, have you gone mad!"

William regarded Charity and the plaid bows scattered over her ballgown and he did not know whether to be furious with her or to laugh. He had been in her company often enough in the past few days to know that this gown was not in her usual mode of fashion. Amusement gave way to any degree of anger he felt—for the truth was that she looked adorable, her blue eyes holding an almost mischievous glint as she regarded her aunt. Not wishing for Charity to know, however, that he was amused, he covered his face slightly, trying to school his features, and upon doing so, Lady Datchworth cried, "And do but look how greatly you have distressed Lord Redbourne. Why, he cannot even look at you, he is so ashamed!"

William swallowed very hard, his eyes watering as he restrained the laughter that still threatened his countenance, but he was determined not to betray his amusement. He wanted Charity to believe that she had hit her mark, for he thought he knew what she was about— that she meant to goad in him what she perceived to be his top-loftiness. And finally when he had gained sufficient command of himself, he lifted his chin and donned what he felt would be an adequately arrogant expression. In a slow movement he reached for his quizzing glass and brought it carefully before one disapproving eye and regarded Charity for a very long moment.

She responded in much the manner he expected her to as she gave her black curls a toss and made her way toward her aunt. He noted that save for the bows, she was exquisitely gowned, for the pink ballgown was split from nearly the waist to the floor revealing an underdress lined with rows and rows of white ruffles. Her black curls cascaded charmingly from the crown of her head almost to her shoulders and through her hair a delicate string of pearls had been threaded. A ruby necklace, however, clashed miserably with the pink gown and William felt the strongest desire to simply walk over to her, unclasp the necklace himself, and begin ripping the bows from her gown one by one.

"But my dearest aunt!" Charity cried. "Whatever is the matter? Oh, you are staring at the charming little bows fluttering about my skirts. Do you not think that they look like *butterflies?* I was enchanted with the idea and had Marie make them up this very afternoon!"

When Charity had reached the spot where her aunt stood staring at her, a hand pressed against her cheek just as Penelope had done but a few minutes earlier, Charity leaned forward and placed a kiss upon both of her aunt's cheeks. "And how very pretty you look in just this shade of blue!"

"Th—thank you!" Lady Datchworth said, her voice sounding quite bemused. "But, my dear, I must say! You cannot possibly intend to wear such a hideous gown to Lady Dunford's ball! You would quite set the *ton* by the ears were you to do so and I am certain that Lord Redbourne would much rather you wore a different balldress entirely—the one you wore last night, for instance."

"Oh, but I could not do that for I spilled an iced cup of champagne down the bodice. Quite clumsy of me, but then I was listening to Miss Widford play upon the harp, and the music was romantical, and my mind naturally turned to William and there it was—iced champagne upon my bosom!"

"Charity!" Lady Datchworth gasped. "For heaven's sake! How came you to speak in so vulgar a manner? You know very well that such a mode of speech is quite frowned upon in society!"

Charity pressed her fingertips to her lips, opening her eyes very wide as she responded, "Should I not have said the word *romantical?* And yet it seemed so very harmless."

"*Bosom!* My dear. One should never speak of bosoms in a drawing room."

"I suppose you are quite correct, and I shall endeavor to remain silent upon the subject of *bosoms* forever." And spying her aunt's kerchief upon the carpet, she immediately bent down to retrieve the object.

Lady Datchworth backed away from her niece slightly as she took the kerchief from her, regarding Charity with a degree of horror in her light blue eyes. Almost she could see tiny little horns sprouting through the riot of curls upon her niece's head and she did not know quite what to do about it—her manner of speech, her gown, everything was so very *changed* and with a sense of helplessness, her mouth slightly agape, she turned toward William and shook her head slightly.

William did not hesitate to respond to this plea for assistance and he immediately moved to stand beside Charity, his expression still quite severe as he let his quizzing glass drop upon its black silk riband, and flared his nostrils at his recalcitrant bride-to-be. "My dear Charity—" he began, but he got no further for Charity surprised him by crying out in a lowborn manner, "Will! It's been ages since I last cast my daylights upon you!" And she threw herself upon him, hugging him very tightly. He was startled by her sudden movements but did not hesitate to return her greeting by encircling her with his own arms and enjoying the very pleasing sensation of being embraced by her—even if she was merely playing at games. After all, a hug was still a hug!

Lady Datchworth backed a few feet farther still from the creature in the pink balldress and fell into the damask chair, giving a little cry of fright. "She is become a monster!" the good woman said, her eyes wide and staring.

Penelope rushed to her mother's side and began patting her hand, murmuring, "No, no! Calm yourself dearest Mama for Charity means no harm, it is but the merest joke she is playing upon William, I assure you!"

"What do you mean a joke, for I see nothing amusing in your cousin's extremely odd conduct!" Lady Datchworth cried. She reached up to adjust the graceful turban upon her head which had become slightly twisted when she had sat down so abruptly. Peppered curls peeped from beneath the blue silk and as always Lady Datchworth presented a charming portrait of elegance and *a la modality*. Shaking her head at her niece, she added, "And if you ask me, Lord Redbourne is hardly laughing in hysterics at your cousin's antics. In fact, he does not seem entertained in the least!"

But William was entertained, though perhaps not in the precise manner Lady Datchworth might have thought for already he could sense that Charity was regretting her decision to fling herself at him, as she struggled to pull away from him. And yet what did she expect? That he would actually spurn an advance which could only pleasure his senses? Silly chit! And he held her more firmly still, as she wriggled against him, trying to break free.

Restraining the laughter that repeatedly rose within his breast, William managed to speak in an austere voice, "How could I possibly be amused, Miss Holwell! For I find your conduct vulgar, your gown atrocious, and the rubies about your neck ridiculous in the extreme. And I suppose in the future I will have to supervise your toilette personally before any event at which we are both to be present, for the Earl of Redbourne most assuredly cannot be seen with a perfect hoyden!"

And how pleased he was with the results of this speech, for Charity lifted her head—though she had great difficulty in doing so since he held her firmly—and scowled at him. "There is another solution to this difficulty, m'lord. We could agree never to attend together the same assemblies, soirees, fetes, or any other of a vast number of social engagements that would come our way during the course of our marriage. Then I should never embarrass your lordship!"

"You speak with some sense," he said, enjoying himself more than he ought. "However, there would always be the chance for an unfortunate accident, an error in the management of our various schedules, and I simply would not be willing to take the risk of ever having you represent me in society in this reprehensible fashion!" And as she tried to disengage herself again, William held her more tightly still, and had all the delight of looking down upon her creamy features and seeing her cheeks flushed with anger as she whispered, "You rogue! Let me go at once! You do this purposefully!"

He leaned down close to her ear and whispered, *I only follow your lead,* my love, though I must admit that I have a great fondness for hugging, and particularly for your manner of accomplishing your schemes!" And as she started to twist herself out of his arms, he released her quite suddenly so that she was thrown slightly off balance and he was able to then slip one arm about her waist, while the other hand held her arm firmly. She was still his captive.

Wheeling her about to face Lady Datchworth, he said, "If it wouldn't be too great a bother, would you ring for Charity's maid and when she has arrived, send her to the library? I think we can remedy this absurd situation quite easily, though I hope you don't find it too improper that I

164

intend to speak with Charity alone for a few minutes."

Charity cried, "But I don't wish to be alone with you! And I am perfectly content to wait for Marie here!"

Lady Datchworth cried, "You do not deserve in the least, Miss Mischief, that I consider your desires in this situation at all. And now, I bid you go with Lord Redbourne at once! You must realize he will very soon be your husband and you must be in subjection to him in everything!" She drew in her breath sharply upon uttering these unfortunate words, for her own situation came forcibly to mind. "And—and perhaps you will go too far, Charity, and will never be able to win his love back, and then what will you do?" Her eyes shifted away from Charity's face, misting over suddenly as she pressed her kerchief to her eyes.

Charity straightened her shoulders at these words and wanted to speak, to comfort her aunt who she realized was suffering no small degree of distress because of Lord Datchworth's anger with her at the present, but she disagreed so strongly with her aunt's old-fashioned philosophy that she merely clamped her mouth shut and glared up at her betrothed.

William did not even try to argue with her, nor attempt to impress upon Charity his view that such a dictum was quite ridiculous, that if ever he found his bride to be such a mousy, sniveling creature, who would always bend her knee to him, he would ship her to the Colonies without so much as a by-your-leave!

Instead he turned her physically about, and began marching her toward the doors. She protested mightily that whatever he wished to accomplish with her in the library, he might do so in the drawing room. But he leaned very near to her and whispered in her ear, "There you are out, for I mean to kiss you a hundred times."

Charity wished that his very warm breath and his scandalous words had not touched her ear, for both had the quite reprehensible effect of causing little shivers to travel down her neck.

"Libertine!" she whispered back.

He continued to pressure her strongly to walk forward, but when she actually tried to dig her heels into the carpet in order to prevent their combined progress toward the library, William wasted no time in lifting her bodily into his arms and carrying her from the room.

His last view of Charity's relations were of Lady Datchworth swooning in her chair and muttering, "What have I done to deserve this!"; of Penelope fanning her mother's features with a wheel fan and repeating that Charity was merely funning with William; and of Anne and George taking the opportunity at such a great diversion to stand very close to one another, their hands clasped and only partially concealed by Anne's ballgown, as they gazed longingly into one another's eyes.

Chapter Eleven

Charity was so angry at being summarily scooped up into William's arms without the least consideration for her sensibilities—and this was just one more example of his complete boorishness—that she spent the entire trip from the drawing room, across the landing and into the library, in trying to persuade him to free her. "Put me down!" she cried, kicking her feet. "Put me down, I say!"

Two maids stood in the hallway watching their progress, large eyes wide with amazement, mouths shaped into round *oh's*, and each carrying a coal scuttle to refurbish the fires in the library, the drawing room, as well as the bedchambers located upon the third floor. They were dressed in dark muslin gowns, stiff white aprons, and starched mobcaps. One of the maids, who wore a red silk ribbon tied in a jaunty bow about the high collar of her gown, cried out, "Bless me, he's got Miss Charity!" And both ladies dropped curtsies to the earl as he transported his bundle in front of them.

Once William had thrown open the door to the library, he turned back upon the maids, and, catching them in the very act of giggling and whispering to one another, he frightened them both by commanding, "Miss Holwell's maid has been requested to attend first Lady Datchworth

167

in the drawing room and afterward to come to the library. Will you please find her and tell her to bring a pair of scissors with her." And when both the maids remained quite still, their eyes unblinking in astonishment, he added in a quiet voice, *"Now,* if you please." And the maids jumped as though he had just shouted at them, and turned quickly upon their heels, fully prepared to do his bidding.

But Charity also addressed the maids, for she was quite unwilling to submit tamely to William's high-handedness. However, her voice was not quiet in the least, but was raised several degrees higher than William's as she called out, "Tell Marie to remain within my bedchamber until I send for her!"

At this point the maids stopped abruptly in their tracks, their coal scuttles rocking in their arms, as they exchanged an anxious look, uncertain what next they should do. For on the one hand, they were perfectly willing to obey the very tall Lord Redbourne, who besides being quite handsome, also had a certain ferocious look in his hazel eyes when he spoke to them. But on the other hand, Miss Holwell was Lady Datchworth's niece, and for a long moment they both remained perfectly still, eyes unblinking, and half-turned back toward Charity and William as they waited for the quarrel to come to a conclusion.

William did not hesitate to turn his piercing gaze upon them and as he passed through the doorway into the library he again addressed the maids, his voice as calm and quiet as it had been previously. "You will do my bidding," he said, "and at once, or I'll see that neither of you work in London again!"

Well! This was quite sufficient for at least one of the maids. Betsy, who wore the ribbon about her collar, had come straight from the poorhouse only one year earlier where her Mama had died of the consumption. Her Papa had died in a coal-mining accident some years earlier, and though her parents had both come from good Yeoman stock, Betsy had no near relations to whom she could turn for assistance, and had been forced to seek employment while still a very young lady, having just turned thirteen at the time of her mother's death. And during the several months her Mama had wasted away upon a bed of straw, Betsy had been approached at least a dozen times by Abbesses to take up a trade that made her ill just thinking about it. And since her lettering was poor, and she hadn't the least knowledge of needlework and stitchery, she felt quite fortunate to have gotten a position as undermaid in Mayfair. Mayfair! She felt the good Lord had been watchin' out for her. But it didn't take more than a simple threat like Lord Redbourne's to remind her how close she was to poverty and the frightening world of the flash-houses. She immediately pulled Sukey's arm, and exclaimed, "Come on, luv. Let's find that Frenchy, just as his lordship wishes us to do!"

Satisfied, William entered the library, closed the door behind him with a firm snap but refused to set Charity upon her feet, even though she was squawking the entire time that he ought to do so instantly or else he would certainly suffer grave consequences. She was by this time fighting him furiously, pushing at his chest and kicking her feet, the white ruffles of her underdress dancing about wildly with her movements.

But only when she had given up a little, and had ceased struggling merely to content herself with scowling upon him, did he kiss her firmly upon the lips, just once, then set her quite gently upon her feet.

"Oh!" Charity cried. "You are the worst beast that ever existed. First you take me quite against my will into this secluded place and then you kiss me! Not to mention the fact that you threatened two poor young maids and frightened them nearly out of their wits in doing so—and I do not hesitate to tell you that had you taken such steps as you referred to, making it impossible for them to find employment as serving maids, I would have taken them under my wing immediately! At any rate, I find your manners insufferable, your arrogance boundless, and the abuse of your power as a peer of the realm quite beyond bearing!" And when he made no response as he leaned his broad shoulders against the door and folded his arms upon his chest, except to smile in that rather infuriating manner of his, she began puffing up the crushed sleeves of her gown, and smoothing out the disordered ruffles of her underdress as she pronounced finally, "What a brute you've become, Will!"

She was deuced pretty, he realized, as he regarded her steadily. But what he loved most was the sparkle, the fire, in her blue eyes. Faith, she was an exciting creature, full of life. He responded with a slight lift of his brow, "I've only treated you this evening in the manner that you deserved to be treated. And if we were to speak of brutishness, how came you to perform this little farce in front of your aunt, who was clearly suffering from a fit of the megrims. I daresay you may not have noticed, but you nearly caused her to faint from mortification. Brutish, m'dear!"

Charity frowned at his words, for he was right, and she wondered how it had come about that Penelope had so sorely misjudged the state of her Mama's nerves. Sighing, she said, "Earlier, I had experienced some reservations about the tone of her mind. And as it happens, I dearly wish the deed undone for she was not at all well, I fear." She whirled back upon William and said, "But not with regard to you, of course!"

William drew away from the door and, walking slowly toward the first shelf of books to the right of the doorway, said, "There, I greatly fear you and my mother would heartily concur." Touching the calfskin volumes gently, he pulled a book forward. But upon finding it was written in Greek, he tapped its cover as though wishing he could translate it with ease, then replaced it upon the shelf.

Charity was so stunned by his admission and by the knowledge that Lady Redbourne had expressed her disapproval of her beloved William—for she had always known that the dowager doted upon her son—that her mouth fell agape as she cried, "I don't believe it!"

A rueful expression stole over his features as he regarded her and said, "Did you think I could not be made to listen to reason? Well, as it happens, she took me sorely to task about the young ladies at Almack's, just as both you and my friend, Hugh, have done and I will at least admit that I treated the chits harshly—though I will still hold to my original motives."

Charity felt this was a somewhat mixed response, but she could not help but be gratified a little and she said, "I honor you for having said as much for I would never have expected you to actually admit you were wrong."

Moving away from the bookshelves, he grimaced at her only slightly as he changed the subject. With a very soft smile, he said, "I wish we were back at the last wedding we attended together. What a cheerful day that was, and you were so pretty, sitting in the swing with your hair all curled and flowing behind you, as I'd push you higher and higher. You were squealing by the time Penelope came to get you! Do you remember that? And do you know that your eyes have a glitter to them that I can hardly resist, an impish quality that has always attached me to you?"

"Oh, William, do stop this nonsense!" Charity cried, his words rippling over her, causing her breath to grow shallow and quick.

The library was well-lit, several branches of candles glowing and flickering about the book-lined chamber, and remained so every evening during the season, into the small hours of the morning. Whenever Lord Datchworth returned from his evening's adventures, he enjoyed sitting in the library for awhile, sipping at his brandy and reading. The volumes he was currently perusing were stacked upon a tripod table near a comfortable wing chair covered in a dark green velvet. The floors were planked and highly polished, and across from the wing chair was a settee in peach damask and covered with a variety of pillows that the ladies had embroidered over the years—tulips and balloons, a cat, a sprig of lavender, a domestic scene taken from the drawing room, a countryside of billowing clouds. Some of the needlework was even of the earliest construction when the young ladies were still taking their lessons in the schoolroom and the stitches were crooked, uneven, and the cloths stained with what might have been droplets of jelly or perhaps even honey.

A writing desk of mahogany sat in one corner of the chamber, upon which flickered a branch of candles. The walls were fitted to the ceiling with elegant oak bookshelves, and finished with a fine piece of carved molding called ribbon and rose that encircled the entire room where the shelves met the ceiling. To Charity, the room felt warm with memories, and smelled faintly of Lord Datchworth's snuff which had over the years stained the armrest of the velvet chair, the powdery grains by their very nature elusive, for next to the stack of books Lord Datchworth kept a tabletop snuffbox, encrusted upon the lid with diamonds and emeralds, and laced on each side with gold filigree.

Charity stood beside the settee, staring down at the pillows and remembering them all, save for a couple of more recent additions which must have been accomplished while she was in Paris. So many memories resided there, that she was for a moment taken back to the schoolroom at Chisley Hall and having a grand time with her cousins playing spillikins. And one of the pillows she recognized as her own. Good gracious, it was of two stick figures, William and herself, when he had first taught her to ride.

"Look at this!" she cried. "This is you!" Charity handed him the pillow and he took it, holding it gently between his hands, his features lit with a softness that surprised Charity as he regarded the childish stitchery.

He smiled broadly as he cried, "How came you to put five legs upon this horse?" He laughed lightly as he continued, "You were such an excellent student, too! Though you always had such an alarming tendency to throw your heart over every hedge! And I am so very glad to learn that you have not changed in the least."

In that moment, as Charity regarded his sweet smile and the laughter in his hazel eyes, she felt caught in the past as well. He seemed to sense that her heart had softened toward him and he did not hesitate to sweep her quickly in his arms. "My dearest Charity, I want you to love me!" And he kissed her very sweetly upon her mouth and then gently placed small little kisses upon her nose and her eyes and her cheeks. Charity forgot everything for just this moment, as he began recounting one of their adventures— after a brief late-spring shower, they had galloped across a meadow, mud spraying their clothes, the sun warm upon their faces and a wind so sweet and presaging summer keeping their brows cool as the horses flew across the long grasses, a flock of blue butterflies springing up suddenly about them, coloring the air, Charity crying with delight.

It wasn't fair, Charity thought, that he should call to mind that particular experience all the while brushing her face with his lips and making good his promise that he meant to kiss her a hundred times, his breath soft against her skin, butterfly-wing soft. "William," she cooed in a whisper, "you ought not to be doing this."

After a moment, William stopped kissing her and, taking her hands within his own, he regarded her with a decided glint of mischief in his eye as he asked, "And now, I wish to pose a question to you that has been haunting me

173

since Wednesday morning."

Charity, who was beginning to feel like the worst sort of hypocrite in enjoying his kisses one moment and then planning to wreak vengeance upon him the next, took a nervous breath and said, "And what, pray tell, is that?"

William leaned very close to her and let his lips drift across her cheek as he asked, "Did you enjoy the highwayman's kisses as much as my own?"

Charity was both angry and shocked as she jerked her hands out of his and stepped away from him. "How could you ask me such a thing, you scoundrel! No, of course I did not enjoy his kisses, that is, well perhaps a little. The truth is that I can hardly remember anything about the experience, save that I was very angry and wished him whipped at the cart's-tail for his wretched exploits!"

"Poor fellow!" William murmured as he moved to stand behind Charity. She was at this moment standing beside the tripod table and tracing the pattern of diamonds and emeralds upon the exquisite snuffbox.

"What do you mean, poor fellow?" she asked. "The man is a rogue!"

"Do but think, Charity. If The Gentleman has made it his business to take up kissing so many females, he must consider himself a master of it, and if you cannot even remember what it was like, well! Then he is to be greatly commiserated for having failed at that which he must believe he does best! But are you certain you cannot even remember his kisses?"

William was standing behind her, very close, his hand touching her arm upon a very sensitive portion of skin above her glove, yet still below her puffed sleeve, and little shivers traveled to the tips of her fingers. She liked being touched in this manner, she wanted him to touch her, to kiss her, but oh, merciful heavens, what was she doing with him, but playing a cheat if after enjoying his caresses so very many times, she would then betray him upon the

174

stage. She felt a decided lump rise in her throat as she responded, "I remember but a little, truly. It was all over so very quickly. However, I do recall being caught up in the excitement of the moment. And I think you should know that I—I actually threw my arms about his neck, but for the life of me I cannot imagine why."

William had been stroking her arm gently, but when she confessed so completely, he was taken aback by the woman before him. No child this, to speak so honestly with him. He had expected her to prevaricate, or to at least avoid telling him anything, instead she had told him all, and a decidedly powerful feeling for her overtook him.

"Are you angry with me?" she asked. "You seem suddenly so quiet."

His voice was rather husky as he slipped his arms about her waist, holding her fast, yet still standing behind her, as he responded, "Charity, I never meant to make you feel as though you must bare all to me. I only meant to tease you a little."

Charity knew the strongest desire to tell him that she had held the highwayman close because her heart and her thoughts, when The Gentleman had kissed her, had turned so completely and inexplicably toward William, but the words were lodged in her throat, her heart still shifting painfully in her breast. And because she was afraid that if he spoke one more kindness to her, or kissed her again, that she would forgive him everything, she spoke in a light, teasing voice, saying instead, "However, I think in many respects, The Gentleman is clearly better at kissing than you are!"

William responded in a similar tone, "How's this?" And he released her.

She turned toward him and said, "For one thing, he is much more charming and dashing and romantic a figure than you—truly he is every girl's favorite daydream! And I think he is more practiced at kissing, for how else can I explain that I hugged him?"

"Then, if this ridiculous highwayman were to seek you out, you would no doubt travel to the ends of the earth with him."

"Such a prospect has a certain charm," she responded with a smile as she sighed deeply.

He stepped toward her and placing his hands upon her shoulders, held her gaze steadily as he said, "Then come with me, Charity. Travel the world with me. Would you care to see the Japans? Or China perhaps! Or, what about some of these islands that float mysteriously about in the Pacific, where the natives run about freely, their babies naked and content. Come with me!" His lips were but a breath away and Charity felt her spirits soar within her at such an invitation. What did William want from her? Why was he saying such things to her? Did he know then that such were her own desires? And perhaps they could travel the courts of Europe and perhaps he would wish for her to perform the ballet? And what would China think of her *ballet romantique?* Almost it was more than she could bear, as his lips found hers in a hard, torturous kiss. He held her fast, nearly claiming her entire body as his own. If only life were so simple. If only one could say, *Let us travel to India, to China, to Africa,* and the deed were done!

After a very long moment, a rather insistent tapping upon the door tore them apart, though neither was willing to give permission for the intruder to enter, even though it was undoubtedly Marie. Charity looked into William's laughing hazel eyes, her heart feeling torn apart completely in this moment, especially since he had actually admitted to behaving unkindly to the young ladies at Almack's. Perhaps his heart might soften further and that somehow he could become friends with Penelope. Her heart ached at the thought, for she was loyal to those closest to her, profoundly so, willing to defend them against any slight or injustice. The rapping sounded upon

176

the door again, and still they both waited. Finally, Charity turned away from him, disrupting the intensity between them and feeling greatly saddened by truths that were too real for her to deny. But he caught her wrist, and cried, "What is it? What were you thinking just now? For a moment, you were as I remembered you, sprightly and charming, but since your return from Paris—Charity, why is it you despise me so much?"

But this time the loud rapping was followed by Marie opening the door and peeping her head in as she said, "I was not certain if anyone was within. I do beg your pardon, Monsieur, but was it you who summoned me?"

"Yes, yes!" William said, somewhat impatiently, a frown now creasing his brow, as he cast a questioning glance toward Charity. He was trying to comprehend her, trying to understand why she had developed so strong an antagonism toward him. He knew that to some degree Penelope would have twisted Charity's opinions, but surely somewhere in his betrothed's heart was the ability to see that he was not at fault in his dealings with Penelope! Or was he somehow, perhaps in a way that he did not yet comprehend! Oh, the devil take it, why did this all have to be so complicated!

Marie waited patiently by the door until Lord Redbourne turned to her and said, "I wish you to remove all of these butterflies—that is, all of these bows, from your mistress's gown. You did bring your scissors, did you not?"

"Well, yes, because I was told to, but you will find that the bows are merely pinned on."

He waved an impatient hand. "Whatever the case, pray remove the butterflies—er, the bows—at once!"

But Marie remained by the door, and though she inclined her head to William and afterward curtsied politely, she said, "I will do only that which pleases my mistress."

William was astonished at so much impudence and would have certainly taken the servant to task had Charity not said in a very cool voice, "And do you mean now, William, to berate my servant? A woman whom I count as friend, whatever her status might be, who has served me for the past four years in the most exemplary manner possible? Will you take her to task for simply expressing her loyalty to me and merely because you cannot order her about as you seem to be able to order everyone else?"

He was shocked, deeply so, that she would speak in such a manner to him, obviously accusing him of yet another fault and he felt so angry of the moment that this time the flaring of his nostrils was very real indeed. "And I do not care at all for this tone of yours, Charity!"

Letting out a very slow deep breath, Charity found all of her newfound sympathy for him vanishing, the faltering love that kept rising within her heart whenever she would remember the past, disappearing in little wisps, even as the early morning mist vanishes once the sun has risen. But, Lord, how her heart ached!

Charity did not answer him, but stared, instead, at the bookshelves, afraid that she might cry. She said, "Marie, please remove these bows. They overset my aunt greatly, and she does not deserve such cavalier treatment from me."

"Tres bien, cherie." And within a few minutes all the bows were in a pile upon the gleaming planked floor at Charity's feet.

Chapter Twelve

Charity sat very tall and straight against the squabs, her head turned for the most part of the short journey to Berkeley Square, toward the side window-glass, where she watched a slight drizzle making little runnels down the window of Lord Redbourne's town coach, the water glistening as each faint lump came into view then vanished into the darkness. Her heart was so very tired of the moment, from hour to hour, the light seeming to shine upon it, bringing her love to William to life, then a dark mist, full of his wretched arrogance, would shut the light out. A black silk cape lined with a soft sable fur, kept her warm against the chill April evening, her pink gown restored fully to its original beauty, her countenance now everything that would add to her husband-to-be's consequence before the *haut ton*.

As the wheels clattered upon the stone streets, the horses' hooves a counterpoint to the rumble of the wheels, a pained, struggling conversation ensued, for the party had decided to travel in two separate carriages, given the fact that there were six of them and that neither Anne nor Penelope wished their balldresses to be crushed. It was decided therefore, that Charity, William, and Lady Datchworth would travel in the first coach and that the others would travel in the second. And without some of Anne's bubbly conversation or Penelope's clever anecdotes, the atmosphere within the earl's coach was stifling in the extreme.

Fortunately the journey was brief, and Charity breathed a great sigh of relief as the coach drew up before the Dunford townhouse.

But when the stately butler opened the door, Charity was shocked to find the worst sort of bedlam in progress, for the guests were met by a much harried Lady Dunford who informed them instantly that three rascals—for she would not call them *gentlemen*—had actually snuffed out most of the candles in the antechambers as well as the drawing room which had had the dubious effect of sending the ladies shrieking through the darkness while at least two of the young men began stealing kisses from some of the prettier, younger ladies, and pretending to be The Gentleman. Afterward, they gathered up as many candles as they could carry and ran to the ballroom, where the young men were now being subdued. And her servants—oh, heaven help her!—were all running into one another, trying madly to relight most of the chambers! It was all so shocking, Lady Dunford cried, as two large tears welled up in her eyes. She was a very nervous lady, high in the flesh, with a huge waistline, and rippling arms. She exclaimed in a truly pathetic voice, "Oh, my dear Abigail! Thank heaven you have come, for you can support me in this my hour of misery. And you, dearest Redbourne—" And here she leaned toward him, pressing his arm, "Your countenance at least will assure some order in my home. But come, Abigail! You may see me to the ladies' chamber, where I have decided to remain until the ball is in a more normal state." And taking Lady Datchworth's arm, she continued, "And did I tell you that one of the young men was quite foxed and cast up his accounts upon the ballroom floor?" Penelope, Anne, and

George, who all gasped in unison, followed behind their hostess and Lady Datchworth, as the two older women began ascending the stairs. Charity thought she ought to follow behind them as well, but she could not resist staying to discover just how the altercation, now sounding furiously from the ballroom, would end.

Lady Dunford continued to pour out her woes, her carrying voice still audible as the small party progressed slowly up the stairs, "Yes, indeed! And poor Miss Widford slipped in it and fell upon her—well, let us say that she left the ball shortly afterward protesting that she would retire to her home in Oxfordshire for several weeks, for she was deeply mortified, poor child!"

Charity and William remained at the bottom of the stairs, for the ballroom was upon that floor, at the back of the very grand house, and shouting and squealing from the ballroom could be heard, as well as some dreadful scuffling and an occasional protestation from a lady or two of, "Merciful heavens!"

"Oh dear!" Charity cried. "What a noise! Why it sounds almost as if a bout of fisticuffs is in progress!"

And as she moved toward the hallway that joined the entrance hall, William pulled her quickly aside, the sounds of a resonant male voice drawing closer as each second passed.

William cried, "By Jove, that's Hugh!"

And Mr. Bramfield's voice could be heard quite clearly as he cried, "Step aside, quickly, quickly! Here comes the first rascal who has expressed the greatest desire to become better acquainted with the flagways!"

A number of ladies screamed and several servants protected the guests by standing in front of them and spreading out their arms, as Hugh came barreling into the entrance hall holding by the scruff of the neck and the seat of the breeches a bleary-eyed young man, whose cheek and eye were swelling ominously. Lady Dunford's butler, as

Charity soon realized, was a veritable pillar of composure as he stood calmly by the door, an expression of boredom upon his face. And once Hugh was close enough, the butler opened the door very wide in his slow practiced movements, and with a gracious inclination of his head, bowed the unwelcome guest out of the house.

But another male voice, both slurred with drunkenness and belligerence, followed down the hall, demanding that The Watch be summoned, for his friend had been bruised badly by that tall fellow and where was he anyway? Hugh turned upon this second swaggering foe, who weaved ominously into the entrance hall amidst the squealing of the ladies he bumped into, and was prepared to do battle again. Catching sight of Hugh, the ruffian hunched over, obviously intent upon taking Hugh in the midsection at a run, but William moved quickly from beside Charity and catching the fellow firmly by both the back of his coat as well as the back of his smalls destroyed any possibility of his doing so. Hugh let out a whoop of triumph, the butler again opened the door, bowing graciously, and William ran this second gentleman from the house, tossing him atop his friend, who was just then unsteadily regaining his feet. The pair of rascals rolled over one another twice together before bumping into the wheels of a carriage directly in front of the townhouse.

Charity moved to stand beside William, and regarded the poor fellows, one of whom was now sprawled beneath a horse. Fortunately for him, the gelding expressed his interest in the proceedings with a mere flip of his tail and a twitch of his ears as he turned about to regard the drunken ruffian.

The third miscreant, who had passed out shortly after disrupting the entire ballroom, was then carted from the house by four husky male servants. These men all wore the Dunford livery, and though their powdered wigs were now sadly askew, their faces shone with the adventure of the moment and a broad smile suffused each of their faces. A season in London was usually dull work and at least two of the footmen had decided then and there to see that a great deal more champagne and other spirits were provided liberally for the guests to imbibe—this was more fun than any of them had enjoyed in the past six months—even at the Five Courts!

Charity watched the servants congratulating one another as they made certain the two fairly stable young men were able to summon a hackney and carry off their friend. And then she turned to regard Hugh and William, who were also offering each other a bow of congratulations in a similar manner and spirit as the servants had done. Several ladies and gentlemen, a trifle breathless with so much excitement, approached the gentlemen at this moment, and began thanking them for their heroic efforts.

The ladies clustered about them, fanning themselves madly and touching their dampened brows, while the gentlemen huffed and complained about the wretched manners of young persons today.

Charity moved to stand near the curved staircase, and watched the gentlemen. She had not really had any great opportunity of observing Mr. Bramfield before but she looked him over carefully now. And though he was perspiring mightily from his efforts and wiping his brow, he was clearly an immaculately groomed gentleman and still stood as though he was in command of his soldiers, his bearing tall and elegant, his deeply set blue eyes filled with amusement as he was approached by the Widow Baldock. This lady drew very close to him, admiring him for being so very strong, and when she reached a hand up in an attempt to tidy his curly brown hair which had gotten a little mussed during the scuffle, he quickly took her hand and drew it slowly to his lips. For some time now, Charity had noticed that very few gentlemen could resist Mrs. Baldock's large, brown eyes and her peculiar manner of practically standing upon the toes of the men with whom she was conversing. And she wondered if William had ever succumbed to her charms.

After watching the men for a few minutes, Charity became aware of a very subtle shift in the demeanor of those who gathered about Hugh and William. For whether they were young or old, male or female, they would initially smile at Mr. Bramfield, and offer him a word or two of polite conversation, but after a moment their eyes would shift toward William, small steps eased his direction, and fairly soon all manner of effusive praise spouted from their lips as they showered William with fulsome compliments. Charity felt ill of a sudden, an angry flush suffusing her cheeks, that these hopeless toadeaters would make such cakes of themselves in deferring so completely to William's position in society as the Earl of Redbourne. Why, they even made it appear as though William had been in charge of some enormous battlefield maneuver, with Hugh but a soldier of the rank and file who had been present merely to do his bidding. And she began fanning herself furiously, trying to cool the fire upon her cheeks for she was quite angry that so many sheep were bleating about William's rank.

But as she watched William, and the drawn look about his cheeks, his nostrils again flaring, she realized with a start that he was equally angry and that it was only with the greatest difficulty that he was managing his civilities as he watched Hugh being ignored. Charity felt the blush on her cheeks deepen with the awareness that in this she had misjudged him. Somehow, she had believed he enjoyed the compliments and fawning which accompanied his rank, and that this was the source of his arrogant, belligerent conduct. But she was clearly wrong.

Her fan came to a complete rest at this thought, and she held it lightly in her hand, her gaze fixed upon Will. Penelope had told her over the years that William loved his rank so thoroughly, that he held everyone else in contempt because of it, and this thought smote some inner chord that shook Charity to the tips of her toes. Penelope was wrong! And the worst suspicion rose within her, that if her cousin had been so very wrong about William, in what other ways had Penelope, unwittingly of course, misled her?

A strong masculine voice surprised her, as Hugh, who was now standing beside her, said, "I was afraid your fan was about to fly apart, for you were fanning yourself with great force."

Charity turned toward him slightly, feeling all of the goodwill toward him that the ridiculous sheep still clustered about William were unable to feel and she extended her hand to him in a friendly, warm manner. And, given his recent light flirtation with Mrs. Baldock, Charity was not surprised when he took instant possession of her hand, saluting her fingers with an elegant, but quite harmless, kiss.

She found herself drawn to Hugh and thought it was greatly to William's credit that he had so good-natured a friend.

"I know it is very improper of me," Hugh cried, "but I had this feeling that if I didn't introduce myself to you, no one else would!" And then he laughed, his blue eyes crinkling as he said, "You are Charity, are you not? I mean, Will's Charity?"

"Yes, of course I am!" she answered. "And you are Mr. Bramfield, I presume!"

"There you are out! My name is Hugh, and I don't answer to Mr. Bramfield, if I can possibly help it—and certainly not to quite beautiful young ladies. No, indeed. Mr. Bramfield is my father and you, most especially, must call me Hugh!" He then begged her to take a turn about several of the rooms upstairs that she might see for herself the sort of mayhem that had overtaken poor Lady

Dunford's townhouse in the past half-hour. And besides, if William caught up with them, he would never have a chance to speak privately with Charity again, he was certain of it! "For you must know that I have a dreadful confession to make to you. And if upon hearing what I have to say you should choose to cut my acquaintance forever, I will understand perfectly!"

Charity looked up at Hugh, her brow puckered slightly, and the smallest fear trembled in her heart, as she remembered that Anne, only this morning, had whispered to her at breakfast, that the latest *on dits* had it that Hugh Bramfield was The Gentleman. "And do you not think it likely!" Anne cried in her little girl manner, her blue eyes wide and glittering with excitement. She took a sip of her steaming hot chocolate and smacking her lips slightly, she continued, "For it is commonly known that Mr. Bramfield has been at an inn near the place where you were attacked so very recently, and at the same hour, too! A most suspicious occurrence! Also, it is rumored that his property is mortaged to the three-percenters! And to think he has been robbing young ladies, that he might redeem his lands!"

Charity had laughed outright at this, giving her head a shake, as she responded, "But he never steals more than fifty pounds! How could Mr. Bramfield—if he is The Gentleman—benefit from such a small sum? No, I cannot credit it, though the circumstances do indeed give him the appearance of culpability!"

And as Charity continued to regard Hugh, she wondered if he meant to confess to her that he was indeed the highwayman. But as she looked up at him, and tried to imagine being held in his arms, and what he might possibly look like were he sporting a black silk mask and a long curling wig, she knew that he could not possibly be The Gentleman—he was too tall! And she felt her entire body relax upon this thought for what could be worse than having one of William's friends be the notorious high-wayman?

"I am trembling with fear!" she cried at last, a teasing smile upon her lips. "For your words sound quite ominous! Pray, tell me at once, Mr. Bram—that is, Hugh! What dark deed have you committed that must now require an ablution!"

Taking her hand again, he tucked her arm about his own, and drew her toward the staircase where they began a slow progress toward the drawing room. He said, "William told me that you were very feisty and now I see that you are and I am glad of it, for my good friend needs a lively female to keep him from becoming too crusty! But let me proceed with my confession ere I lose my resolve— you see, I saw you go into your uncle's office on the night of your party! There, it is out! And now you may slap me if you like, for it was I who informed your uncle and your betrothed of your whereabouts!"

She regarded him in considerable surprise. "Indeed! So it is you I have to thank for spoiling all my fun, not to mention my schemes! Thank you very much, *Mr. Bramfield,* for I will not address you by your Christian name unless you apologize at once!"

Hugh feigned a very sad expression. "But that I am afraid I could never do! And now I suppose I will have to be *Mr. Bramfield* forever!"

"But I don't understand? You seem a stout enough fellow to manage an apology, and you also do not appear so high in the instep as to prevent your consequence from interfering in the business—so I say again, why can't you apologize?"

"The matter is simple," he continued, still wearing an expression of unhappiness. "Because were the truth known, I am not sorry in the least. I had a deal too much fun in making William search for you!"

"Oh, you did not do so!" Charity cried with glee as she

giggled behind her fan.

"Yes, I did and I even had him approach your aunt, who was very much engrossed in her game of whist in the antechamber, and who told him to go about his own business in no uncertain terms for he was disturbing her mightily!"

Charity let out a peal of laughter as she cried, "Oh, it is too good, too wonderful, and how very much like my aunt when she is ensnared by her cards! And was he greatly mortified?"

"William? Never, and certainly not for such a reason as that. He was only irritated that you could not be found and a little mystified at your disappearance. Of course, I had wanted him to take a brief tour of the library as well, but I felt I had tortured him sufficiently."

"Oh, dear," Charity breathed with much satisfaction. "You are a scoundrel! Well, in that case, I have decided to forgive you for revealing my whereabouts but only because I can comprehend perfectly your desire to tease your friend in such a wicked manner, for I feel that way myself most of the time!"

They had by now reached the upper landing at the end of the gracefully curved staircase and walked forward into a large and exquisite drawing room. The long chamber was decorated in golds and reds, the Turkish carpet predominantly the latter color. The curtains at the far end of the chamber were hung with gold silk, and scattered chairs and settees in the well-appointed room were upholstered in silks of the same colors. A large portrait of a suspiciously thinner Lady Dunford, executed by Lawrence, hung over the fireplace, a harp and pianoforte held the delicate forms of the Misses Hardwick, who were at that moment playing a duet they had fashioned from a Bach Prelude.

But as Charity stood upon the threshold, she was struck suddenly by the quite amorous appearance to the chamber, for it was full of couples, heads bent together as though, in the absence of the candlelight, more secrets could be exchanged than were normally done at a ball. And save for a fine glow of coals from the fireplace, the room sported but a half-dozen broken and misshapen candles. Several of the tables, where the candles had been torn from their branches, showed trails of wax droplets. And as Charity glanced about the chamber, she discovered with no small degree of amusement that George and Anne had found the darkest corner of all, and were involved in a serious discussion, both of their faces puckered with anxiety.

Hugh directed her toward the fireplace, where he ensconced her upon a settee and sat down beside her. Not mincing any words he asked, "But what I wish to know is whether or not you mean to marry Will at the end of your charade?" He leaned his arm on the back of the settee his words very low. The chamber was indeed full of whispered conversations, the air almost crackling with the excitement of recent events. Charity was a little shocked at his question and glanced about the various pairs closest to them to see if any had heard his penetrating question. But fortunately the glittering sounds of the duet masked their conversation from anyone else.

Charity could not look at Hugh as she said, "I don't know what you mean! When a lady becomes engaged, she would have to have extraordinary reasons to play the jilt."

"Ah," he said. "Now would not that be a reason there?"

And with the slightest inclination of his head, he gestured toward the entrance to the drawing room where in the shadow of the doorway, her perfectly composed features shaped into a delicate smile, stood Penelope.

"I begin to fear you excessively, Hugh, for you have it exactly right!"

"I thought as much," he said. "And knowing the situation from William's perspective, although I do believe he deserves to be brought down a peg or two, I still feel I ought to warn you to tread *warily*."

Charity narrowed her eyes at Hugh, knowing that since he emphasized the very last word, he had been referring to Penelope. But how very odd! And at first she wanted to dismiss it as merely the loyalty Hugh would feel for William as his dear friend. But she remembered suddenly that even her own uncle had upon more than one occasion leveled accusations at Pen as though his daughter was full of rather wicked machinations. And whatever could Hugh mean by casting such an aspersion upon Penelope's character? She wanted to ask him to explain his meaning but by that time her cousin was nearly upon them, smiling in her quiet manner and fully intent upon joining them.

Chapter Thirteen

Holding Charity lightly, William whirled her about the crowded ballroom as the elegant strains of the waltz filled the long chamber. She felt like the merest wisp of a feather in his arms, gracefully following his lead, her entire body given to the pulse of the music, her feet light and almost nonexistent as they progressed easily from one end of the chamber to the other. Lady Dunford's ballroom became a blur of yellow silk draperies and white molding as William regarded the gleaming black curls upon his errant fiancée's head, a strand of pearls laced throughout.

William had watched her dance before but this was the first time he had actually waltzed with her and the experience startled him. For even though several of his friends had commented upon how Charity seemed to possess wings instead of feet, as well as the ability to make any of her partners appear to advantage, he had felt that they were simply being excessively kind. But now, as he held her hand clasped gently within his own and turned her smoothly about the floor, he understood what his friends had meant. She had an ethereal quality to her movements, at once graceful and delicate, yet so very confident, almost bold. No doubt her years in Paris, where he had always felt elegance superseded form, had given her this decided polish.

He told her so, exclaiming over her abilities and watched her blush which pleased him immensely. They were still not entirely upon friendly terms, for when he had begged her to dance she had at first refused saying she was greatly fatigued. But when he had said that he did not wonder at it since she had been conversing with Mr. Tewin, who never introduced a subject but what he could bring it round to himself, besides being a fish-faced gabblemonger, he had seen the amusement flash in her clear blue eyes. And with such a promising invitation as her exquisite eyes lit with laughter, he had wasted no time in grasping one of her wrists and promising her that if she did not accompany him onto the floor, he would give a series of whoops which would be heard all the way to Dover! It was after the second whoop, which had brought all eyes turning toward them in shock, that Charity, her lower lip trembling with suppressed laughter, had finally agreed to dance with him!

"For I can see," she cried, "that your earlier excitement in having tossed a man onto the flags has quite addled your brain. I shall therefore take pity on you and comply with your request!"

"Whether pity or love, I care not!" he had responded gaily, bowing to her as she passed before him, leading the way to the dance floor.

Lady Dunford's ballroom had finally been restored to order, all of the candles again standing straight within their holders and any broken ones replaced. The room was aglow, as was the remainder of the house, though any number of young ladies sighed and lamented the brief darkened corners in which several scandalous embraces had been exchanged!

William had finally escaped the toadeating crowd that had gathered about him in the entrance hall, sickened by the many quite absurd compliments upon his bravery.

And now, as he looked down upon Charity, he was struck yet again with her beauty, and the lean, almost athletic lines to her arms, and the graceful slope of her neck. If only she was not so firmly set against him, for she seemed to believe that he reveled in his rank when, were the truth known, he spent most of his time amongst the *ton* barely tolerating the deferential remarks and compliments paid to him. Why could she not see that?

She was very silent while they danced and he knew he had offended her deeply in the library at Lord Datchworth's townhouse, but he wasn't precisely certain why. What difference did it matter how he addressed her maid, for was she not but a servant? The task of removing the bows from Charity's gown needed to be accomplished and he simply thought it quite unnecessary for her abigail to cavil about his having issued the command! Such impudence toward any member of the *beau monde* he would never tolerate in any of his own servants, and he said as much to Charity now. "For I simply do not comprehend why you flew into the boughs! And that over your maid!"

Charity looked up at William and said, "I am angry mostly because you don't understand. You have been far too long courted by society, my lord, for you seem to feel that you may dictate to anyone and everyone whenever you please! And that those who serve have no feelings or loyalties themselves."

"Your maid, then, is in league with you?" he asked slightly bemused, trying to comprehend her sentiments.

"Of course," Charity answered promptly. "She is very loyal to me, as I am to those whom I love!"

He was not so much impressed by her words as by the decided glint in her blue eyes, and he felt that couched within these words was a threat of some sort, the same gauntlet that he had experienced from the first. Did she intend, he wondered, at some propitious moment to dissolve their engagement? And he felt certain that that was what she was about, but he could not explain how he knew it to be true.

As he watched her a powerful desire came over him, for he realized with an abruptness that nearly caused him to miss his steps, that he wanted her to be his wife more than anything in the world. He wanted this spirited young woman who would not hesitate to place absurd little bows all over her gown—regardless of how her own career in London would be affected by doing so—to preside over the Redbourne estates.

Charity looked up at him as though she felt his silent thoughts, and he held her gaze for a long moment by the sheer force of his will. Her lips parted slightly, and her brows drew together in a slight frown as she asked, "William, what thoughts march through your mind? Almost you frighten me!"

He held her hand tightly, and said, "I won't let you go, my dear, regardless of what schemes you might be concocting!"

Charity lifted a brow, and retorted, "And I should dearly like to see just how you intend to stop me. I will not be subject to you as my aunt feels I ought. I will not be your slave, William. I will have my own life, my own interests. I will follow my own heart and conscience, wherever that may lead. And I certainly will not permit you any say in the matter whatsoever!"

Tightening the arm about her waist ever so slightly, he smiled at her and in a low voice as he leaned near her, said, "It is not your soul I wish to possess, nor your mind, for I admire your mettle, m'dear. But it is your kisses I intend to keep with me always and you have given me sufficient cause to believe you would not be averse to such an arrangement."

Charity, though lifting her chin slightly, spoke in a breathy quality that satisfied William completely as she said, "And you are a coxcomb if you think I would marry simply for the way a man conducts his flirtations!"

"Then a coxcomb I shall be, and gladly," he rejoindered. "For I value your lips more perhaps than you do mine and only wish of the moment that we were alone that I might move you from your stubborn opinions!"

And when she lowered her gaze from his, staring at his waistcoat in some confusion, he wondered just what he could do to win her love. He might tease her about his kisses, but he knew enough of her that if she was not fully persuaded that she loved him, then there would be no wedding, no black silky hair dressed with a crown of orange blossoms.

Relaxing his hold upon her hand, he decided that he would launch a little campaign of his own, though how, he did not know precisely. Remembering, however, the gossip about a *Lady of Quality* who was to dance *Le Papillon* on the stage at Drury Lane, he thought, given her own abilities, she might be greatly diverted by seeing the performance. Of course just such an evening as he had in mind would also lend itself to his current desire to win her heart.

He asked her if she would join him at the theater, "For I have been given to understand that a ballerina of great skill and artistry is come to London to show us the latest mode of ballet from Paris. I believe it is called the *ballet romantique*. Are you familiar with it, for you were in France so recently?"

William watched an inexplicable blush again darken her cheeks as she said, "Yes, I am quite familiar with the dance. Unfortunately, I will be away from London for one or two days, because my poor companion's mother is quite ill, though expected to recover fully. And my dear Furney, who as you know is like a sister to me, wished for me to attend her in Tunbridge Wells on Saturday evening."

How easily now the whiskers glided from her tongue, almost as smoothly as the flowing movements of the waltz.

William did not offer her the usual condolences at first, for, from the moment she said she would be leaving London, an image rose in his mind that was at once so agreeable that he could do little else but give it full consideration for several seconds. Should he do it, he wondered? Would Charity then guess the truth if he were to waylay her carriage dressed as The Gentleman? And what would she think of him were she to know the truth? And a familiar and quite rebellious sensation began overtaking him, a certain excitement that never failed to cause the blood to rise within him.

After expressing his sympathy for Miss Pelham-Furneux in this distressing time for her, he did not hesitate to ask, "And do any number of people know that you are planning to leave London?"

She nodded but tilted her head slightly at him as she asked, "I find that a singularly odd question. Whyever do you ask?"

"Only that in my opinion you run the great risk of having the highwayman accost you again for I certainly hold to the theory that he is a gentleman of the *ton*. Perhaps even one here this evening! Do you think you ought to inform Bow Street of your intention to leave the metropolis?"

Charity was uncertain how to answer him, for if she did tell Bow Street of her plans to leave London, naturally what would follow would be Mr. Stokes's rather piercing questions undoubtedly with regard to which route she would take to Tunbridge Wells, at what hour she meant to depart, and even perhaps a suggestion that one of the runners accompany her! And she could very well imagine that Bow Street would find it suspicious that instead of leaving London, she went to the City and remained there for two days. She shuddered at the mere thought of having this happen, and having her own schemes uncovered before ever they were accomplished, she swallowed very hard searching for the right words to turn William's suggestion off lightly. And after a moment, she knew precisely what to say.

Affecting an air of disinterest, she said, "I hardly think that would be necessary for now that I consider the matter, the highwayman would not dare to accost the future Countess of Redbourne!"

"So the cat has claws! And if you don't mind my saying so, they are rather sharp indeed! However, what you say contains some sense. But if I find The Gentleman has importuned you again, I shall seek him out myself and drag him to the Magistrate's Court tied behind a cart and horse!"

Charity simpered as she replied, "Oh, my lord! How very brave you are. Why, I feel so utterly protected and cherished when you speak thusly!"

"Vixen!" he cried softly, enjoying the thrust of her words. "But of the moment I have half a mind to accompany you to Tunbridge Wells myself!"

"No!" Charity cried, too quickly she realized, as William regarded her with a quizzical expression. "That is, I am certain you have a great many things you would prefer to be doing, William, than performing a task best left consigned to my maid."

"On the contrary!" he cried. "For if we could but leave your maid somewhere upon the road, I should think such a service as escorting you to Kent could be quite full of enough entertainment to satisfy me completely! I should want for no other diversion than to have you to myself for an hour or two!"

Charity gulped, for there it was again, that rather strange inexplicable ability he had to make her heart pitch about like a small boat on a violent sea. "What nonsense!" she responded sharply, but he merely laughed at her as though he knew precisely how she felt.

Charity sat at the large square table in the morning room, her gaze fixed upon Anne as her cousin, holding her cup of chocolate in both hands, peered at it rather intently. The entire family was gathered about the table, Anne and Penelope sharing one side, while Charity, her aunt, and her uncle, each sat at the remaining three sides. The table was covered in a fine white linen, and they were all partaking of a hearty breakfast of thinly sliced ham, freshly baked apricot tarts, coffee, toast and butter, little muffins stuffed with nuts and raisins, a platter of assorted fruits, and a very sweet, delectable chocolate.

Anne was enjoying her third steaming cup of the rich chocolate, and Charity watched mystified as her cousin proceeded to lift the cup toward the ceiling, almost in a ceremonial manner, as she said, "And I still cannot imagine how it could possibly be done without making a great mess the moment one tried to take a sip of the wine."

Everyone looked at Anne upon these words, several pairs of sleepy eyes blinking at the confused youngest daughter of the house. Finally Lady Datchworth, whose own features were considerably pinched, spoke in a somewhat hoarse voice, "Anne, whatever are you droning on about?"

"Why Byron, of course!" Anne exclaimed, turning toward her Mama, her blue eyes wide.

Lady Datchworth sighed deeply. "And what an exasperating child you are this morning! What on earth do you mean *Byron, of course!*"

"Drinking wine from skulls! For I have been sitting here for the longest time trying to determine how he accomplished the task, for you know it is rumored widely that he did so. But however did he do it?" And she turned her cup of chocolate around and around. "Do but consider, for instance, the various openings in a skull through which the wine could leak all over one's clothes!"

The groans about the table were universal and Charity chuckled softly. For herself, she was grateful that Anne had spoken of something so completely absurd, for her own nerves were stretched very thin this morning and she was afraid that she would betray herself by some thoughtless word or gesture.

However, from the moment she sat down to table with her aunt and uncle and cousins, Charity knew it would be extremely unlikely that they would notice anything amiss. Each of them, as it happened, appeared quite absorbed with their own problems. Lady Datchworth, for instance, had fixed her attention firmly upon her husband, watching him almost constantly, and even pouring coffee directly onto the tablecovers, having missed her own cup entirely because she was scrutinizing her husband's face. She laughed at being so clumsy, but even her laughter had a false gaiety to it, and her fingers trembled when she again poured her coffee.

As for Lord Datchworth, Charity thought he was conspicuously quiet, for he was usually the very first to twit the ladies about how many dances they had stood up for—a silly ritual that, while he had begun doing so when his daughters were first come out, he had continued with them even though Penelope was nearly thirty years old.

But not this morning. He sat eating his ham slowly, his shoulders hunched slightly forward, as though by this posture he meant to keep his heart to himself. And even when Charity asked him what performance he saw at Drury Lane, a question which brought all the ladies' attention to settle upon Lord Datchworth, he merely shrugged. "I can't for the life of me recall the name of it! The entire performance was exceedingly dull save for the moments when the opera-dancers would grace the stage, which for my taste was not frequent enough!"

And this response brooked no further questions as Lady Datchworth gasped, and the cousins regarded one another with expressions of astonishment. Even Charity felt her cheeks burning slightly with this blatant reference to his supposed motives for visiting the theater!

Conversation, needless to say, languished for some few minutes, and Charity pushed a small piece of ham about on her plate. A faint nervous twinge again twisted her stomach ever so slightly, and she found it impossible to bring the ham to her lips. Instead, she put her fork down and took a small sip of her own chocolate, and let out a very long breath of air in hopes somehow of calming her nervous anticipation of the performance that would very soon be upon her.

She turned to Anne, and meant to ask her how she enjoyed the ball of the evening before, but the question died upon her lips as she saw the expression on her cousin's face. Anne was staring into her cup which now sat in front of her, but her expression had grown quite hard, her blue eyes intense, her usually sweet and gentle mouth drawn into a compressed line, a frown creasing her brow.

Apparently having given enough thought to the difficulties of drinking wine from skulls, Anne seemed to have fallen into a brown study as she stirred her chocolate and sighed. Charity was about to ask her if she was feeling quite well, when Anne suddenly lifted her chin in a quite determined fashion. Charity knew something of import was about to happen, for Anne's career had been marked solely by her compliant temperament as she did the bidding of her sister, and her mama and papa. That Anne meant now to rebel against these strong authorities in her life was clearly evident.

Charity watched her swallow very hard, even licking her lips slightly as she said, "Papa, I have something to ask of you and I hope you will give it some consideration."

The mood at the table shifted abruptly and Charity

realized that a subject was being introduced that was all too familiar to the members of the family. Anne took a deep breath and blurted out, "George and I are to be married!"

Penelope rolled her eyes, Lady Datchworth seemed quite irritated as though it was a ridiculous comment, and Lord Datchworth huffed out a breath of air as he responded, "But why do you address the matter to me! You know that I have nothing to say in this, that your mother has already told you her reasons for not wishing for this union for you and I refuse to become involved! Your mother and I agreed long ago that you and Penelope, as well as your respective futures, were her particular charge!" He seemed quite distressed as he regarded his daughter and jerked his head slightly as though his neckcloth had suddenly bitten into him.

Charity watched large tears well up into her cousin's eyes, and remembered how very intently upon the evening before, Anne and George had been conversing. And how was it, Charity wondered, that she had never guessed that Anne's own family—her mother and of course her sister— was in such opposition to her marriage to Mr. Meesden. For it simply never occurred to Charity that her aunt or Penelope would want anything more for Anne than that which would bring her the greatest happiness.

Lord Datchworth raised his voice slightly, his brow furrowed as he said, "Now don't you become a watering pot, Annie! I won't stand for such nonsense, and certainly not during a meal. It is very bad for the digestion."

Anne lowered her gaze to the cup of chocolate which was no longer steaming, and the tears plopped onto a little muffin that she had pulled to pieces upon her plate. In a quiet voice, she said, "Yes, Papa."

Penelope spoke in her well-modulated voice. "There are so many other more suitable young men for you Anne. Why is it you are so set upon having George? You are being quite stubborn and, if you don't mind for a little sisterly criticism, quite ridiculous! You know Mama does not wish you to marry beneath your station."

"But I love George," Anne returned quietly. "Though I daresay you can know nothing of that for you have never been in love."

Penelope held her hand to her bosom, the familiar lace kerchief trailing from her fingers, as she cast her eyes to her lap and with a slight break in her voice said, "Are you forgetting about John?"

Anne hesitated for a moment, and much to Charity's great surprise, finally blurted out, "I don't believe you loved him, Penelope." Her voice shook as she spoke. "I don't think you've ever been in love in your life, else you would not oppose a match that is perfectly acceptable as you well know—you just don't wish for anyone to be happy since you cannot have what you really want—to be Countess of Redbourne!" And then she immediately regretted her words and cried, "Oh, Pen. I am sorry. I didn't mean it."

Penelope, however, appeared as though she had been struck across the face, for her cheeks burned a fiery red against an oddly pale complexion and she weaved slightly in her seat as she regarded her sister. Finally she breathed, "How dare you! How can you or anyone else presume to know what I feel?"

Anne leaned toward her sister, and placed a hand upon her arm as she said, "But I think to some degree it is true, Pen. You've never allowed yourself to love anyone and Lord Meares is so completely besotted with you."

"I think you've quite said enough, Anne. And I do not hesitate to say that Lord Meares is no concern of yours."

Charity watched this interchange feeling slightly bludgeoned herself, for she was seeing truths that cast a terrible shadow over her knowledge of Penelope—and to some extent therefore, her comprehension of William's intense dislike of her cousin. She waited impatiently for Anne to speak, to see what else the younger sister might say to the elder, for Anne's complexion had grown very pale. Finally, she said, "You place too much importance, surely, upon a man's position in society."

Penelope, who by now had regained her composure, appeared as though she had put Anne's earlier words in a careful box somewhere within her heart, and locked it shut. Regarding her sister with a careful smile, she answered her, "And you place too little value upon a man's connections, wealth, and rank. Mr. Meesden possesses the merest competence and he will not be able to give you the daily comforts you require. You will be locked away in the country, with scarcely any society worthy of your dignity as Lord Datchworth's daughter, to console you during the long summer and winter months. Mr. Meesden, for all his fine and noble intentions, cannot clothe you or give you the sort of shelter you have been accustomed to all your life. Do but think of your home, of Chisley Hall, and you have your answer there!"

"But Penelope," Anne pleaded. "You speak as though he resides in a two-room cottage at the edge of his village, instead of in a fine ancient house. And yes, it may have once been merely a lodge, but I don't need more than that and as for comforts, why, we shall keep all the servants we need. He is very economical, as you might say, and has a great many schemes for improving the rentrolls—he has even spoken to William about it! And besides, all I really want is a house full of children. And I want his children!"

Penelope stared somewhat coldly at her sister and said, "And what an indelicate thing to say. You want his children! Why you sound little better than a farmwife!"

Charity was stunned by all that Penelope had said, and her heart gave a funny little twist. She did not remember Penelope this way at all, but then by the time Penelope was come out, Charity was still a little girl, so that she had never shared a London season with her cousin before. But as she considered for a moment, all that Penelope had said, suddenly bits and pieces of Pen's letters came back to her and Charity realized that very frequently she placed her own biased interpretations on the things her cousin would write. But here she could not misinterpret what Penelope was saying. On an impulse, Charity interrupted the sisters and posed a question to Penelope, "Do you feel then, that I am unworthy of William's offer of marriage?"

Both her aunt and uncle protested the question, but Penelope laughed lightly and said, "You are a female, Charity. It is quite a different matter, for your duty is to marry as high as possible!"

Charity felt quite ill of the moment and even Lady Datchworth said, "Penelope, you can't mean that. Why it all sounds so heartless, so conniving."

Anne turned to her mother and said, "Mama, I love George and I wish to marry him. Will you not give us your blessing?"

Lady Datchworth, whose features had already appeared slightly distressed, now seemed drawn together in sheer misery as she said, "Anne, dearest, I don't know what to say to you. I don't quite agree with your sister, that your aim must be to marry as high as you can, but there is some sense in what she has already said—and this we have discussed several times. And however much you might think that you do not need your pin money and furbelows and fine gowns every season, besides a house in town which I know he cannot provide you, these are the very things that can work strongly to undermine the very best of marriages. You must trust me a little in this. If his prospects were even the smallest portion better than they are, I would not hesitate to confer my blessings. I am sorry. I am not unsympathetic, but my answer is no."

Anne again lowered her gaze to the table, although this time Charity noticed that her eyes were very dry. Her initial sadness seemed to have given way to a certain acceptance and after a moment, she said, "I know that you mean what you say, and I will not press you further, I promise."

Lady Datchworth, quite ignoring every proper dictum that forbade her to do so, reached across Penelope's plate, and held Anne's chin in her hand for a moment. "I am sorry, my dear."

"I know that Mama," Anne said, smiling sweetly upon her parent and with a shake of her gold curls, which were dressed in a mass of delightful tendrils at the crown of her head, she turned to Charity and said cheerfully, "Well, I do apologize most heartily for subjecting you to this, cousin, but tell me, are you all packed for your little excursion to Tunbridge Wells? I only wish that you did not have to miss this evening's entertainment! Can you imagine, A Lady of Quality dancing the ballet!" She giggled. "How utterly exciting!"

Anne laughed again and the table was returned to its former state, though Charity felt the strongest sensation that something more resided behind her cousin's efforts to persuade her mother to permit her marriage to Mr. Meesden than she was letting on. And as she regarded Penelope, who was now sitting very straight in her chair and sipping her coffee slowly, Charity shook her head slightly, still quite shocked at all that Penelope had said. But she did not wish to think about her cousin, or the import of her words. At least not yet. Perhaps when her performance of the evening was over she could give consideration to what she had heard, but for now, a little knot of tension twisted her stomach as thoughts of Drury Lane again invaded her mind. And with a concerted effort, she willed her nervousness to disappear as she took another deep breath, and a sip of her chocolate.

But was it truly possible that she was actually to perform her ballet after so many years of preparation? And how very much deception had already gone into her efforts!

Each morning, since her arrival in London, Charity had disappeared from the townhouse with her maid in tow, pretending that she needed to purchase a great many things in order to refurbish her wardrobe. And while Marie was out collecting gloves, ribbons, bonnets, and muffs, Charity was in Hans Town with Monsieur Bovin, rehearsing, stretching, strengthening her legs, ankles and feet, adjusting her slippers time and again until she felt finally that all was ready. This afternoon, at least, Charity could be at ease with one final rehearsal, not worrying that she must return to the townhouse with the appearance that she had just spent two hours shopping leisurely with her maid.

Lord Datchworth interrupted her thoughts as he addressed her, "And so you are to miss the performance of Mademoiselle Novarre this evening, eh? Everyone is talking about her, wondering who she is. But I chanced to be back stage at Drury Lane last night, and met her!"

"What?" the ladies all cried in unison.

Charity, her heart sitting in her throat, nearly overset her cup of chocolate as she cried, "But that is quite impossible!" And all eyes turned toward her.

Lady Datchworth asked with something of a hopeful smile, "And how is that, my dear?"

Charity set her cup of chocolate down on the table, for her hands had begun trembling and she placed them quickly upon her lap, clutching them together as though her very existence depended upon doing so. Laughing lightly, she said, "I suppose what I meant to say was that Mademoiselle has been so very secretive thus far—guarding her identity so carefully—that I suppose I merely did not credit that she would even attend the theater beforetimes. But now that I think on it, I suppose it would be quite logical for her to do so." And turning to Lord Datchworth, she cried, "Oh, do tell us, Uncle! What was she like? Was she very tall, and was she quite pretty?"

As everyone's attention reverted to Lord Datchworth, Charity took a deep breath and pretended great interest as the viscount said, "She wore a mask, for you were very correct in thinking that she was fearful of revealing her identity to anyone. But I did have the opportunity of speaking with her and I found her quite amiable. And as for her presence in the theater, she told me that she had come for the strict purpose of observing the workings behind the stage so that she might be a trifle more comfortable in her performance."

Charity regarded her uncle with no small degree of wonder, for his words made perfect sense as both Anne and Penelope nodded to him. And if she were not Mademoiselle Novarre herself, she would have believed him as much as her aunt obviously did, for Lady Datchworth rose abruptly from her chair, her hand pressed to her mouth as she repressed a little sob, and quickly left the room.

Lord Datchworth's gaze, quite filled with a heart-rending sadness, followed his wife's form as she disappeared into the hallway, her demi-train catching slightly upon a rough portion of the planked floor.

Chapter Fourteen

At one o'clock in the afternoon William sat within his town coach, which was pulled up before his house in Berkeley Square, and tapped his cane impatiently upon the floor of the carriage. A sense of great excitement worked strongly within him as it always did when he was about to don the costume of The Gentleman. This was his own revolt against his society, his own private little rebellion. And though he had already decided—particularly in the face of Bow Street's increased interest in the highwayman's activities—that he would no longer perform this rather silly masquerade, he could not resist the impulse of accosting his bride-to-be at least once more in the guise of The Gentleman.

Beside his legs sat an oversized leather valise, which contained his entire costume and every now and then he struck the battered piece of baggage with his cane, simply for good measure. He was in very high spirits and could hardly wait to see the expression upon Charity's face when he waylaid her carriage. He struck the valise again, trying to release some of the restrained energy that caused his every muscle to feel cramped and tense, but to little avail. He was anxious to be going. And where the devil was Jack anyway?

He was waiting for his servant to return from Grosvenor Square whither he had sent him to spy upon Charity in order to determine the precise hour of her departure. At Lady Dunford's ball, he had extracted from her that she intended to depart at noon, but knowing the feminine propensity for tardiness as he did, he wanted to ascertain for himself precisely when Charity's post chaise would actually pull away from Lady Datchworth's townhouse.

By quarter after one, he had every expectation of seeing his groom appear around the corner of the street at any moment. But by half past one, however, William had grown quite concerned that something had gone amiss. The horses were fidgeting in their harness, and he ordered the carriage to take a turn about one or two of the streets adjacent to Berkeley Square. The whole while, as the matched black horses trotted easily along the streets, the earl felt slightly panicked that his groom would return to Berkeley Square and, not finding William in front of his townhouse, would return to the mews and so miss him entirely. But this he dismissed as ridiculous, for the groom was extremely efficient and would no more fail to wait in the entrance hall for him than he would to properly brush and feed the horses after a day's outing. Jack was a good man, greatly to be relied upon which was why he had chosen him to assist in The Gentleman's exploits. But where the devil was he!

By two o'clock, William quit the carriage feeling decidedly foolish, and returned to his office upon the lower level of his townhouse. There he sat upon his well-worn and exceedingly comfortable dark green leather chair, and rebelliously put his booted feet upon the inlaid walnut desk in front of him. To the side of the desk resided a globe of the world, notorious for refusing to spin properly. The small square chamber fronted the street, and dark green velvet drapes hung beside the window. The sky grew dark and then light in great fits as large clouds moved rapidly over the metropolis, apparently disinclined to cleanse the city of its growing haze of sooty air. Every once in a while, William would reach over to the globe and try to give it a spin, but the globe refused to budge.

By half past two, William still sat in his chair only this time, his feet were on the floor, his elbows on his knees as he bent over trying to spin the globe of the world, one hand propping up his chin. Where the devil was Jack? And when a traitorous clock upon the mantel toned the half hour, William thrust out his foot, giving the globe a hard kick. Continents breezed by in rapid succession as the infuriating globe became unstuck.

Hearing a commotion in the entrance hall, William rose abruptly to his feet, as a rapping sounded upon the door. Bidding the butler to enter, Tebworth, affectionately known as Tebs, and now bent and rheumy-eyed with age, opened the door slowly. William, half-circling behind the desk, fully expected to see his groom behind the butler. Instead, Tebworth bowed politely to William and said, "Begging your pardon, m'lord, but there is a gentleman here who wishes a few words with you—a Mr. Stokes."

William frowned, trying to recall the name as he retraced his steps back to his chair and sat down. "Stokes?" he queried. "Upon what manner of business?"

"He calls himself a runner, which I take it to mean he refers to Bow Street."

William remembered the unattractive man who regarded everyone and everything with a piercing stare, and he started slightly in his seat. For what a moment at which to have Bow Street call upon him, when William fully intended to don the costume of the highwayman!

After considering the matter for a moment, he nodded for his butler to show the runner in and within a matter of seconds, Mr. Stokes, the scar upon his cheek quite red, walked briskly into the room, a scowl upon his face.

"I've come on a matter of grave import, m'lord, and I'll

come straight to the point. We've reason to believe Hugh Bramfield is the man we're after and Lord Datchworth to whom I was just speaking not an hour ago, told me to come directly here for he says Mr. Bramfield is a particular friend of yours."

William was exceedingly grateful that he had already been informed of this news, otherwise he did not know precisely how he might have reacted or whether or not he would have betrayed himself. As it was, he begged Mr. Stokes to be seated, gesturing to a wooden chair near the desk. The runner nodded several times, thanked the earl in a clipped fashion, but made it clear that he kept his wits about him by always remaining on his feet. "You never know when a suspect will try and escape once he's been flushed out, as you might say."

"I wish to thank you for bringing your suspicions to my attention," William said. He wanted a moment to think before he said anything further to the runner and he moved away from the desk, which was situated opposite the door, and walked slowly toward the window. The office was not decorated on a grand scale, for William had little need of fineries, and save for two comfortable wing chairs flanking the fireplace the only other piece of furniture in the room was a curved side table, decorated with a beautiful marquetry, that stood in front of the window. Leaning over the side table slightly, William looked out upon the flags, searching for any sign of his groom. And after considering just how to respond to the runner's accusation regarding Hugh, he decided that a moderate course was best, devoid of shocked denials or outrage and merely responded, "But I wish to assure you that Hugh could not possibly be The Gentleman. I am certain of it."

The runner rubbed a finger alongside his wide, flat nose and said, "The innkeeper reported that Mr. Bramfield had entered the parlor but a few minutes before yer lordship, his face red from riding hard, and seemingly quite distressed. And two days ago we found this mask in the shrubbery near the inn."

William turned toward the runner and immediately saw the black half-mask, his own mask, the mask he had worn to kiss Charity, and the mask he had so carelessly tossed away. He had an odd feeling looking at it, the black silk appearing a little mud-stained, that Nemesis had brought it here purposefully to haunt him.

Glancing out the window again, and still seeing no sign of Jack, he returned to his desk and sat down. Folding his hands atop the polished walnut desktop, William said, "You have no clear proof of his involvement in such a ridiculous enterprise as kissing and robbing young ladies."

"He has a strong motive, however, which is a fact I uncovered during my investigations—he's under the hatches as many of his friends will testify." And pulling his notes from the pocket of his black coat, he scanned his scribblings in a quick manner and said, "A Mr. Tewin, in particular, was more than happy to be of assistance."

"Mr. Tewin is always generous," William responded dryly. "Well, you seem fully persuaded that he is guilty. Do you mean to arrest him?"

"Nay. I haven't enough evidence to do nought but make a fool out of myself, but I mean to find the proof I need. And you might be wishful of speaking with him yourself, in case he should desire to make a clean breast of it. The courts always take a kindly eye to such confessions, not to mention that the crime is more a social one than anything else—for there's an orphanage near Cheapside that gave me a list of The Gentleman's contributions and though it were a matter kept strictly in confidence, each of the ladies who had been a victim of this kissing bandit was given a sort of honorarium. Their names have been inscribed in a book of donations, along with the sums contributed. After speaking with all the ladies in that book, I found that The Gentleman had been quite honest with each of them, for the proper sums was listed next to the proper names. I hardly call it a crime worth a trip to Tyburn Tree. However, this 'ere highwayman has upset many young ladies and their parents—and having two girls of my own, a man running wild about the countryside and kissing innocent maids is something I don't harken to, if you see what I mean."

A man's voice was heard in the entrance hall and William recognized it as belonging to Jack. Glancing at the clock, he could scarcely credit that it was almost three o'clock. And frowning slightly, he didn't think it at all likely that Charity would have postponed her journey for three full hours. However, if he and Jack were to reach an appropriate interception point in time, they would have to leave immediately. Rising to his feet, he said, "Well, I know you've mistaken your man, though I have no means of proving that either. However, I can see that you are doing everything you can to end this dastardly business, and I trust if you have anything further to report, you'll come to me first!"

Mr. Stokes nodded, his eyes narrowed slightly. "I've worked on every manner of crime, from thievery to murder, and I always know when I'm close to the criminal, and that's the sense I have of it now. And I can see by the hard cast to your daylights that you don't care for hearing what I have to say, but I'll tell you again, the man I'm after was in The White Swan Inn on the night of the attempted theft, and somehow or another I'll prove the identity of The Gentleman."

William inclined his head to the man, a little surprised at his doggedness. Moving toward the door, he responded noncommittally, "And I am certain you will. But I do have some rather pressing business of my own to attend to, so if you do not mind terribly much I will bid you good-day."

And he opened the door, holding it wide for the runner.

Mr. Stokes passed slowly through the doorway, turning to regard William in his piercing manner one last time, and paused to bow before he continued into the entrance hall.

Jack, his hat in hand, and a rather strained appearance to his brown eyes, hung back until the runner had quit the house. William then beckoned him into the library, and could see by the sweat upon his brow, and the dirt on his woolen stockings and knee breeches, that he'd been riding hard.

William, tensing suddenly, had barely gotten the door shut behind him when he cried, "What news? Good God man, where have you been? Did she just now depart? We had best hurry!"

"M'lord," Jack began, "there t'ain't no use!"

"Why? Did your horse cast a shoe or run lame? What happened?"

"Miss Holwell didn't go to Tunbridge Wells."

William stared at the young man in disbelief. Finally, he laughed. "What do you mean, she did not go? Of course she went. She's visiting her cousin in Tunbridge Wells. She said as much last night."

Jack heaved a sigh and ran the sleeve of his coat over his dripping forehead as he said, "I did as you bade me. I went to Grosvenor Square and waited near Bruton Street, inconspicuous-like. And I seen her get into a post chaise and pair, though the horses weren't nought to speak of, being quite short of bone—regular gluepots, if you see what I mean—but then the post chaise departs, just as it ought, toward Bruton Street. I'm waiting on the other side of the street, and I mount my horse, and I am preparing to return to Berkeley Square when I thinks to meself, maybe I should follow her a ways, just to be sure. I don't know why, but, I follows the post chaise and the next thing I know, she were in Hans Town!"

"Hans Town! Why, whatever for? Why would she go there? Does she even know anyone there?"

"An old man, as it happens. Very thin and bent over just a little. I didn't see him at first, in fact, I waited there for almost two hours until she come out. That was when I seen the old man."

William frowned, casting about in his mind for anyone of that description. An old man. Charity had no relatives to speak of, save the Datchworths, and as far as he knew, no one in Hans Town with whom she was acquainted. And the only elderly man of her acquaintance was someone from Paris—Penelope once said that the old dancing master that used to reside with the Holwells in Hertfordshire, a refugee of the French Revolution, was mentioned quite frequently in Charity's letters. The dancing master would be quite old by now, but Charity had not even mentioned him since she returned to London. Could he be residing now in Hans Town? "What happened next? You say she did not leave London? But are you sure?"

"Miss Holwell traveled to the City, where I last seen her entering a house. I went round to the servants' entrance and found that a lady by the name of Miss Pelham-Furneux had hired the rooms for the season."

William felt utterly confused, as he finally left his station by the door. Charity had lied to him, then, lied to her family! But to what purpose? He moved to the desk and regarded the errant globe and on an impulse set it spinning. How perfectly it moved now. One hard kick and the world was set to rights! He felt as though he had just been kicked though he wasn't certain that he had completely understood the message. And finally it hit him with the force of a gale wind. Looking sharply at his groom, he scowled at him and cried, "Were these rooms perchance anywhere near the Drury Lane Theatre?"

Jack at first seemed a little surprised, but after a moment began nodding his head slowly. "Yes, I suppose you might say that they are. A couple of streets only, yes. *Oh, sir!*" he cried suddenly. "Miss Holwell is not The Butterfly Lady, is she?"

William nodded his head, and yet still could not believe it was true. "Unfortunately, I believe she is to dance *Le Papillon.* I am almost certain of it."

Jack clicked his tongue. "She oughtn't to do that, m'lord. The *hot ton,* won't like it!"

William could not help but laugh at Jack's twisting of the French words, as he answered readily, "No, the *hot ton* won't like it at all. Charity, my little minx, what have you done?"

Jack then smiled at him quite broadly and said, "She's a bit like you are, ain't she, m'lord. I mean, you oughtn't to be The Gentleman and she oughtn't to be The Butterfly. There's a bit of poetry in that. But what will you do when all them gentlemen rush backstage to offer her the *cart blanchey.*"

William laughed again. "Your French accent, my good Jack, leaves a great deal to be desired! But now that you mention it, perhaps I ought to be the first one to do so!"

"My lord!" Jack cried, much horrified. "How can you speak in that manner about a female what will soon be your wife?"

And as Jack spoke these words, William was struck with the knowledge that if Charity had carried this scheme to the point of actually having auditioned for and winning a place among the cast at Drury Lane, then she must have some quite definite ambitions upon the stage. And a spark of jealousy burned suddenly in his heart, for while he felt perfectly capable of wooing her away from any man who might possibly turn her head, how could he ever compete with ambitions so great that she was willing to risk her position in society forever in order to fulfill her desires!

Chapter Fifteen

William regarded his beloved parent, her white hair drawn regally atop her head, her hazel eyes almost laughing as Finch carefully placed a diamond necklace about her throat. He loved her very much and in a softened voice, said, "Mama, are you certain you wish to attend the theater? Will you be all right?"

Lady Redbourne reached her hand toward her son, and he grasped it lightly as she said, "You made a tremendous fuss, Will, so much so that I felt I ought to attend you this evening at the Theatre Royal. Are you now going to pretend that you would permit me to remain here at home this evening?" She was seated before her dressing table, reclining upon several pillows, her arms supported by padded armrests. The lines about her eyes were deep and pain-riddled, but the laughter remained.

William knelt beside the chair, his mother's perfume familiar from childhood, a faint lavender fragrance, and he said, "You have but to say the word—"

She smiled at him. "And I assure you that I wish to go and fortunately for you, I am perfectly well this evening! Now, what time is it for I daresay the theater will be uncommonly full of spectators. Imagine! She actually calls herself A Lady of Quality."

William rose to his feet, and still holding the misshapen hand, he looked down at her, frowning slightly and said, "Mama, she *is* a Lady of Quality."

Lady Redbourne heard a funny note in her son's voice and glanced up at him sharply. "William, you have been behaving very oddly today. And I don't think I quite understand you. First you positively beg me to join you at the theater and now you look at me as though I ought to prepare myself for something quite dreadful. What are you about?"

William shifted his gaze toward his mother's maid and bade her leave them alone for a few minutes. And when the door had shut behind her, he looked down at his mama and said, "Charity is Mademoiselle Novarre."

The Viscount Meares was a tall, stately man of forty years, who had waited a very long time to select the female he wished to preside over his family's great properties in Wiltshire. He was considered a silent man amongst the *ton*, keeping his own counsel, and rarely making his opinions known except when he had had quite enough of whatever foolishness was going forward. Only then would he intervene and set everything to rights. He managed his life with great care, his needs were simple—the most important of the moment being that he felt it was time to set up his nursery—and in general he permitted events to work themselves out in whatever manner they intended to. He only exerted himself when his comforts were threatened or his goals thwarted.

Of the moment, he was immensely satisfied at the progress he was making with Penelope Ware. She was in every respect the perfect wife for him, particularly since they shared similar tastes—a very pure enjoyment of the privileges of rank unaffected by matters of conscience, a desire for life to be very tidy, and an unerring eye for what was truly tasteful. He glanced at Penelope now who was seated next to him in the very expensive box he had purchased for the season, to the left of the stage. His purpose in hiring the box was strictly to display before the *haut ton* Penelope's beauty and elegance. Her hair was impeccable, and always as he wished it to be, never a single wispy ringlet out of place. And as for her gown, she was dressed in white satin—such a *hopeful* gown, he thought smiling at his own wit—and he wondered if tonight he ought to broach the subject of their marriage. For she would marry him—he was determined upon that score, even if he had to expose Redbourne's identity as The Gentleman in order to do so.

He placed his arm upon the back of her chair and leaning very near her, he whispered, "You are by far the loveliest creature here this evening, my dear." She turned and smiled upon him, acknowledging the compliment with just the correct measure of grace as she inclined her head to him. Sliding his hand back, he purposefully touched the exposed part of her arm and saw the gooseflesh prickle her skin. A slight flush suffused her cheeks and he was satisfied. For some time now he had wanted to kiss her to see if he was correct in his assessment of a certain latent passion that resided beneath her sculpted image.

Turning to Lord Datchworth he asked him several questions about the current bread riots rampant in the West Country and whether or not he felt the Corn Laws ought to be repealed. They chatted for several minutes, Lady Datchworth smiling upon him in that fashion in which mothers always smiled upon the suitors of their choice. After Lord Datchworth had expressed his opinions fully, Lord Meares turned toward Anne, who was sitting just behind her Mama, her blue eyes darting nervously over the crowds below the box, and he recounted a rather silly anecdote to her. Anne giggled but her amusement became replaced by a rather serious expression and he repressed the smallest sigh for he greatly feared that she would soon be on her way to Gretna Green if Lady Datchworth did not immediately plan a wedding at St. James.

The orchestra began tuning their instruments, and he returned his attention to Penelope. The fact was, he didn't care very much for Anne—she was by far too high in the flesh to ever have the least elegance of manner or person.

The theater was full to overflowing with several dandies in the pit arguing ferociously as they minced back and forth displaying their latest costumes. He exchanged the smallest lift of a brow with Penelope at a particularly absurd young coxcomb whose hair was curled and pomaded. He was dressed all in satin, his coat padded as though he had a full bosom, a brilliant pink waistcoat glimmering below a shortened coat, and extremely close-fitting white breeches, that, when Lord Meares lifted a small telescope to regard the dandy, revealed two dark smudges upon each knee. Diamonds glittered upon the sleeves of his coat in the shape of—Good God!—a butterfly. The young gentleman was clearly a Pink of the *Ton* of no mean order.

"Do but look, Penelope," he said, as he gestured toward the dandy. "He wears his diamonds upon his sleeve in the shape of a butterfly—Mademoiselle Novarre ought to be immensely gratified at such an encomium!"

He expected to hear the appropriate response—a delicate snigger—but his beloved had raised her lorgnette to her eyes, her attention fixed upon some object directly across the theater, in a corresponding box. Following the direction of Penelope's gaze, he saw to his extreme irritation that Redbourne had just entered the box carrying a frail, elderly woman who must have been his invalid mama. Why of all the absurd starts, to have actually brought the sickly woman to view the latest scandal in progress. Whatever was Redbourne thinking? He said as much to Penelope, and was surprised when she turned to give him a somewhat blank stare.

Penelope regarded Lord Meares thinking that he was not of the moment quite as intelligent as he generally was. Did no one see what she saw? Did no one but William know the truth? And how was it she wondered, that even Redbourne had guessed it?

She was angry and for reasons she could not even express. Actually, she should have been content with the truth, with her own knowledge that Charity was indeed none other than the infamous Mademoiselle Novarre, for surely William would never consent to accept her as his wife now! The crowded boxes and aisles, the seats overflowing with so many loud and raucous persons, the inquiring expression upon Lord Meares' face, all began buzzing in her head, causing her the worst agony. She hated her cousin in this moment, that Charity had actually risked exposing the Datchworth consequence to the vulgar whisperings of the masses. And what would happen to them all once the truth were known generally— her cousin, an opera-dancer, a disgusting little trollop! And then a twisted sort of peace descended upon her, for she could set aside her consequence if the prize were something sweeter still than preserving one's dignity—the delicate savor of revenge, for instance—William would be twice hurt by an unmasking at Drury Lane!

Lord Meares regarded Penelope steadily, and said, "Have I offended you, my dear, for you seem uncommonly angry with me."

Penelope opened her fan slowly and began wafting it across her features. She systematically rid herself of the anger that had surfaced upon seeing William arrive with his mama in tow, and said, "Forgive me, my lord. It is I who have offended by my inattentiveness and no, of course I am not angry. Now what is it you were saying?"

"Nothing of consequence, my dear," he said with a slight expression of censure in his eyes. And leaning quite close to her, still holding her gaze, he added, "But don't you think it is time that you set aside your obsession with Redbourne?"

Penelope felt her cheeks darken, though she was not so much embarrassed as she was indignant that he would broach such a subject with her. Smiling politely, she asked him if he thought perchance it would rain.

He did not respond to her question, but rather inclined his head slightly as though he understood her perfectly.

By now any number of people had witnessed the extraordinary appearance of Lady Redbourne and before the curtains parted her box was full of well-wishers, exclaiming over her good looks and even Lady Datchworth rose in her seat, apparently intending to visit the dowager's box. But the moment she had gained her feet, the overture to *Don Giovanni* began and the viscountess reseated herself immediately. The crowd settled down to a faint roar, the curtains parted slowly, and measure by measure the opera took command of the frenetic crowd.

Charity heard the music from the darkened netherland of the busy, at some times calamitous, but always fascinating world of the theater backstage during a performance. Nerves were taut, tempers sharp, and the *corps de ballet*, fearful of tripping on some prop and damaging a limb for the remainder of the season, snapped at one another in harsh whispers. She waited in a cramped dressing room, the only place left to her where she might have complete privacy with Monsieur Bovin and Furney to support her. She was dressed in her gauzy tutu that hung to her ankles and upon which had been sewn, for the evening's performance, hundreds of paste diamonds; she would positively glitter behind the footlights. Her ballet slippers were tied to perfection, she was confident in that, and the little wings attached to the back of her costume also glittered with paste diamonds and felt secure.

However, the faint nervous twinges of the morning had become winged creatures that performed acrobatics incessantly in her stomach, but Monsieur Bovin spoke quietly to her about the dance she would be performing, that she was to think about the same things that had flittered through her mind when she had first auditioned for the directors and that she would be magnificent—he knew it! She was as prepared as she would ever be, her black hair powdered and her pearl embroidered mask dangling with ribbons and tied securely about her head. But what if the audience despised her, or worse, what if she fell and their laughter engulfed her?

Monsieur Bovin saw her distress and immediately embraced her saying that when she crossed the stage, even if the audience continued to call to one another loudly during her performance, as they were wont to do, that she was to dance for her parents alone, for their memory, and most particularly for her mama's love of the ballet.

Charity felt tears burn her eyes, but his words were the right ones. Her fears vanished in that moment and a rapping on the door was followed by a shouting voice that bade her move to her position for the first act was almost over and the *divertissement* of *Le Papillon* was about to begin.

The very air whirled about her in a stinging of excitement as Charity stood in front of a nearly crazed audience upon the stage at the Theater Royal in Drury Lane. Her fingers were frozen with fear, and the sounds of the audience gasping and shushing one another, speaking unkindnesses aloud, at first disrupted her every thought. But her gaze caught that of William's in a box upon her left, and his softened smile brought Hertfordshire racing back to her in a rush, just as Monsieur Bovin had wished it to, and all that Charity heard in her mind, as the orchestra commenced the slow, relentless movement from Mozart's Concerto in C for flute, harp and orchestra, was her mother's voice, saying, "Charity, you ought to dance the ballet."

The crowds before her disappeared as the pulsing quality of the *andantino* began pouring into the theater. An imaginary butterfly again appeared before Charity, just as it had during her audition. Dazzling blue wings fluttered before her as she began pursuing the butterfly, dancing *sur les pointes,* very high in the air, her limbs extended in long, elegant lines, the grace of her skirts floating about her ankles, weaving a spell of enchantment. In her every movement, she was a butterfly, metamorphosing before the footlights, the glitter of her skirts becoming an ethereal radiance that caused the spectators to sigh with wonder.

She was beyond the earth now, giving herself to every insistent note that flowed from the orchestra, the music surrounding her and invading her soul. Her world grew misty as the butterfly began chasing her, and she tossed her head, pirouetting, leaping, every emotion streaming through her emanating from the *andantino*. The butterfly lit upon her shoulder, then was immediately off again as she trailed after it, on half-points, then full-points, the creature fluttering just beyond her reach, and darting off in yet another direction. And only when she had given up pursuit, and her feet slowed, her movements gentler, easier as the music drew to a soft conclusion, did the butterfly return. She sank to the floor with a single hand upraised as the butterfly lit gently upon her fingers.

For the longest moment, Charity remained in that position, her heart full, her breath growing easier as each second passed, the butterfly upon her hand slowly disappearing, causing tears to form in her eyes. She did not know at precisely what moment her mind withdrew completely from the dance and reshaped itself before the audience, but she was struck by the complete silence of the theater. She turned to regard the audience, uncertain at first what to do, for there was not a single sound to be heard from a mass of people that usually writhed with the words that flowed from mouth to ear.

She was overwhelmed by the silence, feeling at first that she must have disappointed them greatly, and a sensation of grief struck her that she had failed so miserably. However, she refused to be daunted by this thought and rose to her feet, facing the audience squarely, as she then sank into a deep curtsy, the gauze of her tutu in a graceful circle about her. She remained there for several seconds, her head bowed, and just as she was rising to her feet, a wave of applause crashed upon her with such force that a tremendous dizziness assailed her and she stepped backward, almost stumbling for the force of it. The theater echoed with cries of wonder and approval, and flowers appeared at her feet, dozens of them. She began picking up both single roses as well as several large, fragrant bouquets and she found the hand which cradled the flowers securely was soon covered with droplets of water—her tears. She had not realized, until she felt the moisture on her hand that she was weeping.

The roar from the audience did not subside for several minutes, and after she had curtsied for the third time, she slowly walked from the stage to be greeted by the *corps de ballet* with tears and embraces until she could bear no more and ran to the dressing room where she fell into Furney's arms and sobbed for some time to come.

After she had finally composed herself, and could laugh at having become a watering pot, she turned to her dancing master, who was shaking his head in wonder.

When he could speak at last, his voice cracked ever so

slightly as he said, "You danced with great brilliance. Did you hear the applause—it was like thunder! Oh, *cherie*, I am so very proud!"

Charity embraced him, holding him fast and thanking him for this moment of enchantment. "It was so very much like a dream, even now I feel as though I was never really before the audience." And she let out a great huff of air. "And so many flowers, did you see the flowers?" And she whirled around to gesture toward the bouquets full of roses, lavender, tulips, irises, ferns, ivy. Furney, who kept dabbing at her own eyes with a cambric handkerchief, had begun arranging some of the flowers in a large vase, when a knock on the door sounded. Monsieur Bovin opened the door, and a lad of about eleven, who served to run messages to and fro, bade Charity to come to the Green Room. "For there is like to be a crush of people, Mademoiselle Novarre! Already a dozen gents be wishful of speaking with you and the governors want you in the Green Room."

The knowledge that now she was to meet the very public whom she had upon the evening before danced the quadrille, the country dance, and the waltz, nearly caused Charity to faint. And however would she manage to smile at any number of gentlemen, who would no doubt leer at her, and with whom she was already acquainted? And worse! For what if someone recognized her?

Lady Redbourne sat very still beside her son, her gnarled hand resting lightly upon his arm, her gaze still fixed to a spot upon the stage where Charity had stood but a few minutes earlier and upon which rested a single red rose. She was numb with pleasure, excitement, and dread. And with all these various emotions mixed up together, the most she was able to do was shake her head in bewilderment. The theater was alive with chatter and excitement, everyone exclaiming over the extraordinary performance where the ballerina had remained on the tips of her toes nearly throughout the *divertissement. And was it truly Charity?* Lady Redbourne wondered for perhaps the hundredth time. *And how was it possible that she had effected so incredible a performance.* But of course it was Charity, although with her hair powdered and a half-mask covering her face, unless one knew beforehand—ah, what was to become of so talented and remarkable a female? And what did her son think now?

Turning to regard William, she saw that he, too, was in a state of shock, as he murmured, "I have danced with her. I have felt that she excelled in the dance for she floated about the ballroom floor, yet still I never thought, even when I knew the truth, that she could perform so exquisitely!"

He seemed changed, she thought, some part of him torn from his usual moorings and she felt oddly pleased of the moment.

He looked toward her, but his hazel eyes were unblinking and pinched in something very like confusion, as he said, "I just never thought that anything could be quite so beautiful as this, nor that Char—that is that Mademoiselle Novarre could dance as if with *wings upon her feet!"*

Lady Redbourne, now that the shock of the moment began drifting away, suddenly realized how tense her entire body had been, and she leaned back in her seat, rivulets of pain seeping back into her joints. A wave of nausea flowed over her and she swallowed very hard. "William, I think I ought to return home now."

"Mama!" he cried, as he watched her wince. "Are you all right? I shouldn't have brought you here, it was too much for you. Faith!" he added, running a wild hand through his hair. "It was too much for me!"

With some difficulty, Lady Redbourne reached over to

her son, and with a swollen knuckle, swept back a misplaced tangle of his hair, and laughed at him. "Yes! And I have now concluded that she is far too good for you as well!"

"I begin to think you are right," he answered with a funny expression in his eyes. Rising to his feet upon these words, he lifted his Mama gently into his arms, and carried her slowly from the theater.

When the applause had finally broken over Charity's head, Penelope clapped along with everyone else, but in a quiet, almost soundless manner, her lavender gloves making a dull patting sound as she moved her hands together in a mechanical fashion. She continued to stare at the stage in disbelief, at what she had seen, for her cousin was actually quite gifted. And for a moment, at the very end of the little *divertissement,* Penelope had wiped away a single, inexplicable tear. She had never been touched by the ballet before—or by any theater performance as it happened—and in this case she despised the opera-dancers and their notoriety amongst the gentlemen of her acquaintance too much to feel anything more than contempt for the coquettish females who smiled brazenly upon gentlemen of rank and fashion.

But *Le Papillon* was so different. It was elegant, graceful, and full of a quality which was always elusive to Penelope, *pathos.* She had felt something during her cousin's dance, and she was not at all comfortable with the impact of the short *divertissement* upon her own sensibilities—it felt quite vulgar and she began locking these undesirable emotions away carefully.

And when she was restored to her usual serene state, more familiar sentiments took hold of her heart. The orchestra was silent, and she could logically consider yet again what had transpired before her. Glancing about the various boxes that lined the rim of the theater, Penelope acknowledged the bows of any number of her acquaintance and she saw that while she had composed herself, many of the gentlemen and ladies present were still exclaiming loudly over the performance, fans whirring madly in an effort to cool excited brows.

William, she noticed, was already leaving with his mother, and she hoped that he had not been so foolish as to risk her health by bringing her to watch Charity perform. He was a cretin, she thought.

Lord Meares watched the earl depart, and with a lift of his brows he was struck with the thought, *So Charity Holwell is Mademoiselle Novarre!* And as he glanced at Penelope who was also regarding Redbourne, he laughed to himself for he found much in the situation that tickled his own sense of humor, for he could see that, were the pot stirred a trifle, events might be brought to a satisfactory conclusion.

"Penelope," he said in a quiet voice. "There's something I think you ought to know." And he laughed to himself yet again.

Penelope regarded the boxes nearest to her, as well as her family, and seeing that they were all fully engaged in discussing Charity's performance quite noisily, she leaned close to him and whispered, "I already know who Mademoiselle Novarre is, if that is what you mean to tell me. And yes, I am quite angry, but you needn't tease me about it."

Lord Meares smiled faintly. "I would not be so cruel, but I already knew that you were fully aware of the ballerina's identity. As it happens, I was referring to Lord Redbourne." And brushing her ear with his lips, he said, "He is The Gentleman."

Penelope leaned away from him and stared at him as though he had just bitten her ear. Immediately she covered her mouth with her fan to prevent any sound, any exclamation of horror, from escaping past her lips—or anything worse for that matter, such as an unladylike curse upon the head of the Earl of Redbourne!

When she had drawn in the reins of her emotions yet again, she placed a tense hand upon his arm, her mouth quite dry as she asked, "But are you certain? How do you know this? Bow Street believes the highwayman to be Hugh Bramfield!"

Lord Meares delighted in this moment as he covered Penelope's hand with his own, feeling that he had drawn her in one more inch, as he replied with a smile, "I would never trust any group of men who referred to themselves as *thief takers*. And in this case, I know them to be sadly mistaken. There was another man at the White Swan Inn the evening Charity was accosted by our notorious highwayman—Lord Redbourne, of course. I have always thought it one of the singular advantages of rank that one is never suspect even when the evidence is overwhelming. Indeed, the whole situation is rather amusing, I think." And he inclined his head toward her, as though begging her to think on it for a moment.

She still gripped his arm, the pressure increasing. "But what proof of significance is it that Redbourne, or Bramfield, for that matter, was at the inn the evening Charity was attacked?"

"Penelope," he said quietly, "do but think. Who was the very first person to be attacked and robbed by The Gentleman?"

"You know very well who—I was!"

He inclined his head again. And when she shook her head in response, appearing bewildered and impatient, he sighed. "And what gentleman, though I am loath to speak of it, has always treated your every obsequious act to win his admiration with nothing short of contempt?"

Penelope lowered the fan to her lap, her mouth slightly agape. She felt her stomach turn over and she released his arm, though he continued to hold her hand. "It isn't true!" she cried. "It cannot be true."

"And what gentleman is it that is just bold enough, just rebellious enough in his thoughts and actions to perform so absurd a charade? Why, I heard only a few hours ago at Hyde that Redbourne had actually thrown a young man bodily from Lady Dunford's townhouse last night! Would not this sort of man be capable of sporting a curling black wig, a mask, and avenging his belief that society is full of grasping, hypocritical females who only want his title?"

She lifted her chin to him, her brown eyes black with hate that he had held such a mirror up to her.

He was enjoying himself hugely as he continued, "As it happens, I was playing at piquet with Hugh Bramfield last night at Watier's. I wished to know the truth and after plying him with a great deal of ancient brandy and losing two hundred pounds to him, he was sufficiently in his cups to tell me that he'd known from the first that Redbourne was The Gentleman—that William had always despised ambitious females, and he had come up with the scheme merely to take a little revenge upon the females he disliked the most."

Penelope tried to pull her hand away from Lord Meares, but he held it fast and for the briefest moment she directed all the anger and hatred she felt for William toward him as she cried beneath her breath, "Release my arm, you blackguard! How very much I hate you!"

He refused to let her go as he leaned very close to her and said, "I, on the other hand, have fallen deeply in love with such a grasping female whose ambitions I comprehend fully and which are equalled only by my own! But I want this business between you and Redbourne finished, Penelope, for you are to become my wife and I won't have that man's shadow between us. Do what you must, but be done with it!"

Penelope stared at him, for the first time in her life afraid of him, afraid of any man as it happened, and an odd sensation of respect for the viscount grew quite suddenly in her breast. A novel sensation, she realized. But if he expected her to do his bidding, then he was clearly as foolish as Redbourne! Hah! And she turned away from him, for she had a matter of greater importance to sort out in her mind—just how she was to bring down both Mademoiselle Novarre and The Gentleman!

Chapter Sixteen

As the audience began to settle down, soft swanskin fans moving more slowly over the sparkling features of the ladies and as the gentlemen began to gesture less emphatically with expressive gloved hands, Lord Datchworth turned to his wife. Barely repressing a sudden need to loosen his neckcloth, he spoke politely, "And now, if you don't mind my dear, I did promise Miss Novarre that I would seek her out after tonight's performance. She seemed quite anxious to learn my opinion of her little dance. Do you have a word you wish me to extend to her, for was she not quite beautiful—in her steps, that is?"

Lady Datchworth glanced at her husband but briefly upon his words, and then gazed out upon the audience below them. In a considerably subdued voice, though her chin seemed quite set, she responded, "I am certain you will have sufficient words to express your raptures as well as mine. Though you might tell her, if you wish, that in my opinion, the widow Baldock has the prettier ankle!"

Lord Datchworth felt such a desire for his wife in this moment, that it was with great difficulty he did not cast his schemes immediately aside. And as he regarded her profile, he thought yet again that she was the handsomest female of his acquaintance. He had always loved her, from the time he first saw her at a masquerade at Vauxhall—good God!—was it truly thirty years ago? She had never been precisely needle-witted, though certainly not lacking in adequate intelligence. But she had always pleased him, for she was pretty and lively, and even with two grown-up daughters, scarcely a wrinkle marred the fine bones of her face. But it was more than that, they'd shared a life together. Damme, but this ridiculous gaming business had to be put to an end and if Mademoiselle Novarre would answer, then he'd do it—by God!

Rising to his feet, he bowed to her slightly and she did not hesitate to turn her face away from him. As he moved to leave the box, he addressed Lord Meares proffering a vague excuse that he rather thought a friend of his had motioned to him to take a stroll about the hallways.

And as he quit the box, he turned for a moment to regard his family only to find Anne watching him with a hurt expression in her eyes, a reproachful look. Surely she knew he had no objection to Mr. Meesden. Indeed, he felt her beau was quite suited to her. But what could he do when he and his wife had *agreed?* He gestured somewhat hopelessly to her, lifting his hands slightly, palms up, and shaking his head. Anne was by far the sweeter of his two daughters and the resigned smile that now crossed her face nearly cut his heart in two.

Once in the hallways, he found a large number of the audience gathered about in small, vivacious groups, further discussing the incredible performance they had all witnessed. The same words arose again and again: *ethereal, romantic, the purest combination of form and emotion.*

For his part, the ballet had quite stunned him and he could not remember when he had seen anything quite so riveting save when Edmund Kean had walked onto the very same stage and began, as one reviewer had described it, speaking in *flashes of lightning.* And beyond the fact that he intended to make a great pretense of pursuing the now-famous ballerina, he wished to meet a female who could stand on her toes with the same ease the rest of the world walked about on flat feet!

Monsieur Bovin permitted only three guests to enter the Green Room at a time, and then to remain for only five minutes, so that Charity was able with some degree of composure to shake hands with a variety of people. In addition, she could with great equanimity accept the passionate salutations upon her fingers which any number of hopeful young gentlemen gave to her. For the most part, she accepted their homage with a smile, for the vast majority of them were rather fresh-faced and awkwardly experiencing their first adventures amongst the world of the theater. Large bouquets of flowers began proliferating in the room, the candlelight casting shadows of roses upon the paneled walls. She was still in her ballet slippers, and took a deep breath as Mr. Tewin approached her, his small dark eyes fixed upon her ankles and drifting over her entire costume until his gaze reached her eyes.

From behind her mask she glared at him, feeling that of all the gentlemen present, he was the worst sort of weasel that ever existed and was convinced of it when he pressed his card into her hand all the while placing a lingering kiss upon her fingers.

She nearly slapped his face for such insolent, ungen-tlemanly conduct, but Monsieur Bovin stayed her arm with his hand and addressed Mr. Tewin himself. "You, Monsieur, are not welcome here. My protégée is considerably offended by your manners. Good evening."

Mr. Tewin was quite taken aback as he cried through flared nostrils, "Why, whatever do you mean? She is an opera-dancer! How can she be offended with me? I've never heard of such a thing! She should be grateful for such attentions and not spurn the interest of her betters!"

Charity dropped his card upon the carpet which brought a blush darkening his cheeks, and in a French accent, she said, "You have misplaced your card, no?"

A deep masculine voice laughed aloud at her words, and as Charity glanced toward the doorway she was surprised to find Hugh Bramfield escorting one of the opera-dancers. And gazing at the pretty green-eyed female upon his arm, Charity recognized the French girl—Francoise Minon.

Charity glanced from one to the other, as Francoise looked up at Hugh. And such an expression as entered the opera-dancer's eyes, of affection, of admiration, of the purest love, her eyes shining, her smile soft and sweet! She was deeply in love with Mr. Bramfield!

Mr. Tewin, who had stooped to pick up his card, evidently unwilling to have anyone else discover this blatant rejection of his advances, stood up and squared his shoulders as he turned to meet Hugh. He sneered slightly as Hugh made him an ironic bow and suggested he try his luck at Sadler's Wells.

Mr. Tewin narrowed his eyes and said, "And this from you, Bramfield. A gentleman whose honor is only a fraction higher than this doxy you have upon your arm!"

Francoise gasped aloud, "You dare, Monsieur!"

But Hugh's complexion spoke the depths to his regard for Francoise as his entire countenance stormed over with pure hatred, and he advanced on the smaller man. Charity, quite without thinking, cried out, "Hugh!" which caused everyone to turn and stare at her and she immediately began a long string of commands in French, hoping that she could mask her sudden, and quite thoughtless betrayal of her own identity when she acknowledged her acquaintance with Hugh.

Pausing in his tracks, Hugh regarded Charity with an expression of immense surprise, even of shock, his mouth agape. He stared at her for several seconds, shaking his head in wonderment until he apparently realized the tenuous nature of the situation. Turning back to Tewin quickly, he said, "I suggest you leave immediately, or I shall gladly make you account for your words."

Tewin glared in response and though he hesitated for a moment, he had but to again take in the relative size of his opponent and his decision was made. And with a final glance toward Charity, his eyes narrowed, he flipped his coattails in a ridiculous manner and quit the room.

Within seconds, before anyone else entered the Green Room, Hugh was with Charity, holding both her hands and peering through the slits of her mask into her eyes. Shaking his head all the while, his face covered in disbelief, he whispered excitedly, "Good God, is that you, Charity? Does Will know? How came you—by God, my child, you can dance! I have never seen so exquisite a performance in my life! Was Will in the audience? Of course he was. Francoise, come here my pet!" She joined him immediately, and Francoise, her eyes shining, said, "You were magnificent, Mademoiselle Novarre. Truly! I wish only that I could dance as well as you! My heart aches for the beauty of your performance. But will you unmask and pursue a career upon the stage? Oh, but *cherie,* you give up so much for you are engaged to Lord Redbourne, no?" And with sudden tears in her eyes, she turned toward Hugh and in a voice that broke, she said, "My darling, she is just like you and me. We are all trapped, *n'est-ce pas,* by our society? Even Lord Redbourne!"

Hugh gave Francoise a warning shake of his head, and Charity wondered what Francoise meant with regard to William for she could not imagine in what manner he was possibly trapped by society since he enjoyed the privileges of his rank so thoroughly.

Hugh released Charity's hands as he looked down upon Francoise, his expression suddenly very sad. Taking her arm and tucking it about his own, he nodded slowly and said, "I'm afraid so, my pet. Perhaps we were simply born in the wrong time, you and I." And he turned back to Charity and said, "You see, I wish for nothing more than to marry Francoise, but where in our society would we be accepted?" And he gave a faint, bitter laugh.

Charity reached a hand out to him, but Monsieur Bovin drew her arm back slightly, his expression severe as he regarded her with a slight shake of his head. Only then did the occupants of the room turn to find Lord Datchworth standing by the door, his face ashen.

It had all seemed so simple, Charity thought as she regarded the shocked visage of her dear uncle, to wear a mask and pretend that no one would ever discover her identity as a ballerina. How could she have been so stupid, so naive?

Without hesitating in the least, Lord Datchworth closed the door and remained there as though standing guard. "I cannot credit what I am seeing." His cheeks were drawn and white, his eyes unblinking as he scanned her costume. "And no wonder this morning you cried out in that incredulous tone, *but that's impossible!* Oh, Charity, why have you done this to your aunt who loves you?"

And as though the enormity of her crime broke upon her, Charity burst into tears and ran to her uncle who opened his arms to her and held her very close. He did not repress tears of his own, as he whispered softly, "Foolish child. Foolish, foolish child! Mademoiselle Novarre? It cannot be true!" And then he laughed through his tears as he kissed her hair. "And your aunt thinks that I intended to—that is, well, you know what I mean, though it is very bad to even mention it to you!"

And in her own sobs, Charity laughed too, for the entire situation was absurd in the extreme.

A loud rapping was heard upon the door and Lord Datchworth cried out, "Go away! We are quite busy within!" And a raucous roll of laughter was heard from among several bucks as well as the comment, *It is Datchworth, the lucky dog!*

Charity stepped away from her uncle, and looked at him in the face and she broke into a peal of laughter, for her uncle had just achieved his purpose, though he was completely innocent. For now the entire *beau monde* would believe that she had become his mistress.

Turning back to Francoise she begged to borrow her handkerchief. After blowing her nose several times, Charity finally felt quiet enough to address her uncle. Sitting down upon a settee of rose-colored silk, her tutu spreading out all around her, the diamonds twinkling in the candlelight, she said, "How do I begin to express to you all my reasons. Mama always wished me to dance, though I don't pretend to assume that she ever meant for me to dance at Drury Lane. But from the time I was a little girl, Monsieur has instructed me in the ballet."

"Did you dance in Paris?"

"No. Monsieur Bovin wished for me to return to my family before I made up my mind forever. He wanted me to experience the stage just once and I am grateful for this moment, I do assure you."

"Do you know what you are about?" Lord Datchworth asked, his brow creased with worry. "How very much you risk? Were it to become known, my dear, you would have no life amongst the *beau monde*, even if then you decided that was what you wished for after all."

In a quiet voice, Charity answered him, "I have thought of little else for these four years and more."

He was silent for a moment, looking at her face, at her costume, at the pearl-embroidered mask, at the smudged slippers.

Hugh said, "But did you see *Le Papillon*, my lord?"

"Did I see it!" he cried. "Damnedest thing that ever showed up in this theater! Reminded me of Kean. Well, not Kean precisely, because he's an actor But I've never been so much struck by a performance in all my life as yours, Charity!" And his eyes brightened a little as he took a step away from the door. "But how do you stand on your toes like that, and career about the stage and not fall over!"

Charity stood up and flexing her feet several times, smiled and said, "With much practice and by stiffening the toes of the slippers." And she stood *sur les pointes* and he laughed and applauded her.

"Damme if I don't think you've changed the ballet forever, m'dear."

"Oh, not me!" she cried. "What I have learned is from Monsieur Bovin and from a famous dancing master in Paris, Monsieur Taglioni. Oh, you should see his daughter perform. Her name is Marie and one day, you'll see, she will come to London and then the ballet will never be the same again!"

He took his snuffbox out of the pocket of his coat and taking a pinch, his brow again deeply furrowed, he said, "So, what do you mean to do, my dear? For I daresay it won't be but a few days before the entire *beau monde* knows who you are."

Charity again sat down on the settee and said, "I don't know, Uncle. But I don't think I exaggerate when I tell you that my heart is torn in two."

By Sunday evening Lady Datchworth was lying down upon the rose silk chase longue in her bedchamber with a linen cloth drenched in lavender water pressed against her forehead, and a china house burning her favorite Spanish pastilles. She was utterly miserable, and had regretted losing five hundred pounds at Charity's soiree more than she ever thought possible. Somehow, at the moment she had not considered it a very large sum, after all she had brought a sizeable dowry with her to her marriage to Stephen and besides, Stephen was rich! What did he care that she would lose a few hundred pounds here and there.

But the undeniable fact had been borne in on her the remainder of the evening at the opera as well as all day today that her dearest husband cared so much about her gaming propensities, that he—that he . . . Oh, she could not bear to even think the thoughts and her pitiful moaning brought Penelope rushing to her side, holding her vinaigrette beneath her nose.

"There, there," Penelope cooed. "You must not distress yourself overly much. After all, it is just the worst sort of tittle-tattle. I am still convinced that all Papa did was speak with her! And from what I have been given to understand, she is quite young and has a fiery dancing master who guards her very closely."

"But Mrs. Baldock said that he was only waiting to sell her to the highest bidder and you know your father is excessively wealthy!"

"Mama, I don't like to pinch at you when you are feeling so blue-deviled, but I don't ever wish to hear that woman's name mentioned again. I cannot like her and as far as I am concerned, she is full of mischief and schemes and not to be trusted!"

"I am sure you are correct about the widow—I have never cared for her above half. I just wish I could believe you were right about Mademoiselle Novarre. But you did not see your Papa when he returned from visiting her last night. Why he was more serious and withdrawn than ever I have seen him. And though I am fully persuaded that in the past he made up a great many faradiddles merely to keep me guessing—" and here she sat bolt upright catching the linen cloth in her hand as it fell from her forehead, "Oh, Penelope, I think he's fallen in love with her. He was so serious but every now and again he would chuckle in that way of his, when something quite absurd

243

amuses him, but then he would fall into a brown study. It was most distressing. And who wouldn't fall in love with such a beautiful young woman for she danced so exquisitely!"

"Well, Lord Meares, for one. He thought her technique was excellent but that her presentation was a bit too melodramatic."

"Perhaps you are right, and I make too much of it."

Lady Datchworth sighed. When her beloved husband had actually gone to the Green Room to seek out the infamous opera-dancer, she had not believed that he actually would do so, that he was merely playing at one of his games. But then not only had he gone to visit her, but fifteen minutes later, Lady Jersey, whose nickname, *Silence*, was certainly well-deserved on this score, rushed into her box announcing that Lord Datchworth had locked himself in the Green Room with that, *that creature*. And that Mr. Tewin himself, who had visited the ballerina but a few minutes earlier, reported hearing the drollest laughter and squealing once the door was closed. *Imagine! Lord Datchworth actually shut the door! Although I am told Mr. Bramfield was present within, but he had an opera-dancer on his arm—so there you are!* Could so very many persons of consequence be wrong? Impossible. Her husband, after so many years of threatening to do so, had finally taken a mistress. She collapsed backward upon a mound of rose and yellow silk pillows, her heart fluttering as she cried, "I fear I am having the worst spasm!"

She continued to listen to her daughter's reasonings, but none of them seemed to reassure her heart that all would be well. And when she noticed that her daughter seemed rather to be sighing every few minutes, she finally sent her away with an expression of gratitude, assuring her that all she needed was a quiet evening alone in her sitting room to adjust her thoughts and decide what, if anything, she could possibly do to win back the affections of her dear husband.

But of the moment, all she wanted was a little peace. She tried to read, but the words blurred together—a reminder that she was getting old and ought to see about acquiring a pair of spectacles. And then she lay staring at the coals thinking that it would be a lovely way to pass the evening were she to cut little butterfly shapes from her writing paper and then burn them slowly upon the fire of coals in her bedchamber. Truly, she would find something to ease her mind. But her mind would not be eased and when she thought of Stephen holding an opera-dancer in his arms, her heart felt as though it would burst and finally she simply gave in to a hearty bout of tears.

Half an hour later, when she was resting peacefully upon her chaise longue, she was startled to hear a loud rapping upon her door, and Stephen enter her chamber as soon as she gave him permission to do so. He bore a tray of supper consisting of a steaming bowl of barley soup, a slice of freshly baked bread and butter, peach halves stuffed with clotted cream and walnut pieces, and a bottle of Madeira.

That there were two glasses upon the tray made Lady Datchworth's heart quicken, nor could she misconstrue her lord's meaning when he purposefully locked both doors—the door to the hallway and the door to her bedchamber. "Stephen!" she cried, a very delectable gooseflesh covering her arms. "Why, whatever are you doing?"

Lord Datchworth regarded his wife with a shake of his head followed by an admonishing wag of his finger as he walked slowly toward her and said, "We are going to have an understanding, you and I. And I will not permit you to leave this room until you agree to certain conditions of mine! First you must never wager above twenty pounds in an entire evening." He placed the tray upon her lap and continued his harangue. "Furthermore—"

Her husband's voice became a familiar, happy hum in Lady Datchworth's ears. She remained seated upon the chaise longue, and after adjusting the tray before her slightly, she began sipping the hot soup, her heart rather wild within her breast. Her husband had never appeared to greater advantage, she thought, as she watched him walk to and fro, for he wore his years regally. He was lecturing her with great vigor upon her gaming tendencies, gesturing every now and again with an uplifted hand, beseeching her to curb her compulsions, but she scarcely listened, content instead to watch him, to finish her soup, her bread, and the sumptuous peaches. His silver hair had always pleased her as well as his dark brown eyes in which more than once she could remember getting thoroughly lost. She finished her second glass of wine and began her third. And why wouldn't Mademoiselle find him attractive. All the ladies loved Stephen! All of her friends were mad with jealousy when their own husbands lost all their hair or grew portly or red-nosed and yellow-toothed from drinking too much wine and rubbing snuff upon their gums! But Stephen! The most delicious feeling began settling over her. His very presence made her feel quite loved and though he was in the midst of some tirade or other which she was only but half attending to, she finally said, "Stephen, do shut up and give me a kiss. I'll do everything you say, I promise."

Lord Datchworth stopped in his tracks and turned toward his wife who held her arms outstretched to him. And uttering, "Oh, the devil take it!" he walked briskly over to the chaise longue, at which instant he got rid of the tray as quickly as possible and wasted no time in gathering his wife up into his arms, and kissing her full on the mouth.

Hours later, the very last thing Lady Datchworth remembered as she fell asleep while cuddling very close to her husband most scandalously in his own bed, was that somewhere in all of his rantings, Stephen had said something very odd about how he could never take Mademoiselle Novarre as his mistress because he had known her since the cradle. She had thought this quite odd, for if Stephen had known her since the cradle then the opera-dancer would have to be quite ancient which she wasn't and oh, dear, she'd had too much wine and who cared anyway. She had already promised never to gamble again and her beloved husband told her at least a dozen times that he was still passionately in love with her and besides, he positively detested the ballet!

Chapter Seventeen

Charity stood in the entrance hall of the Datchworth townhouse drawing her gloves of lavender kid off very slowly. Her head was bowed, her eyes focused upon the gloves as though the task were difficult in the extreme. Her thoughts, however, were given to rehearsing for the hundredth time, precisely what she would say to her aunt, for by now she supposed her uncle had informed Lady Datchworth quite fully about her identity as Mademoiselle Novarre. Her hands trembled as she drew off the first glove and then the second.

She heard Hinx clear his throat and was startled to find the butler regarding her with an inquiring expression. "Yes?" Charity asked. "What is it? Is something wrong?"

Hinx frowned slightly and responded with a polite bow, "I was only wishful of knowing if Mrs. Pelham-Furneux is recovered from her illness."

Charity pulled the second glove off with a sharp jerk, feeling furious that she had involved herself in so many whiskers and she said, "Unfortunately, that good lady is still quite ill, though her doctors believe that she will be fully recovered in a fortnight's time. However, Furney has already requested me to return to her—even sooner than I had expected!"

Hinx replied, "I am very glad to hear you say so."

"Are you?" Charity asked, surprised. "Oh. You refer to the health of Furney's mother." She laughed at herself and shaking her head as she pulled upon the cherry satin ribbons of her large poke bonnet, continued, "I am sorry. I am a little distracted this morning. But pray tell me where I might find my aunt and uncle."

"In the drawing room, Miss."

Charity walked slowly up the stairs, the ribbons of her bonnet trailing over her pelisse like two broad red sashes. She did not wish to upset her aunt, who had always been a trifle high-strung, but the moment had come, she realized, to face squarely with her relations the very difficult choices now nipping at her heels.

Standing outside the drawing room for a moment, Charity heard the most delightful giggling and with something of a start realized that trills of laughter and squeals were issuing not from Penelope or Anne, but from Lady Datchworth and on an impulse, Charity opened the door in a secretive manner and peeped her head in only to discover Lord Datchworth chasing his wife about the pianoforte. Her aunt was dressed in a pretty gown of pink muslin and with her peppered curls trailing to her shoulders in a cluster of youthful ringlets, and a beatific smile upon her lips, she looked younger and more content than Charity had seen her in the past five days.

When Lord Datchworth finally caught his wife, who had tried to slip behind the harp and escape into the antechamber, he pulled her into his arms and kissed her. Good heavens! Charity had never seen her aunt and uncle thus and was shocked, but delightfully so. She meant to merely close the door and return to her bedchamber, but Lord Datchworth released his wife in that moment, and Lady Datchworth immediately caught sight of her.

Blushing a little, her aunt cried, "Charity, my dear! You

have come home!"

These words affected Charity mightily. Home. And what a sweet word that was to her as she entered the room, removing her bonnet and placing it upon a curved side table near the door.

Turning to smile upon her aunt and uncle, though even her cheeks quivered, for she was very nervous, she said, "I am very glad to be returned." And in an inquiring manner, she regarded her uncle, waiting for him to speak.

He finally took the hint, and responded, "Oh! I had nearly forgot! I am sorry, Charity! You must forgive my manners for your aunt has been teasing me so this morning that I fear my brain has grown quite addled! But do tell us, how is Mrs. Pelham-Furneux getting on?" And he gave her the barest nod of his head, indicating that he intended of the moment to keep her secret.

Charity nearly fainted with relief as she regarded her uncle. She could not fully credit that he had not told her aunt the truth and she responded, "Furney had hoped to see her parent fully recovered by now, but it seems her Mama will need at least another sennight to regain her health."

Lord Datchworth asked pointedly, "And will your cousin require your presence again?"

Charity nodded. "Yes, but much sooner than I expected."

Lord Datchworth frowned slightly as he crossed the room to the window that fronted Grosvenor Square. He stood facing the window, his hands clasped behind his back and when at last he spoke, his voice sounded quite serious as he said, "You must do precisely what you wish to do, Charity. You are of an age when you must direct your own path for your feet. And please, attend your cousin as frequently as you feel you need to." He turned to smile at her and added, "Only do be careful! That is, I hope that whatever ails Mrs. Pelham-Furneux will not then attack you. One can never be too careful with such sick complaints.''

Charity crossed the room to join her uncle by the window and taking his hand she pressed it. "Thank you. As it happens, I—that is, Furney wishes me to return tomorrow. She is quite distraught—nearly beside herself with worry.''

"Tomorrow!" Lord Datchworth cried. "So soon? But, I thought, that is, I was certain she would not need you until Saturday.''

Charity shook her head. "I am afraid it could not be helped. She *insists* I return tomorrow night.''

Lord Datchworth took both her hands, the morning light streaming in through the window and falling across his concerned features. "But are you certain you wish to return. I mean perhaps she would understand if you simply wrote to her, or something of that nature.''

Charity regarded him steadily. "I want to return, I feel I must. I hadn't meant to go so soon, but there was no help for it.''

Lady Datchworth joined them, and placing an arm about Charity's waist, rebuked her husband, "Why do you tease the child, Stephen? Furney has been like a sister to her, I am sure! And familial obligation is after all one of our first duties.'' She then placed a kiss upon Charity's cheek and said, "Don't let your uncle persuade you otherwise. Your duty is obviously with Furney and not with our rackety pleasures here in London!''

And with a teasing smile upon her lips as she held her uncle's gaze, Charity responded to her aunt's directives, "Yes, ma'am. I heartily concur.''

Later that morning, Charity sat upon the peach damask

settee in the library, all the pillows clustered about her save one. Upon her lap, she cradled the pillow that she had embroidered of herself and William. She had been sitting in the library for some time, reviewing over and over the thrill of her dance at Drury Lane, and afterward the sensation of shock at having been discovered by her uncle. She was glad now that he had found her out, for she was forced to look very hard at the choices before her.

She remembered at the very beginning of her performance how she had happened to glance up at William, and how the warm smile upon his lips had caused her to remember her very sweet childhood days in Hertfordshire. She clutched the pillow to her chest and squeezed it tight, her heart aching, for she truly did not know what to do. Should she give up the ballet forever? But how could she, when her dance had been so great a part of her life from the time she could walk.

On the other hand, she loved her family and the society in which she had been born, and, as she glanced down at all the pillows piled upon the settee, she realized, too, that she had always wanted a family of her own. And a large family, too, if that were possible, for she felt acutely the lack of siblings in her life, particularly when her parents died. And Hugh had been right about one thing—the *beau monde* would never accept his marriage to an opera-dancer any more than they would accept Charity as a ballerina. But how was she to choose? And the funniest thought crossed her mind that she wished of the moment she could discuss the entire matter with William. And she laughed at the thought, for he would no doubt give her the cut direct the moment he learned that she was Mademoiselle Novarre.

At that moment, Penelope entered the library. She was wearing a morning gown of a pretty flowered cambric, her hair in elegant ringlets. Crossing the chamber to the window, she glanced down into the street, and said airily, "It has rained all morning. I had hoped to do a little shopping for I need to replace my silk stockings, but I cannot abide the thought of traveling in this horridly damp weather." Turning back to Charity, she continued, "But what of you? Since your arrival on Tuesday last, you have left every morning to shop for a great variety of furbelows. Have you completed purchasing the necessary accessories to your wardrobe?"

Charity set the pillow aside, and frowned slightly upon her cousin. There was an unmistakable brightness to Penelope's brown eyes as well as a faint blush which actually colored each porcelain cheek. "I—that is, I don't know yet. I have so recently returned from Tunbridge Wells, that I have not had time to confer with my maid."

Penelope walked to the round table that held the bejewelled snuffbox, and lifting the lid to the box, she let it fall with a snap as she asked, "And pray, tell me, how was Tunbridge Wells? How is Furney's dear mother faring?"

Charity did not need to hear more and she said, "How did you guess, Penelope? Or rather I should ask when did you guess, for you were suspicious from the beginning!"

Penelope moved around the table and seated herself in the dark green chair opposite Charity and said, "I always suspected your sojourn in France. Always."

Charity leaned forward slightly as she cried, "Penelope, tell me what you would do. For you cannot know the agony I suffer in the decisions before me. The governors have insisted I unmask on Tuesday night! I am in the worst state of apprehension for I meant to retain the secrecy of my identity for weeks to come until I could know my heart more thoroughly!"

Penelope was immediately on her feet, as she moved to the settee where Charity sat. And after displacing several of the embroidered pillows, she seated herself beside her cousin and possessed herself of one of her hands. And with a heavy sigh, Penelope said, "You cannot know how grateful I am that you have trusted me enough to ask for my poor opinion. Ever since Saturday night, when I saw you upon the stage, and had my every suspicion confirmed, I have been torn as to what I ought to do. Should I tell Mama and Papa? I had meant to, for I feel that they would both be remarkably understanding, yet somehow I thought that the news ought to come from you."

"Your Papa knows, as does Hugh Bramfield and it is very likely that Mr. Tewin knows as well. I made a most unfortunate error that night, calling out Hugh's name for he almost challenged that weasel, Tewin, to a duel!"

"What do you mean, *weasel*, Charity? I don't quite understand for I have always found Gregory Tewin to have just that sense of—well, I suppose it is of little consequence. But tell me, what is it *you* wish to do. For I must say that I was greatly impressed with *Le Papillon*, as was the entire audience. Such a roar as I have never before heard in the theater. It was quite astonishing! And it is little wonder that you cannot decide what you ought to do."

Charity gave her cousin's hand a squeeze, and smiling at her said, "I knew that I could rely upon you to understand. I just don't know my own heart. Could you give up your place amongst society, Penelope, for something that was of great importance to you?"

Charity watched her cousin shift her gaze to the snuffbox upon the round table next to the chair. The rain had finally ceased, and a cool morning light filtered through the windows and danced upon the jewels. How inscrutable Penelope's expression was, as always, Charity thought, save for the smallest tick that affected her cheek, but even then only once. What was she thinking?

Penelope turned finally toward Charity and said, "But

it is of no significance whatsoever what I could or could not do. We are not concerned with what I want in this situation, but solely with your heart and your desires. Do I presume too much in asking if you have the least wish to marry Redbourne?" Her brown eyes were unblinking as she regarded Charity.

Emitting the smallest of sighs, Charity withdrew her hand from Pen's, rose to her feet, and began pacing the length of the room. "I will confess that upon several occasions, he could with but a few words touch my heart. And yet still, I find his own heart so completely hardened to those about him. I fear he possesses scarcely any compassion at all."

Penelope regarded Charity with a soulful look in her brown eyes, and said, "You are so unforgiving and I am to blame!" And removing a lace kerchief that was tucked into the ribbon about her waist, she pressed a corner of the lace to her eyes and said, "I fear that I shall be the very one to separate you forever from so fine a matrimonial prize as Redbourne. But I can't bear the thought of you marrying someone so despicable. One ought to marry for love—if at all possible." She paused for a moment, a tear trailing down her cheek as she tilted her head slightly and said, "Perhaps you were meant to dance the ballet else why would Redbourne be so very cruel and hard-hearted? Perhaps Providence has given you an answer of sorts."

She then lowered her gaze to her lap and wept into her kerchief. After a time, she lifted her head slightly and said, "There is something else I have recently learned, something I fear will shock you greatly. But maybe it holds the very answer you have been seeking." She lifted dewy eyes to Charity who paused in her tracks to stare at her cousin.

How pretty Penelope was, Charity thought, for even in the midst of her tears, her brown eyes merely looked wet, no redness lit the rim of her eyes, nor touched the sides of her nose. When Charity cried, her eyes grew quite swollen, her nose puffy, her eyes red and burning so fiercely that she could scarcely see afterward. Not so, Penelope.

Charity approached her cousin upon these words and said, "Pray do not hesitate, Pen. Tell me everything, particularly if it has to do with William!"

Penelope took a deep breath, and sitting very straight upon the settee, her eyes still cast down, she said, "Lord Meares revealed something quite—quite scandalous to me last night. And I had never meant to repeat what he said, but, given the desperate nature of your circumstances, I feel you ought to be informed of—of the truth." She lifted her gaze again to Charity, another tear again drifting over a sculpted, creamy cheek. Charity waited, her heart near to bursting, as Penelope finally said, "Lord Redbourne is The Gentleman."

Charity felt numb from the top of her head clear to the bottom of her slippers. "William? Impossible! I knew that the *on dits* had it that Hugh was suspect, but not William!"

"Lord Meares believes that Bow Street is merely blind to Redbourne's guilt because of his consequence."

Dropping down to sit beside her cousin yet again, Charity asked, "But how can Lord Meares be so very certain?"

"He had two reasons, actually. One being that I was Redbourne's first victim—and you know how much William has always despised me—but the second was by far the more damaging for Hugh Bramfield, when he was thoroughly in his altitudes, laughed loudly about William's exploits, discussing them in some detail with Lord Meares."

Charity remembered sweet, impulsive Hugh from the night of the ballet, and with but the barest imaginings, she could see this man, who had run into dun territory, laughing innocently about William's adventures as the highwayman. And as she searched back in her mind to that first encounter with The Gentleman, Charity touched her lips and knew it was true. Why had she not seen it before! William was the highwayman. But how incredible to think of William doing anything so completely outrageous and she remembered the moment when the earl had entered Lord Datchworth's office but five days earlier. Mr. Stokes, the Bow Street runner, had been present, and William, though appearing shocked by what he heard, had soon begun referring to the very things he had said to Charity while in the guise of The Gentleman. And all this time, William knew who she was, even though she had worn her mask when he had kissed her! The rogue! The scoundrel! And when, precisely, did he mean to tell her that he had taken up this scandalous occupation? Upon their honeymoon?

Charity now found herself angry beyond words and she rose again to her feet this time to begin beating a path in a circle about the edge of the furniture. "How dare he?" she cried. "And to have subjected you, Penelope, to his wretched, wretched schemes. Why, it is beyond bearing! And to think he stood there in your Papa's office, all the while knowing that I was the one he had kissed, for did I tell you I had worn my mask when he accosted my post chaise? He no more knew my identity at that time than I knew his!" Upon this thought, she paused in her tirade, for tomorrow night she would be removing her mask, and with a swirl of excitement, she returned to Penelope's side, again sitting down beside her, only at an angle this time so that she could take both of Penelope's hands in her own and regard her brown eyes directly. "My mask! I begin to think you've the right of it, my dear, dear cousin. For I believe Nemesis has been pursuing William mightily, but in the shape of a fragile butterfly!"

Penelope shook her head, appearing bewildered. "But I don't quite understand, Charity. Whatever do you mean?"

Squeezing Pen's hands, Charity said, "If I unmask at Drury Lane, what greater comeuppance could such a man as William receive? Do remember how he taunted the young ladies at Almack's and if you are able, do you recall what they had painted upon their fans?"

"Butterflies!" Penelope breathed, her face for the first time that morning suffused with an emotion Charity could recognize—a very pure delight in the prospects of so sweet a revenge!

"Oh, dear," Penelope said in a quiet, though considerably pleased voice. "Why it does rather seem as though Zeus himself has been busily at work in Lord Redbourne's life. And if you did unmask, it would be a sort of retribution for all of William's horrid unkindnesses over the years! And I certainly don't refer to myself in this instance, but rather to all the unfortunate victims of The Gentleman's advances as well as to Redbourne's arrogance amongst the *ton!*"

Charity knew somehow that her cousin was right in everything she said. And she would unmask at Drury Lane tomorrow night without the least twinge of conscience, for how could William possibly believe he could justify his actions now!

Penelope left Charity shortly thereafter, calling for her carriage. And once she was tucked within the barouche, a brick at her feet keeping the April chill at bay, she commanded the postillion to drive her immediately to Bow Street.

At nuncheon, Charity sat beside Anne at the square

259

table in the morning room and noticed that for the third time her cousin had actually dropped something. The first object had been a linen table napkin, the second had been a slice of apple which fell from her fork, and the third had been a dozen green peas which cascaded off her fork and onto the floor. "Oh, dear," she cried, frowning upon the peas that contrasted sharply with the Aubusson carpet in predominantly red shades. A servant was beside her quickly, and all traces of her clumsiness were banished to the scullery.

Charity glanced at her aunt and Penelope, wondering if either of these ladies noticed that Anne was considerably agitated, but they were deeply involved in a conversation about the fabrication of a new turban Lady Datchworth had in mind which would make use of some very pretty seashells she had found in the Pantheon Bazaar recently. Charity wanted to ask Anne if anything were amiss and intended to do so as soon as the servants were gone from the room.

But Anne seemed to have something she wished to discuss as well, for she watched the servants leave and as soon as the door was shut upon them, she interrupted her mother's conversation with Penelope by saying, "Mama, I have a great favor to ask of you!"

Lady Datchworth lifted her gaze to her younger daughter, her expression one of mild surprise. Her features took on a quite loving aspect as she said, "Dearest, whatever you ask of me I shall certainly do. Anything."

Anne seemed to relax visibly as she smiled sweetly and said, "Well, you know how blue-deviled I've been lately because of George—that is because of Mr. Meesden—"

"Yes, I know my dear. But you are being very brave and I am quite proud of you!"

Charity watched Anne's gaze cloud over slightly as she said, "Thank you, Mama. I—I hope I don't disappoint you overly much. I've never meant to be a disobedient daughter."

"Why, Anne!" Lady Datchworth cried. "Whatever do you mean! You are a very good girl. I could not be more pleased with you. Truly!"

Anne swallowed very hard as she said, "Well, I was wondering if it were possible to go to the Pleasure Gardens this evening. You see, there is a masquerade, and I thought perhaps I would not be missing—that is, I thought my spirits might be lifted a trifle were we to attend, if only for an hour or so. And perhaps you might invite along a young man for me whom you feel would be just the sort of gentleman—well, you know what I mean."

Both Lady Datchworth and Penelope exclaimed at the idea as being precisely what was needed to bring poor Anne about. A masquerade at the Vauxhall Pleasure Gardens, the very thing! And were there enough costumes stored in the attic to create a little something special for each of the ladies? Well, after nuncheon they would all have to command the servants to take stock immediately and see what might be contrived. And oh, it would be such fun!

Charity regarded her cousin next to her, and thought for the barest moment that a tear welled up quickly in Anne's eye. But Anne again dropped her linen napkin upon the carpet and though she risked being censured for such an unmaidenly act, she bent down to retrieve it, pausing briefly before returning to an upright position. Charity was certain she had spent that moment blinking back her tears, and she could not be at ease about Anne's sudden suggestion that they all attend a masquerade at Vauxhall.

Lady Datchworth said, "And of course William must be invited, it would only be proper!" And she turned to wag a finger at Charity and said, "But you must promise not to get lost in the shrubbery when the fireworks are displayed!" And she giggled as though she were a schoolgirl, then turned to address her eldest daughter. "Now, Penelope who do you think we might ask to join our little party for Anne. What about Mr. Tewin? Do you not think he would be perfect for our sweet, dear Anne?"

"Oh, indeed yes! You know, I have thought for a long time now that some fine young lady ought to be found for Gregory. And why not Anne, for Mr. Tewin has every advantage any young lady could hope for—elegance of manner, a very piercing sort of wit, and of course he is considered a tolerable-looking gentleman by all of my acquaintance. Why the more I think on it, the more I am persuaded it is a match!"

Charity, by this time, was a little stunned by Penelope's, and to some degree Lady Datchworth's, insensitivity to Anne's bruised sensibilities. Why, Charity had but only to watch the manner in which Anne kept dropping her gaze to her lap to realize that all was not well with her. But neither mother nor sister seemed to comprehend that Anne, for all her intentions of striving to please her family, was still deeply in love with Mr. Meesden. Her heart would require a great deal of time to mend. And when she thought of the beady-eyed, arrogant gentleman whom the ladies had just determined was suitable for Anne—for he was quite wealthy!—Charity felt a trifle disturbed in her heart that Penelope in particular would appear to be so grasping. It was therefore with some difficulty that she applied herself to the cold chicken and lobster patty that sat upon her plate.

And what was she to do about William during an entire masquerade? Except that she knew Penelope would most certainly help her to keep the earl at bay, were it necessary!

Anne said, "But what of Viscount Meares, Mama! Do you not think he ought to be included in our excursion to Vauxhall?"

Lady Datchworth exclaimed that his lordship would add just that measure of elegance and refinement—though admittedly, his presence would make up the proper numbers!—which would assure them all a delightful evening. "And to think I have not been to a masquerade in ages! I only hope that the gentlemen will make some effort and not merely sport a domino over evening clothes. Indeed, Penelope, why don't you send cards of invitations, requesting costumes specifically."

Penelope stared at her for a long moment and finally said, "Why do we not all attend in seventeenth century costumes," and turning to Charity, she winked. "We ladies could wear velvet gowns and stiff corsets, while the gentlemen—"

Anne, suddenly enlivened by the idea, cried, "Why they could all attend as The Gentleman!" And for the first time that day, she actually smiled broadly. "What a famous idea! And George will appear to decided advantage in a long curling black wig, a laced shirt, a velvet coat—"

"George?" Penelope queried, a slightly censorious note in her voice.

Anne blushed and amended, "Gregory! I meant to say Gregory, of course. He will appear quite elegant in such a costume, except that his legs are a trifle thin." And she lifted her eyes as though to gaze at the white scrollwork upon the ceiling, but Charity thought never had she seen so mischievous an expression in Anne's large blue eyes as in this moment!

When nuncheon was concluded and Lady Datchworth and Penelope retired to the attics with a host of servants, Charity walked with Anne toward their respective bedchambers. She could not resist asking Anne precisely what thoughts were going through her mind when she appeared to be admiring the ceiling of the morning room. Anne seemed quite startled at first, and when she had gotten used to the question, she slipped her arm about Charity's and whispered, "I am being very wicked but that is all I will tell you."

Charity whispered back, "And would this perchance have anything to do with Mr. Tewin?"

Anne giggled, covering her mouth with her hand, as they mounted the stairs toward the bedchambers, and responded, "Yes, but only a little and that is all I will tell you!"

"I must admit that I was astonished at how meekly you accepted your Mama's suggestion of Tewin, for I cannot think of two people less suited than you and that mealy-mouthed braggart. Forgive me for speaking so forcefully, but Anne, I hope you do not mean to marry such a man!"

"Never!" Anne returned promptly. "For I dislike him excessively!"

Charity regarded her seriously for a moment as she said, "But will you not be miserable the entire evening?"

Anne went off in a peal of laughter that echoed through the stairwell. "Oh, Charity, and I thought at least you were observant enough to comprehend my schemes, but perhaps you have simply never seen enough of Mr. Tewin to understand! The fact is that Mr. Tewin is in love with Penelope!"

This time Charity laughed aloud, crying, "Oh, no!"

Anne nodded her head several times. "There, you see the beauty of inviting Mr. Tewin along, for not only will I be entertained at watching him try to cut out Lord Meares, but I shall be completely ignored which is all that I wish to be this evening."

Charity still thought that her cousin appeared as though there was another purpose to her suggestion that they all attend the masquerade at Vauxhall, and said as much to her. But dear, sweet, biddable Anne merely smiled in a secretive fashion and responded with, "I only want a little diversion! I assure you!"

Charity could not like the manner in which Anne spoke these words, for her blue eyes glimmered with something more than mischief as she swished into her bedchamber and with another peal of laughter, closed the door upon Charity.

Chapter Eighteen

The box at Vauxhall seemed overflowing with high-waymen as Charity glanced about the table. All of the gentlemen—Lord Datchworth, Lord Meares, William, and Mr. Tewin—wore the long curling black wig that Charles II would have worn, along with half-masks of black silk. She could hardly tell one from the other! And yet, with but a moment's consideration as she regarded each man in turn, she became aware of how singular each of them was even though they were wearing similar disguises. Mr. Tewin, for instance, had a habit of turning his head with an abrupt movement to regard whoever might be speaking, while Lord Meares scarcely moved at all but sat sipping his champagne quite slowly. Lord Datchworth, on the other hand leaned forward in his chair, his usual energy evident in the expressive, almost impatient gestures of his hands while he spoke.

And then there was William!

Charity was never at a loss as to his identity for he was the one who kept finding secretive means and moments for touching her—the rogue! The moment he had arrived at the Datchworth townhouse, she had offered him the coolest greeting possible, and though he was at first considerably taken aback, an expression of hurt passing through his hazel eyes, he had soon taken the offensive, and began his assault. Bowing low, he possessed himself of her unwilling hand, kissed her fingers and whispered to her that whether she liked it or not, she would become his wife!

Charity responded in a low tone, "I shall do as I please!"

But his answer, which rolled quite readily from his tongue, shook her to the roots of her soul when he said, "Then I suppose I shall have to make certain that the thought of becoming my wife pleases you very much!"

And from that moment until the present, he had taken every opportunity afforded him to caress her, to touch her—a hand pressed for the barest second upon her waist when no one was looking, or the same hand brushing against her own as the party waited in the entrance hall for all the carriages to be brought round, or as was the case of the moment, his leg pressed quite scandalously against hers as they sat beside one another in the box at Vauxhall.

She tried to frown him down, and shifted her legs, but with the most unfortunate result that he cried out in a loud voice that he was very sorry, he had not meant to incommode her and made a great fuss of moving his chair. And what mischief brewed in those wicked hazel eyes as he then brought his chair even closer to her own so that this time—the rascal—she could feel his entire thigh pressed against hers! She blushed, and waved a fan over her face. She knew what he was about, which only caused the blush to deepen upon her cheeks. He meant to seduce her! He knew her weakness, and he meant to bring her to the altar through the sheer pleasure of his touch. And given how shallow her breath had become, she greatly feared he would succeed at the task!

Well, she had no intention of crumbling yet again and she tried to ignore him, still fanning herself and remarking to her aunt that of all the costumes, hers in a cherry-red velvet was quite the most becoming!

Lady Datchworth frowned slightly as she noticed how close Lord Redbourne was sitting to her niece—even if they were engaged to be married!—and she, too, began wafting her fan across her face as she said, "Are you certain you are comfortable, Lord Redbourne? For you seem to be quite cramped, as we all are I am sure, about this small table."

But William, his expression considerably grave, responded, "You are very kind to be concerned with my welfare, but I do assure you that I am exceedingly comfortable."

Lord Datchworth could not help himself as he gave a shout of laughter which only brought his wife's censure down upon his head as she cried, "Stephen! You are causing your niece to blush!"

Lord Datchworth apologized to Charity though he still could not keep from smiling at her. He was clearly enjoying her predicament and with just such an expression as said that he felt she deserved to be tortured a little. And glancing from her to William, a slight frown entered his eyes as he addressed the earl, "You were at Drury Lane on Saturday night, were you not?"

William inclined his head and Lord Datchworth drummed his fingers on the table as though wondering just how he ought to pose his next question. After a moment, he said, "Tell me what you thought of Mademoiselle Novarre!"

Charity swallowed very hard and she could not keep from turning to regard William's profile, her heart beating soundly in her ears, as she waited for his pronouncement. He seemed to have conjured up in his mind the performance, for his gaze appeared somewhat unseeing as he narrowed his eyes and said, "I don't think I have ever seen anything so exquisite as *Le Papillon*. Mademoiselle Novarre portrayed an ethereal unworldly creature to such perfection that I felt I had been caught up in a dream." He shook his head. "I am still dumbfounded when I recall it."

Lord Datchworth nodded his head vigorously. "Struck me like the time I first saw Kean playing Shylock! Extraordinary."

William turned suddenly toward Charity and said with a smile, "You ought to have seen Mademoiselle Novarre's performance, Charity. I think you would have enjoyed it greatly, for I have watched you dance our simple ballroom country dances and waltzes and you seem to have an affinity with movement not unlike Mademoiselle. I understand, however, that she is to perform again tomorrow night and you simply must see *Le Papillon!* Would you care to join me at the theater?"

Though Charity had expected this question, her heart was so full of everything he had said, his enthusiasm for her ballet, that she could do little more than respond in a subdued voice, having difficulty all the while, in keeping her breath. "I greatly fear I must leave town again tomorrow morning."

"Your cousin's mother?" he inquired politely. When she nodded her head, he said, "I honor your sense of duty, but I fear you will be missing one of the finest talents to come to London in a very long time."

And as he held her gaze, he added, "Did you know that the governors of the Theatre Royal have commanded Mademoiselle Novarre to unmask?"

"Yes," Charity answered him. "I believe there was something in *The Times* about it—that she is a Lady of Quality and risks everything were her identity to become known. I, for one, cannot conceive of all the difficulties which must lie before her, particularly if she loves the ballet as you seem to suggest she does."

In a sincere voice, he said, "It would be a great pity were her talents lost to the theater forever and of the moment I

270

feel very sorry that she must choose one life over another. I am not unfamiliar, as it happens, with the sensation." And he sat back in his chair suddenly, his gaze torn from her as he considered yet again what his life might have been like had John lived, and had he been able to pursue his desired career in the military.

Anne, who had been listening with great interest to this exchange, said, "Such a decision would be enormously difficult, I would think. For she would be hurting her family as well were she to actually do something so scandalous. And yet, if she was following the impulses of her heart, who could blame her? I mean, she must do what she feels is best for herself, wouldn't you agree, Lord Redbourne?"

He regarded Anne with an expression of surprise on his face, as he responded, "Your sentiments as you have just expressed them, hold an undeniable truth. And though her actions would be considered quite rebellious, if her heart found them necessary, I must agree with you—how could she deny her heart?"

Charity was nearly beside herself with misery, for both Anne and William were speaking of her difficulties in much the same manner as she was wont to think of them. She sat plucking the spokes of her fan somewhat blindly. But what seemed to wrench her heart the most, was that she knew William understood the dilemmas facing her, almost as though he knew that she was Mademoiselle Novarre. She chanced to look up at him at that moment, and saw that he was watching her. His smile was entirely sympathetic and she had no doubt that he was fully cognizant of her role as Mademoiselle Novarre and the thought startled her. For nowhere in his bearing or his manners had she felt the least censure from him. But how was this possible? Surely William, of all people, would have been outraged by her dual existence as well as by the threat her identity as a masked ballerina could diminish his own consequence. Instead, he seemed to understand! Had she misjudged him then, so completely?

The orchestra struck the first chords of a waltz, and he took her hand lifting her to her feet. Somewhere in the confusion and distress of her heart, she knew that he was asking her to dance, but she couldn't speak and merely responded with an inclination of her head as he led her to the floor. If he held her more closely than he ought, of the moment Charity did not care. All she could think was that William knew her heart, that he understood her desires and she gave herself fully to being held gently in his arms as he whirled her around and around.

Charity was grateful for this dance, for these few moments in which to collect her shattered sensibilities.

In a quiet voice, William asked, "What do you intend to do?"

Charity shook her head and answered, "I don't know."

William looked down upon Charity's glossy black curls that were dressed in old-fashioned ringlets over each ear, a style that complemented her Queen Anne gown of royal blue velvet. Her words dug deeply into him as he realized for the first time that Charity might indeed be lost to him forever if she chose to unmask at Drury Lane. What a fool he had been all these years! For while Charity was in Paris following the yearnings of her heart, he had been in London playing at being a ridiculous highwayman in order to mask the loss he felt in not being able to pursue the dreams of his youth. And instead of creating a new life for himself, a life that Charity might have been drawn to when she returned from Paris, he had spent his years in bitterness, his heart growing hard and careless of the feelings of others. He had tortured Penelope—whose own future had been robbed from her in a similar manner as his own—and had punished a dozen other females of the *beau*

272

monde who dared remind him, by their pursuit of his title, of the life he had lost.

And now, when he could have gathered his life back to him, in the form of the woman he held in his arms and whirled about the dance floor at Vauxhall, his bitter heart had all but made it impossible for Charity to love him. He understood that suddenly when he had asked her what she would do, what choices she would make and she had responded that she didn't know. What had he expected? That she would immediately reply that of course she would give up everything just for him? Somehow, he must have expected her to say just that! Why else would he be so stunned at her words?

And the irony was that he had no one to blame but himself. Even his mother, after watching Charity's exquisite performance turned to him in the coach on their way home and said, "And so you thought such a female was yours for the mere lifting of your finger? William, I don't mean to frighten you, but why would such a Lady of Quality marry a man who took pleasure in tromping upon the spirits of chits just out of the schoolroom?"

In a dozen different ways, Charity had tried to tell him that he had gone beyond the line of what was acceptable to her—the pink dress and the green and brown plaid bows, her disappearance at her own soiree, her mockery at Almack's of his own airs of self-consequence. But he had not listened to her, he had not heard her until now, when her words told him simply that he, of the moment, could not offer her more than what her ballet could give her. He laughed at himself with this thought, for though he was a peer of the realm, amazingly wealthy, a matrimonial prize of the first stare, and a decided leader of fashion, Charity saw nothing in his offer of marriage to truly tempt her save an opportunity to take a little revenge upon him. And how pleasing a target Nemesis must have found in him, for he had truly lost himself in his pride and in his bitterness.

The waltz had calmed Charity's spirits exceedingly and she felt a great deal more at ease as they returned to the table where Lord Meares sat alone with Anne, chatting with her in his easy manner. As they resumed their seats, the viscount asked her cousin, "And so I have been given to understand, Miss Anne, that this evening's adventure was entirely of your design."

Anne smiled and said that she had always enjoyed the gardens at Vauxhall.

Charity admired Lord Meares for he was very polite and though he appeared a trifle bored with Anne's conversation, he at least had the good grace to pay her a little attention. Mr. Tewin, as it happened, had attached himself to Penelope's side, just as Anne had predicted he would, but Lord Meares seemed to take most of Gregory's nonsense in stride. However, of the moment, he seemed a trifle concerned, as he glanced several times toward the dance floor, his lips appearing pinched for Penelope and Mr. Tewin were nowhere to be seen.

After ordering another bottle of champagne to be brought to the table, he again asked Anne, "And was it your idea as well that we gentlemen should all be dressed in the guise of the highwayman?"

"Oh, no!" Anne cried. "That was Penelope's idea and I for one thought it a famous notion for I admire The Gentleman excessively!"

William asked, "And how is this? I had thought the ladies despised him as a callous rogue and adventurer!"

Anne said, "Well, I am sure that there are many who would call him a rogue, but it seems to me that in general a man who wished for a little adventure to enliven his days would have some difficulty finding it in London. Except for gaming, which I understand can provide a great measure of excitement! But I have often observed that the results can be disastrous! Why even the Beau lost his fortune in that manner!" Her expression then grew quite wistful as she took a sip of her champagne and said, "Of course, if a man had a property that required a great deal of work and if such a man wished for a wife and a quiver full of children, why I think such an existence could contain a great deal of adventure—domestic adventure, as it were. Do you not think so, Lord Meares?"

But the viscount nodded in a somewhat distracted manner as he leaned back in his chair slightly in order to watch Penelope and Mr. Tewin's approach.

Charity could see that Penelope was very angry and the moment she sat down, she addressed Lord Meares and said, "I would take it very kind in you, if you would do this *man* a great injury, for he actually tried to kiss me!"

Both Anne and Charity gasped, and even William, who was never kindly disposed toward Penelope, cried, "The devil take it, Tewin! You did not do so?"

But Lord Meares lifted a hand and effectively silenced everyone. After regarding Tewin steadily for several seconds, a deathly pause that brought a red flush to Gregory's face visible below his mask, the viscount addressed Penelope, "I am certain you must have misunderstood Mr. Tewin's intentions."

"I most certainly did not!" Penelope cried, aghast.

But Lord Meares silenced her again with a similar gesture as before, and leaning very close to her, whispered something in her ear.

Penelope grew very calm, as she listened to him. And when he had done, she said, "You are very right, of course." She then turned to Mr. Tewin and said, "I beg your pardon for having mistaken your meaning, sir." And she folded her hands upon her lap.

Charity breathed a sigh of relief, for the situation was rife with the worst possibilities for Lord Meares was a known duelist and proficient in both swords and pistols. But Mr. Tewin was not a wise man and to the table at large, he said, "Why it was the most ridiculous thing! Of course I did not try to kiss her! Miss Ware was greatly mistaken!"

Lord Meares sighed apparently bored with the prospect of having to perform a duty he did not in the least cherish. But Mr. Tewin had made it impossible for him to do otherwise and he said, "I hasten to assure you, my good sir, that my silence should not have been mistaken for a belief you were innocent. I only wished to avoid a useless confrontation. And I certainly have no desire to call you out, for it would be grossly uncivil at such a delightful party as this, to do so. But I wish to inform you, my dear Tewin, that if Miss Ware ever complains to me again of even the slightest insult on your part, I will gladly set my dogs upon you without the least twinge of my conscience. And now, have I made myself clear?"

Mr. Tewin was shocked, his black eyes wide with horror, as he sat very straight in his chair and simply stared at the viscount. And from a wisdom born of his fear, he swallowed very hard and turned to converse in an exceedingly polite manner with Anne.

Penelope seemed much struck with the viscount's speech, and pressing her fan upon his arm, she cried, "You would do that much for me?"

Lord Meares responded in a straightforward manner, "Since you are by now fully aware of my intentions toward you, why would you expect anything less of me? Did you not, in fact, ask me to do Mr. Tewin a bodily injury?"

Penelope began fanning herself slowly and regarded the viscount with a measuring look as though she had just seen him for the first time. "Well!" she breathed at last. "I am very gratified."

Lord and Lady Datchworth returned to the table shortly thereafter and much to Mr. Tewin's obvious relief, Lord

Meares did not refer to the incident again, nor did Penelope. Charity then accepted a request to dance the quadrille with Lord Meares, and after that a country dance with her uncle where he warned her that he thought William had somehow learned that she was Mademoiselle Novarre. Charity responded that she was certain of it, whereupon her uncle expressed his fervent hope that she would consider her decision carefully and that his real concern was that she would learn the precise state of her heart, the moment she had set her feet irrovocably upon the wrong path!

After the country dance, dinner, including the delectable wafer-thin slices of ham so famous at Vauxhall, was served. It was not until dinner however, that Anne, who had been unusually quiet for most of the evening, began repeating her pattern of dropping things that had so afflicted her during nuncheon earlier that day—first, she dropped her fork, then knocked over her but partially full glass of champagne, and when her knife clattered to the floor she exclaimed with a thrill of laughter that she greatly feared she had developed *the dropsy!*

Everyone laughed with her for the champagne had been flowing quite freely and a general air of good-will seemed to have settled upon the table—Penelope was more inclined than ever to treat Lord Meares with distinction, Mr. Tewin was on his best behavior, and Lord Datchworth kept saying things to Lady Datchworth in a low voice that would make her giggle and cry out, "Oh, do stop, Stephen!" And she would rap his arm with her fan.

Even William seemed content with the masquerade, for he spoke politely to everyone, initiating conversation as was required and not once did his expression grow haughty or indignant, not even in response to any of Penelope's rather intrusive questions regarding his mother's health and whether or not the dowager enjoyed Mademoiselle Novarre's performance. Instead of answering coldly, his voice was sincere and warm as he said, "My mother's illness has been a great source of distress for a number of years and I have made it a habit in general to merely respond that she is doing well. But it is not the case! She suffers enormous pain nearly every day and I assure you that it is the most difficult business in the world to watch someone you love very deeply endure so much discomfort as she does."

Here, he turned to Charity and in a softer voice added, "But as to the performance of *Le Papillon*, she was both astounded and thrilled to have been able to witness what she feels will be a new epoch in the ballet."

There was not a single person at the table who did not, upon this speech, pause in sipping a glass of champagne, or hold a fork suspended in mid-air, or regard William with a rather stunned expression, for he had never been so forthright about matters so intensely personal. Charity was greatly pleased and as she turned toward Penelope, she could not help but be satisfied to see that her cousin bore faint red splotches of embarrassment covering her neck and chin—as rightly she should for having introduced a subject at once painful and close to the heart of Lord Redbourne.

So much had happened this evening, Charity realized as she regarded William's profile for a moment. Her own identity was common knowledge between them and not only had he understood her dilemma, he had answered her cousin's question, not with the least degree of ill-humor but with an openness that worked strongly upon her own heart. This was the William she had believed lost to her and his sudden reappearance struck her heart as though someone had actually dealt her a physical blow. William then asked Penelope a polite question regarding the peacock she had been embroidering the past several weeks and did she think she would finish it before the season was out?

As the dinner was drawing to a conclusion, Charity happened to glance at Anne for a moment, only to find her cousin staring across the crowd of masqueraders who were waiting for the orchestra to resume their instruments at a figure standing beneath one of hundreds of lanterns hung throughout the gardens. And much to Charity's surprise, the rather short, somewhat portly man wore a costume similar to the rest of the gentlemen seated about the table, and before she realized who the man was she cried out, "Why, how very odd!"

Everyone stopped their conversations or their chewing as Lady Datchworth exclaimed, "What is it? What are you looking at?"

Charity would have answered her readily but Anne interrupted her and said, "Why, it was the most amazing costume I have ever seen! A female dressed like a black page and carrying a very tall palm leaf! She quite put me in mind of the time Lady Caroline Lamb dressed in such a costume. But I fear she has already disappeared into the shrubbery!" Anne turned to catch Charity's eye and said, "And was she not amazingly tall?"

Charity nodded her head somewhat dumbly as the full import of all that Anne had said burst upon her. The gentleman in the shrubbery could have been none other than Mr. Meesden and Anne's readiness to tell a whisker in order to keep his presence at Vauxhall a secret, indicated nothing short of an elopement in progress.

An elopement! Good heavens!

Chapter Nineteen

When at last dinner was concluded, the party rose from the table and moved into the gardens toward the River Thames to watch the firework display. The sound of cannons shattered the night air as the first display burst across the dark sky. The crowds gasped and exclaimed as each roar charged the air.

Charity stood near Anne and was not in the least surprised when her cousin pulled her arm slightly and drew her back from the crowds a few feet. "For I wished you to know how grateful I am that you did not say anything to Mama and Papa about the highwayman standing in the gardens." Another firework exploded over the river, and Anne continued, "Do you know who the man was?"

Charity slipped her arm about Anne's waist and gave her a friendly hug. "I think I have a fairly good notion but are you truly planning just the sort of scandalous elopement I fear you are?"

Anne nodded, her expression at once happy and yet sad, for though her lips were smiling, there was just such an expression in her large blue eyes that bespoke a longing which could not be satisfied—that her mama and sister would accept with open arms the man she loved.

Charity and Anne drifted along behind the crowds, drawing closer to the ill-lit garden paths. Anne whispered, "I never wanted it this way. You must believe that, and I daren't think too much how overset Mama will be when she learns what I have done, else my resolve will falter! But it is not quite as bad as eloping to Gretna Green for I am five and twenty and we intend to be married by Special License tonight at George's father's house. Oh, Charity, whenever I think on it, I want to cry!"

Charity said, "But are you very sure you wish to go through with this? After all, it is not too late to change your mind."

Anne laughed slightly, "Oh, but I think it is, for I couldn't possibly impose upon George in so heartless a manner—not when I *forced* him to wear that costume—and you simply cannot imagine how very much he hates it!" Anne directed her gaze down one of the paths and when Charity followed her gaze, she discovered Mr. Meesden standing beneath another lantern, his stodgy figure quite absurd in a velvet coat that hung very low to his knees, and boots that should have covered part of his thighs but instead were turned down awkwardly below the knees. He stood batting at night-flying creatures which seemed attracted to him and every now and again, he scratched his face wherever the long curled wig touched him. Poor fellow, indeed!

And as Charity saw Anne's mooncalf expression as she regarded her beau, she thought that only love could answer for either Mr. Meesden having agreed to don such a wretched costume, or for Anne to have actually found him a romantic-looking figure.

Both ladies sauntered away from the squealing and shouting crowds as the fireworks continued to blast the air, and when Charity had finally delivered Anne into George's hands, and kissed her cheeks wishing her very happy, she watched them go with a feeling of great sadness in her heart. Would she ever know such love as Anne did, who was willing to give up her parents' approval in order to gain the man she loved? And what of William and all the twisted feelings that had pulled her apart for these past six days. Were these the hallmarks of love? That one moment she had been determined to unmask at Drury Lane in order to humiliate him as he had so humiliated those she loved, and the next moment, when he would but express his understanding of her difficulties, all thoughts of revenge fled her mind? Did she love him? And even if she did, could she give up the ballet for him, or for anyone for that matter?

And just as these thoughts coursed through her heart, she had the very last glimpse of Anne, a cloak now covering her as her precious highwayman guided her lovingly through the crowds milling through the gardens.

Charity turned back down the path, only to find her own highwayman standing not five feet from her. Lanterns danced in the night breeze, casting golden glimmers upon his mask and face. William approached her and in a whisper asked, "And is your cousin content with her decision? I was so very surprised earlier this evening when she spoke of following one's heart's desires, but now I comprehend her reasonings fully. Was her family then so greatly opposed to the match? I don't understand how they could be for George Meesden is an exemplary fellow!"

Charity answered in a whisper, "Both my aunt and Penelope felt that his fortune was not sufficient, that Anne would suffer greatly were she obliged to live upon so small an income."

William stood very near her as Charity again let her gaze drift toward the place where she had last seen Anne, and he asked, "And what is your opinion, though I must presume that since you did not tell your aunt about the elopement that you are not unsympathetic."

"You will be very much shocked, I am sure, to know that when I realized what she was about, I wished for it. She loves Mr. Meesden very much."

"I am not shocked in the least," he said, as he placed a hand upon her arm and whispered in her ear. "Your heart is all that is generous and good. I am not surprised that you would wish for Anne's happiness."

Charity heard his words, the sincere tone in his voice, and she again felt her heart go out to him. "Will," she said, "I had meant to unmask at Drury Lane partly to hurt you and now do you believe my heart so generous?"

William did not hesitate to gather her up in his arms, and holding her fast, said, "And what else did such a fool as myself deserve? Charity, I cannot explain to you what has happened to me in all these years since that time long ago when we rode our horses together. I grew bitter at having been obliged to shoulder what I had grown up believing were John's responsibilities. I had wanted a career alongside Hugh, a pair of colors was the summit of my ambition, and instead I was given a title that had less meaning for me than I could ever express to you, or to anyone. And then you arrived in London, and because of my sentiments for you when you were but a child, I offered for your hand in marriage, believing foolishly that any female was mine for the asking. And there you were spurning me at every turn, showing me precisely what you thought I could do with my rank and my fortune!"

"William, I was very much shocked when I saw your treatment of Penelope and—and other ladies of your acquaintance. My heart was crushed at seeing you so very unkind. You! It seemed so impossible."

He said, "But it was not until your performance that I realized the depth to my folly, that I was to a great degree unworthy of your regard."

Charity placed her hands upon his chest and regarded the lace foaming at his neck, and even plucked the tiny points at the very edge of the lace. He was humbling himself, she realized, and yet she did not know what to say to him. There would always be a part of her that would be drawn to him, but at this late hour, she was not certain that she loved him or that she ever could.

He asked, "I know now that when I made a formal offer of marriage to your uncle several weeks ago, I offered for you in a flippant manner and even to a degree with the intent of hurting Penelope. That is how bad I have become." He took her chin in his hand, and lifting her face that he might look at her he said, "But I ask you now, my darling Charity, can you ever hope to forgive me? And if you could find it in your heart to do so, would you do me the great honor of becoming my wife?"

Charity felt her throat constrict painfully, tears biting her eyes as she said, "I know that you speak with much sincerity, but as from the first, Will, I do not know my own heart. There is a part of me that loves you, that always shall, but you've hurt me very much by the cruelty of your words and past unkindnesses to those I love—to Penelope —that I am not able to forgive you fully. Perhaps that is my besetting sin, that my loyalties are so deep and not easily set aside so that my heart then becomes hardened."

"Will you not at least give my proposals a little consideration?"

"I promise you that I will do at least that much."

"And would you seal such a promise by permitting me to kiss you?"

Charity should have refused, she felt it deeply in her heart, for she had such an inexplicable weakness for his embraces. But then, he was looking down at her with such affection and warmth in his eyes, and he had so sweetly humbled himself that there was nothing for it but to nod slightly and agree to his request.

He was still holding her chin in his hand and placed a gentle kiss upon her lips as he drew her against him tightly. What sweet heaven, as the fireworks continued to explode about them, the breeze cool and fresh! All of his mistakes faded from her mind's eyes and in their stead was the moment she had been ready to dance her ballet and he had smiled warmly upon her. She felt filled with such warmth as he kissed her with an increasing fervency, his lips searching her own hungrily, begging for an answering hunger to fill her and demand to be satisfied.

Charity's heart began to ache as she slipped an arm about William's neck and kissed him very hard in return. She did not want to let him go. His arms held her fast, securely, a bastion against the harshness of the world. If only there was no past between them, to rise up and haunt her, for she felt she would then beg him to fly away with her tonight, just as Anne and George had done.

But as her hand caressed the curls of the wig, she was struck to the core of her being with the thought that he had said nothing to her of being The Gentleman, and she drew back from him.

He cried, "What is it? What has happened?"

She was not certain which thought hurt her more, that he had taken up so scurrilous an occupation or that he had not revealed his identity to her. She asked, "Is there anything else you wish to tell me, William? Anything you think I ought to know?"

He appeared to search his mind, but after a moment shook his head and replied, "No, I don't think so. I wanted you to know how I felt, that I regretted letting my own heart grow calloused and that I wanted to marry you."

She glanced down at her hands which she could see in the shadows had begun trembling. Then she still could not really trust him and she said, "If you don't mind very much William, I should like to be returned to my aunt."

The remainder of the evening was something of a blur to Charity—her disappointment that William would humble himself in so contrite a manner but then refuse to reveal his identity to her, kept her in a state of confusion. She saw the look of pain upon her aunt's face as Lady Datchworth read a missive Anne had left upon their table before she quit the gardens, but Charity was so consumed with her distress that she could hardly respond to the questions put to her, *Did she know of Anne's intentions?* "Yes, that is, no. I only suspected at the very last, though I will confess to you that I saw her leave."

"And how could you not have stopped her, Charity? You should have called me at once! I am as angry with you as I am with my daughter! My heart is so deeply hurt!"

Charity shook her head, feeling badly that she had not done something to prevent Anne from going and yet! She had wanted her cousin to have her heart's desire—to marry the man she loved.

She said as much, and Penelope spoke in a quiet voice, "You were very wrong, Charity. I am grievously disappointed in you."

The party returned to Grosvenor Square shortly thereafter, Lady Datchworth to retire to her sitting room, where it was well-known amongst the entire household that she had begun weeping uncontrollably, though her maid reported that Lord Datchworth was holding her very sweetly in his arms.

Charity remained in her bedchamber, refusing to permit Marie to undress her for a very long time. She sat instead in front of her fireplace, and considered all that the evening had brought to her—William's humility and yet his restraint in revealing all to her, Lady Datchworth's misery and Charity's own part in causing it, her desire to dance the ballet and would she then break her aunt's heart twice? How very complicated the business of living one's life could become, especially when her thoughts turned to William and the sweetness of his lips.

*   *   *

On the following day, the family sat about the table in the morning room considerably subdued.

"I just never thought she would do anything like this!" Lady Datchworth said, her eyes still puffy, though a great deal of her grief had dissipated in a night spent drenching her pillow with her tears. "And what sort of parent have I become that my own daughter, for love of Mr. Meesden, should feel she must elope. I just never understood the depths to her regard."

Penelope, who sat very tight-lipped, stirred her tea slowly, and said, "I am beyond mortification! My own sister involved in an elopement and that to a man unworthy of her consequence!"

Charity sat very quietly, nibbling on a piece of bread and jam. She felt so miserable that she had been part and parcel to the pain of her cousin's elope that she said, "Dearest Aunt Abigail, I do most sincerely apologize to you. I feel so very badly that Anne felt she must elope and yet how can I express to you that she loved Mr. Meesden enough to risk your censure and your love forever in order to live as wife with him. I was wrong not to have prevented her from going, but at the same time it seemed so wrong to make her stay!"

Lord Datchworth, who had been very pensive, his brow furrowed, looked at all the ladies at this point in their conversation and said, "I am to blame. I knew how my dear Annie felt about George, and by God they are well-suited and a more stable young man you could hardly find. She will have a good life and I should have stood up to the pair of you a long time ago, and given her my blessing as she asked me to!"

Lady Datchworth regarded her husband with a sad smile and said, "My dear, I only wish you had, for I could not see the truth then, though now it is clear enough. I suppose I just didn't think Anne's feelings were so very strong. I don't know what I was thinking except that from the time my girls were born, I wanted them to find husbands like you, Stephen—yes, partly of rank and fortune, I will not deny that such things are important to me because I have benefited from them all my married life. Still, I was so blind to the fact that Mr. Meesden is a perfectly acceptable match for Anne. He is an agreeable fellow, who takes great pride in his land and how could I have been such a fool?"

Lord Datchworth rose to his feet suddenly, nearly oversetting his cup of coffee as he did so, and moved to stand beside his wife. He stooped down beside her and took hold of both her hands as he held her gaze and said, "Now you listen here. Enough of these self-recriminations. We both may have been a little at fault, but not for the wrong reasons—we both love her. Let's place a notice in *The Times* and see that this affair has at least the appearance of our foreknowledge and certainly all of our approval. And then perhaps we can have a party for them in the near future, once they've returned from a honeymoon—at our expense, of course!"

"Oh, Stephen, it is the very least we can do!" And Lady Datchworth burst into tears. "One tries to be an exemplary parent but it seems so easy to make very large mistakes without the least awareness that one is doing so!"

"There, there, my pet. Please don't cry again, I don't think I could bear it!"

Only as Lady Datchworth gave her beloved husband a watery smile, did Charity notice that Penelope was staring at her parents in disbelief. "You cannot be serious!" Penelope cried. "Why, Anne deserves no such attention, no such consideration as what you suggest. Everyone will think that we approve of Mr. Meesden and I certainly do not! How could Anne be so addleminded? I have tried to direct her thoughts all these years, to shape her character but to little avail so it seems! But Papa, you cannot really mean you intend to submit a notice to *The Times*? We should cast her off! Indeed, we should make it quite clear that her actions are separate from our own."

Charity cried, "You cannot mean what you are saying, Penelope! You are speaking of Anne, remember? Your own sister! Would you separate yourself from her forever because she loved Mr. Meesden?"

"First of all, I don't think you have any right to sit there in judgment upon anything that I might say—and you know perfectly well why," she laughed somewhat scornfully. "After all, you let her go! I agree with Mama, you are equally to blame for this scandal! Secondly, I certainly hope you do not cherish such ridiculous notions of love as Anne does, for you are destined to disappointment otherwise, and lastly, lest you think me entirely hardhearted, I meant only for Anne to remain outside our little family circle for a year, perhaps two. Long enough for the *haut ton* to comprehend that we do not approve of her conduct!"

Charity sat back in her chair feeling bludgeoned by her cousin's words. If Penelope would do so much to Anne for an elopement, what were her intentions then, were she to reveal her own identity as Mademoiselle Novarre? Charity shuddered at the thought and as she regarded the hard cast to Penelope's pretty face, her chin set, her eyes dark and frowning, her cheeks drawn and pale, she realized that her beloved Penelope was suffering from a similar affliction as William and she said, "I never thought to hear such bitterness flow from your lips, Pen. You, whom I admired more than any other female of my acquaintance. I have been greatly mistaken in your character, and I now wonder if some of the advice you have given me ought to be consigned to the rubbish heap!"

"Charity!" Penelope cried. "Now what has set you upon your high horse? Tell her, Mama, that I am right in this, that we ought to shun Anne until such time as it is perfectly clear to the *beau monde* that we believe her elopement has quite put her beyond the pale!"

But both Lord and Lady Datchworth were silent as they stared at their eldest daughter. Lord Datchworth remained beside his wife holding her hand, and Lady Datchworth pressed a hand to her lips, tears again trembling in her eyes.

"What is it?" Penelope cried. "Why do you all stare at me in this manner? Mama, tell Papa that this is what you wish to do and that his suggestions are quite silly given the offensive nature of Anne's elopement."

Lady Datchworth glanced down at her hands in which she held a crumpled, wet kerchief. She tried to speak but apparently could not. It was Lord Datchworth who shook his head, saying, "I never thought to hear a child of mine speak so coldly about her own sister. I agree with Charity, my dear Pen, *we are speaking of Anne!* And however much I dislike the notion that she eloped with Mr. Meesden, I do not at this late hour intend to cast off my own flesh and blood. We are the ones who appear in the wrong in this situation, Penelope. Not Anne. She did very right to follow her heart in this instance."

"Papa," Penelope cried. "I can scarcely credit my ears."

"And another thing, young lady. You just tend to your own business, for if you don't find a way of bringing Lord Meares up to scratch and settling into a home of your own, I shall hire you a companion and send you to live in Bath for the remainder of your life. I am sick to death of season upon season of your absurd stratagems to win Redbourne, when it is clear he never cared a fig for you! If we were to examine your conduct all these years against poor Annie's one miserable attempt to find happiness in her life, I daresay you would come off appearing quite no-how. So, I wish to hear no more of your nonsense and you may begin by telling your cousin the truth about you and William."

"I don't know what you mean, Papa," Penelope said, and resorted to lifting her delicate lace kerchief to her eyes.

and dabbing at them as though she was crying.

Lord Datchworth huffed out a great breath of air, and said, "If you do not, I will!"

Penelope glared at her father and said, "I refuse to do so and I simply will not remain here and listen to anything you might have to say about *that man!*"

And with that, she rose to her feet, and holding the skirts of her pale blue muslin morning gown in her hands, she walked quietly from the room.

Lord Datchworth turned to Charity and said, "I should have spoken to you much sooner, my dear. For I can see now that many of the difficulties rife in this situation are due to my silence. But you must understand that I love Penelope dearly, but she is something of a fish—though I am perfectly persuaded she has met her match in Meares and I only hope she doesn't give him so great a disgust of herself that he turns coat upon us! Well, enough of that for the moment, for what I wish to tell you is that to a large degree there ain't a man in Mayfair who blames William for his scurrilous treatment of my Pen." He laughed lightly as he released his wife's hands and returned to his seat to take a sip of his coffee. "Damme, but when she gets that curst head of hers set upon a course, it's like traveling down a steep hill without a brake! She's that stubborn! But when John died, Charity, Pen got it fixed in her brain that William would do equally well, and the idea stuck so fast, that he couldn't hint her away no matter how hard he tried. And finally, he just gave up and started this horrid lifting of his brow and giving the cut direct, first to Pen and then to any female who so much as hinted that she would find his advances acceptable. I don't like to say these things to you, because I love my daughter, but she could never let William go—in fact, she still hasn't!"

"But I'd no idea," Charity breathed. "In her letters, she told me of many instances of his cruelty, but I never thought that behind his actions was so much provocation.

292

I am shocked greatly and disappointed beyond words, for I believed her and was loyal to my memories of her."

Lord Datchworth regarded her steadily as he said, "And especially loyal where William was concerned."

Charity nodded her head. "Yes, for from the moment of my arrival in London, I was fully prepared to despise him. And that without ever giving him a chance to explain." She thought over carefully events of the past several days and realized now that she had been given any number of hints regarding the truth—her uncle continually pressing Penelope about her schemes, Penelope's falseness in her letters, revealing only what she wished Charity to know, and what were her intentions now, regarding an unmasking at Drury Lane? She could no longer trust her cousin and wondered how much of Penelope's enthusiasm for Charity's continued career as a ballerina had come from Pen's desire to somehow hurt either herself or William.

And with this thought, her mind turned toward the earl, all of his actions cast in a new light, that again shifted his image about in her mind. He was at fault, to a large degree, she would never deny that, but what young man of three and twenty, who had just inherited an enormous birthright, one he had never expected to inherit, would be able to handle properly all the attending difficulties that such a position in society—however exalted—would bring with it? And her heart softened toward William more than it ever had, for now she understood a little of the torment he had endured in the ten years since John's death. And when she recalled the night of Lady Dunford's ball, and how his friends practically ignored Hugh but fawned all over him, she understood enough of William to know that he loathed such attentions.

Charity finished her breakfast and after a few minutes she said that she must prepare to return to Tunbridge Wells, whereupon her uncle gave her such a beseeching look that she nearly cast herself into his arms and begged him to advise her.

But she knew that no matter what her uncle said, she would never be content with following someone else's advice. No, the course she laid for her feet, right or wrong, must be her own.

Within an hour, she was in Monsieur Bovin's rooms in Hans Town and working through *Le Papillon* yet again.

Chapter Twenty

The late afternoon sun shone upon the glossy black coat of William's favorite stallion, Saturn. The earl was threading his horse through dozens of highly polished carriages that also glimmered in the April sunshine as the *ton* traveled in stately progression along Rotten Row. The ladies favored the open carriages, the landau especially, where they might sit with elegant silk parasols twirling in gloved fingers, and flirt as much as they liked, but at a very safe distance.

The gentlemen preferred their horses that they might move freely amongst the carriages. William, especially, preferred his horse, and if he were to drive to Hyde Park it would be in his light curricle that he could maneuver with similar ease past any dawdling carriage that chose to stop in mid-progress.

Beside him, Hugh rode a handsome chestnut gelding, who snorted and stomped his feet, quite in harmony with Hugh's dashing appearance in a bottle green coat, buff breeches, and Hessians. He wore a decided frown upon his face as he said, "But who is that fellow with the flat nose and the face which looks as though an anvil fell on it!"

"That, my dear Hugh, is Mr. Stokes, who has been following me for the past two days."

"That runner fellow who believes that I am The Gentleman?"

"The very same!"

"The devil take it! But if I am suspect, why has he been trailing you all over Mayfair?"

"I don't know, but I have a feeling he has learned something more of The Gentleman's exploits, but from what source I can only guess. He may be a curst-looking fellow but he's got curious instincts and I've little doubt somehow he knows I am his man!"

Hugh looked a trifle conscience as he slapped his riding crop against his saddle. "William, I don't like to mention it, but I might have said something to Meares about The Gentleman the other night. Not intending to, but the fact is I just don't remember."

"How's this?" William cried. "Hugh, you've not betrayed me?"

Hugh stroked his chin and shook his head. "Damme if I know what I did. I was playing at piquet with him, and the next thing I knew I was in Francoise's room and the devil if I know how I got there. Though I do remember Meares had ordered the finest brandy and halfway through the evening, I recall thinking to myself that the bottle was nearly empty and dash it if Meares had only had but one or two snifters! But that's all that comes back to me except that he asked a great many questions about you."

William frowned, trying to remember the viscount of the night before and was struck by how many times Lord Meares directed questions regarding The Gentleman to Anne. He thought it very likely that Lord Meares was fully aware of his identity, but he couldn't imagine such a man, who always tended to his own affairs, running to Bow Street with any news Hugh might have imparted to him. Of course, now were it Penelope—and he shook his head, for if she knew the truth, then there was nothing more to be said! Only why would Meares have said anything to her?

He cursed beneath his breath, his agitation of the moment communicating itself to his horse, and Saturn sidled toward Hugh's mount, both horses starting to buck. Hugh called to William to have a care but he merely laughed at Hugh and said it was the very least he deserved for having the worst propensity for getting completely foxed on but a thimbleful of brandy!

When William had finally brought his mount under control, he said, "I fear Miss Ware has somehow learned of my exploits, but what could she possibly have gained by informing Bow Street?"

"That lady," Hugh cried, voicing a certain disgust he felt for Penelope, "would not hesitate to bear such a tale to the entire *beau monde* would it serve her purposes. And she has been chomping at the bit to bring you down a peg or two for these past five years and more!"

William nodded. "So it would seem." And he eased his horse between a whisky on one side and a peach, silk-lined phaeton on the other. Both gentlemen slowed perceptibly as they passed the phaeton, and doffed their hats to the Wilson sisters who were the most notorious Cyprians of the day.

Hugh cried, "Dash it, I always wanted to have enough brass to have intrigued Harriette. Prettiest ankles in London and what a wit!" He then doffed his hat a second time as Harriette bestowed a very pretty smile upon him. He sighed with pleasure and then reverted to the business at hand. "But enough of that. What do you intend to do about Charity? Is she not expected to unmask this evening?"

"That she is!" William cried, as they passed beneath large shade trees, the weak sunlight dappling the horses with shadows of leaves.

"Do you mean to let her?" Hugh asked, incredulous.

"I can't say that I have a great deal of choice in the

matter. She is my betrothed, but that only because a notice appeared in *The Morning Post*. She never had the least intention of marrying me and if she dances tonight, she will unmask."

Hugh nodded in an absent manner. "I'm sorry for you then, for I know you love her."

William drew in a large breath and said, "That I do!"

Hugh shifted in his saddle to face his friend, and with a frown, said, "Will, I've something to tell you. I've been meaning to for several days now, but I haven't known just how."

"Now what's that?" William cried in a good-natured manner, fully expecting to hear something frivolous.

"I—that is, we—are leaving tonight. We are leaving England, Francoise and I." He paused for a moment, swallowing hard before he could continue, "We are going to Virginia, as it happens."

William regarded his friend from schooldays, a pain striking his heart at this sudden and unexpected news. "But why, how, though I daresay I already know. Hugh, have the three percenters taken everything?"

"Oh, no!" Hugh responded dryly. "I have these clothes that I am wearing, a collection of three gold, silver, and jewelled snuffboxes of which the moneylenders know nothing, and a pair of dueling pistols. I wouldn't call that impoverished precisely, just a bit under the hatches!"

"I can scarcely credit it," William said, shaking his head. "But you must let me do something for you! I will do something! Can I pay for your passage or perhaps settle some of your debts here? Hugh, I can stand the nonsense—anything you need!"

Hugh reached over and clapped him on the shoulder as he said, "You've always been more than a friend to me, Will. I've thought of you as a brother these ten years and more. But thank you, no. This is my difficulty."

"Well, perhaps you've mistaken my meaning for if I

must give you a wedding present—for I do presume you mean to marry the wench—''

Hugh regarded his friend sternly for a moment and said, "The *lady*, Will, or we shall part company now.''

William was a trifle taken aback, but he immediately retrenched, "Yes, of course. I do beg your pardon. Now, as for a wedding present, what about a tobacco plantation for you to manage. The Sandridges have some interests in the Colonies, though we don't often discuss our connections to a great variety of trading concerns. But there's beautiful land to be had, and if you've an inclination, perhaps we can make some sort of arrangement—purely for profit, of course!''

Hugh laughed lightly. "I wish I had enough nobility of spirit to refuse such an offer, but the fact is, I want a home for my children, and I'll work damn hard, William. You won't regret a thing!'' And as he regarded his friend, he noticed from the corner of his eye that Mr. Stokes had drawn nearer to them, and he added, "What a confounded nuisance that man is. And if I don't miss my mark, he'll not stop until he's got his reward. A thousand pounds, so I've heard! Damme if I don't think it would be a great deal of fun to—Will, by God, I've got it! I think I know what we can do, and end this business regarding The Gentleman once and for all!''

He then bade William return to Berekeley Square where he fully intended to lay before him a brilliant scheme for ridding the earl of the pesky Mr. Stokes forever. In addition, Hugh thought his clever plan would provide William one last opportunity of persuading his bride-to-be to marry him after all!

Once Hugh had presented his daring scheme to William both men decided that not only would Lady Redbourne need to be consulted and involved in at least part of the evening's stratagems, but Lord and Lady Datchworth as well. And when they spoke to William's mama, who reclined upon her chaise longue in her sitting room, frowning and nodding, she gave her opinion at last, "You have both, the pair of you, been rascally from the time you were at Eton together. This entire affair—The Gentleman, indeed, William!—" And she shook her head, scowling at him all the while, "—puts me in mind of any number of scrapes you've shared together. I suppose in its own way it is rather fitting that you would help each other out of these difficulties. Though I must confess that though the whole business seems ramshackle, it might just work. I only ask that you call upon Lady Datchworth and send her to me as quickly as you can for the hour is fast advancing! And William, do try if you can to persuade Charity from her present course, for as much as I admire her talent, her years upon the stage would be quite limited and then what would she have?"

William kissed her upon her cheek, the fragrance of summery lavender assailing him and he pressed her hand, thanking her for being so understanding. The gentlemen walked to the door and Lady Redbourne called out, "We'll miss you, Hugh. Take care of yourself, and your bride, and the best of good fortune to you."

Hugh paused and turned to face Lady Redbourne, offering her his very best bow. And then they were off.

Parting company, Hugh went to Francoise's rooms near Drury Lane and explained the role she would be playing in the evening's farce. Afterward, he hired a post chaise and four and in a goodly amount of time they were both packed and ready for their journey. They had now only to wait until they must arrive at Drury Lane—Hugh dressed in the guise of The Gentleman and Francoise as *Le Papillon*.

William, on the other hand, went to Lady Datchworth's where he spoke privately with both Charity's aunt and uncle. Lord Datchworth permitted him to tell his wife the entire truth, though they were both profoundly shocked to

300

discover that William was The Gentleman. They shook their heads and exclaimed. William apologized profusely, again humbling himself for his wretched behavior, particularly toward Penelope.

Lord Datchworth, however, shook his head in disgust as he said, "I'll tell you what I told Charity this morning, Redbourne. There ain't a man amongst the *beau monde* who blames you for treating my daughter as you have. Mayhap you were quite young when you came into your title, and a little grace might have carried the day, but you weren't of that stamp! What could you do? I should've put a stop to it years ago, but I've always felt children ought to find their own feet—but Penelope never did!"

William said, "I don't pretend to understand your daughter fully, but whatever her reasons, I still have no excuse for my many incivilities toward her." He cleared his throat. "There's only one small difficulty. You see, I am convinced Penelope knows of my identity and that it was she who informed Bow Street against me."

Lord Datchworth nodded, though his expression was one of anger. "That would be just like her to do so!" And after he had made a few inquiries amongst the servants, he discovered that she had indeed gone to Bow Street only yesterday. "The scheming child! She's never really grown up!"

William begged Lord Datchworth's forgiveness again regarding his own exploits as the highwayman and made it quite clear that he insisted upon paying Bow Street's reward, for by the end of the evening he hoped that their plan would give the appearance that The Gentleman was gone from England forever!

Lord Datchworth nodded, and begged to know a few more details of his scheme. When he had been told the whole of it, he asked, "But how will you get Bow Street to Drury Lane?"

William smiled a trifle sheepishly and said, "I was

hoping I might make use of Penelope."

Lord Datchworth gave a crack of laughter, and even Lady Datchworth said that it was the very least Penelope deserved for having caused so much turmoil in so very many lives. "For I am persuaded that had Penelope not been involved, Charity would not have taken her ballet quite this far. I know she possesses a great deal of talent, as you very well know, but I have known her since she was a child and her fondest desires have always been to have a family of her own. Lord Redbourne, I feel very strongly that my niece has fallen deeply in love with you, but because of Penelope's persuasiveness over the years she has convinced herself that she cannot love you. May I make a very small suggestion?"

William nodded.

"Gather together a very large bouquet of flowers, and present yourself in her dressing room—very scandalous, I know, but we are all quite desperate—and then simply tell her that if she wishes to unmask, you still want to marry her."

"I would still desire. I love her!"

Lady Datchworth smiled sweetly. "I never knew you before, William, and I now begin to think Charity almost as fortunate as myself!" And here she turned to her husband, and reaching a hand toward him, had all the delight of having Lord Datchworth come to her immediately, lift her hand, and kiss it tenderly. Turning to William, she said, "Just love her but a trifle and I think she will finally realize her heart. At least I hope so. For as much as I am persuaded she loves her dance, I think she wishes for a family and children of her own just a little bit more."

A very odd thought struck her and she turned to her husband who was still holding her hand and she said, "Stephen! And you pretended to take your own niece as your mistress? I am greatly shocked!"

He patted her hand and with a laugh, said, "But you cannot imagine my surprise when there I was, in The Green Room, prepared to flirt with her and ask her to drive out to Hyde Park so that I could cut a dash and make you jealous, only to find Charity hidden behind the mask. Just before I entered the room you see, I heard her call out Hugh's name—as clear as a bell!" He opened his eyes wide, "I nearly fainted, I can tell you!"

When everyone was satisfied as to what part they were to take in William's schemes, Penelope was brought in and told a slightly different story. William confessed to her that he was The Gentleman, and though Penelope was a little surprised at his confession, she kept her eyes down, her gaze fixed upon the carpet, and murmured that of course she would forgive him. He then told her that Charity was Mademoiselle Novarre and she again seemed surprised, though he was certain she already knew.

Finally, he told her that in order to lay both The Gentleman and hopefully Mademoiselle Novarre to rest, William would abduct Charity from the stage before she unmasked, and race to Dover and then to France where their trail would simply vanish. Later they would reemerge as Lord and Lady Redbourne.

Penelope's cheek quivered upon this final note, and she glanced at William. He could not mistake the hard, unforgiving glint in her eyes and he said, "Penelope, I am sorry we've never quite gotten on all these years and I have treated you abominably. Pray forgive me."

Penelope said that she hadn't the least notion what he was talking about and said that if he had nothing further to say to her that she really needed to be dressing for the theater since Lord Meares and his mama had asked her to join them in his box.

It wasn't but ten minutes later, as William and the Datchworths remained quietly within the viscount's office, that Hinx showed them a note Penelope meant to send round to Bow Street.

Lady Datchworth sighed deeply and pressed her kerchief to her eyes. Lord Datchworth rose from his chair and clapping William upon the shoulder, said, "Then we shall see you later at your mama's house. Very good. And *all's well that ends well*, I trust." And as a frown creased his brow, he said, "However, I think I shall send a little missive of my own to Lord Meares. If anyone can manage my daughter—he can!"

This time, Charity sat in a very fine dressing room, the walls covered in pink and burgundy flowers, the furniture in gilt, and the floor covered with a thick Aubusson carpet in black, green, and burgundy. She sat before a mirror, her mask lying upon the dressing table, as Furney smiled at her in a wistful manner, and made certain that the wings of her costume were still very secure. A rapping sounded upon the door and Charity reached instinctively for her mask. Her hair had already been powdered and she could hear the orchestra tuning their instruments. Her heart jumped at the very sound of the orchestra caterwauling, but not more so than when she heard the messenger boy inform her that Lord Redbourne was begging a few words with her.

Charity was at first going to refuse, but then she remembered that after tonight, after her unmasking, she would undoubtedly be cut off from his society forever, and she suddenly needed to see him. "Please send him here," she responded quietly.

Furney said, "What do you mean to do, dearest? I have never seen you so distressed."

Charity said, "I don't know. I suppose I wish merely to say good-bye to him." She then blushed slightly as she turned back to the mirror and said, "But I do wish to speak privately with him if you don't mind, Furney. He is after all my betrothed."

Miss Agnes Pelham-Furneux was a tall thin female of forty years who had served as Charity's companion for the past ten years and more, since her mama had died. She loved Charity as a daughter, and as a sister and she couldn't bear seeing her charge so torn. As she moved toward the door, she turned to her and said, "I know we've never spoken of such matters before, but don't be afraid to give in to your heart, my dear. I know you have worked very hard for this moment, but can the ballet provide everything you wish for?"

Charity regarded her with much surprise. "Furney, are you saying that you don't think I ought to perform tonight?"

Furney took a deep breath and simply said, "If you do, don't unmask—regardless of what the governors might say to you—and let this be a farewell performance. You were meant for Redbourne as much as he was meant for you. You love him, my dear. You just haven't seen it yet."

And she was gone. Charity sat before the mirror her heart in her throat, uncertain what to think. She had believed Furney wanted her to dance, as her mother did. Oh, Mama, she thought, I need you now. I don't know what to do, what to think!

The door opened slowly, and in the mirror Charity saw William's reflection, his sailor-streaked hair gleaming in the candlelight, his neckcloth tied to perfection and a diamond sparkling in its elegant folds. In his arms he carried a beautiful bouquet of exquisite red roses.

He said, "You appear so different with your hair powdered. How are you? How do you feel? I hope my coming here like this will not upset your performance."

Charity wanted to answer that it would no doubt destroy it, instead she responded, "No, of course not. Do come in and—and close the door if you like. It can become very hectic backstage like this."

He gave her the flowers and she pressed her face into them, letting the fragrance flow over her. "They are lovely, William, thank you."

She put them in a vase by her mirror and was arranging them, when she felt his hands upon her arms, as he drew close to her and said, "I love you, Charity. I love you more than I can ever hope to express to you. From the moment you returned to London I have felt as though the clouds over my dull existence finally parted and the sun had broken through at last. I want to marry you, even if you unmask tonight."

Charity gasped, for she could not believe he could mean what he said, "You would do that because you love me?"

"Because I can't bear the thought of living without you."

"Oh, William," she cried, as she turned around to face him. "I am in the worst state of misery. I don't know what to do."

He slipped his arms about her and holding her very close he said, "I wish I could tell you what to do. I can only promise you that should you desire to wed me we will go to Paris as often as you like. You could perform in London, all over the world, if you wished for it. I don't care, I just wish to have you as my wife."

"No," she said emphatically. "You do not know what you are saying. There is such a clear line for us over which we may not cross. You know that as well as I."

He held her tightly. "I won't let you go. I love you too much, and the world will simply have to understand."

She said, "I would not wish it that way. We should have children, William, dozens of them. And I could scarcely dance then, now could I?"

"Oh, Charity, my love!" And he released her slightly in order to kiss her very hard.

Charity threw her arms about his neck, finally admitting what she must have known since the moment she saw him again in Lord Datchworth's office. She loved him. She loved him more than life itself and she pressed as close to him as she could, afraid that once he drew back from her that they would be separated again and she couldn't bear it! His lips burned against her own, his voice a whisper as he said, "I love you, my darling Charity. I love you."

After a moment, he drew back slightly and said, "There is just one more thing I want you to know. I should have told you last night, when you were probing so carefully, but you will never credit that I had forgotten all about it—the answer is yes, I am The Gentleman."

Charity felt her entire being relax at these words, and she leaned into him. "I am so grateful you told me, but what a rogue you are! And how could you tease me about whose kisses I preferred?"

He smiled down at her, his eyes full of love and he would have answered her but a sharp rapping on the door was followed by a warning that Charity's performance was but minutes away. "Oh, good gracious!" she cried. "Whatever am I to do?"

William saw the mask sitting on the table and he picked it up and helped Charity tie it firmly about her powdered curls.

He looked at her in the mirror and said with a rather wicked smile upon his face, "I nearly forgot. The Gentleman is here tonight, and he intends to see you again."

And with that, he kissed her quickly upon her neck and quit the room. Charity stared after him, completely baffled by what he had said. But she had no time to concern herself with that for Furney appeared in the doorway and said, "Come, come. The stage manager is calling for you!"

Chapter Twenty-One

Lord Meares sat between, his mother and Penelope and was enjoying himself hugely. He had already been apprised of the farce ready to unfold before him, but the most poignant part of the play was his sweet conniving Penelope who was in for the worst shock of her life! And he laughed softly to himself particularly when he turned toward Penelope and saw how eagerly she was watching the stage, her brown eyes glittering with the excitement of events to come!

The audience, fools that they were, stomped their feet in frenzied anticipation of *Le Papillon*. The boxes on the upper tiers, were littered, crowded even, with the *haut ton*, all waiting breathlessly for the revealing of the real Mademoiselle Novarre. What sheep! he thought. And as the curtain parted, the audience fell to an electric hushed silence, as *Le Papillon* commenced.

William and Jack worked frantically backstage with a number of excited stage hands who were looking forward to taking on a few of the runners—them blokes what was always poking their noses into things which didn't concern them anyway!

Pulling his boots on quickly, William finished the final touches to his costume as he placed the long curling wig upon his head and donned his black silk mask. Jack whispered, "Hugh's in position. I spoke with him not fifteen minutes ago and two of the grooms will overturn dung carts in the street as soon as you enter your post chaise. All's as ready as it can be!" And he turned to direct the stage hands and two more of William's servants to the various entrances to the stage.

William heard the music, his heart now pounding in his ears from the sheer excitement of the moment, and he moved toward the wings from whence he would soon enter the stage.

Charity was able, much to her great surprise, to forget William's recent visit to her dressing room, her thoughts focused completely upon the *divertissement*. Once the music began, all she saw was the butterfly, her friend and companion of at least the last year when Monsieur Bovin had choreographed *Le Papillon* for her. She gave herself fully to this performance, uncertain whether it would be her last, but certainly desirous of making it her best and her slippers seemed to have a life of their own as they moved relentlessly about the stage, *sur les pointes,* in pursuit of her butterfly, her dreams.

Too soon, however, the short *andantino* was over and she awakened from her dancing slumber to hear a thunderous applause that rippled over her in waves. She rose to her feet and curtsied deeply only to hear the applause turn to a rhythmic clapping and shouting of "Unmask, unmask!"

Charity finally realized that the moment had indeed arrived for a decision, and she hesitated, staring blindly out at the audience and then searching the boxes for

William's face. But he was not there! How was she ever to make such a decision, and her heart began pounding fiercely. One or the other, a life, a family with William or a heart devoted solely to the ballet.

She thought of her dance and her arms rose to the ribbons keeping her mask securely about her head, but visions of William assailed her and she lowered her arms, the audience frenzied with excitement. Which path?

But something changed suddenly and an obscure shouting occurred from the audience that made no sense to her at all, at least not at first—muffled shouts of bandits and highwaymen. But from the upper boxes, she heard many females squealing that it was The Gentleman! And she noticed that many members of the audience were turned to gaze at something to her right.

Whirling around, she realized just as she saw him, that it was William the audience was responding to. He was dressed in his highwayman's costume, lace foaming at his throat and wrists, long leather boots folded over his thighs, as he swaggered across the stage, as much at home there as any seasoned actor. The audience was wild with excitement!

Charity smiled, her entire being covered in gooseflesh as she laughed and said, "So this is what you meant!"

He approached her and in front of hundreds of shouting people, he kissed her—the rogue! She pushed him away slightly but he held her and regarded her directly as he said, "Whatever you want in this moment, is yours to command. You may leave with me, but if you do, both The Gentleman and Mademoiselle Novarre will die. But if you choose to stay, I will remain by your side."

Charity hesitated only for a moment as the path she desired most made itself quite clear to her. A commotion backstage along with shouts of "Bramfield, be gone at once! Bow Street is here!" distracted her, but only for a second, as she cried, "William, I am satisfied. I'll go with you now."

He drew in his breath sharply. "By God, you won't regret it, my dear!" And he scooped her up into his arms and to the roar of the crowd, crying out their displeasure at having their curiosity thwarted, he whisked her from the stage.

Setting her down as soon as they were in the wings, Jack found them both, calling out, "Follow me! This way!" And they passed by tangles of ropes, scenery, and props, amidst the confusion of the opera-dancers, who skirted out of their way, as they ran to the back of the theater, into the brisk night air where a post chaise and four waited for them.

As Charity clambered into the vehicle she was shocked to find Marie seated within.

"Hurry, *cherie!*" Marie cried. "Bow Street is everywhere! Ah, hurry!"

Jack rode postillion and in a matter of seconds had the post chaise moving at a brisk pace. Behind them, Charity could hear the frustrated cries of any number of male voices, along with the sounds of horses whinnying and snorting. As the coach turned the corner, she was able to see that two dung carts had been overturned making the street impassable behind them. She could not resist crying out in amusement and laughing, though tears somehow tumbled down her cheeks at the same time.

The post chaise very quickly drew to a stop alongside another carriage, which Charity soon discovered was Lord Datchworth's town coach. Within seconds they were inside, the door shut, and Jack had driven the post chaise away. William informed Charity that Jack would return the carriage to the Swan with Two Necks Inn from which hostelry it had been hired.

They did not leave immediately, but in a few seconds

more, an identical post chaise to the one Jack drove pulled alongside their carriage and Charity recognized Hugh's voice as he called out, "We shall write you from Virginia. Good-bye, Will! Now, get along with you! Go!"

"Oh, not Hugh!" Charity cried, tears now beginning to pour down her cheeks. "Where is he going? Virginia? But why? Not his debts?"

"I'm afraid so!" And William called out for Lord Datchworth's postillion to spring 'em. As the coach pulled forward, Charity caught sight of a female within Hugh's coach, her hair powdered and a white mask tied about her hair.

"Francoise! Dressed like me!" she cried.

"Yes!" William cried as he ripped his mask from his face, and pulled the long wig from his head. "She is masquerading as Mademoiselle Novarre and we hope at some point that Bow Street will be drawn away from us and toward them. Our identities should therefore disappear forever. Of course they are to be married."

"At least they will have one another, but I shall miss Hugh very much!"

William swallowed hard and in a tight voice said, "And so will I."

Charity placed a hand upon William's arm as the coach gathered speed, and asked, "Where are we going now? What if one of the runners has spied our trick?"

William covered her hand and responded, "I shan't concern myself with such an eventuality. Right now we have but one mission, to divest ourselves of these garments and return to my townhouse in Berkeley Square where you will be amazed to find an engagement party in progress, hosted by my mother!"

Charity began untying her mask and in a quiet voice said, "Your mother knows then? And does she still wish me to be your wife? But how could she?"

William laughed softly. "You have nothing to fear on that score, Charity. As it happens, she will wonder only that you have decided that I will suit *you* well enough!"

"Oh!" Charity cried.

"But I ought perhaps to warn you that your aunt and uncle are already with my mother."

Charity let out a great sigh. "Then they know all, about both of us, I mean."

William nodded as he began struggling out of his boots. "Yes, my dear, there are no secrets now."

"I must confess that I feel greatly relieved. Are you aware of how many whiskers I have told in the past few days? More than I have in my life, and I mean never to do so again. It is frightfully uncomfortable to be lying to those you love and who trust you!"

William said, "There is just one more thing you ought to know. Even if we do arrive safely at my townhouse, I fully expect your cousin, Penelope, to arrive shortly thereafter with Bow Street in tow. Lord Meares has been instructed to recommend such a course of action."

"But why?"

William removed his coat of burgundy velvet and quickly stripped off his white shirt trimmed with lace at the throat and the wrists. Charity turned her head, feeling quite embarrassed by the nearness of his bare chest, and when he had donned his plain white shirt and began carefully adjusting the folds of his neckcloth, he said with a slight laugh, "You may look at me now, if you wish, for I have my shirt on. But as to why we've included Meares, it seems your uncle believes he's the very one to handle Penelope—and we must lay this last ghost to rest!"

Charity was very quiet for a moment. Finally she said, "I never understood the extent to Pen's bitterness until now. But you are right. Her desire initially was to hurt you and later to punish me! I can see now that I must have truly

314

horrified her when she learned I was Mademoiselle Novarre, for her concern is all in appearances. Did you know she wished to cast Anne off for a year or two when she learned she had eloped with Mr. Meesden?"

He shook his head. "I am not surprised. But I am fully convinced that you may leave all to Lord Meares." He then recommended to Charity to begin changing into the gown Marie had provided for her.

"Only if you now turn away and close your eyes firmly, my lord!"

He did so with a laugh and Marie said, *"Cherie,* we ought first to brush the powder from your hair, and then you shall don this gown. But we must hurry for we still do not have a great deal of time!"

After the performance of *Le Papillon,* when The Gentleman had lifted Mademoiselle Novarre into his arms, the ladies in the upper tiers squealed and gasped with delight. And a few moments later, when two Bow Street runners actually ran across the stage with pistols brandished, the crowd went mad with excitement though two tomatoes did find their way to the stage as the gentlemen in the audience hooted the runners and stamped their feet. In the box next to Lord Meares's, two ladies fainted from so much rapturous hysteria and all the while Penelope sat very still, an expression of intense satisfaction upon her milky features.

Lord Meares admitted to himself that he was a complete rascal as he leaned near to Penelope and whispered, "I think you should know that Redbourne lied to you."

Penelope appeared a little shocked, as she began wafting her mother-of-pearl fan over her features and asked, "What do you mean?"

"He told you they meant to go to Paris, did he not?"

"Yes," she responded, somewhat impatiently.

"And you were the one who informed Bow Street that he would be here this evening, were you not?"

Penelope nodded and immediately attempted to justify such an action, "For I see no reason why he should not be subject to the King's Law as we all are!"

Lord Meares leaned closer to her still as he placed his hand upon the back of her chair and whispered, "Don't gammon me, my love. You don't give a fig for the King's Law. You only wanted to prevent your cousin from winning the prize you could not! And what better way to do so than to inform Bow Street that he would be here this evening! Your revenge would be utterly perfect then, for you would hurt both Redbourne and your cousin with only the smallest effort!"

Penelope lifted her chin as she responded sarcastically, "You seem to comprehend me so completely, my lord, that I see no need to answer you!"

Sliding his hand down her arm he said, "But you appear as though you think I disapprove, when nothing could be further from the truth. I simply feel your immense talents are wasted upon something so paltry as desiring to expose Redbourne. You see, I am fully able to appreciate your abilities and ambitions, but I repeat again, you have been led astray, my dear. Your schemes have been foiled."

Penelope turned to face Lord Meares, narrowing her eyes at him in a speculative manner. "What do you know that you haven't told me?"

"I know that by the time Bow Street finds the vehicle now sporting The Gentleman and Mademoiselle Novarre, the runners will discover only the faintest trail of both personages and any subsequent descriptions of the fugitives will reveal their identities to be, not Redbourne and Miss Holwell, but Hugh Bramfield and an opera-dancer by the name of Francoise, with whom Bramfield so foolishly fell in love. And by the time Bow Street can ascertain precisely where they might have gone, Hugh and his bride will be on a ship to the Colonies."

Penelope leaned back in her chair, numb with shock. She had not foreseen that Redbourne would have lied to her. He might have posed as a highwayman, but he had always been a man of honor in every other respect—it never occurred to her that he would prevaricate and she shook her perfect ringlets in an effort to dispel her disbelief.

After a moment, she closed her fan with a snap and asked, "Where, then, are Charity and William?"

Lord Meares breathed a sigh of satisfaction as he said, "They are no doubt at this very moment heading toward his own townhouse where his mother is presiding over an engagement party—a sly subterfuge of their own just in case Mr. Stokes has a very different idea about what might have become of The Gentleman."

She rose abruptly and said, "I wish to speak with Mr. Stokes if he is about! For I am not finished with Redbourne yet!"

Lord Meares knew that he should have stopped her now, for it was quite wicked of him not to, but he could not resist seeing the final act, and besides, he had his own game he wished to play, for he meant at last to force her hand.

When Lord Datchworth's carriage finally pulled up before William's townhouse, Charity's hair was a glossy black from so much brushing in order to remove all of the telltale powder from her hair, and her scalp tingled dreadfully. The floor of the carriage was covered in a light powder and Charity had sneezed at least three times during the entire process. But she was now begowned in a dress of blue muslin, caught high to the waist and had blushed the entire time she had changed from her costume to the gown, because William had teased her relentlessly though he was very good about keeping his eyes closed! Her cheeks still burned slightly as she stepped down from her uncle's town chariot. About her throat was a delicate necklet of sapphires and in all appearances, save that her ringlets were not as curly as they usually were, Charity appeared as though she had just emerged from her toilette.

As soon as they both stood upon the flagways, the town coach departed, taking Marie and the accusing costumes back to Grosvenor Square.

As Charity took William's arm, a marvelous peace descended upon her and she knew in the depths of her heart that she had made the proper decision. Smiling up at him, she said, "You look very dashing, William, though your shirt-points are not as crisp as they usually are and once we are inside you may want to brush your hair for it is sticking up in the back in a very odd manner."

He smiled in return, and said, "You, however, are dressed to perfection—your maid is quite a talented female." And as they crossed the threshold to stand in the entrance hall, he turned to her and said, "Charity, you will never know how glad I am that in this moment you are with me. I was so afraid I had lost you forever!" And even though his butler was looking on, he did not hesitate to kiss her very soundly upon her lips, which only served to deepen the blush upon her cheeks.

When they entered the drawing room, Lady Datchworth gave a cry of relief, and she said, "Oh, thank heaven you have decided to quit the stage. I was so afraid—and yet, your performance was so extraordinary on Saturday—I could not have blamed you, not really, and yet—oh, my dear, I am so glad you are to marry William!" She was on her feet then, and mingled her tears with Charity's as they embraced.

Charity begged forgiveness of everyone present, even placing a tear-drenched kiss upon Lady Redbourne's soft, lavender-scented cheek. And when her eyes were dry, and Lady Datchworth had become quite calm, Lord Datchworth demanded to know every detail of their escape from the theater.

Lord Meares had warned Penelope against saying anything to his mother about Redbourne, and Lady Meares's presence as they sought out Mr. Stokes prevented Penelope from revealing the truth to the runner. And since they traveled in separate carriages, with Mr. Stokes following behind in a hackney coach, the runner was still ignorant of the true state of affairs when the entire party entered Redbourne's drawing room.

Mr. Stokes, for his part, seemed quite distracted, since he was still operating under the belief that Lord Redbourne, in the guise of The Gentleman, was being pursued by runners back at Drury Lane—and that by fellows less talented than himself! He feared someone would make a grave error in judgment and bungle the entire operation before he was able to return. But Miss Ware had convinced him that he ought to come with her to Lord Redbourne's residence. Mr. Stokes didn't trust her above half for she had a shifty manner of looking at people. It was therefore, with a great deal of astonishment that he found Lord Redbourne seated beside Miss Holwell, as content as he could be!

"There he is!" Penelope cried, leveling her arm at William. "He is The Gentleman, the man who crossed the stage at Drury Lane not half an hour past. And there is Mademoiselle Novarre!"

The assembled guests in the dowager Lady Redbourne's

drawing room all appeared quite shocked, as Lady Redbourne cried, "What is the meaning of this! Miss Ware, I take great exception to your bounding in here in this extremely hoydenish manner—and very late as well—and then accusing everyone present of the most ridiculous notions! Your manners are beyond bearing!" She then shifted her gaze to Lady Meares and called to her in a much gentler voice, "Why, Henrietta! I did not know that you would be joining us this evening, but I am very happy to see you. Do come here and let me look at you! Why it has been ages!"

Lady Meares, who was still looking at Penelope as though the tall young lady next to her had just gone mad—and was this really the female her son hoped to marry?—found it very difficult to shift her attention from Penelope to her hostess. But when she was finally able to do so, she crossed the room in her skittish manner to greet Lady Redbourne as she called out in her little girl's voice, "What a pretty gown you are wearing! And how very much purple agrees with you! I could never wear such a color or even lavender for that matter. My complexion will only bloom when surrounded by roses and delicate pinks!" She paused before her hostess and curtsied slightly as a means of displaying her elegant rose-colored silk gown. And after smiling brightly upon Lady Redbourne, she asked, "But how do you go on?"

Penelope wanted to take the situation in hand, but at every turn her desire for control seemed to be thwarted, for how could she argue with Lady Redbourne—her hostess and a poor invalid!—who leaned against several pillows, her gnarled hands held lightly upon her lap. And besides, the dowager had ignored her so completely as though the pronouncement she had made was the mere rantings of a child rather than the intent of a grown woman to see justice done! Well, perhaps not justice so much as her own

320

form of vengeance, but that was hardly the point! However, the moment her gaze settled upon Charity and William who sat opposite Lady Redbourne her anger bubbled over again.

She was about to interrupt Lady Meares's suggestion that Lady Redbourne try the baths at the Cheltenham spa, but Lord Meares checked her at the precise moment she opened her mouth to speak by telling her she looked quite pale and was she feeling all right? And in a solicitous manner that infuriated Penelope, he took a firm hold upon her elbow, guided her to a chair near the dowager, and bade her sit down. For good measure, with a wicked twitch of his lips, he added, "And where is your vinaigrette, my dear, for I would be happy to hold it beneath your nose!"

Staring up at him in surprise, Penelope cried, "What are you about, my lord? I—I am perfectly well, thank you! But, you ought to see to Mr. Stokes—"

"Yes, of course," he responded in his polite manner as he turned to the runner and said, "Do sit down, sir. Yes, there by the door, we will attend you in just a moment." And Lord Meares very properly joined his mother in greeting Lady Redbourne.

Though Charity had been prepared for Penelope's arrival and that most likely she would have found a means of bringing Mr. Stokes with her, she was still shocked by the entrance of the entire party. Part of her wished to believe that her cousin was not so very bad as this, but with such a willingness to expose William, she rather thought that now every ill-opinion of Penelope had been confirmed.

The guests were grouped near the fireplace—William and Charity seated together upon a settee across from Lady Redbourne, while Lord and Lady Datchworth sat in wing chairs between the dowager and the fireplace. The drawing room was decorated in rich contrasts of white, dark blue, and rust. Peacocks danced about the room—upon the andirons, carved into the gilt border of the mirror above the fireplace, and hidden within a flowered wallpaper *à la Chinoise.*

Lord Meares said, "And we do apologize for being so very late to your son's engagement party, but Penelope insisted upon seeing—as it turned out—Mademoiselle Novarre's last performance."

Lady Redbourne scowled upon Lord Meares, though a mischievous twinkle glimmered in her hazel eye, and in a frosty voice which carried clear to Mr. Stokes's burning ears, said, "Such a gross uncivility on your part I find quite difficult to overlook. But for my son's sake, I shall do so, only what is the meaning of your bringing *that man* along? Who is he and what does he want—and furthermore, what does your betrothed—" and here she gestured to a much startled Penelope, "—mean by leveling such ridiculous accusations against William and Charity?"

Penelope cried, "And what do you mean that you refer to me as Lord Meares's betrothed?"

Lady Redbourne lifted an austere brow at Penelope but remained silent.

Lord Meares moved to stand before Penelope, removed a thin gold snuffbox from the pocket of his waistcoat and after taking a pinch, regarded his beloved Penelope and said, "Am I mistaken, my dear, that matters are indeed not settled between us? I thought we were of one mind, that we were agreed upon every important subject in the world, including our future together! However, if I have grossly mistaken your desires, then I apologize at once. You have but to say the word and I shall *never* importune you again!" Faith, but he was enjoying himself.

Penelope, who had appeared quite angry throughout the proceedings, now turned very pale, her lips clamped tightly together. She spoke in a low voice, her brows furrowed in a decided scowl as she whispered, "Then you are in league with them."

He responded quietly, "Of course. I want a decision from you on both scores. All or nothing, Penelope. And I want your answer now. I told you on Saturday that I wanted a certain matter finished, and I meant it."

Charity could see that strong feelings worked within Penelope's breast, that her spirit was torn between wanting her revenge and knowing that if she did not accept the viscount's hand now, she would never have another opportunity. Penelope's gaze shifted to her father.

Lord Datchworth spoke cryptically, "I have always thought the city of Bath an excellent place to retire, to live out one's years in solitude and tranquillity."

These words appeared to have a strong effect upon Penelope, who gulped visibly and in a very small voice, smiled upon the viscount and said, "Of course we are engaged, I was only teasing you but a little."

Lord Meares bowed to her, satisfied, and after seeing his mother settled into a chair next to Lady Redbourne, crossed the room to take up a seat beside Charity.

At this moment, Mr. Stokes, who apparently did not at all care for being relegated to a chair by the door when he had business of great import to attend to, stepped forward, facing Lord Datchworth as he cried, "I should like to address your lordship, if I might!"

The viscount rose to his feet and said, "And what is it my good man. Why are you here? This is a very important celebration for my niece, and you disturb us. I sincerely hope that you've good reason for coming."

Mr. Stokes glanced about him in a nervous manner as he bowed slightly and said, "As to that, I've reason to believe that Lord Redbourne is The Gentleman."

"And by what cause do you make such an outrageous charge?"

"By the cause that I've received certain information of

late that directed me toward him. Your daughter, Miss Ware, told me a certain person, as yet undisclosed, heard Hugh Bramfield speak of Lord Redbourne's many exploits as the highwayman!"

Lady Redbourne winced slightly as she sat forward and exclaimed, "How dare you come in here in this extremely impudent manner, and denounce my son! I am excessively displeased. Lord Datchworth, you have my permission to toss this man out onto the flags!"

Penelope, though she regarded her newly acquired husband-to-be with much trepidation, chose to continue her original scheme. Rising to her feet, she said, "I refuse to permit this man to leave until he has spoken. I saw Lord Redbourne dressed in the guise of The Gentleman at Drury Lane. He told me this very afternoon that he meant to dress up as the highwayman and to abduct Charity, who is Mademoiselle Novarre!" She glanced toward Lord Meares, but he merely lifted a faint brow as he watched her, and her knees began to tremble.

Charity, who had suffered sufficiently from Penelope's schemes did not hesitate to say, "What are you talking about, Pen? Oh, you must be funning since we have been planning this party for these three days and more!"

Lady Redbourne turned to Penelope and said, "You must calm yourself, my dear, for I greatly fear you have been seeing phantoms for William and Charity have been with me the entire evening." And in a softer voice, she said, "And I would think, simply in memory of John's love for you, that you would not wish to brandish about such ridiculous accusations."

Penelope cried, "But you do not understand! Don't you care that your son has been masquerading as a notorious bandit?"

Lord Meares decided the farce had continued long enough, and clicking his tongue from across the room, addressed his bride-to-be, "I thought it excessively odd in you my dear that you chose to go to the theater tonight rather than to your cousin's engagement party and now I begin to feel you are developing a fever for your face is uncommonly flushed! However, all might be settled if you would but produce this witness you have been referring to, though I cannot help but wonder if your witness desires to give any such evidence."

Penelope drew in her breath sharply as she regarded Lord Meares's rather piercing gaze. Charity knew full well that the viscount himself was the witness, but she could also tell by his expression that if Penelope dared to say anything, she could expect to suffer grave consequences— such as the fulfillment of Lord Datchworth's threat of sending her to Bath for the rest of her life.

Penelope lowered her gaze to her hands folded neatly in front of her. Charity had never seen her cousin so full of emotion as in this moment, her cheeks flushed, her jaw working strongly. But avarice carried the greater weight in her heart, and revenge was forfeited. After a long moment, she lifted her gaze to the runner, her expression cloaked in her habitual demeanor of polite womanhood, and she said, "Do you know, Mr. Stokes, that it has grown very warm in here and of the moment, I cannot seem to remember who it was precisely who revealed such information to me. I have the worst memory, as it happens, and unfortunately once something leaves my mind, I fear it is gone forever."

Mr. Stokes glared, first at Penelope and then at each person in turn. Huffing out a frustrated breath of air, he cried, "I don't know what this means, but I know when I've been humbugged! And I'll get to the bottom of this if it takes all night. Now, how long did you say you were here, Lord Redbourne?"

William was about to answer him, but at that moment a

large commotion was heard in the hall, and in a few seconds, another runner burst into the room, exclaiming, "Mr. Stokes, you'll never credit what has happened!"

William's butler began an apology all the while trying to force the runner to leave the room, but the earl signaled to him to let the man alone. When the butler bowed and quit the room, Lord Datchworth said, "Go on, man! Let us hear all that you have to say. We've each an interest in this business!"

But the man seemed to have lost some of his daring as he glanced about the elegant chamber and could not at first speak. Stripping the hat from his head, a sad muddied object which he began turning nervously between hands that trembled, he cleared his throat. "It was Hugh Bramfield after all. One of our men caught sight of post chaise on Drury Lane and lit out after it on foot. He got within five feet of the carriage and what does The Gentleman do but take off his mask and wink at Timmons. By God, it were Bramfield staring back at him. But the lady's identity still remains unknown, but she were Mademoiselle Novarre for she was masked and Timmons could see her little wings since she was turned away from him and her hair was all powdered!"

Mr. Stokes stood listening to this recital, his mouth agape. He glanced first at Penelope, who remained in her chair, her skin alarmingly pale. Lud, but she was the coldest fish he had ever seen. And first she said she weren't engaged to Lord Meares and then she said she were teasing. He sighed. The lady was obviously one of those flighty females, who wanted a little adventure in her own life and had made up a tale just to set everybody in a spin. And here he was calling Redbourne The Gentleman just because a lady says she has heard things from a proper source—more like from funny little voices in her head!

He began his apologies and after a moment, Lord

Datchworth called out, "That's enough, good fellow. We all make mistakes. You just see that Mr. Bramfield is brought before the magistrates court and you shall have your reward."

"Thank you, milord. You are most kind!" He then retreated in quick form, dragging the trembling runner with him, and when the door was shut behind them, Charity breathed a very quiet sigh of relief.

Lady Meares exclaimed, "What an impertinent fellow! And how buffleheaded to have actually accused Lord Redbourne of being The Gentleman. I have known all along that it was Hugh Bramfield, for I saw him not two days ago, dressed as the highwayman and kissing a lady in front of her own townhouse on Upper Brook Street. Imagine how very shocked I was! Though I did not see the lady's face, it was clearly Hugh Bramfield!"

Charity watched Lady Meares's face and heard Lord Meares next to her chuckle softly, and she could not resist addressing the dowager, "Lady Meares, was he wearing his mask? How did you know it was Mr. Bramfield?"

"It was the look of him of course, the way he held himself as he so scandalously embraced that female! My goodness!"

And very soon Lord Datchworth began to laugh as did Lady Datchworth and even Lady Redbourne smiled and told the dowager Lady Meares that she was just as big a wet goose as she had ever been.

Soon afterward champagne was brought from the buttery and two engagements were summarily toasted. Some few minutes later the Datchworths drew Penelope into a secluded corner where they spoke quietly with her for a long time. Penelope dabbed at her eyes with her lace kerchief all the while, her head bowed, and though Charity was not at all convinced she felt the least remorse, she at least had the good grace to hug each of her parents in turn once they had finished with her. But as she rose to her feet, her expression was the same—cool, elegant, controlled.

Charity shook her head. She could not comprehend her cousin in the least, and found herself drawing a little closer to William, who reached down and gave her hand a quick squeeze.

Lord Meares then congratulated Charity upon her many talents, and she could not resist teasing him, "If we were to speak of talents, my lord, I daresay I am but a farthing candle to you. I have only recently learned the strength of my cousin's, shall we say, will, and only a man with exceptional abilities could hold such a female so firmly in check with but the merest lift of his brow."

He bowed to her and responded quietly that he and Penelope were very much alike and that he foresaw a quite productive union since he had a great many ambitions in Parliament, an arena in which he was persuaded Penelope could make much better use of her own vast repertoire of skills.

Charity responded, "I begin to think you are very right! You are a wise man, my lord, and I wish you every happiness."

He nodded again, and seeing that Penelope was just then crossing the room to join him, he moved to greet her, taking her hand and kissing her fingers lightly.

A month later, William and Charity were seated beside one another in a post chaise and four, heading toward Hertfordshire on the Great North Road where they would spend the first week of their marriage at William's country seat, and later to travel south to Dover, crossing the Channel to enjoy a prolonged honeymoon in Paris.

Between William and Charity sat a small wicker basket

which Miss Finch, her eyes glimmering with tears, had thrust into Charity's hands just before the post chaise pulled away from the flags. The basket was from her ladyship, a wedding present of sorts. Charity could not imagine what was in it, but Miss Finch had said that they ought not to open it until they reached Little Digswell!

They were nearly there now, and Charity could hardly contain an odd sense of excitement, her gaze creeping often toward the basket. What had Lady Redbourne given them at this late hour—Miss Finch nearly breathless in running out to the post chaise—to express her hope that their marriage would be a happy one.

Charity regarded her husband of but a few hours, and still could not credit that everything had ended so well. Lord Meares had marched Penelope down the aisle but a week earlier—the bride, if not radiant then certainly triumphant, and the groom well-satisfied.

All had been forgiven between herself and Penelope, though Charity did not think she would ever be truly close to her cousin again and she shook her head, wondering how she had ever thought she had known Penelope.

Anne had returned to attend both weddings, creating her own little stir with her mysterious disappearance of a few weeks earlier only to reemerge in society as a dignified matron. She and Anne had formed a new bond, their enjoyment of one another increasing with each day as Charity discovered in Anne the openness that she had always credited to Penelope.

Lady Datchworth had persuaded Lady Redbourne to accompany her to Bath for the summer, where she fully intended to see that the dowager was taken daily to the baths, renowned for their healing qualities, particularly of arthritic complaints.

Lord Datchworth had given Charity away and expressed over and over again that he was certain her happiness was assured, and that in William she had met a spirit as adventurous as her own. "And your Papa would have been greatly pleased with Redbourne." He breathed a great sigh of both satisfaction and relief as he cried, "Imagine having you all married within a month of one another! Very tidy indeed!"

"Oh, Uncle!" Charity cried through her tears as she hugged him very hard.

When Charity later spoke with Monsieur Bovin, she was gratified to learn that the governors at Drury Lane had hired him to serve as their new choreographer as long as his age and health would permit, and Furney, though kissing Charity through tears of her own, returned to Tunbridge Wells where she decided to remain as long as her mother needed her.

After a great deal of consideration, William decided to visit each of the ladies he had importuned—calling upon them in Hugh's name, of course—offering them the return of the largesse he had once stolen from them. He was pleased however to find that since Mr. Stokes had already proved to them that the funds had indeed benefited an orphanage, most of the ladies—many of whom swooned at the mere thought of their experiences in the arms of that handsome rascal Hugh Bramfield—refused to accept any money.

In fact, there was only one lady who demanded a return of her fifty pounds—Penelope, of course—and William immediately complied. However, when Lord Meares learned of it, he bade her return the fifty pounds instantly, with an elegantly composed apology for her ungenerous attitude toward the poor orphans!

William had lifted his brows at the letter and when he showed it to Charity, she said, "I am now convinced that she has met her match! My uncle was very right to have supported his cause with her!"

Charity could laugh about all of it now, as the post chaise rumbled toward the village of Little Digswell, though at the time any such evidence of her cousin's selfishness hurt deeply.

A few minutes more and the post chaise arrived in the quaint village, full of ancient timber-framed buildings, and very soon drew into the yard of the White Swan Inn. The large wooden sign above the inn, painted dark green and sporting an elegant white swan below the lettering, creaked in the growing wind.

William helped his bride, who carried the basket over her arm, down from the post chaise where they were met by the landlord of the inn. He wore his linen towel draped over his arm which made both William and Charity smile as he led them to a parlor.

"I could hardly credit it, m'lord!" he cried, as he begged Lady Redbourne to be seated.

Charity started at this appellation, turning around to see if the dowager was present, then blushed at the realization that the landlord was referring to her! Lady Redbourne! William's wife! And she turned to smile upon her husband, her heart suddenly full of love.

William returned her smile and would have accosted her save that Mr. Boles continued, "And to think that highwayman fellow were Mr. Bramfield!" He clicked his tongue. "I was never more shocked than when them Bow Street runners came up here poking about in the shrubbery and asking all manner of impertinent questions. One fellow in particular, with a face that looked like a dozen horses had trod all over it, kept asking one question after another, first of Bramfield and later of your lordship. I hope I never said nothing that might have gotten your friend in trouble. Why, were a week later that I read in *The Times*: "Bramfield, believed to be The Gentleman, narrowly escaped capture as he boarded a ship for The

Colonies." Hardly a crime worth Bow Street's efforts—kissin' ladies is more of a lark, if you ask me!" And with a wink, he quit the room promising a very nice tea tray, for his wife was an excellent cook.

When the door closed behind the friendly innkeeper, William did not hesitate to lift Charity's poke bonnet from her black curls. "For though I admire your hat, I can hardly kiss you if you are wearing it!" And once the offending object had been removed, he gathered her up into his arms and said, "And now, for a little *lark* of my own!" And he kissed her very hard.

Charity felt his lips touch hers, her heart again full to overflowing, her mind returning to but a few weeks earlier when she had received the lips of a notorious highwayman and thought only of William. And as before, she slipped her arm about his neck and returned his kisses with all the love that now filled her heart.

After a moment, William drew away from her slightly, though he could not resist kissing her forehead and keeping an arm closely about her waist as he said, "Now, let us see what Mama bought us for our wedding. She has been hinting for the past two weeks that she had the worst time finding one of the articles, but Miss Finch was able after a long search, to discover it in a funny little shop on Bow Street."

And when he had lifted the cover of the basket, tearing the silver paper to reveal his mother's gift, he gave a crack of laughter. "Of course! I should have known," he cried.

Charity peeped into the basket and there sitting in a nest of paper, were two masks—William's black silk mask, the muddied one that he had tossed into the shrubbery nearby, and Charity's pearl-embroidered mask. She gave a cry of delight, saying that Marie had said she had misplaced the mask somewhere—and all this time Lady Redbourne had taken it into her possession.

A short missive accompanied the present, written in

332

Miss Bracken's fine script, "May your marriage be filled with all the bounty of two such fine spirits!"

Charity fingered both masks, and frowned. "William, we came so very close to being separated forever. I am afraid just thinking on it!"

William again took her in his arms. "Then don't think about it ever again. I am convinced we were meant to be together even from the time we took a toss into the duck pond so many years ago, and you came up sputtering and laughing!"

And as Charity gave herself yet again to the sweetness of his love and the tenderness of his kisses, she thought perhaps that William was very right indeed!

GOTHICS A LA MOOR—FROM ZEBRA

ISLAND OF LOST RUBIES
by Patricia Werner   (2603, $3.95)
Heartbroken by her father's death and the loss of her great love, Eileen
returns to her island home to claim her inheritance. But eerie things begin
happening the minute she steps off the boat, and it isn't long before
Eileen realizes that there's no escape from *THE ISLAND OF LOST RU-
BIES.*

DARK CRIES OF GRAY OAKS
by Lee Karr   (2736, $3.95)
When orphaned Brianna Anderson was offered a job as companion to the
mentally ill seventeen-year-old girl, Cassie, she was grateful for the non-
troublesome employment. Soon she began to wonder why the girl's family
insisted that Cassie be given hydro-electrical therapy and increased doses
of laudanum. What was the shocking secret that Cassie held in her dark
tormented mind? And was she herself in danger?

CRYSTAL SHADOWS
by Michele Y. Thomas   (2819, $3.95)
When Teresa Hawthorne accepted a post as tutor to the wealthy Curtis
family, she didn't believe the scandal surrounding them would be any concern of hers. However, it soon began to seem as if someone was trying to
ruin the Curtises and Theresa was becoming the unwitting target of a
deadly conspiracy . . .

CASTLE OF CRUSHED SHAMROCKS
by Lee Carr   (2843, $3.95)
Penniless and alone, eighteen-year-old Aileen O'Conner traveled to the
coast of Ireland to be recognized as daughter and heir to Lord Edwin
Lynhurst. Upon her arrival, she was horrified to find her long lost father
had been murdered. And slowly, the extent of the danger dawned upon
her: her father's killer was still at large. And her name was next on the
list.

BRIDE OF HATFIELD CASTLE
by Beverly G. Warren   (2517, $3.95)
Left a widow on her wedding night and the sole inheritor of Hatfield's
fortune, Eden Lane was convinced that someone wanted her out of the
castle, preferably dead. Her failing health, the whispering voices of death,
and the phantoms who roamed the keep were driving her mad. And although she came to the castle as a bride, she needed to discover who was
trying to kill her, or leave as a corpse!

*Available wherever paperbacks are sold, or order direct from the
Publisher. Send cover price plus 50¢ per copy for mailing and
handling to Zebra Books, Dept. 2824, 475 Park Avenue South,
New York, N.Y. 10016. Residents of New York, New Jersey and
Pennsylvania must include sales tax. DO NOT SEND CASH.*

ZEBRA ROMANCES FOR ALL SEASONS
by Bobbi Smith

ARIZONA CARESS   (2727, $3.95)

One day Chance Broderick threw his hired boy, Rori, into the river for a bath and got a big surprise: his helpmate was no boy! Dazzled by her raven tresses, her silken copper-colored skin, her luscious curves under the wet buckskin, he was no longer in such a hurry to get his trip over with. Rori's savage beauty was rarer than any gold, and he knew he must possess her.

CAPTIVE PRIDE   (2160, $3.95)

When independent Cecilia Demorest discovered Noah Kincade would be in her father's home, she swore that somehow she'd get the privateer's weapons to the Colonial cause! The untouched beauty plotted to promise him her charms—and then double-cross the enemy. But the moment she felt Noah's sensual lips trailing down her throat and his muscular frame pressed hard against her, her scheming thoughts gave way to burning need.

DESERT HEART   (2010, $3.95)

Rancher Rand McAllister was furious that circumstance had made him the guardian of a scrawny girl, Lorelei Spencer, from Arizona's mining country. But when he discovered the pig-tailed brat was really a ripe, voluptuous beauty, his resentment turned to arousal. Her emerald eyes sparkled with the promise of ecstatic nights; her supple skin flushed with desire. As her guardian, Rand didn't have a clue what to do with her . . . but as a hot-blooded male, he didn't have to think twice about how to handle his luck!

Available wherever paperbacks are sold, or order direct from the Publisher. Send cover price plus 50¢ per copy for mailing and handling to Zebra Books, Dept. 2824, 475 Park Avenue South, New York, N.Y. 10016. Residents of New York, New Jersey and Pennsylvania must include sales tax. DO NOT SEND CASH.